FLEET SURGEON TO PHARAOH

FLEET SURGEON

TO PHARAOH

SHELDON A. JACOBSON

OREGON STATE UNIVERSITY PRESS

LIBRARY
The University of Texas
At San Antonio

*To the seafarers of my faith
who on the decks of modern explorers,
from Columbus to Byrd,
have played the man,
this tale is proudly and reverently dedicated.*

FOREWORD

IT MAY SEEM STRANGE that a university press, accustomed to publishing solemn works of profound scholarship, should publish a novel. But this work, *Fleet Surgeon to Pharaoh,* is a novel based on scholarship in many fields.

The author, Dr. Sheldon Albert Jacobson (Capt. USNR, Ret.), is Associate Clinical Professor of Pathology at the University of Oregon Medical School in Portland, Oregon, and Pathologist at the United States Veterans Hospital in Vancouver, Washington. He is a student of the history of medicine, of the history of sailing, and of ancient philosophies, particularly the Hebrew tradition. As a young man he sailed the Atlantic coast in his own boat. As a youth he served briefly in the merchant marine. As a medical officer in a Navy fleet tanker he became acquainted with more of the Atlantic. Wherever in this novel Belnatan and his mariners sail into a harbor on the coast of Africa, Dr. Jacobson has established that it exists.

Scholarship, however solid, would not be enough. The Oregon State University Press believes this to be a fascinating as well as a worthy novel. It invites the reader to sail with Belnatan and Asa ben Abdiel along the coasts of Capricorn 2,500 years ago.

CONTENTS

The wind goeth toward the south, and turneth about unto the north; it whirleth about continually, and the wind returneth again according to his circuits.

ECCLESIASTES I, 6.

Necho, king of Egypt, ... sent Phoenicians and ships, charging them to sail on their return voyage past the Pillars of Heracles till they should come into the northern sea and so to Egypt. So the Phoenicians set out from the Red Sea and sailed the southern sea; whenever autumn came they would put in and sow the land, to whatever part of Libya they might come, and there await the harvest; then, having gathered in the crop, they sailed on, so that after two years had passed, it was in the third that they rounded the Pillars of Heracles and came to Egypt. There they said (what some may believe, though I do not) that in sailing round Libya they had the sun on their right hand.

HERODOTUS, Wars of the Persians, IV, 42.

What song the Syrens sang, or what name Achilles assumed when he hid himself among women, though puzzling questions, are not beyond all conjecture.

SIR THOMAS BROWNE, Hydriotaphia, V, 4.

THE ACTION BEGINS IN THE YEAR 600 BEFORE THE COMMON ERA.

PART I

THE HILLS OF JUDEA

B etween the desert and the sown fields rise the stark brown hills of Judea. From north to west, tantalizing in their nearness, appear the snows of Mount Hermon, the verdant Galilean slopes and the fruitful plain of Sharon. But south and east, peak after parching peak, the jumbled wastes stretch to Arabia. When the west wind blows, the thirsty limestone hoards the scanty rain, to yield it up in springs and wells which, few, are infinitely precious; when the simoon blows, life suffers and endures. With ceaseless toil the husbandman works the narrow valley farm and leads his thin lines of olive trees up the lower slope; above him the shepherd guards his hungry flocks.

Small wonder that in that hard land arose a people who knew that they hung in the hand of heaven; and yearning upward like their own cypresses from the stony soil, they sought the Unknowable. In the merciless sun they dreamed of mercy; on the hardness of rock they dreamed of love.

But not alone by drouth and desolation were they tried. The wars of the winds have their counterpart in the kingdom of men. From the fertile lands the teeming empires spewed their armies of conquest, and in the intervals, marauders from the desert raided incessantly and pillaged and killed.

So has it ever been; so is it today.

THE EDOMITES STRUCK AT DAWN. Up from the south they had come, unseen under the moon, but seeing their path well enough; and slinking barefoot to lurk downwind from the village, they had aroused not even the dogs to sound an alarm. Now a door opened, and from one of the two score stone huts a woman started with a water jar; now another, and another; and a man appeared driving a scrawny cow. His glance swept the landscape. He stiffened, pointed, screamed an alarm, and fell with an arrow in his belly. Villagers burst from the doorways. A dozen arrows swished, some home and some astray; women screamed wildly. Rallying cries of the more cool-headed villagers were lost in the yells of the Edomites sweeping in for the kill. Although slightly more numerous than their assailants, the Hebrews in their surprise stood no chance to win or to escape. Alone and in pairs they found themselves ringed by spears, and were quickly despatched. Many were cut down before they could reach their weapons. Some were slain with the sleep scarcely out of their eyes. Within minutes, no male capable of combat remained alive.

Methodically now, the band turned its attention to the noncombatants. Old and middle-aged slaves had no value; swiftly the Edomites killed the aged and the aging. Infants and young children would fetch a price eventually, but would be a hindrance during the escape; laughing tribesmen impaled them while the mothers, shrieking, struggling, imploring, were held back. The raiders then divided. Small bands ascended the hills to drive in what flocks and herds they might find, while others made a systematic hunt for booty—grain, oil, clothes, and what scanty silver the villagers possessed. A detail meanwhile secured the captives.

Within two hours the caravan was ready. A few of the young women, too maltreated to travel or intractable from fear or despair, fell to the spear. The rest, as well as some of the stronger animals, were laden with the plunder. The marauders started southward, driving before them the cattle, sheep, goats, and helpless humans. Wells and cisterns were polluted with dead bodies. An ax-stroke apiece took care of the young trees, assuring that they would never bear fruit. A few hammer blows wrecked the scanty household furniture and utensils. Long before the sun was high overhead, only the dead and the dying remained.

2

The last of his patients cared for, Asa, son of Abdiel, the priest, set his face toward home. His lean, muscular mountaineer's legs carried him effortlessly up the steep path, but his mind was troubled as he reviewed the events of his visit. He knew that he had done well with the carbuncle on the neck of the man Simon. The fig poultice had brought it to a head; he had incised it thoroughly and had established satisfactory drainage. Healing now was only a question of time. Of his other cases, some were progressing well and some not so well. The girl Zilla presented a diagnostic problem. What was the nature of the spreading whiteness of her skin? He had seen her on several occasions. He had faithfully ordered the quarantine according to the book of priestly instructions, and yet he was unable to arrive at a diagnosis. The scalp hairs in the affected areas were white, and the lesion had not regressed during the periods of quarantine. In fact, a steady advance had taken place. Yet he could not bring himself to consider the disease malignant. If leprosy it were, why then did the lesions look exactly like those which hale old Malachi had been carrying for twenty years? If he gave the girl a clean bill of health and thereafter leprosy appeared he would have exposed a community to a source of contagion. He could not find it in his heart to break this girl's life by sentencing her to the permanent isolation of the leper.

The diagnostic uncertainty, he reflected, was only a part of a larger and much more serious dilemma. The method of differentiating leprosy from other skin affections was laid down for the priests in one of the six books which were the authentic voice of God. And yet he had had occasion several times to see that the rules did not fit his case histories and his physical examinations. He tried to believe in the scriptural prescriptions rather than his own experience, but as a conscientious physician he could not indefinitely doubt the accuracy of his own observations. They simply did not agree at times with what Abdiel, his father, and the other members of the priesthood had taught him. Zilla's disease, he felt, was not leprosy. With a sense of deep disturbance he entertained unwelcome doubts of the perfection of the written Word.

Well, the directions were wrong and that was all there was to it. But that was not all there was to it. If the directions were wrong, how much else might be wrong? The fundamentals that upheld his entire world, his entire cosmology, were in danger of crumbling. Doubt did not come easily, but it came. If instructions in this case were false, how much else might be false that he had been taught to revere as the authentic word of the spirit of God? Was it indeed the word of God? Or the word of man, interpolated in the Divine utterance? How much in scripture was man made, how much God made? How much of the absolute might be impugned by medical fact that was not fact?

Asa had never been inclined to cynicism. For the scoffer he had only contempt, but to close one's eyes to either manifest truth or error was equally not in his nature. Nor did he believe that man was required to give faith against the evidence of his senses. The universe was a logical whole, the work of a single creation by a single Creator. Nothing in it, therefore, could be false or misleading. It all pointed together, rightly understood, to its Divine source.

Meanwhile, the spell of a beautiful day had been working upon Asa. He was young—only 22. He was healthy and he was a mountaineer afoot in his native hills. His thoughts became less troubled as they turned more and more to the landscape about him. A plainsman would have been appalled to find himself among these bleak Judean slopes with their scanty browse not even concealing the limestone outcroppings. He would have felt crushed by canyon walls and overhanging cliffs, but Asa looked upon them with growing delight.

The trail led for a while along the slope, and on the level Asa joyed in the effortless stride that carried him swiftly over its relatively even surface. Far below him, to his right, he could see the tiny white stone houses of the village he had left and the bustle of activity about it as men worked in their scanty fields, women clustered about the well, and animals grazed further and further afield.

He stopped to exchange a few words with a bronzed boy of nine who herded a flock of goats. "Sholom aleichem, Kohane! Peace be with you, priest!" said the lad, smiling, and "Unto you be peace," was Asa's courteous rejoinder. "How is it with the broken arm?"

"Oh, no more trouble," replied the lad, "thanks to you." By way of demonstration he unfastened the sling from his belt, picked up a stone, and with a vigorous whirl sent it flying through the air.

"I am glad," said Asa with a smile on his regular features under their short black beard. "Let me try your sling. It is not so long since I was a boy like yourself and took my turn with the village flocks in these same hills." He picked up a stone, put it in the bight of the sling and let fly. The bush he had selected as target was not stirred as the stone crashed to the ground some distance away. Well, that was to be expected. For accurate slinging one needed round stones, but those were found only in the beds of brooks. Here on the hill the split rock fragments did not permit an accurate cast. For practice or in an emergency they would serve, but the provident shepherd carried some better ammunition with him for use against foxes and wolves that might menace his charges.

Yes, a beautiful day, and as Asa climbed upward to the ridge his thoughts reverted to his boyhood. How proud he had felt at the repulse of the four-footed marauder! How, wrapped warmly in his cloak among his flock, he had loved to lie at night and look upward at the sweep of the stars! Like every shepherd and wanderer he knew them well. Every constellation was a friend. Yes, there were worse lives than that of a shepherd lad in the hills. For that matter, he admitted to himself with a smile, there were worse lives than those led by the priesthood. He for one had no quarrel with the destiny that had set him down in these remote hills to minister to goatherds and husbandmen. As long as the rains came and the land was quiet, even Jerusalem, the capital, held nothing better. That village below toward which he was beginning to descend, for instance. Where was there more warmth and joy than there when their priest-physician came among them! He smiled in anticipation of welcome. Yes, a pretty little town. "How goodly are thy tents, oh Jacob! Thy dwelling places, oh Israel!" And in an access of reverence and gratitude Asa's lips shaped the words of an ancient song.

I lift up my eyes unto the mountains; whence shall come my help?
My help is from the Lord, the maker of heaven and earth.
He will not suffer thy foot to slip: thy Keeper doth not slumber.

Behold, He slumbereth not and He sleepeth not—the Keeper of
Israel.
The Lord is thy Keeper: the Lord is thy Shade, he is on thy right
hand.
By day the sun shall not strike thee, nor the moon by night.

But something was wrong. It did not look quite right down below. Of course, that was it! There was no one stirring about the houses. He did not see any cattle. On this side of the hill he looked in vain for sheep or goats. Something must be amiss. He became anxious and hurried his stride.

Turning a corner of rock half way down the hill, Asa almost ran into a man who was hurrying up the trail as fast as his legs could carry him.

"What has happened?" Asa asked.

"Peace to you, Kohane! Edomite raid," the man answered him, even in his haste not forgetting his deference to the priesthood. "One of our shepherds saw them fleeing southward with booty and captives and gave the alarm. I am going to raise forces from over the hill to pursue them."

"And the village," Asa asked, "any survivors?" The man shook his head. "I don't think so. I do not know. I didn't stop to see. There is someone taking charge down there. We are going in all directions to rally some spearmen. It must have been a raid in force. We may be too late to catch them, but we can try." He ran up the hill.

Asa hurried on down past the orchards and into the village. At his call a man stepped out of a house.

"I am Asa ben Abdiel. Are there any who need me?"

"In here, priest. There is a man still alive, but I think not for long."

Asa passed between two mutilated fig trees and entered the small square stone hut. In its single room the far side was a low platform. There, on a crude bed, he saw his patient. A pool of blood on the nearer floor showed where his rescuer had found him. There was a reddening bundle of rags on his abdomen. Asa pulled them aside to look at the wound.

"A spear thrust," the man whispered. "Sholom, priest. There is nothing you can do. I am dying."

"That will be as God wills," replied the priest, looking at the abdomen for signs of distention. With His aid we can save you yet."

"And for what?" murmured the man, his eyes closing.

For what indeed, thought Asa, as he went for a bucket of water. The patient's loved ones were dead, or, perhaps worse, slaves to the Edomite. His hard-won livelihood was ruined. The ministrant knew, as he wrung out a cloth in cold water for a compress on the fevered abdomen, that he could not save him. For all that, the man would not die at once. There would be hours, perhaps days, of suffering before his tormented spirit would be permitted to depart.

Asa sat by his patient doing the pitifully little that he could do. Not the most skilled of the priesthood could save this man. Could an Egyptian? Possibly. Egypt was the land of science and art. Egyptian physicians were renowned throughout the world. Could they achieve anything with a belly wound? Asa did not know. Hebrews scorned Egyptians as idolators and slaves of Pharaoh. Nevertheless, he had to admit admiration for what he had seen of their metalwork. He longed for their fabled medical knowledge. Perhaps an Egyptian would have been able to diagnose the girl across the hill and would know at once whether she was a leper or whether she could live out her life in health and happiness. An Egyptian physician might be brought to the capital, though the priesthood discouraged the servants of idols. But he would not come out to the Judean hills, nor could the sick and wounded of Judea be sent to the land of the red earth.

It would be a wonderful thing, though, if the priests of Israel could be armed with the medical skill of the children of the Nile. How much suffering might be avoided! How many deaths might be postponed! Should not the wise man be willing to learn from any, no matter what his nation or his God?

Shortly after noon his patient slipped into a merciful coma. Asa stepped outside the hut to find that a number of spearmen had assembled from the villages roundabout—hillmen from Gan-Shemesh, Beth Hanegba, and Ge-etzer—lean, muscular men armed with spears, bows, and short swords. Even as he looked, another dozen approached.

The three village headmen were conferring amid a press which quickly made way for Asa to join the central group. Elimelekh ben Gedaliah was a local chieftain of some military reputation.

"Peace be unto you, priest," was his salutation. As Asa returned the greeting he was aware of the irony of those words uttered under circumstances like these. "With those now arriving," said the captain, "we are two score and seven. These are enough to attempt a rescue. If we wait for greater numbers we may never overtake the Edomites. As it is, it will be a close thing if we cut them off before they get to safety in their own territories. We must start at once. Will you come with us, physician?"

"Of course," Asa replied.

If they should be able to overtake the fugitives, it would be near the border. There was grave doubt that they would ever return home. Nothing was said about the risk. It was one of the risks of life. A tiny people stubborn and foolish enough to refuse to be overwhelmed must be prepared to accept danger again and again.

"The fastest way," Elimelekh was saying, "would be to pursue them in their own tracks. They're encumbered with captives, beasts, and plunder. They can't travel as fast as we can, but we don't dare make an open pursuit. They'll certainly have a rear guard; as soon as we're seen those cursed Edomites will massacre the captives, hamstring the animals, and be off."

Heads nodded. They knew only too well that he was right.

"We must ambush them. That means a longer distance to cover and a less direct route. The Edomites have to keep to fairly level ground on account of their train. We must take the ridge trails and keep high on the shoulders of the mountains so that they won't see us as we pass."

The goat-skin bottles were filled at one cistern that had escaped defilement. A bite of bread, a fleece or two against the biting mountain air of night, and they were off to the southward.

For several hours it was safe to follow the easily negotiable valley. There was little talk; breath was too precious to waste. In the late afternoon there was a brief halt for rest. Then began the climb.

Higher they went and higher. To mountain-born sinews it was not tiring to climb effortlessly over the rock and ledge, through scrub and gravel, until far above the now-distant valley floor they encountered a trail which ran along the shoulder of the ridge. Then they turned south again.

Tireless feet ate up the miles. Not until nightfall brought shadows and made the trail first unsafe, then impassable, did they halt. In the dark they made a hasty meal of bread washed down with water, and lay down to snatch some sleep.

Several hours later when the moon rose and cleared the eastern crest there was light enough for them to see their way. Now was the great opportunity to pass their foes unseen. Southward again they went. No one spoke in the eerie surroundings. It was bitterly cold in the frost before dawn, but not a man complained. They circled westward of a peak so that it would be between them and their enemy.

Dawn broke. When the sun stood three hours high, the peak was behind them over their left shoulders, and a dry wadi cut downward and eastward to the valley that was their target. They hurried down, keeping in the depths to be as inconspicuous as possible. Presently the wadi debouched into the narrow valley. Its rock furnished ample cover. The pursuers sat and ate a scanty meal.

Here, if luck was with them, they could cut off the raiders. If the foe had passed this point it was useless to pursue him further. This was Edomite country.

Luck was with them. They had crouched in concealment with the valley empty before them for only a few minutes when around a curve in the trail came the raiding party. A tense word ran along the line of ambushers. Asa's stomach turned cold. He felt for his knife, making sure it was loose in its sheath. No question would be asked in the melée about priest or physician. His life could be worth no more than those of his companions, even though by reason of his office he was expected to keep to the rear of the fighting.

The Edomites came closer, their force strung out in a long line on the narrow, uneven valley floor. As they urged on the captive women and animals, the interval closed. From the lips of Elimelekh the headman came a bark like a jackal's. Then came a twanging, and a dozen arrows found their targets.

The Hebrews rose with a yell and bounded forward. Numbers were about equal, but this time the northerners had the advantage of surprise and position even over an armed and wary opponent. In a compact group they fell upon the vanguard of the marauders and cut them down. Stabbing and slashing, they swept along the Edomite line, rolling it down upon its rear, wiping out those too slow of wit or foot to drop back in time. There was a flurry of fighting at the tail of the column where those who had escaped from its head had rallied on the rear and for a few minutes attempted to fight it out. Within an incredibly short time, half the raiders lay dead and the other half were scrambling up the valley slopes. There was a brief exchange of arrows. Then the raiders melted into the hillside and were gone.

Pursuit was out of the question. The Hebrews had penetrated too far into enemy territory to delay. Because of the weak ones they had rescued they must start back immediately.

They had fared better in the fighting than could be hoped for. Observance of the military maxim, "To be stronger than the enemy at the point of contact," does more than facilitate victory. It reduces the losses of the superior party to a figure disproportionately low. Not one of the northerners, accordingly, had been killed or mortally wounded. One was found unconscious with a gash on his head. His pulse, Asa found, was strong, and there was no great loss of blood. A second, with a downward parry, had deflected a spear thrust from his belly to his thigh; the general effect of the wound had not been severe, but with a severed tendon he was in no condition to march. A boy of sixteen was lying, white and weak but still aware, with a slash through the thick of an arm. He was almost exsanguinated before Asa's dressing stopped the hemorrhage. The hand was already numb and cold, and the priest feared subsequent gangrene. Asses would carry these three, and Asa could quickly attend the less seriously wounded.

The recent captives were in worse case. All were exhausted by violence and terror and by the fatigue of their enforced flight. A few were casualties of the engagement. There had been those of the Edomites who had found opportunity for a few vengeful blows before the Judeans won the field. A corpse of a woman lay sprawled with her throat red in a ghastly gape. Another woman, propped in the arms of a friend, was coughing out her life from a pain-wracked chest, still transfixed with the arrow. Asa's stomach churned sickeningly at sight of a ten-year-old girl, silent, her eyes wide with fear and agony, whose bloody bowels tumbled out of a slashed abdomen. Her case was hopeless. His binding and unguent were only a merciful pretense.

Even among the others, grateful as they were, there was no jubilation. Widows, mothers whose little ones lay butchered, and orphaned youngsters turned in silent anguish homeward. Only the mother of the dying girl wept uncontrollably as she plodded beside the beast that bore the final ruin of her hopes, and two half-grown boys sobbed behind their mother's corpse.

Asa fell in on the other side of the doomed girl, who was already mercifully unconscious. He sought desperately for words of consolation for the mother, but he was unable to think of any which would not sound like an impertinence. It was not merely the loss in itself. It was the utter pointlessness and senselessness of the whole catastrophe. Even if the Edomites had made good their escape with their plunder, it would only have necessitated a stronger punitive expedition to discourage repetition. Evil piled upon evil.

He gave up the attempt to find words of his own for the woman, and began softly to chant, "With my voice I cry unto the Lord; with my voice I make supplication to the Lord. I pour out before Him my grief: my distress I recite before Him. When my spirit was overwhelmed within me—and Thou knowest well my path—on the way whereon I desired to walk they had secretly laid a snare for me. I cried unto Thee, O Lord: I said, Thou art my refuge and my portion in the land of life. Listen unto my entreaty, for I am very miserable: deliver me from my pursuers, for they are too mighty for me. Bring forth out of prison my soul, that I may thank Thy name: with me shall the righteous crown themselves, when Thou wilt deal bountifully with me." As he murmured, the woman mastered herself and became silent.

The caravan halted for a few minutes to bestow the injured more easily upon their mounts. The priest joined the motherless lads. As they started he stepped between them and laid a hand on the shoulder of each. The younger burst out sobbing afresh, crying, "Mother! Mother!"

"You will not be alone," said Asa. "We will find you a father and a mother." He was silent for a minute and again, softly, he chanted, "O Lord, hear my prayer. Give ear to my supplications: Thy faithfulness answer me, in Thy righteousness. The enemy hath pursued my soul; he hath crushed to the ground my life; he hath made me dwell in darkness, as those that are dead eternally. And my spirit within me is overwhelmed: in my bosom is my heart astounded. I remember the days of olden times; I meditate on all Thy doings; on the work of Thy hands do I reflect. I spread forth my hands unto Thee: my soul longeth for Thee, as a thirsty land. Hasten, answer me, O Lord, my spirit faileth: hide not Thy face from me, that I may not become like those that go down into the pit."

When he had finished the psalm the boys' crying was more subdued. Asa too was relieved. After a day's activity and a night's forced march, it was not easy to spare breath for the psalm while hurrying toward safety.

3

Bone-weary, the priest plodded into the stone-built village of Beth Hanegba where was his home. The place was compactly built, as were most villages and towns in that time of peril. He passed modest huts, big enough for one or two rooms, until he came to a slightly higher building built in the form of a right-angled "U" opening upon the street. The gap was closed by an eight-foot stone wall. He opened a wooden door set into the middle of it and entered his courtyard. In the center stood the well. There were a fig and an olive tree and a number of flowers in the unpaved corners. Three doors gave access to the building that formed the inner three sides, and on the left stone steps climbed along the wall of the house to the flat roof. From one of the doors a comely auburn-haired young woman emerged and threw herself into his arms.

"Thank God," she said, "that you have returned safe. You are all right?"

"All right," he replied, and kissed her. "That is, all right except for being heartsick, tired to death, and thirsty—which is well enough compared to some others."

He drained a goblet that she proffered. He doffed his woolen cloak and stood in short linen breeches. Prescribed for the priesthood for occasions of ceremony, these were affected by many of them for daily wear. He tossed his headcloth to a nearby bench. As he did so, his wife drew water from the well and filled a basin. While he washed off the dust and sweat of the journey, she set about the preparation of food. She built a smouldering fire up to a low flame, and a cut of lamb was soon broiling over it. She brought out a large, rather flat, circular loaf of bread, some grapes, and a carafe of wine and poured some water. Soon after Asa had completed his bath, they sat at their meal. He suddenly discovered that he was ravenous.

As he recounted the events of the previous days, he was struck, as every sensitive man has always been, by the dualism of his reactions. Despite the harrowing scenes through which he had passed, here he sat enjoying, even in his sadness, the tasty meat, the presence of his lovely Michal and the coolness and peace of his garden. Yet he felt no guilt, as he would have had he lived in a more ordered country.

The meal finished, early though it was, they sought their bed. During the previous forty-eight worrisome hours she had slept and eaten as little as he, and when, late the following morning, he opened his eyes, she was still beside him.

Asa would have liked to spend a lazy day, but the victims of the raid—those who had survived—would need his attention. As religion prescribed, he washed, prayed, and fed his cow before sating his hunger. He then took to the trail again, and an hour's walk brought him to the settlement where the people had been temporarily housed.

There was much to do. His medical duties, of course, came first. Most of the wounded were doing well, but the hand of the sixteen-year-old boy had, as feared, begun to mortify. There was no pulse, and the finger tips had a dirty blue coloration. Amputation was essential. But at what level? If he cut too high, both the shock and the subsequent crippling would be unnecessarily severe; if too low, the gangrene would advance, and there would be a second terrible ordeal which the boy would not survive.

Despite a fever, the hand and wrist were cold. The wound, on the contrary, was fairly clean, and the flesh of the elbow, although swollen and somewhat discolored, appeared viable. Asa determined upon the mid-forearm as his operative site. That would be safely above the danger zone and low enough to preserve useful elbow-function for the stump. He applied a tourniquet above the elbow. Experience had taught that compression lower than this could not adequately control hemorrhage. Then while four men held down the youth, Asa, working as quickly as possible, made a circular cut through skin and muscle. While he sawed the bone, the youth writhed but was silent. In a remarkably short time the severance was complete. Asa shifted the tourniquet downward close to the free end and applied a dressing. The whole operation had taken no more than two minutes.

Having left directions for the post-operative care—mainly a matter of cold packs and administration of water and wine—Asa returned to his other problems. The question of providing for the bereft must be met. Where the duty of the next of kin was not clear cut, the priest's dictum was requested. He made his adjudications as best he could, and in general they were uncontested. Behind him was the force of community opinion, and behind this, ultimately, was the authority of King Jehoiakim in Jerusalem.

They could fairly easily find homes for children who had lost both parents. A few of the widows were automatically provided for; a man was duty bound to marry the childless widow of his brother in order that he might beget offspring on her. The first born of such a union would by law bear the name and inherit the property of the dead man. Since plural marriage was permissible, a prior wife was no bar, and indeed a small people fighting desperately and unremittingly against powerful neighbors could not afford to turn its widows adrift. Widows with children would be supported by relatives insofar as means permitted. In an agricultural and pastoral society, the labor of an extra woman was by no means to be ignored.

The most trying task Asa had left for last. With a heavy and a helpless feeling he visited the mourners. A priest might not approach a dead body (save of his own close kin), but it was his duty to offer such consolation as Judaism could afford. The heathen to east and south offered elaborate assurances of a happy future for the pious dead, with a continuance forever of the pleasures of this world—provided always, of course, that the living were able and willing to purchase the costly comforts of organized religion. Otherwise were the austere beliefs of the Hebrews. Man's duty was to live the godly life on earth; what followed was God's province, unknowable to man.

Most of his flock accepted Asa's ministrations gratefully. Not so the woman beside whose dying daughter he had trudged on the way north. When he had finished his words of comfort she waited for a minute and then shook her head.

"No, Kohane. My husband was a good man, and a kind one. Yet it may be that he deserved his fate. Who can know the heart of a man? It may even be that this has been visited justly upon me. I do not think so. I have not been sinless, but I can think of nothing that I have done that deserves this. Still, I submit myself to the Divine Justice. But what of the child? What guilt could have called for her to be cut off when the morning of her life is not yet ended? And for her to die so horribly! Where is the justice of God?"

Asa gave her the answer that he had been given. "We cannot understand. We cannot know. We can only submit. Somehow, this is for the best! 'The judgments of the Lord are true and righteous altogether.' "

The woman shook her head. "Though I go down to destruction, yet will I say that my child's fate was unrighteous and without mercy."

Asa sighed. He could find no answer, and in any event, the woman was not now in condition to receive one. He blessed her and departed.

In the days that followed, the problems raised afresh by the raid continued to bedevil the young priest. He made his rounds as hitherto. An old woman complained of general indisposition with no very definite symptoms. Asa, guessing at the visceral sluggishness of the aged, prescribed extract of cassia. There was a broken leg to set. He did it, he thought, well. The alignment was good, and there should be no deformity. For a patient dying slowly of some malignant disease, beyond his powers to diagnose, and still more to heal, an extract of hemlock brought some relief of pain. Examination of old Ukiah showed nothing to the physician's eye and hand, but the man was obviously failing; and indeed, why should he not fail? The loss of his son and only grandson meant the loss of all interest in life. Asa gave what comfort he could and prescribed coriander seeds in a hope that they would stimulate the appetite. On the other hand, another oldster complained of his inability to interest a young wife. Asa, although not very sympathetic, suggested caperberry pudding. The old fool should have anticipated the difficulties of so unsuitable a union.

As Asa worked, the question of evil haunted him. He had said, only the other day, as many a time before, that we could not understand, but he felt an urge to understand. He remembered an answer that his father had given him during the time of his training.

"A dove in a cage," the old man had said, "is safe and well fed. Even if it passes under the hand of the slaughterer at last, its death is quick and painless. And yet what is a dove in a cage? A creature flabby of mind and body. It can scarcely fly. It has no craft. If it escapes it cannot fend for itself, and more often than not, returns willingly to its cage. The doves in the wild, on the other hand, are harried by hawk and eagle. They bake in the sun when water is scanty and often starve when seeds are lacking. But the beauty of creation is in their flight, and in their wariness and resource is the wisdom of Providence. Son, man without his woes would be a bird in a cage, and instead of the Divine Idea of his Creator, he would be a useless thing living in a greyness of neither joy nor sorrow."

These words had satisfied Asa then. They did not satisfy him now. Was the recurrent agony which spread through the land part of the Divine Plan? Did a merciful Providence intend its creatures to suffer so atrociously?

An incident of his practice at about this time pointed up the problem in a new light. One morning a young woman came to fetch Asa to see her sister. He knew them, of course, as he knew all the inhabitants of his district. The girls, although for some years marriageable, lived together. Their parents were dead and they supported themselves by casual labor in the fields. As they walked, the priest took history.

"Gomer has been well," said his informant, "until two days ago. Her usual time came upon her, but not as it has done in the past. She has had much pain and has bled much. She seems to me to be very sick. Now she is unable to get up. She keeps calling for water—I think she is feverish—but she will not eat. She sleeps badly."

They passed by a tiny garden in which lilies bloomed opposite a sycamore tree. As they entered through the narrow wooden door, Asa was aware that his conductress pressed unnecessarily against him. He gave no sign of having perceived it.

The sick girl lay on her back. Asa noticed the drawn countenance, the flushed face, the rapid breathing. He laid his hand upon her brow and found, as he had expected, that it was hot. At his word, her sister raised the patient's garment and Asa perceived a slight swelling of the abdomen. He pressed it gently and the girl moaned and writhed. A suspicion formed in his mind.

"When was it last with you after the manner of women?"

"Four weeks ago."

"Listen to me. You are a very sick girl. With help you may be saved, but death is close to you. I cannot help unless you tell the truth."

The girl hesitated. "Three months."

The priest sighed. "I had heard that you burned incense to the Queen of Heaven, and that you worshipped in the grove of Ashtoreth. I had hoped that it was mere gossip." He shook his head sadly. "Who did this, and how was it done?"

"I did it myself, with a pointed stick."

He spent much of that day and that night and the next day and night at the bedside of his patient, but it is doubtful whether his ministrations did her any good. He purged her and applied cold compresses. Pity and anger struggled within him. Would they never learn, these fools and backsliders, to cast off once and for all the vile worship of the Canaanite goddess of love? What business had a Hebrew girl living the free and easy life of a Canaanite? She had brought her misery upon herself by her own perverseness.

For all that, no young man of any feeling can be unmoved by the spectacle of a girl in serious trouble. As, worried and weary, he gazed upon the young woman, now white and still, he wondered whether any code of morality could be justified if it brought a human being to the desperate point where, to avoid ruin and disgrace, she played at dice with death. Better, he was almost tempted to believe at the moment, if she could have had her baby without condemnation by the village, rather than be brought so untimely to her grave.

As it happened, she lived, but this happy circumstance did not resolve his problem. Asa held by the austere rule of his people. Otherwise he was well content and gave thanks daily for his lot. Between joy and shame he reminded himself that he was one of the fortunate ones, though his happiness was bought with a ransom of a river of tears.

4

But now was the season when the routine of life would give way to an ever-joyful experience. Spring had come. The Passover was almost upon them.

Since ancient times, the spring festival had been celebrated with public prayer over unleavened bread, or matzos, made from the first of the barley harvest; while in each home the paschal lamb had been prayerfully eaten at night with gratitude to the Giver. Of late years, however, both observances had been combined and dedicated to the Almighty who in a springtime some six or seven centuries earlier had freed the nation from slavery in Egypt.

Like as many of his people as could make the trip, Asa with his wife prepared to go up to Jerusalem. Three times a year they journeyed to the Temple to refresh their spirits by communion with God and to pay Him their tribute of Temple worship.

So Asa and his Michal joined converging lines trending toward the north. Mounted upon asses, they rode among the pilgrims. Most were afoot with their burdens over their shoulders. Many herded before them the sheep, goats, or cattle that were destined for the Lord. A few rode upon camels, a very few upon horses. In holiday mood they traveled gaily northward in the now green mountains. The miscalled Rose of Sharon, the lilies, the blossoms in the small orchards brightened their way. There was an overnight stop at an inn, at whose broad hearth tasty viands were cooked for those of fatter purse, while dates and barley cakes sufficed the rest. Both within and without, the air reeked with the pleasant smell of frying olive oil. The courtyard was crowded. As befitted his priestly status, Asa and his wife were lodged within a room, but most travelers slept in large family groups irregularly scattered through the bursting inn.

At noon the next day they skirted the Vale of Hinnom and took the road at the summit of which they saw the walls of Jerusalem, City of Peace. With happy anticipations the throng swept through the gates. Asa was soon welcomed in the home of his mother's brother.

The house of course was in a turmoil of orderly confusion. Asa's aunt embraced her visitors, and then the older woman and the young one were immediately engrossed in the endless tasks that confronted the Hebrew housewife on the eve of the Passover. A thorough house-cleaning was underway. All leaven (yeast) and all bread and other such foodstuffs as had been exposed to its action, were burned. The last of the unleavened bread was baking in a large stone oven in the courtyard. The wine, in earthen crocks wet on the outside for cooling by evaporation, was being readied for the ceremony on the morrow. The women aired and inspected their best rainment. After hurriedly washing and changing his dusty clothing, Asa walked to the Temple to pay respects to his old teachers and friends.

In the cool of the evening, bathed and fed, they sat at their ease upon the roof as every other family in Jerusalem was doing. Asa told the news of the countryside. He told of the Edomite raid and its aftermath. In happier vein, he commented on the fields of young wheat and barley sprouting after the abundant winter rains. Then he asked his uncle about the news in Jerusalem.

Shealthiel, portly, well clothed and carefully groomed, dignified (or just a little pompous?) frowned. "The court," he said, "grows more and more hectic. His majesty's foreign office senses unrelenting pressure from the Babylonians. I must say that we are of no mind for surrender. What we can do to preserve the independence of Judea we will certainly undertake. In fact," he said, and frowned, "sometimes I think that the king will undertake more than he can perform. For every farmer or shepherd that we can muster and arm, the Babylonians can field a company of superbly trained and equipped infantry, to say nothing of tremendous numbers of chariots, which to be sure cannot perform to advantage among hills such as ours. If we are to survive it must be by a combination of courage and wile—especially the latter."

"And what of wile," asked Asa, "can we use against Babylon?"

"Much," answered the old courtier, with a smile. "Our relations with Egypt grow ever more cordial. Judea in the hands of Babylon is a lancehead thrusting toward the red lands. Judea in the hands of Egypt would be a lancehead thrusting toward the land between the rivers. It is our hope that while Egypt and Babylonia growl at one another from across opposite borders, we can maintain a position of neutrality—a precarious one, it is true—between them. The status of a buffer country is delicate and difficult, but often it is the only status in which a tiny nation like ours can survive."

"And can we survive in it forever?" asked Asa. "How long can we walk a knife-edged trail on the ridge?"

"Long enough, perhaps. We will not have to walk it forever. Egypt has been weakened before now. It is not long, as you know, since she was conquered by the Nubians and again by the Beduins from the West. There have been civil wars and famines. The power of Sais waxes and wanes. And as for Babylonia, the kingdoms between the rivers have been overthrown many times and will be again. Ur of the Chaldees was a strong city in the days of our forefather Abraham; today it is forgotten, except by us. Where is Sumer? Where is Akkad? Hammurabi is dead and his power is long since broken. A diplomat must always hope that time and chance will weaken his enemies, even when he cannot meet them himself. In the meantime, he must use what craft he can to await that weakening."

"So—" asked Asa.

"So, as I have indicated, we of the foreign office feel that for the time being our interests lie with Egypt. Since Pharoah Psammetichus reestablished the kingdom at Sais in the delta, Egyptian power has been growing. Necho is a vigorous monarch, and it behooves us to cultivate his support against the East."

"Might he not swallow us?"

"Necho has his own problems. He will have enough to do to maintain himself and will be glad to have us as a bulwark against Babylon."

"Do all the court share your view?"

The older man laughed. "Even if they did, politics would force many into opposition. The isolationists dream that Judea can stand in her mountains against the world."

"Are there many such dreams?"

"Some, but curiously the main opposition comes not from the court, but from the mob. Even in your villages, you have, I am sure, heard of a rabble-rouser named Jeremiah. He holds mass meetings in which he inveighs against the people for their sins—I could count plenty myself among our political opponents, of course—and threatens them with Divine retribution by the hand of the Chaldeans—it used to be the Scythians—and many of the people are spellbound enough to want to placate the rulers—Babylonian, Assyrian, or what you will—of Chaldea, even to the extent of turning our backs upon Egypt." Shealthiel raised a goblet of wine.

In the sphere of international politics, Asa reflected, it would seem reasonable that a minister like his uncle, trained almost from the cradle to affairs of state, should exercise more competent judgment than a preacher from the hills.

Yet this was questionable. Despite the self-sufficiency and supposed omniscience of men of affairs, their machinations broke down at least once in a generation, and the spearmen had to go forth to retrieve if possible the errors or failures of the makers of policy—errors or failures which many had denounced in advance even though the denouncers might be and frequently were unerudite farmers, herdsmen, or potters.

There was indeed grave question as to whether the palace was less fallible than the hovel. Certainly, mused Asa, the carpenter knew more of woodworking than his fellow; the shepherd was the best judge of where to pasture sheep; and the priest could give a better opinion on the Law than could a layman, but when it came to world affairs, the relations of people to people, he more than half suspected that the common denominator was the human heart; which the farmer might understand as well as or better than the politician. His uncle's faith in Egypt was perhaps tragically misplaced.

Well, that was no concern of his. Healing was his business, and if the Nile had anything to teach him about the relief of pain, why, from the Nile he would seek to learn.

"I have thought much of Egypt of late," Asa mused aloud. "It will be no secret to you, or indeed anyone, that in our medicine we of the priesthood are far from being able to achieve all that we will. The priesthood of Egypt, on the other hand, despite its darkness in things spiritual, has sciences that we do not possess. Again and again I have been baffled by a diagnostic or therapeutic problem. That my experience is limited, of course, I freely admit. That an older head could solve all—I might even say most—of my problems, I do not admit. And how often, even knowing the diagnosis, do I find myself powerless to arrest or even to modify the course of disease! Do you think it would be possible for an Egyptian priest to be brought to the Temple to teach us what they know of disease?"

His uncle smiled sceptically. "From what I know of your profession, Asa, I find it hard to believe that the priests of the Temple would tolerate such an arrangement. Professional jealousy alone would forbid it, but to do them justice, I think they would have sounder reasons for an objection. As you are all too unhappily aware, the war of the priesthood against Baal and Ashtoreth, although at present it goes well, is far from concluded; and to accept an exponent of strange gods; nay, more, to sit at his feet and to honor his teachings, might be to strike a serious blow in the minds of the credulous at the exclusive worship of our God." He thought for a moment. "I tell you this in confidence," he said in a lower tone, "your aunt is aware of it, and your Michal is a girl who can hold her tongue, and in any event," he said with a smile, "gossip does not travel readily from your village to the capital. The fact is that King Jehoiakim has about determined to send an embassy to the Pharaoh. It is entirely possible—I say it is possible—that your uncle may travel there as the representative of the King."

Asa expressed his surprise and gratification.

"Your sentiments, though welcome, are a bit premature," said his uncle with a deprecatory laugh. "At any rate, what passed through my mind was this. I imagine that the secrets of the priests of Ra are closely guarded. It is conceivable, nevertheless, that the prestige of an ambassador may be sufficient to win from them some of their medical texts."

Asa's eyes lighted up. "Do you think so?"

His uncle nodded. "I rather think so. Of course, one cannot be sure. The commissioning of a translation, however, would almost certainly be something that Egypt would not tolerate. It might be well if you set about the study of the hieratic script. I think that I could obtain

for you some of the court manuals that are used in diplomatic cor-
respondence."

It was an eager and excited Asa who tossed upon his bed that night.
There was much—too much—to do in the few days following. To
every Hebrew who was not the veriest clod, study was as the breath
of his nostrils. To a provincial such as Asa, the opportunity to sit at
the feet of the Temple elders while they lectured on theology and
medicine was an infrequent privilege. Then there were drugs to buy;
sounds and lancets to be sought out; there was personal shopping to
be done (in which pursuit he was eagerly assisted by his wife) ; and
last and most important, devotions had to be made at the Temple. The
priests offered no sacrifices of their own. By law they were forbidden
to own farm or pasture, receiving their livelihood in a share of the
offerings brought by the public.

On an evening Asa assisted his uncle in a final search through the
house for the sour dough that was used to raise bread, that with it all
undiscovered leaven might be burned in a symbolic fire. Thereafter,
the house was ritually pure for the Passover.

The next day passed much like the preceding one. At sundown the
family, now swollen to some two dozen by guests from all parts of
the tiny kingdom, gathered to celebrate the holy day. A treasured
linen cloth was spread, and the table set with copper dishes preserved
for this feast only. Silver carafes and bronze goblets provided the wine.
As the priestly member of the family, Asa received the lamb that had
been purchased for the feast, symbolic of the Paschal lamb that had
been slaughtered by the forefathers in the days of Moses. He solemnly
consecrated the feast to God, tested the knife blade upon his thumb,
bent back the animal's head and with a swift to and fro motion cut
its throat. The lamb died almost without a struggle. Quickly it was
skinned and dressed. The meat was roasted, and the hide and the discarded parts set aside for burning. While they sat at table, the story
of the exodus from Egypt was retold to the children. As they ate the
good roast meat and drank the wine of freedom, with frequent bless-
ings upon the Provider of food and of freedom, they discussed and re-
discussed the tale of their wanderings and sang of the Divine Guidance
under which they had won from slavery and doom to liberty and life.

On the following day it seemed incredible to Asa that a good part of the kingdom could assemble, not only in the city, but within and about the Temple itself. Shealthiel and his household entered through the great bronze gates. The family then separated, the females and young boys remaining in the Court of the Women, while the men crossed the threshold into the second space. Then Asa alone, as entitled by his priestly caste, entered the Court of the Priests and joined his fellows about the Altar. Beyond this was only the Holy of Holies, whose floor none but the high priest himself might tread. The choir chanted a psalm, and then another psalm. Presently the high priest himself appeared, clad in snowy linen. Upon his bosom was the golden breastplate with the twelve jewels of the twelve tribes of Israel. After a prayer, the sacrifices were offered, and while the altar flames consumed them, the story of the deliverance from Egypt was chanted again.

Before departing for home, Asa paid a final visit to his best-loved teacher. Azariah, portly and aged, sat long at wine with his visitor. Their talk ran from personal news to details of Asa's medical practice and suggestions by the older man.

"You have enjoyed your visit," said the older priest, sitting back at last.

"I have indeed," said Asa.

"But not as much as you expected. Is that not so?"

Asa, surprised, only then realized that he was obscurely troubled on each visit to Jerusalem.

"I have often thought," said the older man, "that a door once closed should not be reopened. One thinks back with pleasure to the place where one has lived happily, and yet when one revisits it, it is with a certain sadness. A joyous time need not perhaps have come to an end, but once ended it cannot be relived. The age, the activities, the friends who made it what it was are irrevocably lost. The very walls, as one wanders among them, seem to whisper, What do you here? To us you are the dead, and we have to do only with our living. Go and return no more!"

"There is something of that feeling," said Asa. "I realize that it has been true—that is, I am realizing it now. It is paradoxical that to me who spent years of study in and about the Temple, the prescribed visit of three times a year is perhaps less joyous an occasion than to the countryman who has never dwelled happily in its shadow."

"I have heard old soldiers say the same," said Azariah. "They would visit the palace guard to seek out fellow campaigners of the years of their youth. There was a pleasure in the greeting and pleasure in the talk—that I know—but their faces were wistful as they turned away. Just as man cannot live twice, he cannot drink twice the same cup of wine. Why sadness must mingle with joy I do not know."

Asa frowned. "I have seen overmuch of sadness of late," he remarked and went on to tell his mentor of his fruitless efforts with the woman who would not be comforted. "I had nothing to give her. How could I resolve for her the problem of evil?"

"You could not. You never will, nor will anyone, save in part. This much we know. If there had not been darkness the Lord would not have created light. Perhaps joy can exist only side by side with sorrow. If you had a child, as I hope soon you will, you would not raise him by indulgence alone. If you did you would regret it. You would temper his delights with trial because only thus are strong men and strong women developed."

Asa nodded. He had encountered that reasoning before. When in his childhood he had asked the reason for pain, he had been told first that it was the will of God. When a little later he had asked why God inflicted pain upon His children he had been told the story of man's Fall. That had sufficed him for a long time, but his maturer questioning had brought answers such as the old priest had just given him. Now he felt himself not wholly satisfied. Nevertheless he let it pass.

As Asa took his leave he broached another matter.

"We do our best in the hills. Occasionally a priest of the vicinity, a little older than I, will see a patient for me and make a suggestion. That of course is by no means enough. Would it be possible to arrange for a more experienced physician to come occasionally to the back country, to see some of my difficult cases?"

"We have been thinking of some arrangement. Perhaps it can be done."

The following morning, their leavetaking completed, Asa and his wife started for home. His uncle had been better than his word. In Asa's baggage was a manual of elementary Egyptian, with a comparison of the hieratic script, favored by the Egyptian priesthood, with the Hebrew alphabet, as well as a comparative vocabulary of the two tongues, and some notes on Egyptian syntax. Moreover, there was a half promise by a priest-physician who was visiting with the Egyptian embassy of the loan of some of the medical writings of his people. It was Asa's task now to prepare himself to read them.

He studied hard in the months that followed. The hieratic syllabary was a much more complicated form of writing than the simplified alphabet that had been developed by the Semitic peoples, and it demanded a mastery of far more symbols than the twenty-four Hebrew letters. Nevertheless, Asa mastered it and passed on to study of the language, although his pronunciation would indeed have been laughable in the land of the Nile. Yet all of his labor might have come to naught had it not been for a mangy fox near Damascus, far to the north.

5

Abdadon was an insignificant trader. Not directly connected with any of the prosperous Damascene exporters, he could not hope for a share in the lucrative commerce between Damascus and Jerusalem. He was, however, a distant cousin of a royal tax-gatherer. This relationship was sufficient for the larger traders to tolerate his presence in the protection of their well-manned caravans. Upon arrival in Judea, he would leave the fertile field of the capital to his betters and carry his wares into the villages. Here he did a small but profitable business exchanging Syrian metalware for oil, honey, balm, and occasionally, other products. Too poor or too stingy to afford much of a retinue, Abdadon was not without patience and enterprise. He had found that a couple of well trained dogs would do the work of several men guarding his wares and person against thieves of the night.

Just after the beginning of one such business trip, Abdadon was very much annoyed when, with Damascus not yet out of sight, his dogs scented game and, despite his angry command, took off from his train. Mule and camel drivers laughed heartily at him as, cursing and impotent, he watched his dogs start a scrawny vixen from the shelter of a thorn-bush. As it happened, however, he might as well have kept his temper, for the chase was a short one. The fox, obviously in poor condition, had run for only a minute or two before the dogs were upon her. She turned, snarled, sank her teeth into the ankle of one of her pursuers and died under their fangs. The jeers of Abdadon's companions turned to compliments as the two dogs happily trotted back.

The march to Jerusalem was rapid and without incident. Abdadon made an appointment for the return journey and continued southward. He had recently covered this territory and judged it expedient to commence operations some distance beyond. It would be a good opportunity; his companions were remaining in Jerusalem a little longer than usual, and he, his assistant, and his pack animals had stood the trip well. But one of the dogs seemed sick. The animal had not been eating lately; it had a dull appearance and took but little note of his commands or of its surroundings. He hoped that it would recover. Training a new dog would take time and trouble.

Abdadon arrived at a village that was new to him. He arranged with a resident for shelter for himself and his animals and exhibited his wares. Business was good. Judea had had a fairly wet season. The villagers had an abundance of oil and honey and some grain, and they were willing to trade. He preferred silver when it was available, but of this they had little. In any case he knew they would have distrusted his scales, and not without reason. Well, a man took his opportunities as he found them.

There was one minor sour note in his satisfaction with the day's merchandising. His dog was definitely worse. It had lost flesh. There was an expression of dull misery upon its face. It could not rest. After lying down briefly it would come to its feet and start wandering aimlessly, only to return and repeat the performance. There was a thick, brownish secretion dripping from the corners of its mouth. Twice it had snarled at him as though not recognizing its master. He doubted that the dog would be fit to travel in the morning.

It wasn't. A breakfast eaten and his goods packed, Abdadon paused at the well for a final watering before taking the trail over the ridge. The dog dragged itself wearily toward the well curb and lay down. A woman approached with her bucket. The dog was in her way. She set down her foot close beside him; the cur snarled and slashed her ankle. She screamed. A neighbor snatched at a stick and threw it at the animal. He yelped and bit at the face of a little boy nearby. Abdadon flung a stone. A man stooped for another and the dog ripped his arm.

More stones thudded against the mangy body. The animal turned as a sheep was driven by and slashed its shoulder to the bone. He bit a second sheep before the shepherd's flung knife took him between the ribs and made a merciful end.

For Asa, the first result of this little misadventure came some three weeks later when he was called upon to decide a petty point of law.

"Kohane," a woman hailed him as he returned from his rounds one afternoon, "will you advise me?"

"What is your difficulty?"

"My little son has not been well. Today I thought to tempt his appetite with some chicken. Since my man died, I can ill afford luxuries, but for the sake of the child I decided to kill a chicken for him instead of for the market."

"What is the matter with your child, and why have you not brought him to me?"

"I thought that his illness would go away. I did not want to bother you about a trifle." She crimsoned. "I have but little to offer the priesthood."

"And when have I refused to treat those who could make no offering? Thus sayeth the Lord: 'I am the father of the orphan, and the only judge of the widow.' Let me see your son."

He followed her through a wooden door that opened directly off the street into a small, one-room house. On half of the floor a few chickens were pecking at some scattered grain and a goat lay chewing his cud. The other half of the floor, higher by the height of a man's knee, bore a low table, some chests and a bed on which the sick boy lay and listened to the first rain of autumn.

"For several days he has been restless and irritable. I think perhaps it is because that dog bite on his cheek has begun to hurt again. Yesterday he would not eat." As she spoke she stroked the youngster's hand.

Asa lifted the clumsy dressing on the cheek. About the tooth marks there was some redness. Swelling had subsided and had not recurred, but the forehead was hot to the touch. Asa wondered why. Obviously the wound, however irritated, was too slight to cause a general systemic reaction.

"What's the matter, sonny? Does it hurt?"

"A little," the boy said, and as the priest poked at his belly he frowned in irritation and drew back.

"Did I hurt you?"

"No," sullenly.

His mother rebuked him. "The priest is here to help you, son." She turned apologetically to Asa. "He never acts like this."

There was some significance, the priest was sure, in the lad's altered behavior, but it was beyond him. His probing fingers and questions alike failed to produce a diagnosis. Unsatisfied, he prescribed hot steeps for the wound. Then, "What was it you wanted to tell me about your chicken?"

"My neighbor was killing for his own table, and I asked him to kill one of mine. He did so. Then he noticed a wound on its back from something—hawk, rat, I know not what—that had attacked it. He told me that it would not be lawful to eat it, and the headman, passing by, agreed with him. The bird had seemed perfectly well, and I can hardly afford its loss." She uncovered a pot, and displayed the plucked fowl.

Asa looked at the partly healed wound on its back. Unquestionably, according to the law, the bird was not kosher—not fit—for the table. Unquestionably, also, the family would undergo a real deprivation if it were thrown out. The priestly authority allowed considerable latitude in interpretation of the Divine mandates.

"Prepare your dinner," he said. "I pronounce this chicken kosher," and left amid her thanks.

As day followed day, the boy grew steadily worse. He had small appetite, and when he attempted to eat or to drink a spasm seized his throat so that he could take in nothing but a little water. Fear appeared in his face and it was mirrored by the greater fear in his mother's. Still Asa could do nothing. One day the sudden clang of a dropped copper kettle stiffened his whole body with an uncontrollable jerk, while his lips drew back and bared his teeth. In terror, the mother fetched Asa, and when the priest arrived the boy was irrational.

In his home, two days later, Asa was predicting to his wife that the boy would be dead before the end of the week. "There is nothing that I can think of to try. I have not the faintest idea what is the matter with him. It wrings my heart to face his mother."

She tried to distract him. "Zachariah was in today. He wanted some advice concerning his flock. Two of them are sick, he says— the same two, by the way, who were bitten by the dog last month."

Asa looked at her sharply. Facts were falling into a pattern. The child—and now the sheep—all three bitten by the same dog! Still, it could be coincidence.

It was the very next day that, as Asa left the village to visit some patients in the next settlement, he noticed a man and wife in an olive grove. Spying him first, the woman turned to her husband and spoke. Asa could not hear what was said but saw the man shake his head. She went on speaking to him, something urgent in her manner, and now Asa could hear the anger in the man's voice as he bade her hold her tongue. It puzzled him. He knew the farmer as a mild-mannered man. He wondered what, apparently connected with himself, had provoked the man's anger. Well, he could hardly interfere, unsummoned, in a domestic dispute.

Much further along the trail he was accosted.

"Peace be to you, priest."

"And to you, peace. My wife told me that you were having trouble with your sheep." He followed the shepherd into the pasture, listening.

"It is those two who were bitten by the dog," said the shepherd. "They are not eating. It seems to me that they are becoming thin, and their noses are hot and their mouths dry. This has been going on for a week, and they are getting worse."

Asa looked at the animals. Here, too, the wounds were somewhat red, but the prodding fingers discovered no pockets of pus and elicited no sign of pain from the animals.

"I do not know what to do for your sheep," said Asa, "but I think that you would do well to keep them strictly out of contact with the rest of the animals. Whatever this may be, I fear that it is no trifle."

Later in the day, as he approached the village on his return, he saw the couple of the olive grove again. This time the woman succeeded in urging her reluctant spouse to approach the priest. It was she who spoke.

"Peace be with you, priest."

"And to you, peace."

" I have been trying for days to get my man here to visit you, but he is stubborn like all of his family. He is sick but is too obstinate to try to get help."

With mounting apprehension Asa looked at the arm on which he had dressed a dog bite some six weeks ago. "The bite is hurting you a little," he guessed.

"A little."

"And he has been irritable and without appetite." He addressed the woman.

"He has," she answered in surprise. "Usually he is as good tempered and placid a man as you will find, but for the past week he has snapped out at me for every little thing. He has not been eating."

The priest knew in advance the little that his examination would reveal. Nevertheless, he went over the man conscientiously. There was nothing that he could prescribe except bed rest—and obviously, that would soon be forced upon the man in any case. He went on home, cold with fear.

The boy died that night. All day he had lain in a coma, and his mother, rising to see to him before dawn, found him already stiff.

The second evening after that, the shepherd came to Asa's house to tell him that both of his sheep were very sick, one of them dying. Scarcely had he left when the orchardist's wife came in wringing her hands, to tell how her husband had arched his back in an uncontrollable spasm upon the slamming of a door.

Asa grew rigid. He felt the blood leave his cheeks, and terror kneaded his spine. It was a full minute before he forced himself to turn his head and look at his wife's foot. There was a slight redness at the margin of the almost healed dog bite on her ankle.

6

Again Asa was bidding farewell to his old teacher in Jerusalem. They stood with clasped hands. "Once more," Asa said, "thanks, with all my heart, for coming so promptly."

The older man waved a deprecatory arm. "I wish that I could have accomplished something."

"You did your best. No one could have saved her. No one could even have diagnosed her or the others." He paused. His eyes narrowed. "An Egyptian, perhaps?"

"Who knows?" The other sighed. "Though I rather doubt it."

"Peace be unto you," said Asa.

"And you—God give you peace!"

It would be a very different homecoming from the last. In fact, it would not be a homecoming at all. He no longer had a home, he reflected, as he strode southward. He had a house, but it was merely a shelter. Well, so be it. There was work to be done, and there was one good thing about his present state of mind. When one has reached the bottom, he told himself, there was no place to go but up.

Did he want to go up? Did he want anything? For himself, no. (But you will, a tiny voice whispered from his innermost being.)

He stifled the whisper furiously. Perhaps he had rejoiced too much in his good fortune. From now on he was living only to serve his people.

And serve them he did. While the modest rains of autumn came and went and snow visited the hilltops, he dispensed his myrrh and cassia, splinted fractures, quarantined contagions, and advised his people in a thousand problems of daily living—but he found no satisfaction in his work. Weekly, monthly, his discontent grew. All too clearly he saw his limitations—or better put—the limitations of the medical knowledge of his age and country. Nor did he have any sense of a growth of medical science. So far as Asa could see, physicians were traveling eternally in a track that led nowhere, like an ass harnessed to a millstone and going round and round the same worn path. Not that he felt he was by any means a charlatan. He did his best and, within the limits of his time, he felt that it was good.

His concern with the problem of evil was of course intensified by his own bereavement, but at no time after the first shock of his loss was he preoccupied by his own grief to the exclusion of the more general suffering. Here too, it seemed to him, he was going round and round a treadmill in trying to understand. Acceptance—yes; resignation even. Beyond that, he felt a consuming hunger to know. In a reasonable world there must be a reason for evil as there is for good, but the conventional explanations failed to suffice him.

He was wearily aware of the maneuverings of the parents of eligible daughters. Indeed, not a few frank propositions of matrimony came to him, but he was utterly uninterested. Not that he had vowed or resolved to spend the rest of his life in celibacy. It was a matter which he had successfully avoided exploring in the recesses of his own mind. Deeply, he knew that the time must come when he would come to terms with life. A man, like a people, though wounded, should recover or die, but he was young and had plenty of time.

For all that, as the spring approached, he found himself becoming more than a little uneasy when the fresh wind molded the clothes of a graceful girl against her body; and it began to require some self-discipline to keep his attention to an attractive female patient entirely on a professional level. When at ease at home, he pored over his studies of Egyptian, it was frequently hard to keep his imagination from details of evenings that he had spent quite differently in this very house.

It was the last year in which his life was to flow in its natural channel. The pattern came to an abrupt end on his next visit to Jerusalem for the Passover.

7

The letters had not exaggerated. His uncle was indeed a sick man. In fact, to the physician's eye, he was plainly doomed. The pain in the upper abdomen had become continuous, so that his uncle slept poorly. Asa could palpate a firm mass below the breast bone, and the whites of the eyes betrayed the beginning of jaundice. The rapid loss of weight, the bloody vomitus, the weakness, all foretold an early demise. The older man did not ask Asa about the outcome. That in itself told the young priest that he had guessed the end.

Nevertheless (and this, thought Asa, was an inspiring lesson!) the patient could still interest himself in the world of affairs. "The ambassador to Egypt will be sent very soon," he told his nephew. "As you can see, I shall not be the one. My friend, Malachi ben Ittai, will represent our interests at the court of Egypt. The choice, I think, is a good one. As you are aware, there are three parties among the advisers to the throne. The neutrality group, to which, I am afraid, the

King inclines, thinks that we can remain aloof from the rivalry between Assyria and Egypt. I do not think so. Neutrality as between great powers is something that little nations, caught in the sphere of their conflict, always desire but never achieve. There is a more numerous faction that wants to throw in our lot with the Chaldeans. I think that would be suicidal. They are hypnotized by the spectre of the Assyrian armies which throughout our lifetimes have marched irressistibly through our part of the world. To me, however, it seems very plain that Chaldea is approaching her doom. The Assyrian terror has done nothing to win support for her in her dark hour. Revolts spring up in all quarters of the empire, and the Medes will be pressing from the north. But no one has ever subdued Egypt for long; Necho will be a strong Pharaoh. He is capable, aggressive, and rich, and I think that he will hardly lose the chance to snatch what he can from the wreck. Our policy must be directed toward the south. Malachi thinks as I do, and I hope that he will be able to cement an alliance. There are many who still look with dread and suspicion upon the land where we were once enslaved. I can understand that point of view very well, but modern policy must be adjusted to the needs of the times. Ancient history should be let die."

"I agree," said Asa.

"Naturally, I am disappointed that I cannot undertake the great task, as I had hoped, but the Lord seems to will otherwise. Be it so. I have not forgotten, either, about my offer to try to get you some Egyptian medical texts. How have you come along, by the way, with the language?"

"I have mastered something of it."

"I am afraid your labor has been in vain. It would have been a delicate task at best, and I have no hope of being able to persuade ben Ittai to undertake it."

'This is a blow." Even as he spoke, Asa realized the selfishness of being more concerned over his own loss of opportunity than over the denial to his uncle of the fruition of his life's work, but even as he thought it Asa still did not put the feeling aside. "Don't you think that there is some possibility that you might persuade him?"

The dying man shook his head. "I would not try, even for you. The negotiations will be delicate. Necho is, as I have said, a strong king, but the priests are at his right hand. Anything that might, even in small measure, antagonize them would prejudice the mission. Malachi is somewhat more conservative than I, and I know that the barest possibility of risk would deter him. Besides," with a faint smile, "he would not take kindly to the idea of helping to introduce foreign ways into Judea."

Asa hesitated a moment. "Will you at least give me a letter of introduction to him and let me try? It is not for myself I ask it. You know only too well, obviously, how limited are the resources on which as physicians we draw. Is not the health of the Hebrew people worth even a much greater risk?"

"I will do that."

In asking for the letter, Asa had meant no more than he said, but it was with a very different request that he presented himself in the home of Malachi ben Ittai on the next day.

"You are welcome, priest." Ben Ittai clapped his hands and ordered fruit and wine. The servant brought a salver of figs and pomegranates, goblets, and a carafe of chased copper. There were the usual questions as to the health of the uncle's family and a brief period of small talk. Then Asa broached the purpose of his visit.

"My uncle tells me that you are to be King Jehoiakim's ambassador to Egypt."

"Apparently. There can be last minute changes, of course, but if the king's purpose holds, I shall be leaving in two months."

"As my uncle has probably informed you, I am a physician. We do the best that we can. As my uncle's condition testifies, our best is too frequently not good enough. I have been more and more dissatisfied with the state of medical knowledge in Judea. It is simply not adequate. In Egypt you will have the benefit of far more skillful practitioners of the healing art."

"And so I too have heard," admitted Malachi cautiously. "Whether it is true, of course, I do not know."

"No more do I, for the matter of that. But if it be so—and reports tend to confirm it—it would be hard if the Hebrew people were to continue to suffer for the lack of such relief as could be given them in other quarters."

"Joseph brought us down to Egypt once. Despite his good intentions, the results were disastrous."

Asa smiled in response. "I would hardly transport our people to Egypt, even if I could; and I see no prospect, even if it were desirable, of importing the Egyptian medical profession wholesale. It was my thought that the Egyptians could be induced to spare us some copies of their medical texts. My uncle, at the time when he hoped to make the trip himself, promised to try to obtain some of them for me. I know that you would be unwilling to risk offending the priests of Isis with such a request. I have a better idea."

"Your uncle, for all his friendship, does me less than justice," said the older man slowly. "I entertain no such narrow concept of the ambassadorial functions as you impute to me." (Why must these bureaucrats be so pompous in their language? thought Asa.) "An ambassador may conceivably fail in his main purpose. Any consolatory profits that I could salvage would be all to the good. Everything that Egypt might contribute to the welfare of Judea will be within my province. But what do you purpose?"

"Nothing less than this. An ambassador has the right to bring with him his own priest for embassy worship." Ben Ittai nodded. "I am asking you, therefore, to take me in that capacity. Once in Egypt, I want the help of your influence to obtain for me the privilege of studying their medicine."

Malachi whistled. "That is a large order. So far as I am aware, it is without precedent. I do not think that the priesthood of Isis would take kindly to the idea of introducing a foreigner into their mysteries." He thought for a moment. "I shall take the matter under advisement and let you know. Naturally, inquiries must be made."

"Azariah, the priest, is my teacher and friend. The head men of my district may also have something to tell you."

There was some desultory conversation and the young priest took his leave.

Apparently Malachi's inquiries were satisfactory, because within the week Asa received his appointment as priest to the Hebrew embassy to Egypt. A flurry of activity ensued. Asa went immediately to the Temple to see about a replacement for himself for the village practice. Azariah undertook to supply one from among his disciples.

This attended to, Asa turned southward to wind up his affairs and await his successor.

There was no long delay. Eleven days later the new young priest-physician reported in, and with a curious twofold emotion Asa introduced him to the local men of authority and discussed with him the status and history of his cases.

For all that Asa's life had lost much of its savor, with extra sadness he went about closing his house and saying goodbye to the villagers whom he had known and served. Deeply affecting, and of course gratifying, was their reluctance to part with him. But he never thought of canceling his plans, and soon he went up to Jerusalem from his village for the last time.

"You had best stay at my house until we set out," said Malachi. "Thus, we will all become better acquainted. It will not be necessary for you to purchase much in the way of supplies and equipment. Egypt can furnish all that you need, much of it better and perhaps cheaper than are available here. I have given the same advice to my wife and the girls," he went on, with a rueful smile," but they are in a frenzy of shopping nevertheless."

The girls? Asa frowned. He was still in no mood for romance and did not wish to be thrust into contact with unattached young women. Besides, he wanted to devote all of his time to his studies. But ben Ittai's next words relieved him.

"My household will consist of my wife, of course,"—Asa had met her—"my two youngest sons, aged 11 and 14, and my daughters. I call them both my daughters, although in fact only one is actually our own child. Zeruiah is engaged to be married to Joel ben Eliphas. He is to be secretary of the embassy. The other one is Tamar, the daughter of my old friend Jehoiada. She was orphaned of both parents at once in her eighth year. Worse, some insidious disease has left her blind since two years thereafter. She is now eighteen. Despite my best efforts, I have been unable to arrange a suitable marriage, on account of the combination of her affliction and some very serious political errors that make her inheritance something of a liability. Azaryahu ben Daniel, whom you have met in this house, has been confirmed as commercial attaché. I am taking my old body-servant Sallu, and my wife and the girls insist on their maid Yehoaddan. Whatever additional servants we need we will hire when we arrive at Sais. I have no doubt," he added with a smile, "that they will be hand-picked by the secret service of the Pharaoh."

That evening they assembled at dinner. Malachi's wife, an aristocratic-looking woman who claimed kinship with the king, greeted Asa cordially. The daughter Zeruiah was a vivacious red-head. She seemed very much wrapped up in her fiancé, and if to Asa young Joel seemed to be self-centered and rather a cold fish, that was her and Malachi's affair. Tamar was a reserved dark-haired girl with a good figure and a face that was neither beautiful nor plain.

Asa and Azaryahu took to one another at once. The commercial attaché was a merry, outgoing sort of fellow, obviously intelligent and, as was to appear, quite capable and serious under his veneer of wit.

There seemed little time in the ensuing weeks to spend in one another's company. A thousand preparations had to be made. Asa worked feverishly at his Egyptian, and in fact turned out to be the best linguist of them all, with Azaryahu a close second. Time passed rapidly. The king favored them with a formal presentation at court, at which Asa, used though he was to the Temple, was more than a little impressed by the cedar, bronze, and ebony of the palace. He acquitted himself well enough, responded fittingly to the king's hope that he would inaugurate a new era of health and longevity for Judea, and bowed himself out.

PART ii

The Egyptian Plain

Day after burning day the sun-god wheels through the Egyptian blue. In vain the traveler listens for the patter of the gentle rain; those scornful skies change never. The baking land swelters in the glare. But the young corn stretches luxuriantly upward beneath it. Great is Ra, lender of light to his children!

The mercy of the land comes from the south. Year after year in unvarying rhythm rise the waters of the river, gift of the monsoon clouds so far away; in late spring they rise, they flood the flatness of the valley, they slake the thirst of anguished earth. Great is Nilus, bringer of bread to his children!

In the narrow monotony of the plain, the changeless glare of the heavens, the recurrent bursting of the banks of the river, all is measured, all is counted, all is allotted by the servants of the king. Not here the unforeseen—not here the variant—not here the rebel. The armies, the tax gatherers, and the priests have made the Pharaoh into a divinity among men, feared and revered in Egypt and afar. Great is Amun, giver of glory to his children!

Surely this endless and unchanging cycle was established to sustain man for more than the moment of his mortal span. Surely his ka may endure forever, there in the western reaches where all is joy. And so, to house the living clay and dead of king, noble and priest, rise palace and temple, pyramid and tomb, incredibly ancient, incredibly huge. What though the peasantry groan under the burden of their rising? Great is Osiris, lord of life everlasting!

1

On a warm day at the end of summer the little caravan started on its way. Mounted on asses, as befitted those who came in peace (horses in that age and region betokened warlike intent), they came down from the hills. A squad of royal guards accompanied them to the borders of Philistia, where it was replaced in succession by a like number of swordsmen of Gath, Ziklag, and Gaza. The Philistine city-states were approaching the end of their history and their power was crumbling, but they still retained a quasi-independence. Asa looked curiously at the kilted soldiers with their circled feather headdresses, their small round shields, and their iron swords. So these were the men who once had dragged down King Saul!

Like most people, Asa had never been beyond the borders of his own land. The seas were free to all—at great risk, it was true—but not the land. A caravan route, its recognition won by intricate negotiations, might be maintained; but even so, any expedition could end in disaster. An embassy such as theirs could count on a measure of safety. Otherwise, to visit strange lands without overwhelming force was to court almost inevitable enslavement or death.

So they passed over the succession of low ridges below the mountains, across the narrow, fertile plain and southward along the sandy shore. All of them had seen the Great Middle Sea from their hilltops, but not for several generations had the Hebrew power extended to where one could bathe in sea water. Curiously they sipped the briny fluid, then headed toward Egypt.

Four days' travel brought them to Migdol, the Egyptian frontier station. The kilted corporal of the Gaza guards saluted the swarthy Egyptian lieutenant and requested shelter and provision before leading his men back north. From now on the party would be in the land of Egypt. This first sight of it was far from impressive. Did these few score mud huts huddled about a well under some dozens of palm trees, these lackadaisical soldiers, unkempt, their uniforms awry, these slatternly women and filthy, sore-covered children represent the power and the wealth of the Pharaoh? Seeing them was something of a letdown..

Tahpanhes, reached five days later, was slightly more impressive.

A huge stone fort came first into view. Nearer, they saw a cluster of huts around a stockade that was twice the height of a man. Ushered through the gate, they found themselves before a building which measured some fifty paces in each dimension. If seen from above it would have the form, roughly, of two granite cubes set side by side against one another but with considerable overlap. The walls receded slightly toward the top. There were two narrow, bronze-studded doors, each at the top of a flight of steep steps. Otherwise there were no openings in the walls except for a row of loopholes just below the roof.

Lycurgus, commander of the Greek garrison, made the visitors welcome. They spent a day resting from the desert. These Ionians and Carians, the best troops of the Egyptian army, in this fortress secured the northeastern gate of Egypt. Other detachments were scattered throughout the delta.

The ensuing few days of travel brought wonder to the Judean hillmen. A land which stretched absolutely level as far as the eye could see was remarkable in itself. But this was the season of the flooding of the Nile. Fully half of the land that they traversed was under water, and their progress through such areas was over a series of low causeways which served to retain as much as possible of the water through the following season. The abundance of water was the greatest of marvels to the dwellers in the parched highlands. Added to this was the circumstance, known to them, of course, but never before seen, that the water came not as rainfall (even in the delta the skies of Egypt were almost always blue) but exuded, as it were, out of the very earth. From this plain rose on very low mounds the houses and villages. The construction was mostly of mud. The more pretentious buildings were of brick; of stone, the universal building material of their own land, the travelers saw nothing.

This richness of moisture, they discovered, brought its own problems. Sewage disposal in their own country was governed by rigidly enforced laws which were adapted to the terrain. All human excrement was deposited outside of the zones of housing and there buried. In the half-flooded delta this was impossible, and the stench of man's making was unpleasantly evident almost wherever they passed. Added to this was the plague of gnats and mosquitoes, controllable at night only by the use of netting supplied them by the Ionian light infantrymen who were their escorts.

Strange as was the countryside, Sais, the capital, when they reached it, was as great a marvel. Here was a city beside which the architecture of Jerusalem appeared crude and primitive. The poorer quarters presented the same mud construction that they had seen before, but from this there was a transition to row upon row of uniform, attached brick dwellings that housed many of the workers and the humbler class of merchants. The heart of the city, however, was made up of the very ornate, beautifully faced brick mansions of the well-to-do, sloping slightly toward the roof and decorated in pastel colors. Even these were far surpassed by the magnificent dressed-stone construction of the temples and the Pharaoh—the Great House of the King—from which the monarch took his title. Here were broad flights of steps, huge pastel-colored columns with leafy capitals, statues of crouching lions, bulls, men, and gods, all painted to the life. Even Malachi ben Ittai, despite an attempt at professional imperturbability, confessed his amazement.

A representative of the vizier met the travelers at the edge of the city and conducted them to a small palace that had been set aside for their use. The women in the party exclaimed in delight at the broad halls, beautiful murals, high-ceilinged rooms, and exquisitely wrought furniture. Not the least of the delights was the enclosed garden with a rectangular reflecting pool amid a riot of flowers.

The house was adequately staffed, and to the perfunctory query as to whether or not all was satisfactory, ben Ittai naturally answered in the affirmative. His wife's first duty was to instruct the cook in the dietary laws of the Hebrew religion. The flesh of cattle, sheep, and goats alone was to be used, the animals to be slaughtered painlessly under the supervision of a member of the household. All shellfish were forbidden; scaly fishes were acceptable, as were the locusts, universally esteemed in that part of the world.

The travelers were allowed a week in which to rest and adjust to the new surroundings before ben Ittai received a summons to present his credentials before the king.

Psammetichus, first of the Saite kings, and Necho his son had stimulated a vigorous revival of the ancient Egyptian arts in this new capital, even though the means at their disposal were limited. The great house would not have stood comparison with the palaces of Thutmose or of Rameses the Great, but it was distinctly impressive, especially to those who had no standard of comparison higher than the court of Jehoiakim at Jerusalem.

On the broad, gently sloping steps of the palace, Ranofer the vizier stood waiting to receive them. On either hand crouched a granite lion. Behind the vizier was a portico of rose-tinted, fluted columns. Passing through these and through several large antechambers, the ambassadors found themselves in the throne room.

Rose-red walls and pillars, the latter with green lotus capitals, supported a carved and painted cedar ceiling. At the far end of the hall sat the Pharoah on his golden throne, which was raised by a dais to the height of ten or a dozen low steps. Behind him two servants slowly waved ornate fans of ostrich feathers. Beside him stood a shaven-headed, white-robed priest of Amun, staff in hand. On the right of the dais was a file of Egyptian infantrymen, naked to the waist, armed with spears, swords, and shields of leopard hide. On the left was a like number of Ionian hoplites, the heavily armed Greek infantrymen, with horse-tail-decorated helmets, shining breastplates, and greaves on their shins. Like their counterparts they were armed with spears, swords, and oval shields. Next to the dais sat a lion cub, its leash in the hand of a palace servant.

The Pharaoh was a moderately tall, well built man of early middle age dressed in a white robe. On his head the tall, mitre-like double crown, white above and red below, symbolized upper and lower Egypt. His right hand held the golden whip, his left the blue and white miniature shepherd's crook, the two crossed on his breast. Ranged about under murals of battle scenes were the courtiers. In former times these would have been simply garbed, but in the court of Sais they wore sweeping, brilliantly colored robes.

The ambassador and his staff bowed deeply, advanced to the foot of the dais and bowed again, after which the vizier presented them to the Pharaoh. Then turning to the visitors, he intoned, "His Majesty King Necho, Son of the great Psammetichus, the strong bull, the Divine Osiris, Lord of Upper and Lower Egypt, greets his brother Jehoiakim, King of Judea, and welcomes Malachi ben Ittai and his staff to his court."

"Brother" was purely courtesy. Jehoiakim was incomparably weaker than the Pharaoh and everyone present knew it: Egypt had set him upon the throne in the place of his brother. Malachi produced his letter and put it into the hands of the vizier. "Let my lord the king read the words of my master Jehoiakim, King of Judea. He sends his greeting by his servant Malachi ben Ittai and therewith his prayer that the days of my lord the king may be many and that his land may be fruitful in all of them. We have come that we may know the will of my lord the king, that there may be peace for all time between Egypt and Judea and that the caravans may travel north and south for the increase of the two lands. Let therefore the words of thy servant find grace in the eyes of the king of Egypt that I may hear his wisdom and enjoy his favor."

Compliments ran on back and forth for almost half an hour; then the audience was concluded.

The household settled into a routine fairly easily. Zeruiah was much taken up, naturally, with her fiancé and with the bazaars of Sais, so that the ordering of the home was shared by her mother and Tamar. The ladies were thrown into a fever of anticipation with the receipt of an invitation to a formal reception in honor of the Judeans, to be held at the home of the vizier.

The party began at about noon. Tables had been set under a large covered portico opening upon the garden of the vizier's house. The host certainly spared nothing for the entertainment of his guests. Upon arrival, each was crowned with a small cone of perfumed ointment, which gradually melted down upon his head. Slaves served a variety of rich foods. Baked and roasted mutton and beef appeared between dishes of onions, beans, cucumbers, and olives. There were fish, boiled and fried in olive oil. Wheat and barley breads were set out. Fruits included dates, grapes, figs, and melons. For the thirsty there were milk and water, beer and wine. The roast duck garnished with leeks was particularly delicious.

Beer, a perennial favorite of dwellers on the Nile, was new to the Judeans and they did not particularly relish it. They had, however, to confess that the Egyptian wine deserved its fame.

Servants of both sexes went to and fro among the guests to replenish empty plates and goblets. Physician though he was, Asa was more than a little disturbed and embarrassed by the proximity of serving girls clad only in a narrow girdle or a diaphanous skirt. He carried off the situation as well as might be. He suspected that Malachi, despite his years, and Joel, despite his air of sophistication, felt the same way. As to the reaction of Malachi's wife and daughters, he could only guess with wry amusement. Azaryahu frankly enjoyed the display. Not that Asa was immune to the effect of unveiled female flesh. Priest-physician though he might be, Asa was a normal male. Female nudity produced the effect that it might be expected—indeed, that it was designed—to have. These courtiers of Sais were no artless primitives but strove deliberately to whet an appetite to the end of its more voluptuous satiation.

The entertainment too, although parts of it might have been furnished in certain very special circles in the Judean capital, was in part purely Egyptian. A pair of wrestlers highly skilled in their art battled to several falls to Egyptian cheers. Naked dancing girls performed, while others accompanied them on harps and pipes. In beer- and wine-bibbing Malachi's party without exception exercised restraint. Some of the Egyptian guests, however, were far gone in drink by evening.

Among the company was Irj, Greatest Physician of Lower and Upper Egypt, ranking member of the profession. Watching his opportunity, Asa caught his superior's eye and glanced meaningfully at Irj. Ben Ittai sighed and gave a permissive nod. Asa drew Irj aside and bared his desires.

Irj was non-committal. "I would not say that it is out of the question," he said gravely, "but the matter will take some doing. We have an excellent medical school here at Sais. The students are carefully chosen from among the better families. We want none of the vulgar among our colleagues. Many of the young men, moreover, have some standing in theological circles. Medicine here, as obviously is true in your own country, is closely tied up with divine worship. Your status in that respect certainly qualifies you, but the priesthoods of Sekhmet and of Thoth must give consent to have you initiated into their mysteries."

"I must make plain at the outset," explained Asa, "that I may under no considerations participate in the worship of any but my own God."

Such at least was his sense, although he struggled sadly with the strange tongue.

Irj looked at him with some surprise. This hillman was really narrow and bigoted, like all barbarians. Still, one must be polite to a member of the embassy of a now friendly power, even one so backward and tiny that only by courtesy could it be called a power at all.

"The authorities will have to consider that," he rejoined. "Your foreign nationality of course poses another difficulty. It has not in the past been our policy to permit the export of our technologies and arts. If the ambassador can prevail upon the vizier to speak a word in your behalf from that point of view, I will see what can be arranged with the priests of Sekhmet and of Thoth, Bes, and Thoeris. Above all, Amon must give consent."

"I shall certainly be most appreciative of any help you can manage," said the Judean. "I am sure that the ambassador, and even my king, would also be grateful."

"Frankly, I am more interested in obliging them than you," answered Irj, with a smile that robbed his words of unpleasantness. "Meanwhile, may I make you acquainted with the Lady Nektanebis? Asa ben Abdiel, my lady, priest to the embassy of King Jehoiakim."

Asa bowed to a slender young woman half a head shorter than himself. Her features were regular and delicate, her smile friendly but with some reserve.

"And how long, son of Abdiel, shall you be drinking the water of the Nile?"

"That will be as my king wills. Suddenly I find myself hoping that it will be for long indeed." Aptly said, mused Asa, but why in the world did I say it?

"I see that the arts of gallantry are known beyond the borders of the land of the black earth." Then, "Is it not ill for a priest to be so far from his temples?"

"I am not that kind of priest. In my own land I have but little to do, professionally, with worship, and nothing with the Temple, although when there are calls upon me, I do what I can. Primarily, I am a physician."

"I have met the ambassador's lady and her daughters, but nothing was said of your family. Have you left your wife and children at home? Or is yours one of the priesthoods of which, as I have heard, celibacy is the rule?"

"Definitely not. The priesthood is hereditary," said Asa, "but my wife died, leaving me no children." It no longer hurt to say it.

"I am in like case, and have been for these two years." There was a brief silence. "You will be lonely."

"If my hopes are realized, I will have little time to think about my loneliness. The physicians of your land are famous throughout the earth. It is my hope that I may be permitted to study here and drink from the fountain of their knowledge."

"And that I suppose is why you are really here?" Asa nodded. "Did you mention that to Irj?"

"I did. He neither encouraged me nor did the reverse."

Use of a barely mastered foreign language is quickly exhausting. When Nektanebis' attention was claimed by a group of guests, Asa felt constrained to seek his countrymen.

Azaryahu ben Daniel had been observant. "Aha! I find our priest, our hermit, our bookworm, monopolizing the most charming woman in Sais!" Asa made a disclaimer, although pleased, like any other man, at the sally.

"Penta-Oser has invited our party to his country seat for several days. The ambassador has accepted for all of us, and we are to leave in a week."

Asa made the proper acknowledgments. He had no desire to absent himself from the capital, but he had to follow the ambassador's lead in social life. It might be interesting to see how Egyptian nobles lived on their estates.

Life at the embassy had fallen into a routine. Malachi was engaged constantly in receiving official or semi-official visitors and paying visits on his own account, when he was not informing himself on the thousand and one aspects of Egyptian politics and economy. Joel, the secretary, was usually at his side. Azaryahu prowled through the bazaars and interviewed an endless succession of shippers, craft-foremen, and merchants. Zeruiah was rather idle, surrendering herself to the shopping and party-going of the city with a zest that Asa found difficult to understand.

It was amazing to him that Tamar could carry as much responsibility as she had voluntarily assumed. The blind girl moved quickly and surely through the palace despite her brief occupancy of it. She could sense a wall or a right-angled turn in a passage. It was of course a rule of the household that furniture was not to be moved without warning, and obstacles were never to be deposited except in specified places against the wall. Nevertheless, her performance was still impressive, and no one would have thought on casual observation that she could not see. She seemed to divine what the domestics were about. Beyond that, it worried the family that she was beginning to pass through the adjacent streets.

It was Asa who found time hanging heavily on his hands. Impatient as he was to begin his medical work, he had little to occupy him beyond the studies in Egyptian which all members of the embassy were pursuing. His duties as chaplain were very light. Under these circumstances, he frequently joined Azaryahu in his prowling. The result was that he often found himself involved with that outgoing young man in convivial gatherings in home or tavern. The two were very unlike, but enjoyed one another nevertheless.

2

"Tomorrow," Penta-oser had said, "I am going to give you a sample of a sport which I know will be new to you, mountaineers that you are. We are going into the marsh to hunt ducks."

The ambassador and his wife begged off, but the five young people accepted. In Judea, Malachi would not have permitted his daughters to go unchaperoned into so lonely an area with three young men. Up to a point, however, he was willing to fall in with the freer customs of this country.

Accordingly, the party had risen before dawn, made a brief chariot journey in the dark, then walked some distance through increasingly marshy country. In the first of the greyness they embarked in three reed boats and pushed off into a narrow waterway between head-high stalks of papyrus. Penta-oser set out several tame ducks as decoys and the group settled down to wait. They heard the calls of ducks and other fowl and at times an exciting whir of wings as the birds sought feeding grounds after their night's sleep.

The day brightened until Penta-oser could clearly see a pair of ducks, circling to settle by his decoys. Strongly they flew and beautifully against the sky, finally stiffening wings and legs for a landing. Standing suddenly, he drew back his arm and hurled a curved stick slightly longer than his forearm; it sped to intercept the flight path of one of the birds. As the bird fell, Penta-oser released a hunting cat that clambered out over the papyrus stems and soon returned with the bird in its mouth.

Joel and Zeruiah, in the boat with their host, congratulated him upon his marksmanship.

"My favorite throwing-stick," he answered, as he held out the retrieved weapon for their inspection. "Beautifully shaped. A straight stick would follow a straight path, and a swift and graceful flyer like the wild duck would avoid it with ease. But the bend in the stick gives it a curved path, and the duck does not know how to allow for it."

Asa described for Tamar the scenery and the occurrences of the hunt. It had surprised him, in the first place, that visionless as she was, she should care to go on such an expedition; yet she was obviously enjoying herself. He also noted with astonishment how much more of the surroundings he observed when retailing them for another's benefit.

She showed an interest in the smallest details of color and form. Several times she spotted a flight of ducks by the swish of their wings before the others had become aware of it. She asked Asa about the flowers, the birds, and even the fish. Asa noticed a school of tadpoles darting by overside. Half playfully, he made a scoop out of a piece of open mesh cloth. He retrieved a few and dumped them into a water-filled gourd.

"But these are not tadpoles," he exclaimed and fished one out for a closer examination. "They are of the same size and more or less of the same shape, and like tadpoles they are black, but now that I look at this one closely, I perceive that it has a pair of pincer-like jaws, and it has a head and body division which tadpoles lack."

He looked overside again. "Here, clinging to a papyrus stem, is a tiny, whitish, worm-like creature. I am putting it into the gourd. It wriggles about. One of the tadpole-things is investigating it. He seems to be attacking it! Now two of them are tearing at it. Apparently they are hunters, and this is their prey." He looked into the swamp water once more. "Here comes another school of the same—no, these I believe are really tadpoles. They are suddenly darting straight away. Ah, I see why. A fish as long as my hand has flashed in among them and is devouring as many as it can catch."

He paused. "Behind us, some three boat-lengths away, a small green frog sits on a floating leaf. An insect flies past. A blurred flick about his mouth and the fly is gone. Oh, a serpent has flung himself from the thicket and seized the frog at the shoulder! The frog struggles, but he cannot free himself. The serpent has wound him in its coils. Now it has taken him by the head to swallow him."

Tamar shivered. "This peaceful scene, this rich land, and yet in so tiny a bit of space and time, so much killing!"

"It almost seems," Azaryahu put in, "as though the more plenty, the more strife."

"Worse than that," answered Asa, "the more plenty, the more life; and the more life, the more devouring. We have seen a struggle for existence in our own hills, where the fox preys upon the lamb, the hawk upon the dove. Lions, fortunately, have become scarce, but this blind death-struggle among the tiny crawling things seems to me infinitely grimmer, more unceasing and more relentless."

A grim struggle indeed, he mused. These were all creatures of God, and yet they pursued and devoured one another with unremitting hunger. Were they so different from the hawk and the dove, the fox and the lamb? It might well be that all flesh was as one in the eyes of its Creator, each being sent forth with permission to seek, as it could, its meat from God. Were not man, man's struggles and man's drive for meat and mate, of a piece with this bitter warfare of the wild things?

But if this were so, and if all life were viewed with an equal eye by the Creator of life, how account for His declaring some flesh clean, other kinds unclean? Why had the Lord forbidden most kinds of meat to His people? Did the Lord care indeed which form of life preyed upon which? It did not seem so, and yet, there was the word in Holy Writ. If this were indeed not the decree of God but merely the codified prejudice of some human lawgiver, how much else might have been inserted unbidden into the Divine decree? It was a deeply painful train of thought.

The Egyptian had had fair luck, but as the day broadened the ducks flew higher and seldom came within range. The party repaired to a nearby island to eat, rest, and while away the time until the approach of evening twilight should send their quarry once more to seek food. Asa's perplexity continued to gnaw away at the back of his mind.

As late afternoon came upon them, the six re-embarked as before, Penta-oser's attendant departing in one boat with the remains of the meal. The others resumed their former station, but few birds came their way, and the impatient hunter poled off to try his luck elsewhere. Asa, Tamar, and Azaryahu remained where they were. Once a strange boat passed them, poled rapidly by two strangers who made no answer to their greeting. Time passed and twilight came. They were becoming uneasy when there came a hail in Joel's voice. Minutes later, the other boat reappeared in the gloom.

There was Joel, disheveled, sweaty, anxious, leaning on a pole, while in the bow sat Zeruiah, Penta-oser's bleeding head cradled in her lap.

"What happened?" exclaimed Azaryahu, as Asa began to examine the unconscious man.

"A thrown stone caught him in the head. I don't know whether the motive was robbery or revenge, or even whether it may not have been aimed at a duck. I caught a glimpse of the thrower as I retrieved Penta-oser from overside. Since then we have been wandering around trying to find you."

The gash was on the right side of the head above the ear. There was blood in the ear, but it seemed to Asa to have come from without rather than from within the auditory canal. This was a favorable sign. He could palpate no depressed area in the skull.

"There is little that I can do here. We must get him back at once."

"We certainly must," remarked Joel, "before the attacker arrives armed to finish the job—and us."

"Easily said," remarked Azaryahu, "but we could not find our way unguided through this swamp even in the daylight, and now it is dark. I would almost as soon be knocked on the head as be eaten alive by these mosquitoes."

"I can take you back," said Tamar quietly.

"You!" the four ejaculated as one.

"To me the night is no handicap, and I have long been accustomed to relying on other senses than sight. Turn the boat to the right until I bid you stop." They did so. "Now paddle ahead." They went for some distance. "Now turn sharply left," she commanded. Soon the boats grounded. With the paddles and some clothing, they improvised a litter for Penta-oser and, Tamar leading, the party started off. A few times she hesitated, and twice she changed direction. Presently she halted. "If you shout now for help you should be answered."

It was much later when she explained. "The wind had been blowing steadily all day, and I judged our original course by it. True, it might have changed at sunset, but some chance I had to take. Where we changed course in the boats we must have been near an island on which an animal had recently died or been killed—I had smelled the stench of the carrion on our way out. Our landing at exactly the right spot was a piece of good fortune, but we could have found it by exploring the bank to both sides. At any rate, there was a wooden post there to which the boats had been moored. I started walking, again according to the wind, until we came to a point where I had noticed a very intense perfume of some flowers whose name I did not know. Some fifteen paces beyond there we made a half turn to the right, and when I felt some particularly firm ground again, as this morning, under my feet, we turned left. A few minutes brought us to the point where I remembered having heard a clucking of hens, and I knew that your hail would be answered."

"Unbelievable!" exclaimed Asa.

"Not so unbelievable, if you know Tamar," Zeruiah answered. "I have known her to perform remarkable feats before."

"Partly luck, nevertheless," was Tamar's disclaimer. "Had the distances been wrong, I might well have walked astray, or I might have led you into any number of obstacles. Had I given you time to consider all this in advance," with a mischievous smile, "you would never have trusted me, and we had to do something at once."

The denouement of this little adventure was amazing to all parties concerned. Penta-oser made a rapid and a complete recovery, but his erstwhile guests found themselves the target of veiled accusations. For a week or more they encountered more than a few scowls on the part of people in the street. It was not, as the vizier explained to Malachi, that any blame could possibly lie with the Hebrews for the attempt, if such it were, on the life of the popular princeling. The government was known to be conducting conversations with the Hebrews, which was sufficient reason for the opposition party to be hostile to its aims. It had seized, therefore, on this opportunity to arouse public feeling against the Judean embassy.

The only apparent effect of the affair was to bind more closely Asa and the other members of the embassy. With Joel indeed he had but little in common, but he became even faster friends with the commercial attaché. Tamar's exploit had definitely brought her more prominently to his attention. He noted with appreciation the efficiency with which she discharged her household duties and the grace and sureness with which she moved in her darkness.

3

As months went by Asa's mastery of the language progressed. He spent as much time as possible in conversation with the Egyptians, carefully repeating each new word and every new grammatical construction as it came to his ear.

"Many disagreements," he remarked to the lady Nektanebis in the garden of the Babylonian ambassador one day, "are based solely on nuances of meaning. If that remark be banal—as I know it is—in the personal field, it may still have a certain amount of freshness in world affairs. I think the recent war between our countries may well have been a case in point."

"Perhaps," she suggested smilingly, "a royal semanticist could have saved Josiah's kingdom for him."

"Seriously, I think he could have. There was no essential conflict of national aims."

"I have never followed the details of politics, even though my family has always been attached to the court. Are you interested in statecraft?"

"Every one who is interested in his future—or in whether or not he will have a future—must be interested in statecraft," Asa reflected aloud. "Naturally I am concerned for the welfare of my country and am therefore interested in its foreign policy. I should like to see more general interest. There was a time when my people had no king, and each ordered his affairs as seemed best to himself, but even in a kingdom public opinion exerts pressure and makes itself felt."

"I am not sure that what you say has been true in Egypt," said the woman thoughtfully. "True, Pharaoh Necho must balance the elements of his people against one another, but in the days of the older and stronger monarchs, only the priests might influence royal policy. Be that as it may, don't you think that such things are best left to statesmen? A professional is almost always more competent than an amateur."

"In medicine, yes," said Asa. "In craftsmanship, yes. In most fields, yes. But in statecraft, I am not so sure. Naturally, I would not criticize Malachi ben Ittai even if I thought him wrong, and I have not been associated with him long enough to think him so. A foreign minister generally has come to be a man of such intellectual arrogance that he conceals his purposes not only from his people but frequently from his king. If I had a field and engaged a husbandman to work it, I would not for one moment tolerate his telling me that he would not explain what he was doing because I could not understand or because he feared lest an incautious word of mine would betray his plans to my enemy, to my undoing. Yet on no better ground do these gentlemen of the diplomatic service pursue their machinations in remote inaccessibility."

"But will you not admit, priest, that they may well know their own business better than a layman?"

"I will not admit it. It is, as I see it, the function of a foreign office so to reconcile the apparently opposing desires of two nations that there need be no conflict; or failing this, to persuade its own or another government that it is in the long run advisable to accept even the decision which seems to run counter to its immediate interests.

"And yet, once a generation or oftener, the diplomats fail in their task and have to call in the generals to get them out of the mess into which their own obstinacy or knavery has plunged them."

She laughed, "You are hard on them indeed." Then, leaning languorously backward, "sometimes I think you are hard on yourself as well."

It was not easy for Asa to pretend to be completely obtuse, but he did his best. "As priest or as physician," he replied, "one must be hard on one's self or drift into a sinecure and fail his God, his people, and his own soul."

But Nektanebis was not deceived.

4

Malachi took up with Ranofer the vizier the question of Asa's admittance to the school of medicine. Shortly thereafter the dean of the faculty was summoned to the palace.

"I do not like the idea at all," said Nebamon with a frown. He was a tall, patrician-looking priest of Sekhmet somewhat archaically clad in a plain white linen kirtle and cape. He affected the ancient fashion of a clean-shaven skull and bore a long staff with its handle carved in the representation of a lion's head. "Irj has already broached the matter to me. I told the Greatest Physician that I considered it most unfitting that I, a servant of Sekhmet, should introduce into her mysteries this savage who, in his presumption, states in advance that he will not pay her homage. He, a worshipper of some obscure deity who has neither shape nor statue that anyone can find, to deny her rites to our lion-headed Lady of Pestilence! Nor would it be pleasing in the sight of Thoth or Bes or Thoeris, to name but a few of the divinities we may offend."

"Your point is well made," said the other diplomatically, "but I think that His Majesty, as the earthly incarnation of the divine Osiris, can answer to the Great Ones for any slight that this Judean may put upon them."

The other frowned in distaste. "There was a time when a Pharaoh would have scorned to have any of his servants instruct a barbarian. This principle was specifically affirmed, you remember, in our ancient treaty with the Hittite king."

"And as specifically waived, you remember, in a subsequent covenant with Phoenicia!"

"A great mistake, in my opinion, and it would be a greater to share our knowledge with foreigners in these troublous times."

The vizier looked at him sardonically. "And how long will Judeans be foreigners? The Pharaoh is still strong and ambitious. Babylon is beset in the East. Need I say more?"

"Have your way," conceded Nebannon, "but you will live to regret it."

The temple of Sekhmet stood at the edge of the town. Here her priesthood conducted a medical clinic and school. In a bygone age, when the great cities of Egypt were upriver to the south, the temples were built in outlying desert areas; but there was no desert in the rich alluvial delta of the Nile.

The building was massively walled, but except for carved and painted roof beams, supported by walls and columns, it was open to the sky. Statues of the goddess, represented as a draped human female with the head of a lioness, stood about the central enclosure, and before the largest burned a flame fed by spiced and perfumed oils.

The medical curriculum was divided into several courses of study, as specialization was highly developed. General and internal medicine was under the patronage of the god Thoth, who had revealed to man the arts of writing and healing, as well as several others. Future surgeons were under the protection of Sekhmet, the lion-headed goddess, Lady of Pestilence, who delighted in blood. The eye was the chosen field of other students, with hawk-headed Horus as their patron. Midwifery and diseases of women were the province of Thoeris (represented as a belly-swollen hippopotamus), ugly, dwarflike Bes, and occasional lesser divinties. Dentistry was still another of the medical disciplines.

The daily activities began by an admission of patients to the clinic. The instructors would examine them under the eyes of the students, pointing out signs and symptoms, indicating the diagnosis, the treatment, and the prognosis or guess as to the probable outcome of the disease. This would consume much of the morning. The early afternoon was taken up with a classroom exercise which was usually a lecture or a reading from a manuscript. Books were scarce and expensive, and it was a rare student who could acquire his own. The junior instructors were known simply as physicians. Over them were set the Chiefs of Physicians. A few bore the title Inspector of Physicians, but only Nebamon, the head, was entitled to call himself Superintendent of Physicians.

Judean physicians, of course, were general practitioners, and Asa accordingly had arranged to spend time successively in each of the specialties. It was with considerable excitement that he seated himself for his first lecture and saw his professor unroll a papyrus scroll and begin to read its archaic content.

The physician's secret: knowledge of the heart's movement and knowledge of the heart.

There are twenty-two vessels in man; they carry the air to his heart and also carry the air to all his limbs.

There are two vessels in him to his breast; they make burning in the anus. What is done against it: fresh dates, leaves of fig, of sycamore, water, pounded together, strained, to be taken by the patient for four days until he is well.

There are two vessels in him to his thigh; if he is ill in his thigh or his feet ache, then thou shalt say concerning him: it is that the vessel of his thigh has received the illness. What is done against it: a viscous fluid and natron are boiled together and drunk by the man for four days.

There are two vessels in him to his neck; if he is ill in his neck and his eyes are dim-sighted, then thou shalt say concerning him: it is that the vessels of his neck have received the disease. What is done against it: decoction of myrtle leaves, washerman's slops, pinion, fruit of the vine are mixed with honey, applied to his neck, and the neck is bandaged with it for four days.

Most of the pharmacopeia consisted of substances known to Asa, although some of them, such as human and animal feces, the milk of a woman who had just borne a male child, womb of she-cat, and others, were substances which he would never have thought of using medicinally.

It was, it appeared, the custom of the Egyptian physicians to divide their cases into three categories: illnesses which they expected to treat successfully, illnesses which they would treat but with doubt as to the outcome, and illnesses with which they would attempt nothing. Asa was reluctant to make such sharp divisions among his patients and particularly to abandon the incurable to despair.

Indeed, Asa's studies in internal medicine were a tremendous disappointment to him. With much of the treatment he disagreed. Some of it he considered nonsensical. Much of it he considered impious. The keenness of observation of the Egyptian medical men and the care with which they took histories and evaluated symptoms he appreciated, but to dismiss a patient with a charm or an amulet or to have him drink the water in which a papyrus sheet bearing an invocation to an idol had been boiled he considered at best charlatanism and at worst blasphemy.

It is probable that he gave his hosts less than their due. A physician traveling abroad is, unconsciously, overly critical of all that he sees in his field. He is but too aware of the deficiencies of his colleagues and takes their accomplishments for granted. Had the medical practitioners of Egypt been as inept as they seemed to Asa, it is unlikely that the profession could have retained its prestige.

Naturally, Asa had better sense than to voice his criticisms to Egyptian ears. Even in the embassy he refrained from adverse comment for the most part, fearing, probably correctly, that he might be misunderstood. Before a minor embassy function, however, waiting for the guests to arrive, he found himself alone in a corner of the garden with Tamar, who drew him out.

"I have heard quite a bit about symptomatology and diagnosis," Asa admitted, "but in therapeutics—treatment—I suspect, between ourselves, that Egypt has fewer secrets than we had thought. One point I must concede—we had believed that in Egypt the art of medicine was only for the rich. This is not so. The temple physicians are adequately supported by the worshippers; payment is not a consideration when medical advice is sought. One would think that this would lead to a rapid and perfunctory examination of the patient, but at the school at least, this is not so. However, there is a difference in the dispensing of drugs. A patient receives only such medicines as he can pay for. The more expensive materia medica are out of reach of any but the wealthy."

"Then the medical care that the poor receive is actually of small value," observed Tamar.

He made a wry face. "I am not sure that they suffer a disadvantage in that direction as against the rich. Sometimes I find it very difficult conscientiously to prescribe as I am bidden."

"Do you not then approve of the medical art of Egypt?" Asa whirled in embarrassment to see the Inspector of Physicians, Iwti, who had come up behind him. Zeruiah, Joel, and several guests were approaching.

The priest thought fast. "My complaint is on theological grounds. I am, as you know, forbidden by my God to serve any other divine beings. I cannot therefore with honesty give a patient a charm inscribed with a prayer to Horus."

Iwti laughed. "You young men are either too irresponsible or you try to carry the cares of the world upon your shoulders. The gods, I suspect, have more attractive occupations than keeping a continual eye upon the petty misdeeds of men. I have marked you, Asa. You are hard at work all day, and I can tell from your recitations that you spend much of your off time with borrowed manuscripts. I would suggest more relaxation."

"Allow me to prescribe for the physician," put in a younger Egyptian, grinning. "I shall be glad to direct him to a source where he may purchase a lovely and lively dancing girl."

Zeruiah giggled.

"Unfortunately, that is not lawful," said Asa, uncomfortably, but aware that he would like nothing better.

"How unlawful? Do not tell me that the men of your people are forbidden to enjoy women and that you must call in foreign assistance to propagate the race?"

Asa ignored the jibe. "Although the men of my people are not specifically forbidden to know women other than their wives, the Divine word exhorts against it. To the priesthood, consorting with loose women is expressly banned. In fact, it is more or less expected, and of the high priests it is required, that there be only one wife."

Zeruiah giggled again. "As if there could be any doubt how you men spend your leisure time!"

Asa wondered, as countless men have done before and after him, at the imaginings of a circumspect, well-brought-up young woman. In general, her idea of the private life of the average male was not fit to be spoken aloud, an incongruity that no man has resolved and none will. At the same time, the possibilities involved in the purchase of a woman were tantalizingly and delightfully imaginable. As a priest of the Holy One, he should be the last to befoul the bed of any woman, but to voice this principle, he knew, would be to sound mawkish. He shrugged and made as if to turn away.

An Ionian captain of the palace guard could not resist a jeer. "Has the possibility occurred to you that you might be something of a prig?"

"It has. I do not think so, but it is possible."

"Oh, come," and Zeruiah spoke up for him. "Our priest is somewhat stuffy, but nice."

Asa knew, of course, that in some quarters his scruples made him an object of scorn, but that bothered him not a whit.

"For all that," offered an Egyptian, "one of our Egyptian girls may yet surprise him."

"For all that," murmured Asa to himself, "she might."

5

There was an unexpected sequel to the hunting party. Asa was handing a female slave a packet of dried liver of a swallow pounded with viscous beer. "The chief of the clinic bids you take this to your mistress," he said, "and rub it on her breasts, belly, and thighs. This should restore her quickly from the effects of the miscarriage." At this moment an Egyptian soldier entered with the request that Asa accompany him to the hall of judgment. Asa washed his hands and complied.

A scribe pointed to a dirty, unshaven man clad only in a torn loin cloth. "Have you ever seen this fellow before?" he asked. There was something familiar about the man, but Asa could not place him.

"Ever seen him in a boat?"

Of course! That was it! This was the man whom Asa had glimpsed poling past on the day that Penta-oser had been assaulted in the marsh. He told the scribe so. The latter nodded grimly.

"His trial will take place on the day after tomorrow. You will appear and give evidence."

It was with considerable disturbance that Asa spent the next day and a half. Despite the man's offense, there was something desperate and pitiable in his appearance. It is not pleasant for a normal man to injure a person who has not harmed him, although of course Asa recognized his duty under the law. Malachi assured him that he had no alternative but to testify.

"I hope they don't flog the poor devil too hard," remarked the younger man. Malachi, who by now knew something about Egypt, gave him a sidelong glance, but said nothing.

The trial was brief. There was little doubt that the accused, a rascal of no property and no family, had launched a murderous assault with the purpose of robbery upon the person of the nobly born Penta-oser. The fact that, terrified at his own deed, he had fled without attempting to follow it up, constituted no extenuating circumstance in the eyes of the law. The culprit was found guilty and sentenced to be impaled alive.

A horrified "No!" burst from Asa's lips. All eyes were turned toward him. The judge frowned.

"Does the foreigner take exception to the justice of the Pharaoh?"

"Far be it from me to criticise the Pharaoh or his court, but may not some mercy be shown? After all, despite his wicked intention, the man neither killed nor stole!"

The judicial lip curled in a sneer. "I do not know how you Hebrews order such things. Frankly, I do not care. We of the black lands are lovers of justice and haters of crime, and I should advise you, young man, to conduct yourself more in accordance with courtly procedure."

"Let me look again. Perhaps I was mistaken in my identification," burst from the frantic priest.

"In that case, not only will the prisoner suffer as he should, but you will be subject to the penalty for perjury."

Ranofer the vizier said, "Really, ben Ittai, you will have to keep your juniors better in hand. The whole town is laughing at him, and therefore at us."

Malachi said, "You are in Egypt, Asa, and not in Judea. Do not meddle with what does not concern you."

Nebamon, dean of the faculty, said, "This comes of throwing wide the gates of the medical school to all comers. A scholar this Hebrew may be, but a gentleman he obviously is not."

Only Tamar had a kind word for Asa.

It was only the next day that Asa was examining a woman who, successfully carried through a severe febrile illness, came to seek help in replacing her fallen hair. The instructor looked at her, and said to Asa, "Recite on the castor plant and its pharmacology." Asa quoted:

List of the virtues of castor: it was found in an ancient book concerning the things beneficial to mankind.

If its peel is brewed in water and applied to a head that suffers, the head will be cured immediately as though it had never suffered. If a few of its seeds are chewed with beer by a person who is constipated, it will expel the feces from the body of that person.

The hair of a woman will be made to grow by means of its seeds. Brew, mix it to one mass, and apply the grease. Let the woman anoint her head with it.

Its oil is made from its seeds. For anointing sores with a foul discharge it will be very effective. Anointing thus for ten days will cause them to disappear. Anoint very early in the morning in order to expel the sores. A true remedy proved millions of times.

The instructor nodded. "Proceed accordingly."

As he turned away, a servant appeared leading a man in a yellow livery. "Greetings from the Lady Nektanebis," he said. "She invites the Physician Asa ben Abdiel, Priest to the Judean Embassy, to a feast at her mansion on the fourth day following."

The prospect of seeing this attractive young woman was very pleasant, and Asa made a suitable acceptance.

The group that gathered in Nektanebis' palace consisted of some dozen persons. The hostess, beautifully garbed in a white and scarlet tunic, gave a cordial welcome to Joel, Zeruiah, and Azaryahu. They were introduced to Ineni, a lieutenant in the palace guard, Re'meryptah and Hapu, each cast in the international and unchanging mold of the polished courtier, and Puymre, a priest of Amun-Ra. Harpagus, a merchant of Media, Belnatan, a Phoenician, and a young physician named Snefrunofr arrived together. Greeting the other members of his embassy party, Asa wondered, naively enough, why Tamar had not been included. There was the usual profusion of food and drink that the Hebrews had come to expect at Egyptian parties. Presently the hostess, seated next to Asa, clapped her hands to silence the harpists and the conversation. "In honor of Belnatan, our Phoenician sea captain, and his prospective fleet surgeon Snefrunofr, we will hear a ballad of peril and toil at sea."

A middle-aged man, bald and wigless, clad only in a white loin cloth and bearing a sort of lyre, approached and began to chant. He sang of himself as a sailor who had put to sea in a mighty ship with scores of young men, the flower of the navies of Egypt. The ship was cunningly wrought by shipwrights of Tyre (this was a graceful tribute to the home city of Belnatan), with sails and oars of purple and bulwarks bright with beaten gold. For days it danced over the waves. Weatherwise, they could read each shift of wind or sky a day before it befell. And so, when a storm roared out of the north they made all secure and spread all canvas to take full vantage of the breeze. (The Phoenician smiled and shook his head.)

But wild and wilder blew the gale. Huge and huger rose the waves. The high hearts of the voyagers failed within them and loudly they prayed to the image of Horus in the eyes of the ship to save them against fell sea-chance.

But Horus heard them not. On a moonless night, exhausted, despairing, they felt a terrific shock as the ship drove upon a reef. In a trice they were drinking the bitter brine. All save the singer sank and died. He alone, lashed to a timber, was borne ashore. He staggered up out of reach of the waves and the darkness took him.

Great is Ra, who darts his golden rays upon us! He sheds his beneficence upon the two lands of the Nile and upon the Ethiopians to the south; the sea-peoples praise him in the cities of the Greeks, and he smiles upon the sand-ramblers of Asia and upon the isles of the sea. Great is he in the red of his setting, and great in the gold of his dawning! Praise be to Ra!

With the morn the sailor stirred, waked and opened his eyes. There on the strand at his feet stood the figure of a woman, magnificently tall, beautiful of body, and vested like a queen; only her face he could not see, for her head was swathed in fold on fold of dark green stuff in which were glints of carnelian, of turquoise, and of emerald. He sprang to his feet, and with hands hanging humbly before him he spoke: "High-born lady, surely you are mistress of this land! Pity, noble one! I implore your mercy on a wretched castaway, who has lost his all in shipwreck and escaped but barely with his life!"

A moment she stood in silence, while doubt grew within him; then she took him by the hand and said, in a whisper that was almost a hiss, "Put fear from you, sailor; come, and you shall enjoy my bounty." She led him through groves where figs and pomegranates hung from the trees and vines rich with grapes twined about. Over a carpet of wild leeks she brought him, by a brook wherein the swarming fish were sluggish and fat, to a pavilion of cedarwood. He washed the brine from his flesh and found a razor for his cheeks and fresh raiment that would garb a prince. In a chamber sumptuously furnished was a table set with the most delicate food and wines. She waited as he sat and dined. Then she led him round the isle—for so it proved to be. Lovely it was, and musical with birdsong. Save only for his conductress, he saw neither man nor woman and heard no voice save hers, always in that hissing whisper like no other woman's voice he had ever heard. He wondered greatly.

The evening came, and he ate and drank. She brought him into a chamber where was an ivory bed. She shed her cloak and the queenly bosom swelled white in the gloom. Then his manhood stirred, and he pulled her to him, and his lips sought her throat. He would have undone her head-cloth to see her face, but she prevented him, saying, "All else I will bare to you for your delight, but only my head you may not look upon. Forbear to try, lest it go ill with you." He removed her skirt; he bore the resilient buttocks down upon the bed; he explored the hidden promise of the parting thighs; and the frenzy seized him.

Yet even in the sweet delirium was he aware that the body beneath him, for all that it was convulsed like his in the divine madness, was cold, as the flesh of no other woman he had ever known was cold. The smell of her was unlike the fragrance of the hair of other women beneath his nostrils. She neither cried out nor sobbed nor gasped her passion but passed silently under the amorous yoke.

For three days the sailor abode with the lady of the isle, and for three nights she was his lover. He saw naught of any other than she, neither high-born nor slave, yet the viands appeared on his table and clean linen by his bed. His wonder grew.

On the fourth day he told her that he was fain to try fishing in the brook. She brought lines and hooks and bait for his pleasure, and he made pretense of pleasure in his angling. During the night, as they lay on the goodly bed, he fixed the hooks to the frame just beyond their heads.

Then in the morn he seized the woman, as though in amorous sport, and thrust her upward so that the hooks snared her head-cloth. He then of a sudden jerked her downward, and the cloth was held, and her face and head were naked to his eyes.

He screamed aloud.

For there, rising from the soft pale shoulders, swayed the flaring neck and giant head of a cobra!

The goddess Renenet rose slowly and sternly to her feet. Her eyes glared at the gibbering figure before her, and the fangs showed cruelly in the gaping mouth.

For a moment she poised to strike. Then her whisper came again: "For the sake of the egg that is even now growing within me I shall spare your life."

Then the cobra goddess hissed loudly, and from afar came an answering hiss. She thrust him forth from the door, and led him, trembling with terror, to the strand, and departed. Forth from the wood came a serpent whose girth was that of a man and whose length was as the palace of the king. Trapped on the beach, he could not flee, and in terror he realized that he was lost to this world and the next. He must be devoured, and no priests would prepare him for the Hall of Judgment and the far journey to the happy lands of the west.

But it was not so. For when, hands hanging humbly before him, he implored the monster for mercy, the snake spoke to him kindly and said, "Fear not, oh sailor! For I spill no blood and crunch no bones of the sons of men. In three days I shall return and I shall bear you over the waste of waves to the many-templed river of your country."

Thus it befell. The sailor, fear still in his heart, bestrode the neck of the mighty beast. Far through the foam it swam and fast he clung. Night followed day, day dawned after night, and on the third day the seaman set foot safely on the coast of Egypt. The serpent swam back to his island.

An appreciative babble came from the company. "Let us hope, Belnatan, that your journey comes to no such end." Nektanebis turned to the Judeans. "Belnatan is about to commence a long voyage of exploration in the service of His Majesty. Since earliest times our people have known that to the north lies the great Middle Sea and beyond it Crete and the isles of Greece. What lies to the south has ever been a mystery. By land the desert, swamps, jungles, and savage tribes bar the way. Perhaps the great Ocean-Sea which washes the edges of the world will offer a road. Belnatan is assembling a fleet of ships on the Red Sea, which lies toward the rising sun, and will take them far to the southward to find what may lie there. Ever following the coast, he will sail until his ships have circled the great land on which we live and will enter the Middle Sea and return home from the direction of the setting sun."

The mountaineers from Judea were aghast. Of ships and the sea they had heard. Brief voyages through known waters they could understand, but what might be an endless search into the unknown filled them with dread. Even the more sophisticated gentlemen of Egypt could see it in no better light. Puymre shrugged. "It is well known to all that the Phoenicians are going to their deaths. To the south one comes to a region so torrid that no life can exist."

Belnatan smiled. He was a stocky, powerfully built man with a broad face and a thick, full black beard. "It may well be so. Be that as it may, His Majesty the Pharaoh has honored me with his commission to explore the coast of Africa, and I shall try to do it."

"I have heard," said Asa, "that at sea there are storms in which the wind whips up waves so mighty that they swallow the stoutest ship afloat."

Snefrunofr answered. "Ships have been lost at sea. It is true. But other ships have survived. Belnatan is the foremost seaman of Tyre—which is to say, of the world. In his forty years he has not only repeatedly sailed the length and breadth of the Middle Sea to our north and west, but has ventured out through its western portals onto the great Ocean-Sea itself. There he has voyaged to the islands of tin in the far-off seas of fog. He has also sailed out of the Red Sea to the coasts of Chaldea, the richest land, after ours, on earth. In fact, Harpagus here took passage with him from those shores on his last voyage. His seamanship will overcome all perils, and I am proud indeed that Irj, Greatest Physician of Lower and Upper Egypt, has recommended me as fleet surgeon."

"The appointment took some doing," put in the courtier Hapu, with a touch of malice. "We had thought that the medical profession of Egypt was esteemed abroad almost as highly as here at home, but only the insistence of Ranofer, His Majesty's vizier, overcame Belnatan's reluctance."

"I yield to no one in my admiration for your medical science," rejoined Belnatan diplomatically, "but I will confess to some doubts as to how well a gentleman of Egypt will fare in the crude life of a Phoenician galley."

Snefrunofr laughed. "Let me worry about that."

"How long will your voyage last?" asked Azaryahu.

"No one knows. We plan to be absent for perhaps as much as a year."

Re'mery-ptah spoke unctuously in the hope that someone would carry the report of his praises to the ear of King Necho. "It is known to all that the second Necho is a pharaoh whose equal has not been seen since the day of the second Rameses. He will give to Egypt glory and conquest enough to match those of his great predecessor. We have been checked—temporarily, of course—to the north, but the Pharaoh is not one to let Babylon stay the advance of his empire. This expedition will add new, wide, and rich lands to Egypt."

Asa said nothing, but to him the project was fantastic. Truly, the Ocean-Sea remained as at the dawn of creation, void and desolate, when only the spirit of the Lord moved upon the face of the waters. Granted that the spirit of the Lord still moved in that vastness, he for one would far sooner lift up his eyes toward the mountains, whence cometh help. He, indeed, was a child of earth, and the way of the sea-rover was not for him. To journey endlessly over the barren sea, along desert coasts peopled, if at all, with swarms of enemies; to press into the zone of intolerable heat; to encounter none knew what manner of monsters by land and sea; to thirst and starve without hope of succor—

this was madness! But to step between a fool and his folly was also madness, and so he held his peace.

The talk veered to other subjects. Hapu turned to Asa with the question everywhere put to the foreigner, "How do you like our land?"

Asa made the appropriate rejoinder.

"I seem to remember," Hapu went on, with the dash of acid characteristic of him, "that you were not very happy about a certain legal proceeding."

"I was not, but I suppose, as a stranger, I should have held my tongue."

"Are not criminals executed in your land?"

"For murder, yes. For attempted murder, no. And in any case, never so slowly and painfully."

"In what fashion do you put men to death?"

"As I implied, we inflict the death penalty but seldom. When we do, it is by stoning. The condemned is thrust into a pit, whereby, if he is fortunate, his neck is broken. If not, rocks are thrown upon his head. This is painful, no doubt, but it lasts for but a moment or two."

The Egyptian shrugged. "You are, it would seem to me, overly tender-hearted toward the undeserving. However, that is your business."

"I will not have such grim conversation at my party," Nektanebis interrupted and summoned the dancing girls.

Again Asa watched disapprovingly what he considered the conscienceless degradation of fellow human beings, but again the spectacle had upon him its natural effect—the effect, in fact, that Nektanebis had intended. A girl such as these could be his for the asking. He was single, vigorous, youthful, and cut off for the time being from the mass of marriageable maidens of his people. Who would blame him, in Egypt or even perhaps in Judea, if he vented his ardor on some willing Saite lass?

Asa carried on through the evening as best he might, striving, not unsuccessfully, to mask his turmoil with a manner of urbane unconcern. When at leave-taking his hostess, goblet in hand, invited him to tarry for one last drink, it took all his resolution to plead the morrow's early surgery and turn his back upon the delights so vividly imagined and so ardently desired.

6

The patient brought in to the clinic had the sweat of terror upon his brow. He exhibited two tiny puncture wounds in his right thumb. He had thrust his hand into a pile of rubble to retrieve a dropped chisel and had not seen the lurking asp.

Phiops took charge at once. He sent an attendant to fetch the statuette of Dje-Hor, a figurine of black basalt set in a basin of the same material. Incised upon the crossed arms and the carven drape of the god were magic incantations. Invoking the aid of the divinity, Phiops poured water upon its head. In this water, collected in the basin, a linen binding was steeped, and then applied to the wound.

"A sovereign remedy for snake-bite and scorpion stings," said the physician, "but it must be applied promptly."

"When so applied," asked Asa, skeptical but polite, "is it always effective?"

"That, naturally, depends upon whether or not the patient and the priest are in favor with the divine Dje-Hor."

Iwti, Inspector of Physicians, entered the clinic at that moment. A glance told him what had happened, and he had an approving word for Phiops. "I am bound for the neighborhood of your embassy," he said to Asa. "The clinic is closing for the day. You may accompany me."

It was the afternoon of the sixth day, and Asa was due at Malachi's home to preside at the welcoming of the Sabbath at sundown. He set forth with the older man.

"Perhaps," advanced Iwti, "we can get you a statuette of Dje-Hor to take back with you to Judea."

Asa shook his head. "I am most grateful, but we Hebrews can have nothing to do with other gods than our own."

"True—I had forgotten that you worship only one god. It is strange to me that a people can be satisfied with so restricted a religion. I should think that many whose prayers were not granted would turn elsewhere."

"Frankly, they do. It is a continuous battle of priest and prophet to stamp out the service of strange gods. This is a problem with which you, of course, have never had to contend."

"You happen to be wrong," said Iwti after a pause. "This is a matter of which the people know nothing, though I see no harm in mentioning it to a priest, even a foreign one. Long ago, some three-quarters of a thousand years, in fact, Egypt had a heretic king. He broke up the worship of Amun and the other gods, putting in their place only the sun god, Aton."

Asa was amazed. He had always thought of his people—the faithful among them, at least—as the only worshippers of one supreme God. Was not Israel His chosen people, to whom alone He had made Himself known, whereas all other nations bent the knee to wood and stone? The revelation that monotheism had been attained in Egypt came as a shock. It was painful and disillusioning.

"Moreover," Iwti continued, "he tried to set at naught the eternal law that the stronger nation, the more powerful man, shall enjoy the fruits of his supremacy, at the cost of the weaker. The results were what you might expect. The gods raised foreign powers who overthrew his armies. No clergy can tolerate a king who spurns it and its worship. The priests of Amun stirred the army and the people to revolt, and the Pharaoh died in despair. His new religion died with him, and the curse of oblivion was put upon his name and that of his god."

Later, left alone, Asa tried to rally from the shock of Iwti's disclosure. He had the usual amount of chauvinistic pride in his people, and it was galling to realize that in another nation too the high concept of monotheism had been achieved. And so long ago—even before Moses! True, Israel had known God centuries earlier than that—it must have been at least five hundred years before that that He had been proclaimed by Abraham. That was a comforting reflection.

Asa reproved himself for the tenor of his thoughts. As a priest of the Most High, he should be delighted to learn that anyone, Hebrew or foreigner, had come to know Him! Had not Moses, when apprised of a rival, said, "Would that every man might be a prophet?"

It was, therefore, with a feeling of some humility that at Malachi's board that evening Asa consecrated their Sabbath rest unto the Lord. Nevertheless, he was moved later to detail to Malachi his conversation with Hapu on capital punishment—so stubborn is the old Adam in man.

"It is strange," he remarked, "that these well-born and well-bred Egyptians should deliberately inflict the extreme of suffering on a fellow mortal. In most ways, I must admit, they have won to a higher plane than our Judean tribesmen. Their art, their technology, their medicine, their political organization, their whole manner of living is infinitely superior, but in spirit they seem more akin to the nomads of the wastelands." (This was somewhat unjust, he realized vaguely, but kept on.) "Why this senseless cruelty, especially when it profits them nothing? No, their code of ethics is far inferior to that of our people. Apparently the gods of Egypt do not enjoin upon their worshippers that reverence for the bodies of their fellow men which the God of Israel has ordained for His people."

Malachi disagreed. "To give them their due," he said, "these Egyptians are a decent lot—as heathens go, of course. Fundamentally, you are right; all idolators are lovers of blood. But compared to the Hittites, or the Scythians, or especially to the Assyrians, the subjects of the Pharaoh are a mild people."

Azaryahu broke in, "There was—to me—more important talk at Nektanebis' than this of executions. Malachi, I told you this morning about the Phoenician's voyage. He could discover something interesting, although I doubt whether a soul will return alive. Then there's Harpagus, the Mede. Now, there are two commercial possibilities worth developing! Malachi, how about holding a reception and inviting those two?"

"Oh yes, do!" put in Zeruiah. "I am dying to wear a new dress made out of one of the most exciting fabrics I have ever seen!"

"We cannot support a commerce with Media, even if a route could be established, which I doubt!" was her father's rejoinder. "Nevertheless, that decision is not for me to make. So, Azaryahu, I shall do as you ask."

Later, in conversation with Tamar, Asa spoke again of the depressing cruelty which, outside of their own land, was so universal. "When I hear of an instance of brutality," he remarked ruefully, "I am filled with the unholy desire to give the perpetrator a dose of his own medicine. That, of course, makes me, scarcely less than he, an agent of evil."

"Up to a certain point," she replied, "we judge our acquaintances by their deeds and opinions. Once convinced, however, that they are of the true precious metal, we judge the deed by the doer. Always bearing in mind, of course, that we may have made a mistake.'"

Asa silently acknowledged the tribute. He did not, of course, fail to note that this girl had attained to an understanding that those of maturer years often failed to reach. Was it that her shadows spurred her inward vision to wider scope? A layman's love of paradox would have led him to assume it, but Asa did not know.

"That had not occurred to me," he confessed, "but now, as you say it, I realize that it is so. By the same token, I realize that I have been taking for granted a certain freedom of movement—of bearing, shall we say—on your part, that I would have thought out of place for a well-brought-up Hebrew maid. Yet, since it is you who act so, I have been accepting it as right and proper.'"

She colored prettily. An Egyptian woman, he reflected, would have been too tanned for the blush to be so readily observed. He remarked aloud upon this, adding, "There are, you see, indirect dividends for modesty."

"I should have thought that men preferred the more revealing lack of costume among the women of the Nile."

"It has its attractions, I will confess. It also has it drawbacks. We observe modesty as a divine command, but Heaven, I believe, has given us its laws to make the final and licit unveiling the more delightful. The Egyptians have in their nudity more pleasure than we, but by that much the less ecstasy in the final privileges."

He felt a twinge of regret, immediately, at having spoken so. Perhaps he had cast an even deeper shadow upon her darkness. Would any man ever take this luckless woman to wife? He hastened to turn the conversation. "At any rate, the Egyptian artists have no lack of inspiration. I have learned to enjoy and appreciate their work, forbidden to us though it be."

Blunderer! he thought in vexation. Again he had unintentionally taunted her with her defect. But she was armored against such gaucheries. "Yes, I have felt many of their statues, and miniatures as well. Naturally, I can best apprehend the carvings in the middle sizes."

"It is hard for me to guess what you perceive and how you feel about it. Sometimes I am afraid that I have been tactless."

"Never fear, I have learned long since how to live with myself and others."

"I have the deepest admiration—I think everyone who knows you does—for your resignation."

"Not resignation, Asa. Make no doubt about that. Acceptance, yes. I have, as I say, learned how to live as I am, but there are hours of rebellion. Never think otherwise. Still, I must accept my fate or be, in one way or another, destroyed."

She was silent for a moment, then went on. "It took time to learn that I could accept it. At first, when I lost my sight, I wanted to die. I would hear no one, speak to no one; I hardly ate. Then, one day, hearing some thoughtless child comment aloud upon my state, I was suddenly angry. I remarked to my aunt that I was worth more blind than he with his sight. It was a petulant remark, but that night, as I lay in my bed, I suddenly realized that it might be true! That was the beginning of my recovery. From then on I set out to prove to myself, child though I was, that I was abler than the sighted! By the time that I realized that it was not so, I had mastered my world sufficiently to be sure of my own worth, sight or no. In some ways I can excel."

"I have seen ample proof of that," said Asa.

"There still come hours of weakness when I surrender to 'if only' thinking, but the hardest thing is to make others think of me as a person. Somehow, those who have escaped a major physical defect look upon those who have one as personifications of their lack, rather than as complex, otherwise normal people with a defect which, however major, is a mere overlay upon the personality. Somehow, too, we are expected to be saintly characters who have been purged of all selfishness and evil. I am not evil, Asa, but neither am I a saint. I will not be held as a poor fragile creature to be pitied and indulged, nor as one to be taken advantage of for the profit of my supposed betters."

"I did not understand," said Asa.

"Even my family has not fully understood this. Not that I am complaining of them—Malachi has dealt generously with me and was under no legal or moral compulsion to do so—but even they sometimes feel that I should be thankful for any crumb of happiness that a busy world may cast at my feet, while at the same time I must be protected from anything that reminds me of my difference, and I will not have it so—not from the world, or from them, or from you."

For all her courage, she could not tell Asa what most she wanted to tell him.

Zeruiah's summons to her foster sister ended the situation. Asa thought sadly, not for the first time, of the mischance that had blasted this life. Why? How could he reconcile the concept of a loving Father with the cruelty that had robbed a child of the world of light and color?

7

The instructor Bitiu passed through the clinic. Asa looked up as he paused by the student on his left. The elderly patient rose, wincing as his knees straightened. He held out his hands, the finger joints knobby and swollen, the wrists stiff.

"Your diagnosis?"

"Rheumatism."

"Correct. And your treatment?"

"Upon a piece of papyrus I shall inscribe, 'O pain, and son of a pain, thou who wrackest the limbs of man, depart from this sufferer! Foulness and evil! Thou shalt oppress him no more! Begone! Begone! Begone!' This is to be boiled in water, and the patient is to drink it."

"A good remedy, well attested." Bitiu turned to Asa. The Hebrew demonstrated a deformity of his patient's left arm, just above the wrist. The man's face was drawn with pain and anxiety. "You can feel the displaced ends of the fractured bone. There is no overriding."

"Right—a fracture of the forearm. What shall you do?"

"After setting, linen bandages soaked in a mixture of flour and honey reinforced with wood."

"That should splint it well. Very good."

By the time Asa had dismissed his patient, Malachi's steward Sallu was waiting for him. "Sholom, Kohane!"

"And peace to you!" replied the priest.

"I need your decision on the law of Kashruth. I have bought and slaughtered a steer for ben Ittai's reception, but at the butchering I saw something on which I need advice."

"Then let us go."

Looking after them as they walked away, Bitiu remarked to Asa's fellow-student, "It is curious, but much as these Hebrews may try to imitate our thinking, they remain essentially barbarians, unenlightened and ridden by superstition. The idea of needing a priest to pass upon the acceptability of meat for the table!"

Asa was musing aloud to Sallu, "It is strange that for all their science, these heathens cannot free themselves from superstition. The idea of giving a patient a charm to be boiled down and drunken!"

"But we use many charms against sickness in Judea."

"True, unfortunately, but you do not get them from the priesthood."

The linings of the right and left chest cavities of the slaughtered animal were abnormal. Instead of transparent membranes through which the red muscles between the ribs could be perceived, there were whitish, pearly surfaces. In the tissues above and behind the heart were several roundish masses as large as an eyeball with satellite tubercles about them, and as the steward's knife sliced them, cheesy, whitish matter escaped. In the lungs were several masses of similar matter replacing the normal tissue; this, when removed, left cavities of irregular shape and ragged lining.

"I have seen this before," said Asa, "but usually in a scrawnier animal. It is a consumption of the flesh. This meat is not kosher—not fit to be eaten. Take it away and bury it."

Malachi's steward nodded with a sigh. A beggar woman, who had come in hopes of some offal from the butchering, sprang forward eagerly. "My lord, if you are going to throw the meat away, pray give it to me."

Asa shook his head. "Our God has given us a commandment that such meat may not be eaten. No good can come of flouting His will."

"My lord, pardon, but I see by your garb that you are not of Egypt, and likely your God is not of Egypt, either. To us worshippers of Amun your meat is not forbidden."

"I may not. The meat must be destroyed."

"My lord, please, please let me have it. For many months my man has lain with a broken leg that refuses to mend. My children are starving. There is nothing ahead of us but death. We can eat of this meat while it is fresh, and for gift of what we cannot eat our neighbors will give us grain for many weeks. Be pitiful, my lord, and let me have the meat!"

The steward looked enquiringly at Asa, who shrugged and spread his palms outward. "It has been said, 'The Law was created for man, not man for the Law.' If the meat means her life, give her the meat."

To bargain for a new steer, cut its throat, and butcher it for Asa's inspection did not take very long, and the chief dish for Malachi's feast was provided.

Harpagus the Mede, guest of honor at Malachi's board, drained his goblet appreciatively. "I am agreed with you that we mountaineers can never be happy in the lowlands. There is nothing like the city of Sais in my native country. The palaces and temples, the murals and statues of the black land fill me with amazement and admiration, as I know they do you. I have seen the pyramids, and the mightiest of them is but as a pebble compared to the lowest hill of Media. This sun-baked plain is ugly, filled with grain as it is, compared to the soaring forests of the Median hills. True, the plain is bounded by bluffs at the edges of the valley upstream, but they are a poor substitute for the sky-reaching ranges at home. Although I freely admit," with a laugh, "that I am more than eager to bring back with me a caravan load of the metals, fabrics, drugs, and perfumes of Egypt."

Azaryahu nodded. "Yes, we too are glad to do business with Egypt, even though, like you, we shall not be sorry to walk a mountain road again."

"I must say," the Mede went on, "that there are even worse surroundings than this flat-topped terrain. I have never in my life known such misery," turning to Belnatan, "as in your ship. Here at least a man can walk and stand erect, and his stomach does not threaten at any moment to heave itself together with its contents into the waves."

Belnatan laughed. "We of Phoenicia have long learned to accommodate ourselves to life at sea. I must confess that some of us have initial difficulties; certain few can never adjust to a heaving deck. Others of us, however, are happier afloat than ashore."

"I suppose a man then can even come to love the rack if he spends enough time on it. I for one should almost prefer it to the prospect of returning by the way I have come, but I suppose there is no help for it."

"None," rejoined the Phoenician. "To take a caravan north through Syria, around the headwaters of the two rivers, across the land of the Babylonians to Media would be ruinous, even if you could bring it in safety through so many petty kingdoms and thieving tribes."

"Is there no danger of loss by sea?" asked Asa.

"Danger? I should think there is," the Mede took up. "One never knows at what moment those hideous seas will swallow ship, cargo, and all, and you are sunk in the sea without a trace. Every strange ship is a probable pirate, and the crew must be prepared to stand to arms whenever they sight a sail. Not to speak of reefs, shoals, and all the other perils of which I was told on our late voyage by my well-meaning host—in kind attempt, no doubt, to cheer me up and make me enjoy the journey."

"Yet," put in Engidu, the ambassador from Babylonia, "our Phoenician friend is planning a far longer voyage to the south."

"I know, and if a mountain of gold stood at the end, I would have no part of it."

"There is no mountain of gold." Engidu shook his head. "There is no food. There is no water. There may be no pirates, but the shores swarm with savages who kill for the pleasure of killing. The rocks and shallows are unknown, and at the end there is only an intolerable heat that blasts man and beast, and from which none may return."

"No doubt you are right," murmured the Phoenician. "Still, His Majesty has honored me with his commission, and we are going."

"And that," said Engidu, "will be the end of you and your five ships."

"It may be so, but who, incidentally, told you that I am taking five ships?"

"So runs the story in the marketplace. Five stoutly built vessels. Is it not so?"

"Very likely. His majesty, of course, will make the final decision."

Asa gazed at Belnatan in bewilderment. What sort of madness was this? To leave the sweet earth with its springs and trees for the endless, horrendous, shifting ocean? A place where only the the fish could live and the very birds ventured timidly but a little way from shore?

Where the warm consciousness of a friendly village beyond the next hill, a city of refuge a day's march away, was swallowed up in the cold emptiness of the great deep?

The courtier Hapu tossed in his usual bit of venom. "Engidu's kindness of heart extends to the men of all nations, and he is deeply disturbed over the danger to Belnatan. In fact, he has even made strong representations to Ranofer, the vizier, against the voyage. Or is it your sovereign, Engidu, who is disturbed at the prospect?"

Engidu's face darkened. "The proposed exploration happened to be broached in conversation. We of Chaldea feel that we know, as well as any, what little is known of those waters. We should be sorry to see the Pharaoh waste treasure and men in an impossible task."

Belnatan smiled sardonically. "I am sure that his majesty is deeply appreciative of Babylonia's concern for his prosperity. Just as I am grateful for your efforts to avert my destruction."

It was Tamar who hastened to relieve a strained situation. "We all wish you well, Belnatan, but it is time for some music!"

Nature, however, changed the program. One of the Egyptian rains —rare in this delta region, unknown on the upper river—began. Most of the party stared in pleasure at the slanting drops, but Tamar stepped out into the garden to enjoy it upon her shoulders.

Her thin robe was soon soaked, and the young priest noted with quickened interest how the wet cloth molded itself to her form. Considerably to his surprise, however, he found himself resenting the fact that others too might appreciate the trimness of her figure. As Tamar went in to change, he found himself indulging in amorous speculation. The girl's defect would be no handicap in the supreme function of wifehood. Her face was less fair than Nektanebis,' to be sure, but as to the rest, she need not fear competition.

Yes, Nektanebis was the better looking, the young priest noted a few evenings later, but he was uncomfortable, just the same, sitting opposite this young woman with very little covering above her waist. With an effort, he kept his gaze on her face or on the sennit-board between them.

Inlaid in its wooden surface were ten rows with three squares each of blue faience. Near his end of the board were a half-dozen little cones of the same material. Near her end, the squares bore as many short, round, concave-sided pegs.

Nektanebis threw down onto the mat-covered floor four carved sticks, two of wood and two of ivory. She glanced at their lie and shifted her pieces on the board. "It is your move, priest," she said, looking into his eyes with a barely perceptible smile.

Asa picked up the sticks. He wondered how successful was his pretense of stupidity. In another sense, he thought wryly, perhaps there was no pretense about it! His hand felt clumsy as he picked up and cast down the little rods in his turn. He moved his pieces.

"Not well done," she rallied. "I do not think, priest, that you take advantage of your opportunities."

He thought briefly of the shock with which his erstwhile fellow-villagers would behold him now. They would have something to say about these opportunities!

Nektanebis threw and moved a piece between two of his. "I do believe, priest, that I am getting through your defenses!"

Well, maybe she was. Was ever man so bedeviled? If he accepted the bounty being flung so unconditionally at his feet, who would have the right to blame him?

I would, he answered himself.

His hostess lifted the empty carafe. "There is wine in the jug over there." They rose simultaneously to fetch it, and suddenly, somehow, she was in his arms, and their lips pressed.

It was no use. He knew, despite his hunger, that he would go no further. In that moment he touched the nadir of humiliation. He had acted shamefully toward her, he knew. He should have checked the relationship long ago. She felt his embrace relax, and looked up, puzzled.

"I don't understand. I know I'm not ugly, and I know you like me. Is it a vow? Some religious duty?"

"A religious duty—yes, in a way. If we became lovers, I should immediately have to clarify, in my own mind, my responsibilities to you. Because I'd have them, and I could not escape them, regardless of what anyone might say."

That, essentially, was it. He could not take a woman and thereafter be indifferent to her fate. The light touch was not for him. "I cannot ask you to forgive me for having gotten you into this position. You cannot excuse what you cannot understand."

"Perhaps I understand more than you think." Asa was perplexed, as so many men have been, that while the woman of discretion does not see that a man too may have his sexual aesthetics, her looser-living sister can perceive and realize his problems.

Asa walked homeward that night in a black depression, loathing himself. He had put Nektanebis—or permitted her to put herself—in what he regarded as an impossible position. He desired her, certainly; he was even fond of her. But love her, with an ardor that would admit no obstacles to marriage, he did not, even were she willing to exchange her guarded, luxurious Egyptian living for the harsh realities of the Judean plateau. For one thing, he held her very accessibility against her. He was not proud of it. Nektanebis was a woman who had known a husband's bed. How could he judge her for the loneliness of her nights? Nevertheless, judge her he did, fond and pitying though he was. He did not excuse her transgression, albeit he recognized much in extenuation.

Was he merely a self-righteous prig, he wondered. He was too close to his problem to tell, but, to put it crudely to himself, he could not see himself buying dearly—in marriage—what he could obtain cheaply. And at a cheaper price he did not want it. He was not bargain-hunting.

As was not infrequently the case, Asa slept badly in his lonely bed.

A few days later Nektanebis kissed him for the last time and gave him his dismissal. Asa found himself deeply saddened, but he did not try to change her resolve.

Nektanebis was not the woman to brood alone. By the favor of Khnum, the Potter who shapes the babes within the womb, men looked upon her with pleasure, and Engidu, the Babylonian envoy, was among them. When, therefore, Engidu invited her to accompany him on a trip upriver to Thebes, she accepted.

Engidu did an expert job of stage-setting. The crescentic hull rested lightly, gracefully upon the river, its high bow and stern beautifully wrought with carvings and burnished bronze. The deck was sea green, the bipod mast and square sail yellow. Aft rose a deck-house of scarlet, covered by hides striped in green and yellow, its partitions and side panels removable for a breeze. Between this and the oarsmen's benches forward sat a trio of harpist, flutist, and tympanist. A steward kept the cloth wrappings of an earthenware jug sufficiently moist for evaporation to cool the wine within. They moored early and supped moderately but well. The crew was sent to sleep on the bank. Only the Babylonian, his guest, and her maid remained aboard.

Where the sun is a tyrant, grateful is the fall of night. Nowhere is this lovelier than in the exceptional clarity of the cloudless Egyptian sky. When one floats, sated and at ease, between the upper and the nether spaces and lets their peace and beauty steal into the soul after a day of sail and hears a plaintive melody from not too near nor yet too far away, the scene is set for a masterly performance.

The Egyptian, as has been indicated, had been no inconsolable widow. She was very much a woman of the world. As such, she thoroughly appreciated Engidu's virtuosity, at the same time that she recognized it for exactly what it was—a masterly performance. Had he been less accomplished an amorist, he might have been more credible, and more nearly to the heart's desire. As it was Nektanebis' surrender did not include an inner core of objectivity in her less rapturous moments.

8

Weeks passed, and months. Asa labored faithfully in the clinic, relaxing as necessary in the household of Malachi. He was receiving a patient one morning when a slave slipped a note into his hand. Pentaoser was holding a reception in honor of Benanu, Admiral of Babylonia, just arrived on Egypt's Red Sea coast with a squadron of galleys for a visit of ceremony. All of the embassy staffs were requested to attend. Grumbling, he crumpled the papyrus. He would have preferred a quiet evening with Malachi, Azaryahu, and of course, Tamar. Public business was a nuisance. He turned again to the peasant.

"Doctor, I seem to have no strength lately. A little labor tires me out, and I must rest. I can no longer do a hard day's work."

The man was in good flesh, but his complexion was poor. Asa pulled down his lower eyelids and noted how pale a pink was their color.

"Is your urine bloody?" asked the priest.

"Whose is not, among us who work in the irrigation ditches?"

Asa nodded. He had come to recognize this sickness as the scourge of Egypt. He opened a jar and transferred four spoonfuls of a white powder into a large beaker.

"Your treatment is correct, though lacking in ceremony," came the voice of Phiops, who had come up behind him. "No medicine is fully effective without divine assistance." Taking the spoon from Asa's hand, the Egyptian intoned, "As for this measuring utensil, this prescription shall be measured with it. It is the mouthful measure with which the god Horus measured his eye lotion. It is tested; there is found through it life, well-being, and health. This prescription is measured with this measuring spoon in order to remove therewith every sickness which is in this body." Then to Asa, "Continue."

"Four ro of powdered dates," said Asa, and added the four mouthful-spoons of brown powder. Then, "Eight volumes, or one jugful, of barley-paste. I shall boil the mixture down to six ro—three handfuls—and he is to take it in four portions on four successive days."

The instructor nodded. "It is sometimes useful to add one ro of decoction of juniper berries, for diuresis," he suggested. "The flow of urine often needs stimulating." He passed on.

At Penta-oser's reception Benanu the Babylonian was slim and elegant in a knee-length tunic, with curled and scented hair and beard. He presented his three captains to his host. Further introductions were made, and it developed that the three, like so many of the mariners of Chaldea, were Phoenicians—in this instance, men of Sidon. Belnatan and the three fell into shop talk. Asa, to his surprise, found himself listening with considerable interest to this discussion of a world that was so alien to him. Despite the fact that the talk was in Phoenician, so similar to Hebrew that he should have had no linguistic difficulty, the seamen's language contained much with which he was unfamiliar.

Wearying of the effort, he strolled into the garden with Tamar. Soon he was telling her of the languid patient of the other day and commenting on the grip that this disease held on the peasantry of Egypt. "Frankly, I am more than a little skeptical of the efficacy of our treatment of it. The poor generally are affected, and I am told that it has always been so, as far back as the medical records go, which is some two thousand years. Think of the aggregate human suffering from this cause alone! One cannot grasp so large a problem. And why? That is what troubles me, because I cannot understand the reason." (A priest, he warned himself, should not express such doubts to a layman; nevertheless, he did not stop.) "One might look on it as God's punishment of a wicked and idolatrous country; but in that case, why are the rich and powerful, most responsible for the evils, generally spared? I have not seen or heard of a case in a priest or noble, except once or twice in the mildest form. Nor is it the way of God to continue a plague so long."

"Besides," put in Tamar, "are we not taught that the Egyptians too are the children of God?"

"We are, certainly. You remember the legend that after our escape from slavery in Egypt, when the pursuing Egyptian armies were overwhelmed in the returning waters of the Red Sea, the angels began to sing Hosannas of joy. Whereupon God rebuked them, saying, 'The Egyptains too are my creatures, and they are drowning. Do you then rejoice?' In any case, punishment is futile if no one relates the penalty to the trespass and points the way to penitence and pardon." He sighed. "These problems trouble me deeply."

"Asa, you had the woes of all the suffering ones of Judea on your heart, and now to them you add those of all the sick of Egypt. The patriarchs and the prophets could not remove evil from the lot of mankind; no more can you."

"What would you?"

She turned her eyes, with the illusion of sight, full into his. "I would have you take thought for your own happiness."

The priest looked upon the graceful girl and felt a stir of tenderness. Perhaps, indeed, happiness lay here! He laid a gentle hand upon her arm.

Penta-oser came around a corner, with him Malachi and Azaryahu. "I was looking for you, to offer some refreshment. Won't you come to the table?"

Asa turned. "I am afraid I have been boring Tamar with talk of medicine. It's as well that you have rescued her."

"Go ahead, please, all of you," said Tamar. "I'll join you in a moment." As they disappeared, she buried her face in her hands and tears of disappointment welled.

Youth is the dramatic time. The drama of despair and death offers it a role which, despite its boundless powers, it loves to play. But in Tamar's life there had been too much of despair and renunciation for her to savor the part; it was hope that flourished in the weeks that ensued. Indeed, the young priest's obvious enjoyment of her company gave ample food for her hope to grow on. It cannot be said that his mood when with her was one of rapture, but there was a deep and growing enjoyment whose current, strong though quiet, set in the same direction. For Asa began definitely to think of marriage.

He was not wildly, thrillingly in love with Tamar, as he had been with the poor dead bride of his first youth, but he had for her a growing affection and a deep respect alike for her understanding and her integrity. And, what to a young man is most essential, though insufficient in itself, she could and did inspire him with delicious imaginings of the nuptial chamber.

It must be confessed that the priest, despite his high regard for womankind, was by no means devoid of the usual bump of masculine conceit. In his daydreams of Tamar, he did not neglect to admire his role of savior. He could not help knowing that he was something of a catch. As a priest of Israel, a descendant of Aaron, brother of Moses the lawgiver, he carried the blood of the aristocracy, highest of the three castes of his people. Intermarry the three might and did, freely, but the child took its status from the father. A priestly family, even if not wealthy, could never want for bread. To these were added the love and gratitude that the countryside showed to its physician and therefore, in a measure, to his wife. Asa could offer, finally, youth and health. That some women, at least, looked upon him with favor had been often evident.

All of this was, frankly, more than a girl in Tamar's situation might reasonably expect. There was, therefore, just a suggestion of conscious virtue in his image, as seen through his own eyes. Not that he pretended to himself, even for a moment, that he might espouse the girl out of generosity. He would take her, if take her he did, because he desired her and because the prospect of passing with her through the long years ahead was becoming more and more pleasing. It was to his own happiness that he had an eye even as he might hope, thereby, to make hers.

9

"Doctor, the child has gradually been growing sicker. A month ago she became listless and pale, and her appetite began to fail. Two weeks ago I noted that her body was becoming warm. She seems weaker."

Asa looked at the worry-worn face of the mother. It seemed familiar. "Have you been a patient of mine?"

"No, sir. You were kind enough to give me the carcass of a steer a few months ago. Remember? I was very grateful."

He remembered, with some uneasiness. The meat had been unfit according to the law of Moses.

The four-year-old girl, small for her age, had a pasty complexion under her tan. Face, arms, and legs were thin, but her abdomen was protuberant. No mass was perceptible in it under his hands, but there was a tenseness of fluid under pressure. The navel was prominent, like a nipple. The girl's flesh was distinctly hot. Her expression was drawn. Bowel and bladder functions, he was told, were not disturbed.

He did not like the look of what he saw. The case would require observation and study. Meanwhile, he would try to build her up.

"The broth of doves, boiled in a pot, with leeks," he prescribed, "every other day. A half-glass of red wine before every meal. Bring her back in a week."

"There is another patient, doctor. My husband's broken leg is mended, but he has been failing for six or seven weeks. He has not been willing to come for treatment until now."

The tall, thin young man had flushed cheeks and fever-bright eyes. "I have seemed to be weak, doctor, and I tire easily. I can't work as before. I feel hot in the afternoons and evenings, and lately I have been waking up during the night, soaked with sweat." A fit of coughing put an end to his complaints.

In Judea, Asa would have isolated the man in some unused hut at the edge of the village. Here, he had not the authority to compel obedience, and the couple, he knew, would not cooperate voluntarily.

He prescribed a mixture of honey, chalk, and myrrh for the cough, ground peas in beer for the fever. The man was instructed to return with the child.

The physician was very uneasy in his mind about the family. His mood, however, was considerably alleviated by the next patient who presented herself. Following his examination, Asa announced smilingly, "I shall give you a prescription for your nausea, but it is of no consequence. Six months more, and you will sit on bricks!"

The young wife looked up joyfully. "Will I really have a baby at last?"

"I am sure of it. In half a year you will be crouching on a pair of bricks for your delivery!"

As the happy patient left, Azaryahu walked in. "You have been keeping too much to yourself lately, Asa! I'm going to drag you off for some relaxation over a glass. Come along!"

"Can't, and won't be able to this week. Several of the staff have left for some festival to Amun at Thebes. I've been rushed. What's the news?"

"Oh, nothing that greatly concerns us. Our sweet-tempered friend Hapu has been trying to undermine Ranofer, but the vizier has found out about it, and for the while, Hapu is in bad odor. The Chaldean ambassador asked Ranofer for an audience with Pharaoh. He took his admiral along, and they talked down Belnatan's projected trip of exploration. Babylon, I suspect, would like to reserve the southern ocean with its lands and trading privileges for herself, but the Pharaoh was not persuaded. Harpagus, my Median friend, is departing soon. We have concluded a trade agreement, but I am not as optimistic as I was that much can come of it. Well, if you won't come along, I'm off!"

The priest turned back to his work. Throughout that day and successive days, however, his thoughts reverted from time to time to the stricken father and daughter.

When, a week later, they returned, there had been no improvement. The man looked appreciably sicker. His cough had become steady and he was bringing up thick, tenacious white matter, and there was worse news.

"Doctor," said the woman, "you were right about fearing the anger of your God. Another of my children is coughing. Several other people have been taken sick—all of them of families to whom we sold the accursed beef. Give us a charm to avert His wrath!"

Asa looked at her sadly. "There is no charm. I will treat your family and neighbors as well as I can—or you can be treated by another doctor, and I will pray for you. I fear that I sinned in letting the meat be eaten, but you told me that you were in desperate case. I will not conceal the fact that I am worried about this sickness."

The woman set down a little bag of weighed pieces of copper. She stripped a few cheap bangles from her wrist and throat. "Doctor, this is all we have of value. Take it and make sacrifice to your God, that he heal us."

"We may sacrifice to Him only at the Temple in Jerusalem, but it matters not. Our prophets have taught us that He wants justice and mercy, not sacrifice."

"Take these for yourself, then, and pray for us."

"Keep your goods. I am His priest, and I will pray for you, with all my heart."

He did. He also consulted with the older staff members of the medical school. Their unanimous advice could be summed up in the words of Nebamon. "I have seen such cases. They are a consumption and always fatal. Refuse to see or treat them, for there is nothing that you can do."

Asa could not refuse. He was not an Egyptian. He was a Hebrew, and mercy was a sweet savor in the nostrils of his God.

On the next day, when the woman came running to him in terror, Asa hearkened and followed her home. "Last night she complained of a headache, and when I tried to lift her head that she might sip some wine, her neck was stiff. Then she had a convulsion. Now she has had another."

Sadly the priest looked at the dying girl. He could not bear to betray the poor distracted mother with a vain hope. She read his verdict in his face and went down on her knees before him. "Lord, take our home, and all that is in it, and sell me a charm wherewith your God will cure my children and their father!"

"I have no charm. There is none. If there were, I would gladly give it."

"Do not tell me such a tale. The physicians and priests of Sekhmet and Thoeris have charms to sell and so must you."

"I swear to you that I have no charm. I can do no more."

"Lord, take our all and sell us as slaves, but give me the life of my child!"

His heart wrung, the priest fled from the house.

"Yes, I'll go to your drinking party, Azaryahu," said Asa. "Indeed, I need some distraction." He soon found himself at a busy inn, seated with Azaryahu, Remery-ptah, Harpagus the Mede, Belnatan, and Snefrunofr, Belnatan's fleet surgeon. Azaryahu called merrily for wine.

Harpagus, Asa's right-hand neighbor, commented on the priest's obvious melancholy. Asa related the events leading up to it.

"For all my faith, I cannot see why the good God has made these wretched beings to suffer so atrociously."

"The gods," said Belnatan, "do not greatly concern themselves with human griefs and joys, any more than you and I interest ourselves in the destinies of those flies."

"If they could afford the proper ritual entombment," offered Remery-ptah, "and their good deeds outweighed the evil, they would have the reward they merit in the afterworld. As it is, I am uncertain."

"Does God ever give man a second life?" asked the priest, sceptically. "And if so, what to Him are poverty or wealth? If a man has sinned, is there no mercy on high?"

"There is mercy but not omnipotence." It was the Mede speaking. "Ahura-Mazda, creator of life and of good, loves man and man's welfare, but opposed to him is Ahriman, Prince of Darkness, creator of evil. It is he whom you must blame for your patient's woes."

Asa shook his head, but before he could speak again Snefrunofr forestalled him. "We are not here to discuss theology, but to drink and to make merry."

It was at that moment that Asa noticed a vaguely familiar face at the door. The newcomer looked about, noted the group, and at once withdrew.

Snefrunofr began a love song, and Remery-ptah joined in. Soon they began to improvise, first the one, then the other, producing humorous couplets directed, more or less broadly, against one another.

As they subsided amid laughter, Azaryahu told a humorous tale about the amorous misadventures of a Libyan muleteer. In the middle of it, Asa, less in the mood for bawdy stories, saw the stranger re-enter the inn. The man kept his gaze averted, speaking to a muscular, coarse-appearing fellow who studied the group with lively interest. After a minute, both departed again.

Asa turned to Belnatan. "I have just remembered where I saw a man who entered a moment ago. He is one of the Sidonian captains of the Chaldean fleet."

Belnatan's brow furrowed thoughtfully.

"Why so worried, honey?" asked a waitress, petting the Tyrian on the cheek as she passed.

Snefrunofr leaped up with a laugh. "No wonder that Belnatan gets the female attention, in the largest chair, and with that dashing purple tunic! Were I so equipped, I could do as well!"

Belnatan smiled and tossed the garment around Snefrunofr's shoulders. He handed over his conical white cap with the purple border. "Take the chair, too," he offered, and changed his seat. The Egyptian physician accepted the chair and beckoned to the charmer. She approached coyly, and a verbal skirmish ensued.

Other drinkers had been drifting into the inn. From a knot of men, voices rose in anger. As the party looked that way, one man pushed another. A fist crashed. Some one swung a stool. There was a flash of metal, and as a rioter ducked, a bronze knife flew through the air.

Snefrunofr crumpled, the knife handle projecting from the purple tunic on his chest.

10

Malachi ben Ittai had listened gravely to Asa's story. "You have had a trying day, to say the least. I am glad that you have come here to relax among us for the evening." He was silent for a while, looking out at the darkness. "I have been wanting to talk to you, Asa. It might as well, perhaps, be now. Come into the garden. If what I am about to say does not please you," he went on as they strolled into the night, "please tell me so at once, and we will not mention it again. In that case I ask your pardon for bringing it up at all. It has seemed to me that you have been seeing rather more of Tamar than mere politeness would require, and I have the impression that you are rather fond of her. It is hard for me to tell how my ward looks in another man's eyes. Some women are simply not romantically appealing to some men, and there is nothing to be done about it. Tamar has little portion of her own, and I can not spare her any considerable dowry. Most of my family's substance was used up in the war."

"I am not concerned about a dowry," Asa answered.

"I know that it is presumptuous to offer a priest the hand of a maiden with her blemish, but if you could be persuaded to take her to wife, it would be a most blessed act. Well, I need not tell a scion of Aaron how the Lord is pleased by charity to orphans. Tamar has been to us as a good daughter, and I know that she would be a good wife. We have been more and more troubled concerning her state. Once I had arranged a very suitable marriage with a young man of excellent family. He was also blind. Tamar refused—rather bitterly. Surprisingly, she said that never would she wed a blind man. Who can understand women?"

"Not I." Asa shrugged.

"Her father, as I told you, made a serious mistake in his politics. You have no political ambitions, and need not, therefore, suffer for it. Her youth is passing, and time presses. What say you? Would you be willing to take Tamar to wife, as an act of compassion, meritorious in the eyes of God and man?"

"I will take her." Asa paused to pick his further words, but he had not enough time to utter them.

"Indeed he will not!" and Tamar stood furious before them. "Am I a beggar, to seek charity? Will a normal man wed me only out of mercy? I will be a maid to the end of my days, Asa, rather than have you throw yourself away, without love or desire, on a wretched creature such as you could not freely choose!"

This, of course, did Asa and herself considerably less than justice. He had been embarrassed by Malachi's depreciation of the girl, but there was a germ—no more—of truth in her outcry, and it was enough to rob his stammered protestations of the ring of truth. Straight and proud, the young woman stalked off to her room.

Malachi threw out his hands in despair. Asa was less disturbed.

"You are both wrong," he said. "I shall be proud and happy to have Tamar as my bride. It will be no mere act of benevolence on my part. I understand how she feels. Her pride has been deeply injured. I don't think that she can be persuaded now. Tomorrow, or the next day, when she is approachable, I think I can convince her that I really want her."

By the time the evening was over, Tamar was praying that he would do just that.

But he was not to have the chance.

About to enter the clinic on the following morning, Asa was confronted by the mother of his little patient of the day before, her face contorted with grief and bitterness. She spat at him. "Murderer!" she shrilled. "My child is dead. My husband is coughing up masses of blood. Heart of stone! May the divine Osiris cast your soul to the crocodiles of the lower world!"

A neighbor took up the cry. "What of my little son? I bought some of your cursed meat. Are your charms for sale only to the rich?"

A third woman hissed at him. "Have you no bowels of compassion, accursed foreigner? Am I too to die and leave my children?" Her words broke off in a fit of coughing.

The temple attendants pushed the women away and dragged Asa inside. Too shocked and bewildered to work, he spent a useless morning. The staff and his fellow students looked at him askance. At noon Nebamon sent for him.

"A mob is forming outside," the dean said coldly. "I cannot remember such disgraceful doings about this institution of healing. Only you, who have held yourself above the service of our gods, have brought shame and riot upon us. I was opposed to your admittance among us in the first place, but the vizier would have his way. You have clearly demonstrated your unfitness for the medical profession— at least, for that of Egypt, though in your own country the standards, apparently, are lower. I would suggest that you return there. At any rate, I must ask you to leave here and not return."

When Asa passed out of the building, he was the target for a shower of stones. Hapu, the intriguer, had seen his opportunity to embarrass the administration, and a mob had been recruited for a "spontaneous" demonstration. A platoon of Carians charged through and escorted

Asa from the clinic toward the palace of Penta-oser. There were shouts of "Death to the foreigner!" "Darling of Ranofer, back to your desert!" "Down with the vizier!" "Back to Judea, Hebrew murderer!"

Dazed and incredulous, the priest was delivered, according to instructions, to the mansion of Penta-oser. Here, at the Judean embassy and at the home of Ranofer, Greek guards were stationed to confront shouting, mud-slinging mobs.

It was not worth Ranofer's while to face up to the challenge. That evening a letter was delivered to ben Ittai. It recalled the disturbances after the assault upon Penta-oser in the marshes. It recounted the rebuke which the court had felt it necessary to administer to Asa. It alluded finally to the current incident.

"In view of these circumstances, His Majesty's Government finds itself under the painful necessity of declaring Asa ben Abdiel, priest to the embassy of the kingdom of Judea, persona non grata at the court of the King of the two Egypts. It is confidently expected that his Excellency the Ambassador of the King of Judea will take immediate steps to sever the connection with his mission of said Asa ben Abdiel. On the second morning hereafter an armed escort to the border will be provided."

In Asa's mouth was the bitter taste of ignominy. Malachi's explanation of the political intrigue behind his ouster made no difference. He was a failure and was being sent home in disgrace. He had failed to learn enough medicine to treat his people's ills. That there was, really, not a great deal to learn that he had not already known would not be reckoned with—perhaps not even believed—in Judea. He had failed Malachi, had embarrassed, perhaps jeopardized, the mission. He had failed the kindly Ranofer, his sponsor. He had failed that poor, misguided peasant woman. He had even, for that matter, failed Nektanebis. He had, finally, failed Tamar. He shrank in an agony of shame from the prospect of such homecoming, but there was no way out.

In anguish of spirit he poured out his soul to his God.

Asa's first impulse, when Penta-oser's steward announced Belnatan of Tyre, was to send his regrets. He wanted to see no one. Nevertheless, it was an unexpectedly kind gesture if the sea-captain had come to console with him, and Asa forced himself to receive his guest. To

Asa's amazement, the Phoenician had another purpose in mind and came at once to the point.

"You can no longer stay here, as I have heard. Under the circumstances, you will have scant joy of your homecoming, and it will be pointless to return."

"What alternative have I?"

"I have come to offer you the post of fleet surgeon in my expedition."

For a moment Asa could only gape. This was the very last role in which he could have imagined himself. Then, "Fleet surgeon? Me?"

"You."

"But what do I know of ships?"

"You can learn. There have always been more than a few of your people sailing in our ships. Long ago there were very many."

"That was in the reign of King Solomon. He even maintained a fleet, sailing out of Ezion-geber on the Red Sea, but after his time, we lost control of the seacoast. As a matter of fact, even in very ancient times certain of our tribes took to the sea. I remember that in her taunts Deborah sang, 'Dan lay in his ships.' Some of my people have followed the sea ever since." By now the priest had begun to collect his wits. "It was generous indeed, Belnatan, to think of helping me in my distress."

"Generosity played no part. To do myself justice, I am not averse to doing you a good turn, but in this case, I am thinking only of the welfare of my crews. It will be a piece of unparalleled good fortune if I can persuade you to sail with me."

"I appreciate the compliment. I certainly need good opinions now! But there are many physicians who can . . ."

"I daresay there are, but I have not picked you for your professional acumen, although I have made certain of your competence and dependability. They are, of course, essential. The one reason I want you, and no other physician in Sais, is that you are a Hebrew."

"I don't understand."

"Doctor, I am setting out on a voyage to no one knows where and for no one knows how long. I have no idea what we will find. I know that there will be dangers of many sorts, terrific labors, sometimes under impossible conditions. There will be no fresh crews to recruit.

We have no colonies in that part of the world. The men I take with me must live to be the men I bring back—or I do not come back, and the voyage fails. They must live through wounds, through hardships, through hunger, through thirst, through plague. I have seen the cities and the caravans of many nations. Nowhere have I seen a higher level of health than among your people."

"God is good to us," said the priest.

"He may be. I do not dispute it, but what impresses me is your low rate of disease. As to medicine, narrowly considered, I am, frankly, somewhat skeptical. Surgery I take more seriously, but any Phoenician sea-captain can do a fair job of surgery if he has to—not as prettily as a doctor, perhaps, but we get by. I have seen your Judean caravans. Your camp hygiene is unique—and town hygiene, too. You Hebrews alone never deposit your excrement among tents or houses. You recognize and segregate the carriers of contagious disease—some of them, at least—living and nonliving. Above all, you have rigid food inspection. You, Asa, recognized that steer carcass as unwholesome and condemned it."

"I merely did as God ordains."

"Be it so. Then your God has taught you which meats are dangerous to man. I want you to do all this for me and my ships. Besides, there is no Phoenician surgeon at hand, and I do not want an Egyptian. Snefrunofr was forced upon me. I am sorry for his death, but I am, frankly, relieved that he will not be with us. We Phoenicians like to keep the secrets of the seas to ourselves."

"But I am not a Phoenician."

"No, but Judea is not a maritime power. Were you a Greek, for instance, I should want no part of you."

Asa hesitated only for a moment. This was the answer to his prayer! The unforeseen and unguessed, the perfect solution to his problem! "I will sail with you."

"Excellent! I can have your travel orders changed to route you along the canal which Pharaoh has been digging to connect the Red Sea with the Nile and western waters. In a few days you will begin your duties with my crews. In a month, we sail. One thing, though, must be understood The discipline of a Phoenician ship is strict. You will always be under my orders or those of my deputy."

"Agreed—with two conditions."

"Name them."

"One—under no circumstances am I to be kept from the worship of the God of Israel and of Him alone."

"Your religion is your own affair. I shall not interfere. And the other?"

"I shall obey your orders and so will the working people of your ships, but over my patients I am to have complete and undisputed authority."

"As long as they are on the sick list, they shall be under your hand."

Thanks to the prospect of action, Asa was no longer in the apathy of despair. At the same time, as he rode his mule, he could not at once throw off the effects of his misadventures. What troubled him most, however, was the realization that such evil—not merely the eclipse of his own prospects and reputation but, worse, the sicknesses and deaths of the wretched Egyptian families—had resulted from an act of good will. If the Lord had punished them for a transgression, he would have seen the justice of it. If they had been deliberately brought low by human malice or greed, he could at least have understood. Here was a case where obedience to the spirit, if not the letter, of the Divine directive had entailed suffering and death.

There was in the Hebrew language no word, as in the Jewish philosophy no concept, of charity as this was known to other peoples. The expression used in Hebrew for such an act was "mitzvah," literally, a commandment. In giving to the poor or in performing any other good deed the pious Judean considered that he was merely obeying a Divine decree, as in duty bound.

Asa therefore would have had no sense of self-righteousness about the gift, even had it not been, as in this case, something worthless to him. His intention had been good, not evil. True, he could conceivably have bought the beggar woman a healthy steer, but then another would have begged the forbidden beef, and another, and not even King Jehoiakim's purse could have fed all the poor of Egypt.

Why, then, had the Lord turned his gift of life into one of death? Why is it that so often in this world the best of intentions go badly astray? How can a good and loving Father permit some of the noblest impulses of man to be perverted to hideous ends? Does it not seem (and Asa shuddered inwardly at the concept) that God deliberately works evil?

If He could thus work woe to mankind, it would mean, apparently, that He was not the fount of goodness that Israel believed Him to be. The priest's soul shrank in anguish from the blasphemous thought. After all, even human agents of suffering, as he had just realized, might not have willed that which they effected. His own intentions, in the matter of the meat, had been of the very best. The preacher Jeremiah sprang suddenly into his memory. His uncle Malachi and the rest of the pro-Egyptian party considered him a dangerous demagogue who would, unchecked, pull down Judea to destruction. Yet Asa knew in his soul that Jeremiah, mistaken or not, was a man of God and good to the core. But if Jeremiah were right, then his opponents were destroying the kingdom. Yet Asa felt definitely that they, too, meant well.

It is one of the greatest tragedies of mankind that so much of the evil of the world is wrought by people who are essentially good! A year ago Asa could have found God as a voice of quiet surety within his bosom, but he knew now that some at least of the priests of Sekhmet and Hathor, Moloch and Ashtoreth, had the same still small voice whispering its falseness into their hearts. In his anguished search to know his God, Asa could find nothing more definite than that same "I am that which I am" which had come to Moses out of the burning bush so long ago. That which had been as a spring of cool waters within him had become that which burned on and on and would not be consumed.

So Asa wrestled with his soul and his God. It was in no vain or shallow spirit that he questioned. He investigated every doubt at painful cost. He knew that he would follow, doggedly, wherever the way was pointed. Had he been less devout, he would not have felt thus constrained to understand why Divinity moved in the dark ways He did; had he been more, and more blindly, devout, he would have accepted without faltering nor permitted himself to question and doubt.

The question and the doubt equally with the acceptance and the devotion were inherent in the philosophy of Judaism. The Hebrew prophets, more than those of any other of the nations round about, had a burning passion for justice—justice in the tribunals of God and man alike. Who seeks justice must strive for it—against wrong or even the appearance of wrong. In this striving, however humble his mien, he may not be overawed by judge or monarch, human or Divine.

As he strove, Asa called to mind those of his forerunners who, loving and fearing God, had yet striven with Him in the courage of their manhood. Abraham, the first of the prophets, had fearlessly called God to account for the lives of possible innocents before the whelming of Sodom and Gomorrah. Jacob had wrestled night-long with the angel and had wrung from him a blessing with the acknowledgment, "Thou hast striven with man and with God and hast prevailed." Job, the righteous dweller in Uz, had long and bitterly protested the divine judgment until persuaded.

" 'Come, let us reason together,' saith the Lord."

PART iii

THE SOUTHWARD WIND

God said, "Let there be a firmament in the midst of the waters, and let it divide the waters." And God made the firmament to divide the waters under the firmament from the waters over the firmament; and it was so. And it was evening and it was morning of the second day. And God said, "Let the waters under the heaven be gathered together unto one place, and let the dry land appear." And it was so. And God called the dry land, earth; and the gathering together of the waters, He called seas; and God saw that it was good.

Now God hath made the mountains to skip like rams, and the little hills like lambs; and man, even man, hath He appointed to furrow the face of the plain with a hook. Only His sea endureth forever, unchanged; he rolleth his waters now as in the days of the beginning; the waters thereof roar, and foam. Who has entered into the springs of the sea? or wandered through the bottom of the deep? Cloud is the garment thereof, and thick darkness its swaddling band.

Now there be they that go down to the sea in ships, and have their business in great waters. But touching the waters above the firmament, know ye, that every man goeth a voyage. And if he be fainthearted, he setteth forth, but turneth back into the mouth of the haven; but if he be mighty of spirit he voyageth afar through the Great Deep, seeking the land which the Lord will show him.

And some wander for forty years in the wilderness of waters, and some are whelmed therein. But some shipmen voyage even unto Ophir, and fetch them thence amethysts, and sandalwood, and ivory.

To an inlander, there are few activities of civilization which present a more bleak and dispiriting aspect than the operations of a long disused, out-of-the-way shipyard. Asa stood on the shore of Egypt gazing across a narrow arm of the Red Sea. With sinking heart he beheld in the distance the ghastly, dun-colored Sinai desert. About him clustered in disorder barracks, sheds and shops, their surfaces scoured colorless by sand under the drive of the eternal wind. Some dozen and a half ships, in various stages of completion and repair, were drawn up on the beach, the areas between a litter of line, lumber, tools, boxes, scaffolding, and sailcloth. Unpainted, some of them with gaping holes in their sides where the planking was unfinished, the nearer ships looked as clumsy, helpless, and out of place as any other sea creatures stranded by evil circumstance. About them laborers and slaves in paint-stained scraps of clothing wandered and babbled in apparent confusion. In the rear straggled the miserable hovels of Baal-Zephon, and everywhere the sifting, shifting, endless yellow-brown sands and the roasting sun of the midsummer desert.

"Lord have mercy!" thought Asa in dismay. "What have I let myself in for!"

There was, as has been remarked, little difference between the tongues of Judea and Phoenicia; yet when accosted by a sailor of Gades, Asa had difficulty in understanding the outlandish accent with its interlarding of Iberian words. He was soon, however, conducted to Ethbaal, senior officer present, who like his commander was a stocky man in early middle age. He read Belnatan's letter and bade the priest welcome.

"Glad to have you aboard, doctor! You must be tired after that long and dirty journey. Fresh water is not a plentiful item here—it is all brought overland from the Nile—but we can spare enough for a bath. Hereafter, most of your bathing will have to be done in sea-water.

"You'd best take what's left of the day to rest and get settled. Do you want to stay here at officers' quarters or would you prefer to find a woman with a hut on the beach? The local females aren't much, as you can see, but I can arrange for one to be put at your disposal."

"Where are the officers' quarters?"

"That palatial shed yonder—fit for a king! If, of course, he has been driven empty-handed from his kingdom."

"I think," Asa said with a smile, "that I should like to live like a king."

"Good enough! Then you'll join the officers for meals, of course. Mattan!"

A pleasant-looking, wiry man, slightly older than Asa, approached. "Yes, Sir?"

"Mattan, this is Asa ben Abdiel, our fleet surgeon. He is a Judean, further trained, as Belnatan writes, in Egypt. It seems that the Egyptian surgeon we were expecting has met with a fatal accident. Mattan, doctor, is master's mate—second in command, that is—on Belnatan's ship here, the *Ayelet Hashakhar*. You, no doubt, will sail in her."

His ship, then, had a name—*Doe of the Dawn,* or *Morning Star.* Asa looked at her disreputable state with churning bowels.

"My own is the *Ishat Yom,* beyond her." Asa forced out some complimentary nothing about the *Seawife.* "Mattan, have the doctor's duffle taken care of and make his arrangements for living with the other officers. See you at dinner, doctor!"

Asa found the room assigned to the fleet surgeon small and poorly furnished but gratifyingly clean. Cleanliness, indeed, he was to learn, was a passion with Phoenician seamen, no less than with his own people, whose faith prescribed a ritual of washing before each meal and after answering a call of nature. This was a welcome discovery, familiar as he was with the filthy habits of the Canaanites, Syrians, and other peoples of his part of the world.

On the morrow Asa was introduced to his brother officers. On the *Morning Star,* besides Belnatan, the fleet commodore, who doubled as captain, and Mattan, the mate, they included Chelbes, the quartermaster, and Abbarus, the boatswain, a ranking petty officer. Chelbes was a stoutish, outgoing man in the middle thirties. In contrast to the others, whose speech and bearing evinced some education and family background, the lean and greying Abbarus had obviously risen from among the mass of the seamen.

Among the officers of the other ships, Ieoud commanded the *Ruakh Tsofonis,* or *North Wind;* Abdemonus the *Avzeez Habor,* or *Brant,* and Balsachus the *Ayal,* or *Stag.* Each in his turn formally introduced his master's mate and quartermaster, and Asa looked upon his companions for a future at whose length and character he could only faintly guess.

Mattan then proposed to take Asa on a tour of the *Morning Star.* "I know nothing of ships," warned the priest.

The other smiled. "I could tell that by the way you looked at them. Our fleet consists, as you know, of five galleys—four men-of-war and a storeship."

"Why men-of-war? Do you expect to fight?"

"As to that, who can tell? All at sea are enemies except other Phoenicians, and even they, if they have taken service with a hostile king. We may have to fight off barbarians bent on plunder, although I hardly think we shall need this much strength. We would do better to have the greater cargo capacity of four storeships and one man-of-war to protect them, except for one thing. The storeship is a merchantman—deep, beamy, and heavy—"roundships," we sometimes call such. They are much harder to row than the war galleys and make less speed under oars or sail. We know enough of these coasts to be able to count on favoring winds for the first few months. Thereafter there may be calms and we may have to row. Or we may have to force our way against a river current to gain a needed harbor. We may even have to flee from an overwhelming enemy force. So speed is essential. At the same time we are taking the storeship for all the extra supplies it can carry. When it is emptied, the commander could at need abandon it if we have not completed our journey."

"If we may have to run in any case, why not just one speedy vessel, with the storeship to transfer its crew and be abandoned?"

"Entirely too risky. A ship can rip her bottom out on a reef. She can founder in a storm. An epidemic can make her crew too weak to save her. Many other things can happen. We are sailing with five ships; we shall be lucky to return with three. The four war galleys are being built to the same plan, so that parts and supplies will be interchangeable as necessary. The timbers and hardware were floated up the Nile, then shipped here by caravan. If Pharaoh Necho had finished his canal, ships could sail from the Middle Sea up the Nile, then directly across the desert to the Red Sea at this point."

"How many cubits long is the *Morning Star?*"

"We have adopted the more convenient unit of the ell—twice the length of a man's sandal. It is easier for rough measuring. Each of the four ships measures 30 ells overall, not including the ram at the waterline. They have a beam—that is to say, a width—of six and a half ells and draw one and a half as ordinarily laden. There is another ell and a half of freeboard between the waterline and the gunwale. Come over here, doctor.

They moved a few feet. "You can see the construction through this unfinished side. The keel is of fir from Sinir, as are the kelson lying on top of it, the false keel projecting below, and the smaller bilge keel on each side. The latter are for protection when the ship is being beached. They also help to keep the ship on her course. Without any projection from her bottom, she would yaw badly in a seaway and make too much leeway."

"Yaw? Leeway?"

"Yaw—turn continually from side to side, with a sinuous instead of a straight course. Leeway is progress sidewise, like a crab's. It can occur with a beam or even a quartering wind—I mean a wind from the side, or from over your shoulder."

"Oh." Asa had never seen a crab.

"The ribs are of Bashan oak. They are rabbeted into the keel at one and a half ell intervals. As you see, they curve outward, upward and slightly inward, the last producing what we call a tumble-home in the bulwarks. Each pair is connected by a beam which serves as a rowing bench, except for five ells at bow and stern, which are decked over. For extra bracing the ribs are also connected just above the kelson by short beams called floors.

"The stem," Mattan continued, "also oaken, is *scarphed* to the bow (front) end of the keel; so at the after end is the sternpiece. Inside, the joint is reinforced by an oaken apron. Planking, deck, and spars are our own Lebanon cedar. Fastenings are of iron, the outboard ends countersunk and covered with wooden dowel sections set in pitch. Pitch makes the seams water-tight, too. The oars will be of oak, the sailcloth of Egyptian linen. One and an eighth ells above the waterline, each side is pierced by a row of holes for the oars, with another pair of holes through the poop, aft, for the steering sweeps. A leather collar keeps out most of the water. The one-man oars are six and a half ells long. When the ship is heavy-laden and low in the water, the oars are pivoted on thole-pins set in the gunwales."

The mate then talked of the crew. "Normally these ships carry two men to a ten-ell oar (except for one-man bow oars), making fifty rowers in all. These ships therefore are called pentekonters, or fifties. We are halving the number of men in order to stretch our supplies. The rowers will be able to make less speed—a parasang and a third, or 10,000 ells, per hour in a spurt, instead of half again as much, but it cannot be helped. There are also two quartermaster's mates for the steering sweeps, a flutist to give cadence, and an acting boatswain. Each ship, therefore, will carry three officers, a boatswain, and 29 men, plus yourself on the *Morning Star* and the fleet supply officer on the storeship."

Mattan turned again to one of the ships under construction.

"Notice the waling-pieces, the long timbers affixed to each side at the waterline, running the length of the ship. They meet at the bow and distribute the shock of the ram. The *Brant*, our storeship, is essentially of the same construction, but her dimensions, as you can see, are very different. She measures 48 ells overall, 16 beam, and her depth of hold is six and a half ells. She is a beast to row when heavy-laden."

"What are the ships further down the beach? Aren't they part of our fleet?"

"No. The half dozen nearest are ships of the Royal Egyptian Navy. You can see that their lines differ appreciably from ours. Note the rocker keels and the generally delicate structure. Their rigging, when the masts are stepped, differs even more. The further vessels, off by themselves, are the Babylonian fleet."

"The Egyptians seem much the better."

Mattan was kind enough not to laugh at him. "The Egyptians are more beautifully painted and carven, but they haven't nearly the sea-keeping qualities of the others. Nor are their seamen as good. The Babylonian ships were designed and built by men of Phoenicia; their crews, too, are largely Phoenician. The Egyptian genius does not run to the sea. This is strange, because the first ships were developed in Egypt."

"Then how do you account for it?"

"I can give you part of the answer. To develop a great maritime industry, a nation must have unlimited shipbuilding facilities. The Nile valley is completely lacking in timber; all raw material of that sort must be imported from us. Secondly, a seafaring nation must have distant bases where their ships can refit and their crews recuperate and where they can find protection from enemies. The Egyptians have never been a colonizing people. They seem to suffer from uncontrollable homesickness when they leave their crocodile-infested river."

The conversation was interrupted.

"Rofay!" Asa turned. He had realized during the day past that among the Phoenicians he would be addressed as doctor rather than as priest. "This morning I tried to catch a falling timber, but it struck my finger on the end." The seaman exhibited an index finger already swollen and somewhat discolored. Asa could not detect any crepitation or undue flexibility, but he would hardly have expected to even if, as he suspected, the bone had been broken. He splinted it lightly with wood, then inquired as to the location of the medical stores. Mattan passed the word for Benadon. A somewhat corpulent man in his thirties reported.

"Benadon is the ship's loblolly boy. He will assist you as necessary and will nurse the sick and injured as you direct. There will be a man on each ship assigned to this duty. Benadon, show the doctor the inventory of the medical stores and the stores themselves."

Asa busied himself with his duties. He prepared few draughts, for watery solutions would quickly go putrid under the Red Sea sun, but day after day he ground materials into powders, compounded his ointments, shaped splints, cut bulk linen into roll upon roll upon roll of bandages, large and small. There were bronze instruments to inspect and sharpen, spoiled drugs to cull and favorite materia medica to order from the capital while it was still possible. He also held classes for the five loblolly boys as their duties permitted and instructed them in his own notions of nursing, dressing, and dietetics.

"Once we set sail, doctor," Ethbaal had warned him, "there will be no possibility of replenishing your supplies. You must foresee all needs. What you haven't brought along, you will have to do without. The Pharaoh has granted us fairly generous funds, but you are limited by weight and stowage space."

And again, "You will have to exercise great thought, doctor, in the disposition of your materials. There must be a fairly even distribution of them among all ships; not so much for each ship's own use, but so that if one or more vessels are lost, you are not left without essential supplies or equipment. In each ship they must be carefully and systematically stowed. You have probably not the faintest conception of how lively a ship can be in a seaway. We cannot have your gear going adrift below decks in an unholy jumble. Furthermore, every one of the thousands of articles on board is so to be bestowed that it can be located instantly without light, on the blackest night, and that even in a storm, when the ship is standing alternately on her stem and on her stern, and rolling her—and your—guts out to boot." This, thought Asa, is patently an exaggeration. He was later to learn that it was not.

A few days after Asa's arrival Belnatan came. After a careful inspection of everything, he called a council of his officers.

"You have not done too badly," he told them, "but it's not good enough. All ships must be ready for sea four weeks from today. Our sailing, as most of you know, must be by midsummer, and that time is the deadline. We cannot sail much sooner because beyond Cape Comorin—he caught Asa's eye, and explained, "the easternmost point of Africa—the winds will still be southerly, and we should have to lie there and consume, uselessly, food and water. That coast is very dry. We cannot delay beyond midsummer, because after that time the winds of the Aualite Gulf, between the Red Sea and the Cape, will have turned against us. Heavily laden as they are, the ships cannot be rowed hundreds of parasangs to windward, especially in this heat— which will get, if anything, worse. Each of you has his assignment. Are there any questions?"

There were none.

"Get on with it, then, and drive the men! Drive!"

The tempo of work increased under Belnatan's eye. The sides of the ships no longer gaped, and the cheerful clink of the caulking irons mingled with the lower pitched thud of the mauls on the decking. In the shade of the tarpaulin by each ship her sailmaker and his mates stitched endlessly. Tabnit, fleet storekeeper, divided the mountains of supplies. To Asa it seemed impossible for such an enormous volume of goods to fit into those four little holds. Now the painters were at work clothing the bare hulls in royal garbs of vermilion and gold (where absence of pitch permitted), while the carpenters turned their attention to the few interior fittings or worked on the ships' tenders. Huge jars in protecting wooden frameworks were filled with water and sealed. Aft on each ship the five-ell deck was at once steering platform and officers' quarters. Slightly forward of amidships was set a little tabernacle for the butt end of the mast.

"Why is a pair of eyes painted on each bow?" Asa asked Mattan.

"Without eyes, how could the ship see her way?"

Asa looked amazedly at the other until the mate laughed. "Well, that was the original idea, anyway, and we keep up the custom out of innate conservatism."

That same evening, paying a courtesy call on the aged priest of Amun stationed at the Royal Naval Yard, Asa recounted the exchange. The old man shook his head. "People always invent an explanation for a custom whose origin they have forgotten. Sailors in general will give you the same reason as your mate, but the painting of eyes on ships actually began quite differently. In the beginning of time, the divine Osiris was slain by his jealous brother Seth. The body was cut into seven pieces, which Seth scattered widely through the world. But Isis and Horus, the faithful wife and son of the murdered god, resolved to re-assemble the pieces and inspire them again with life. To accomplish this, they traveled from land to land to collect them. One piece, however, had fallen into the Nile and had been eaten by a crocodile. Not knowing this, Horus descended on his quest into the underworld and in a boat explored the river of the dead. He failed, of course, but returned and carved a piece of wood in the necessary shape. Isis and he then restored Osiris to life. In memory of his filial piety and of his voyage on that dread river, Horus was made the patron of such as fare upon the sea. For long the statue of the hawk-headed god was set up in the bow of every ship. Gradually, however, his head alone came to be mounted and then merely painted on each side of the bow. So the arts of Egypt declined from their glory, until only his seeking eyes were represented, but even today, in some of the coasts of India, whither the art of boat-building spread from Egypt (as well as to the north), the fishermen paint the head of a hawk upon their bows.

Except among a few of us of the priesthood, the reason has long been forgotten."

Then, in a different tone, "But let us talk of newer things. My letters tell me that a colleague of yours, Nebamon, priest of Sekhmet, has fallen into disgrace. He is blamed for the death of a chamberlain who was his patient."

Asa smiled grimly. "I am not sorry," he said. "Had it happened sooner, it might have spared me much pain," and proceeded to relate his misadventure.

The old man shook his head. "Do not gloat over the misfortune of another. Some may think as badly of you."

The fleet surgeon bowed his head in deep shame. He, a priest of Israel, had been given a lesson in charity by a heathen!

It was during this period that Asa was introduced to the pleasures of sea bathing. Every evening the hot, sweaty workmen refreshed themselves in the tepid sea, and Asa, whose home boasted hardly a brook to wade in, let alone a waterway large enough for swimming, stared in amazement at the spectacle of human beings living on and moving through the water.

Mattan undertook his instruction in the art, and Asa made rapid progress. The priest's limbs, cramped from the year-long sojourn in the unaccustomed city, also rejoiced in long climbs over the barren hills. He exercised his arms by a resumption of his boyhood practice of slinging, although in this country of sand, stones were not numerous on the beach.

"Enjoy yourself, doctor," remarked Chelbes, the *Star's* quartermaster. "You'll not be treading the earth of any civilized land for a year or more."

"How do you know it will be a year?"

"Why, doctor," expansively, "any old sailor can figure that. It can hardly be less, and cannot be much more, as the captain obviously figures. These fifties, loaded deep as they are going to be, displace roughly 30,000 sep each. Take off 10,000 for the weight of the hull, and they can float 20,000." He dipped a pointed stick into some paint, and made his calculations on a plank. "We carry a crew of 3 officers and 30 men—say 75 sep each."

Asa nodded. Seventy-five double pounds was a fair average weight per man.

Chelbes continued, "Each man needs 14 sep of arms and armor and half a dozen sep of clothes and personal effects—total, 95 sep per man and gear. Multiply by thirty-three and you have"—he hesitated "3,135 sep of men and their gear—say 3,200. Take that from 20,000, and you have—let's see—16,800. Take another 6,000 for ship's equipment (a lot of replacements there, of course) and you have 10,800 left."

"You're quick at figures."

"You have to be, in shipping. Well, there's 10,800 sep for provisions. Each man needs, per day, a sep and a half of food, one sep of firewood and two kab of water. That right, doctor?"

Asa nodded. A man could hardly do, over a long period of time, with less than a double pound of fuel, half again as much food, and two half-gallons of water a day.

Finding an eager listener, the quartermaster continued, "Two kab, stowed in jars, comes to five and a half sep; altogether, eight sep a day. That, times 33 men, gives you 264 sep of consumable supplies daily. Divided into 10,800, you have forty days' provisions on each of the fifties.

"But the bulk of our stores, of course, are in the *Brant*. The *Brant* displaces about 245,000 sep; of this, about 40,000 are for weight of hull. That leaves 205,000. Subtract, again, the same 14,000 for her people, their gear and supplies for forty days, plus 38,000 for another forty days, water for the whole fleet, plus 48,000 of ship's gear (she being a much heavier ship) and replacements for the others, and you have over 100,000 sep of food. That's over a year's rations. Plus our original six weeks. Water and fuel, after the first two or three months, we expect to pick up on the way. Every desert comes to an end somewhere. We can go on short rations of food and water for a while, if we must, and stretch our supplies out further. I'm sure, doctor, that in years of drouth you drank much less than two kab a day in Judea."

Asa nodded.

Chelbes pointed out the prospect of picking up a little—perhaps much—extra food on the voyage and the certainty of some spoilage. "Obviously, then, the captain plans to be gone for a year to a year and a half before he reaches our colonies in northwest Africa or Iberia, at the far end of the Middle Sea."

"But how can he possibly know the length of a journey that no human being has ever made?"

"Doctor, we Phoenicians don't believe in telling all we know. Our ships and our trade routes are our life, and what we don't know, we can often infer. I daresay that our mariners have charted the coast for some days' sail, at least, south from Cape Comorin, but beyond that, how the captain can guess at the length or nature of our journey is beyond me."

One by one the ships were ready for launching. With gangs of men pushing and hauling, the vessels made their majestic way on rollers down the beach and into the shallows at low tide. When the rising water refloated them, they were towed further out and moored. Water spurted in through wide-open seams and the galleys sank almost to their decks. For a week their planks and timbers soaked and swelled, squeezing together and shutting off the inflow. Meanwhile their crews finished the small craft, spars, oars, weapons, and miscellaneous accessories. When the hulls could be bailed dry, they were laid alongside the wharves, and under the watchful eyes of the boatswains' and storekeepers' mates, the food, water, oil, wine, and other supplies were carefully and systematically stowed. Sailcloth, flour, dried meats and fish, cheese, beans, peas, and onions were protected from moisture. By lamps and torches the crews worked frantically through the final night.

The longboats, utility tenders, would tow astern in good weather; in bad, they would be taken aboard. Each had a length of twenty-four sandals (a dozen ells) and a beam of three ells and a quarter. The captains' gigs, six ells by one and three-quarters, lay aft of the masts or nested within the longboats.

2

Five days before their projected departure, Belnatan's crews had watched the Babylonian fleet set forth on its homeward journey. Larger than the explorers' ships, they were double banked, with two rows of oars on a side. In line astern the gleaming ships, their purple sails bellying forward, had swum grandly into the south.

"Well, that's the last of them!" remarked Asa to his commander.

"One never knows," replied Belnatan with a speculative squint.

On the morning of a brilliant, windy day, Belnatan and his crew sacrificed a splendid white bull to Baal-Melkarth, tutelary divinity of Tyre. They then consulted the omens; these were favorable. (Belnatan had seen to that.) The Egyptian priest invoked the blessing of Horus on his sovereign's venture. Apart, Asa knelt in communion with the God of Israel. By noon Belnatan gave the order to embark. In each war galley a small image of one of the Kabirim, the dwarfish, ugly, glaring Tyrian deities of navigation, was set up as a figurehead. A horse's head graced the stem of the storeship.

Asa's heart beat high in excitement as with the aid of Benadon, the *Morning Star's* loblolly boy, he carried his sea-chest onto the poop-deck where the upward-curving stern made a taffrail and a breast-high lee for officers' quarters. Even Beltnatan, his glance on a thousand things, noticed the brightness of his eye and relaxed in a smile.

"Well, doctor, not so glum about going to certain destruction in the unknown?"

Asa laughed happily. "I think you know pretty well what you're about, Captain!"

"I sensed how you felt about the cruise two months ago," said Belnatan. "I've noticed many a time how a man's thoughts are colored and changed by his company. Most of my seamen would think it madness to face a charging lion with spear and shield. Put them among a party of Libyan lion hunters for a few weeks, and—you, there! Drop a piece of metal that close to a water-jar again, and you'll feel a rope's end kissing your backside!"

The decks were a litter of small boats and unstowed gear in seemingly unresolvable confusion. Lines lay in an apparent tangle. Men rushed hither and yon in what to the landsman's eye was frantic, aimless activity. The four subordinate captains came aboard and reported their ships as ready to sail.

"You have your orders," said the commodore. "I repeat the salient points. We will proceed in column astern, following the Egyptian ships. The interval between ships by day, in clear weather, will be four shiplengths. At night, or by day with poor visibility, you will close in as necessary, with due regard to keeping clear. At hourly intervals during the night, weather conditions permitting, you will show a torch for two minutes over the sternpost—oftener in thick weather. Should a galley or galleys be separated from the flagship, we will rendezvous first at Berenice, then at the Royal Egyptian Naval Station at the mouth of the Red Sea. Do you understand your orders? Very well, gentlemen—good luck!

"Mr. Mate!"

"Aye, aye, sir?"

"Get the ship under way!"

"Aye, aye, sir! Rowers!"

The ship lay along the southern side of the wharf, her prow toward the shore. She was therefore moored by her starboard side. One man took his seat on each of the benches to starboard, one to port. Mattan raised his voice again.

"Special sea details!"

Two men sprang to the hawsers at each end of the ship.

"Cast off, fore and aft!"

The mooring cables were released and dragged aboard. The pressure of the wind slowly widened the gap between galley and wharf.

"Out oars and steering sweeps!"

The twenty-six oars rose as one. They were extended outboard, secured by a line to each. Then the oarlooms were passed in through the thole-holes. The two steersmen took their stand on either side of the afterdeck, each of them with a huge steering sweep in the water.

"Stern all!"

Standing in the bow, the boatswain half called, half chanted, "Heave, oh! heave, oh!" As the oars dipped in cadence, the galley moved and gathered sternway.

"Starboard your helms!" The looms of the huge steering oars moved to starboard, their blades to port, and the stern of the galley turned downwind.

"Hold water!" The oars were braced, blades vertical in the sea. The sternway was checked.

"Give way together!" To the rhythm of the boatswain's mate's flute the oars beat the water. The galley began to move forward. At Mattan's word to the helmsmen, she turned her head offshore, then downwind.

Two Egyptian galleys, bound for the naval station controlling the straits at the southern end of the Red Sea, waited as their escort.

One by one the other ships fell into line, *Morning Star* first after the Egyptians, then *Stag,* with the storeship *Brant* midway among the Phoenicians; then *North Wind,* with the vice-commander in *Seawife* bringing up the rear. They turned their prows to the south. Now most of the rowers shipped their oars, only a few still pulling to keep steerage way. The masts rose, their butts in the kelson steps, secured at gunwale height in the tabernacles. From the truck of each, twenty-two ells above the decks, a forestay was led and belayed to the stem, a backstay to the stern, and a pair of shrouds, leading slightly aft, to the gunwale on either side. Seamen laid hands to the halyard that led up the mast, through a dead-eye at its truck and down to the yard. Now to a chant the eighteen-ell yards or cross-spars rose to the mast heads, their sails bundled close by brailing lines. From either yard-arm a trimming line or brace led to a kingpost at the forward end of the poop deck. The brails were slacked off, letting the sails fall and fill with the north wind. From each clew, or lower corner, of a sail a sheet-line was tensed to a samsonpost. Braces and sheets squared the sails to the breeze, and the voyage had begun.

Asa stood by the carven prow of his ship and drank in the new sights, sounds, and smells of the sea. The deep blue waters of the Heroöpolitan Gulf churned to milk under *Morning Star's* forefoot as she sped south with a bone in her teeth. On either shore the sombre brown earth rose to the ridge-tops, but the sun shone splendidly on the scarlet hulls and the purple sails of the fleet and flashed blindingly back from a thousand wavelets. A white wake trailed from the Egyptian ahead. Some of the seamen were still engaged in stowing gear and making fast for sea. Others were erecting an awning of woven palm-fronds—needed indeed in the intense heat. Ithobaal, a lad making his first trip, stepped onto the foredeck, and carefully scanned the waters ahead.

"Looking for something?" asked the priest.

"Yes, sir, the mail buoy. There may be letters from Tyre which have come overland and been dropped by a ship in a sealed leather bag. It would be moored to the bottom and marked by a blue spar buoy."

Asa looked at him incredulously and started aft. As he did so, he became aware of grinning faces turning toward the prow.

Mattan laughed. "Have they pulled that old one on the youngster? It's tried on every novice. Probably it was done on the Cretan ships, a thousand years ago."

"And on the earliest Egyptian ships, before them?"

"I doubt it, doctor. The Egyptians have never been famous for their sense of humor."

Chelbes, the quartermaster, approached as the mate turned away. "Your gear all stowed, doctor?"

"All shipshape, I think." Asa mopped his face. "The wind has dropped since we set sail."

"It only seems that way. Look overside at the waves. Feel the pull of the sail on the sheets, those lines from its lower corners to the after samson posts. We're running with the wind; therefore we don't feel all of its force. Besides, we are standing in the shelter of the poop. It'll be hot as blazes for many weeks to come, unless the wind changes. And it won't."

"You are right, come to think of it, the waves are higher. The wind must be freshening."

Chelbes laughed. "Wrong again, doctor. We are running out of the lee provided by the head of the bay. It takes a good long fetch for the wind to work up a sea. Within an hour, though, we'll be rolling."

"How fast do you think we're going?"

The quartermaster stared speculatively overside. "A good parasang per hour."

Asa made a rapid mental calculation. A parasang, or triple mile, meant nine thousand ells.

"We could do better by sheeting the sail further in," said Chelbes, "but *Brant,* so much deeper and beamier, cannot."

Belnatan rolled up the chart he had been studying and put it into a sea-chest. "Mr. Mate!"

"Aye, aye, sir?" was Mattan's response.

"Pick your crews."

"Aye, aye, sir," again. Then, "All hands muster aft!"

On the poop deck stood the four officers, as well as the two steersmen gripping the handles of their sweeps. The rest of the men, most of them stripped down to loincloth and cap, gathered just forward.

"When we sail day and night," Mattan explained to Asa, "we stand watches to relieve one another. The evening watch begins at the end of twilight, after the evening meal. It ends at midnight, when the stars which have been above the eastern horizon after dusk have swung to an overhead position. The dawn watch then begins and lasts till first light and the morning meal. The morning watch goes on till noon, with the afternoon watch from then till dinner-time."

"Then each man gets only six hours of sleep."

"No; because it doesn't take a full watch to handle the ship under sail. One-half of the watch is awake at a time, the other half is on call. Chelbes and I will dog the afternoon watch—that is to say, we will split it in half—so each can get a couple of hours of rest. When the ship is under oars, it is of course a full crew operation. We then generally sleep ashore or, occasionally, aboard, lying to a mooring."

"Doctor," said Belnatan, "you will share Mattan's watch. You will be under instruction and will learn seamanship. Before this cruise is ended you'll find ample opportunity to exercise your knowledge. Chelbes, you will have the boatswain as a junior officer of the deck. For the first several months, Mattan, until the doctor understands his job, I will relieve you for two or three hours every night."

The crew was soon mustered.

"I take Chips," said Mattan. The ship's carpenter, lean, middle-aged and grizzled, stepped to the starboard rail.

"Abdelim," picked Chelbes, and the sailmaker moved to the port side.

"Bodo."

"Tamasus."

The choosing went on until port and starboard watches had been made up; whereupon the men were told to resume the work of stowing and making all shipshape.

Southward swam the fleets through the blue and gold of the afternoon. Asa felt no little pride in being a part of this beauty, strength, and daring. He felt his cares receding behind him with the soil of Egypt. Again, as many times recently, he sighed inwardly as he thought of Tamar, but for that affair there was no help. He brought his thoughts back to the present.

Yes, the wind was freshening a bit. Lacy white crests decked the wavetops. The *Star* rolled rhythmically as one swell after another overtook her, passed under her hull, raised her amidships in unstable equilibrium, her ends unsupported, so that she reeled now to port, now to starboard, until the wave passed under her bow and away. The motion was delightful—or was it to everyone? Asa became aware of a greenish hue in the face of a man near him, and the lad who had been looking out for the mail buoy suddenly vomited overside.

Benadon grinned. "Seasickness gets a lot of them at first, and some of them get it again at the beginning of every cruise." And, indeed, another of the crew was obviously feeling ill.

Asa examined the sick man with interest. He had heard during the past month of seasickness. He remembered having seen a similar disorder in a man who had ridden a camel for the first time. There was nothing that he could suggest. He felt embarrassed to make this confession but relieved that no one seemed to expect any treatment. He had a brief period of queasiness himself, but it soon passed away.

They had their evening meal—roast meat still fresh from the shore, bread, onions, and fruit—while a glorious sunset flamed over the purpling hills of the Egyptian desert. Then, while three quarters of the crew disposed themselves to sleep under the benches, Mattan took the afterdeck for the evening watch. The sea and the sky darkened until the hills were a blacker line against the brilliantly starry heaven. The priest looked upward to the same constellations that overarched the hills of Judea. Like old friends following him to strange, new places, they greeted his eyes—the Great and Little Wains, the Swan, Boötes, the Scorpion, and the Archer. To his surprise there were lights in the sea as well—glows and sparkles in the bow wave and wake and in the curling crests of the waves.

"It is strange," Asa remarked, "to think that I am sailing in a ship where my ancestors walked dry-shod three-quarters of a millenium ago."

"That was when your people escaped from slavery in Egypt, wasn't it?"

"That's right." Asa was surprised at the mate's knowledge. "They fled to the east. 'And the Egyptians pursued after them, and they overtook them encamped by the sea; and between the camp of the Egyptians and the camp of Israel was a cloud and darkness all the night. And Moses stretched out his hand over the sea; and the Lord drove back the sea with a strong east wind all that night, and made the sea dry land, and the waters were divided. And the children of Israel went into the midst of the sea upon the dry ground; and the waters were a wall unto them, on their right hand, and on their left. The Egyptians pursued, and went in after them, all Pharaoh's horses, his chariots, and his horsemen, to the midst of the sea. And Moses stretched forth his hand over the sea, and the sea returned, when the morning appeared, to its strength; and the Lord overthrew the Egyptians in the midst of the sea. The waters returned, and covered all the host of Pharaoh; there remained of them not even one. Thus the Lord saved Israel on that day.' "

"I know about it," said Mattan. "As fine a yarn as ever I've heard spun. But seriously, doctor, and with no disrespect for your theology, no seaman can believe for a moment that the sea could behave in that fashion."

"Beg pardon, sir," said the quartermaster's mate at one of the steering sweeps, "but I can believe that story. I seen that sort o' thing happen."

"What do you mean?"

"I been around these parts a lot, sir. I used to be on the caravan route through the Sinai Desert. Up here at the head of the gulf, you can get as much as a three-ell tide at springs. After a couple days of particular strong winds out of the north, a lot of water would be blown out of the gulf, and, 'specially with a moon tide, I've seen bottom that I've never seen before. The Israelites might 'a crossed a narrow arm of the sea that way. Most o' them Egyptians don't know nothing about tides. The only salt water they know about is the Middle Sea, where there ain't no tide. If the general was from up-country, he wouldn't even know nothing about that. So they might 'a tried to follow. If in the meantime one o' them khamsin winds started to blow from the south, the water would 'a come rushin' back in a flood tide that would drownd a camel, let alone a horse or a man. This here Moses might 'a knowed about the tides and winds in these parts, 'specially if he'd spent any time east o' the Nile valley."

"He had," said Asa.

"Well, sir, there you are. He might 'a smelled a change in the weather and took advantage of it."

Mattan had listened with interest. "It could have happened that way, certainly. But what then? Water and browse are scarce in the peninsula of Sinai. A large expedition, moving slowly, cumbered with women, children, old people, and baggage, could not possibly pass the desert."

"When all other food failed," Asa answered him, "the Lord sent down manna like dew in the night, and they found and ate it in the morning. When water failed, Moses struck the rock and the Lord brought forth from it sweet water."

"Now that is a little too much."

"Beg pardon again, sir, but I've ate this manna the doctor tells of. There's a certain shrub, what there's a lot of them in the Sinai Desert. Now there's a boring worm that lives in the stems, millions and millions of 'em. The sap leaks out of the bore holes, and in the cold of the night it hardens, like, and you can scrape it off and eat it in the morning, like the doctor says. I done it many a time. It's sweetish. I ain't never seen no water knocked out of a rock, but I heard of it. I heard tell that there's places there where, if you take and knock off the surface of some of this limestone with a hammer, you can find water underneath. Might be Moses had spent some time there and knowed those places."

It might be thought that the priest's faith would be strengthened by this vindication, but the opposite was true. The effect of the seaman's revelations was indescribable shock. Was the strong hand of the Lord to be replaced by a mere clever—even brilliant—utilization of perfectly natural phenomena? In place of the Mercy of the manna, was he to be left merely with the senseless and wasteful prodigality of blind nature? If so, perhaps all of the other miracles which God had supposedly manifested for His people were also, in fact, spectacular happenings which, properly understood and interpreted, had nothing of the preternatural about them! Asa's literal faith was badly shaken.

Of course, he reasoned as he began to recover, the helmsman's naturalistic interpretation might not be at all pertinent to the facts. Even if it were correct, it did not necessarily follow that other wonderful events in the history of his people were susceptible of the same sort of explanation. Even if the helmsman were right and the wonders that had awed generations of Hebrews were, in their essence, spurious, did rejection in toto of the Hebrew theology necessarily follow? Suppose his forefathers had not been preserved by marvels on their transit of the Red Sea. The important point was that under the good providence of Heaven they had gotten across. Suppose God had not engraved the two tablets of stone for Moses on the dread summit of Sinai. Under His inspiration, nevertheless, then and thereafter, Moses and the later prophets had formulated a code of law and morals by which a people might fittingly live and die.

Lying on the poop deck of a tossing ship, Asa strove valiantly against the winds of doubt that sought to blow him into the outer darkness of shoreless seas far from the radiance of God and the warm brotherhood of man; strove valiantly, and as he was driven from under the friendly guide-stars that he knew, charted new constellations by which to steer his course according to the commandments of his Captain; strove valiantly and won. The winds of doubt went whistling off to leeward and away. They went; but the coldness of their passing remained with him.

3

By the day following, the ships were in their cruising routine. As may be imagined, Asa entered with enthusiasm upon his instruction and found the seaman's lore fascinating. The wisest of his people's kings, Solomon, had recorded the way of a ship upon the sea as one of the four things that he did not understand. To this extent the priest was in a fair way to surpass him. Indeed, his mind, trained both to priestly abstractions and to the natural phenomena that concern a physician, made rapid progress in the nautical art during the ensuing weeks.

All through the hot, flawless day they ran, with the highlands of Egypt and the Sinai peninsula on either hand. Through the night they continued smoothly on their journey. By the following dawn they debouched from the Gulf of Heroöpolis into the wider expanse of the Red Sea proper. Over the port quarter Mt. Sinai, where Moses had received the Law, disappeared from Asa's ken. Crossing a wide and deep bay, they approached the western shore.

Along both its coasts, the Red Sea is foul with coral. Here, therefore, they could run only by daylight, with a lookout at the masthead to con them clear of the reefs. The gulf had been narrow enough so that even in the hours of darkness they could keep a mid-channel course that would carry them clear of all dangers, but in the wider expanse this was too uncertain. Accordingly, the man aloft watched for the sharp transition from amethyst to turquoise where the coral formations approached the surface. To run upon one would mean to rip the bottom out of a ship. From a height they were much more readily perceived than from deck level—with some difficulty at the two extremes of the day but very easily when the sun was high.

During this stage of the journey the ships spent every night at anchor. Sometimes they swung in the shelter of reefs at a distance from the shore. More often they enjoyed the luxury of cooking fires on the beach and beds in the sand, with only an anchor watch to guard the vessels and check their hold on the bottom against drift. Asa asked Mattan about the ground tackle.

"In the days when the ships of your people and mine sailed these seas together," Mattan told him, "sailors could not have known the same relaxation. Formerly we moored our ships with rocks, which dragged easily, but since the invention of the anchor, in the last century, we sleep more securely. Not but what anchors have been known to drag or to foul with a turn of the mooring-line about a fluke. Even today the watch officer must be vigilant."

Day followed day with little change in their routine. In the narrow confines of the vessel, Asa's trail-wonted legs ached with inaction. The wind fell lighter and the almost unbearable heat grew ever more intense. Ashore, the breeze had helped them to endure the sun and had dried the sweat as it appeared, but the ships were running with the wind and it was not felt. Despite such shade as they could achieve, the sunlight was reflected burningly from the wavelets. Even the desert of Judea had been less trying. The bodies, wrung dry with sweating, thirsted continually, but Belnatan would not increase the water ration.

Mornings and evenings, Asa held sick call. Under his direction, Benadon dispensed his concoction of figs to those in whom the cessation of physical activity had resulted in constipation. He bound up cuts and massaged sprains. Other medical aides were doing the same on the other ships when under way. Ashore, Asa saw all the crews. Twice in this time another galley was laid alongside the *Morning Star* that Asa might discriminate between sprain and fracture. There were no more dramatic calls upon him.

Occasionally the escorting Egyptians would locate a well ashore, but the scanty water did little to spare their supplies, especially since, as Chelbes remarked, the Egyptians took care of themselves first. He remarked it without malice—the men of Tyre and Sidon would have done the same.

Now and then a few huts appeared but their dwellers had sought the slight coolness of the hills. The long, brown coast offered little greenery to relieve the barrenness. A break in the monotony occurred some two weeks after their initial departure. "Tomorrow," Belnatan announced, "we put in to Berenice. We should arrive early enough for a good rest."

This port, Chelbes informed Asa, was a transshipment center. Northbound ships from Chaldea and even India unloaded here and their goods were carried by caravan to the Nile, then floated downstream to the cities of Egypt.

"Is the overland route shorter here," Asa asked, "than where we started?"

"As a matter of fact, doctor, it's a little longer, but it is not practicable for merchant ships to voyage north of this point unnecessarily. In the upper part of the Red Sea, the wind blows almost constantly from the north, and ships would have to be rowed against it slowly and at great cost. Below here, on the other hand, winds are lighter and somewhat variable, so that by picking his season a shipmaster may bring a cargo to this point quickly and cheaply enough to show a larger profit, and there are good wells here."

The town, when they reached it, was mean enough, albeit more of a place than the one from which they had started. Reaching it at midday, they rested until the following morning. Asa stretched his legs among alleys in which vice wore so sordid and wretched an aspect that it sent him, sickened, into the desert at its doorstep.

Most of the crew were less sensitive. They came staggering aboard in groups or singly. Some were carried to the wharfside, disheveled, bloody, and comatose, by members of the garrison. Asa worked late that night on lacerated scalps, loosened teeth, and bloody noses, and for days thereafter prescribed hot sitzbaths and sandalwood for incautious devotees of Ashtoreth.

"Too bad you didn't like the town, doctor," Belnatan remarked to him. "It's the last you'll see for a long, long time. After this there will be only the Royal Naval station in the straits and then nothing."

More slowly thereafter they proceeded southward. Twice they had to lie up for a day while the air was calm or an adverse breeze blew itself out. The heat by now was hardly to be borne. Some of the water acquired the odor and taste of rotten eggs, but it could not be replaced. Crew members held their noses and drank the stinking stuff down. Hilly, brown and desolate, and seemingly devoid of life, the shore passed them by. Equally desolate was the surface of the Red Sea.

Equally empty, that is, of human life; of the presence of marine creatures they had frequent evidence. The islets became increasingly numerous. Some were scantily green, more were barren; rock and sand, sand and rock met the eye. Astonishing mirages appeared shimmering above the waters. Islands floated in the sky; their mirror images danced below; castles and towers resolved themselves into pinnacles of rock. The glare of the sun, redoubled by the shining sea, beat at eyeballs and seared the skin.

A month of voyaging, a month of gasping on the hottest sea in the world, a month of thirst. The water ration no more than maintained them—it afforded no relief. They raised again the eastern coast. Toward the straits, the two sides of the Red Sea approached each other to within the range of visibility. Ahead, in the strait, they saw the island of Perim.

"We won't find very much at the naval station there," Chelbes remarked. "I doubt whether there are three Egyptian galleys—certainly not more. And the facilities are scarcely enough even for them. Piratical activity is not marked hereabouts, and in peace time it does not take much of a force to control this southern gate to the Red Sea" —the last for Asa's information.

"We will also find our friends from Chaldea," Belnatan put in softly. "They have been damaged by running aground near here and have put in for repairs."

The others stared at him in bewilderment. "I don't understand,

Captain." As a tyro Asa could most easily afford to confess his incomprehension. "How can you tell what has happened to a fleet that left days before us and which we have not spoken since?"

The captain only smiled. Suddenly Mattan let out a long whistle, but to the inquiring looks he said nothing. For the rest of the day he was very thoughtful.

Perim Island was less clearly seen than might be; a fine sand, blowing over the surface of the water, constituted a low haze that hid detail. The island was not very high or large; nevertheless, Asa gathered that it had to be approached with care because of strong currents in the strait. They coasted along its shore until they opened a deep, narrow harbor on its south side. The sails were lowered, the masts unstepped, and the ships entered under oars.

Hauled up on the shore were two Egyptian galleys and one of the Chaldeans. "I was only partly right," Belnatan observed. "Call away my gig."

In a moment the smaller of the ship's boats was in the water and Belnatan was being pulled by two rowers to pay a courtesy call on the Egyptian commandant.

"Happy to meet you, Captain!" said Menes. "Did you have a good trip?"

"As good as could have been hoped for, thank you."

"Splendid! This Chian wine is, some of us think, superior to any of our own vintages. We keep it in a porous pottery jar covered with a wet cloth; it is as cool as we can get anything to be in this wretched, God-forgotten corner of the earth. The facilities of the station, such as they are, are at your disposal."

"Thank you. I must unload, beach and scrape the bottoms of my ships."

"Of course. I can put a few dozen men at your disposal."

"That will be very kind. I notice one of the Chaldean ships that sailed before us."

"Another cup, Captain? Yes, that ship ran on a reef just outside the harbor mouth, and remained behind for repairs. Although, to tell the truth, I saw little evidence of damage, and little haste to repair what there was. At any rate, her captain announced only an hour ago that he would be ready to proceed in the morning. Perhaps he has had his own reasons for wishing to be out from under the eyes of his commanding officer."

"Perhaps."

In the meantime, Captain, you will be my guest. Oh, but I insist. And your captains must take dinner with us. Not at all—not at all. The lady Tekoschet and I have so little company here."

"Thank you, sir. No more now, thank you. I think we shall be ready to sail in four days, allowing for a rest of the crews. What ships will constitute our escort to Cape Comorin?"

"Escort? My orders said nothing about an escort, Captain."

"Didn't they, now? Well, I suppose these feather merchants are all alike. His Majesty was very specific and emphatic about it. He sets great store by this expedition and will be most indignant if it comes to any harm at the outset. Of course, in your own case, I know that your friends stand close enough to the throne to absolve you of blame for any untoward happenings in your district. It is very disappointing, all the same."

"Oh, come. I haven't said we can't provide you with an escort. His Majesty himself, eh? Yes, I'm sure something can be worked out. Ah, your bath is ready, Captain. One of the wenches there will take care of you. Which one do you prefer?"

4

Three days later, the hulls scraped free of their infestation of marine growth, drinking water replenished, and the ships reloaded, the men were resting. Belnatan addressed a council of his officers.

"I must assume that the Chaldeans will attempt to wipe us out in the vicinity of Cape Comorin. Ever since the days of Tiglath Pileser the kings of the Land between the Rivers have had ambitions concerning sea-power and seaborne commerce. They will not willingly see Egyptian interests expand at sea, any more than they did on land. They have already made two attempts to do away with this expedition. The first was by their ambassador, who tried to talk the Pharaoh out of it. He failed. The second time they had a try at my assassination. The doctor was present when his predecessor was killed. That was no accident. One of the Chaldeans had identified me. The doctor will remember that, immediately before the murder, I happened to yield my place and my cloak to the luckless Snefrunofr. He died instead of me. Now I find one of their ships delaying here, on a flimsy excuse, to carry our time of arrival and departure to the fleet. I was able to bluff the commandant into furnishing us with an escort as far as Cape Comorin."

"How will you answer for that deceit to the Pharaoh?" asked Balsachus.

"If I don't return, there will be no need to answer. If I return successfully, I'll be able to snap my fingers at such a peccadillo."

"Suppose we ask for an escort for a month's sail past the Cape?" Abdemonos asked.

"Not a chance. These Egyptians would sooner venture to Hell than south of the Cape."

"We might delay our departure until they have given up and left," said Ieoud.

"We'd use up too much of our stores. And the Gulf wind is due to turn against us."

"One, or even two, Egyptian galleys will be scanty protection."

"But enough. The Chaldeans will not risk an open rupture by attacking an Egyptian vessel, or us under its convoy."

Ieoud spoke slowly. "Sir, I respectfully submit that in view of your disclosures, the project must be abandoned. The Chaldean ships are biremes. With their double rows of oars on either side, they are faster as well as heavier than we. We must inevitably be outmaneuvered. They have some sixty men in a ship against our thirty; we cannot even hope to board them successfully. Any one of them, sir, is more than a match for our whole fleet; she can ram and sink us one by one. I propose, therefore, that we return to Egypt; or if you dare not do so, let us offer our ships and our services to the king of Babylon."

"We have engaged to sail around Africa," said Belnatan, "and around Africa we are going. I believe we are safe as far as Cape Comorin. Between Cape Comorin and Socotra Island are some forty-five parasangs of open water. We may be able to slip past the fleet at night. And if not—well, I have fought superior forces before, and so have you."

There was a grimness about the men who put to sea on the day following, a resentful ship's company leading the way in a galley of Egypt. How the word had leaked from officers to men no one knew; but leaked it had, and now to the hardships and hazards inherent in the enterprise was added the prospect of a battle against desperate odds. Had Perim been other than the remote, inaccessible spot that it was, desertions might have been expected; but a deserter there could hope at best for enslavement; barring that, for speedy death. Even for a free man, life on hot, lonely, barren Perim was scarcely endurable.

The fleet put out from harbor to begin its second month's voyage. The ships steered south and approached the African shore. With a moderate southwest wind they ran down their easting. On the first night on which they carried through on their course, as the sun went down in glory behind them and darkness shrouded the restless, tossing sea, Asa was aware of a profound perturbation. He had not yet sailed all night in such open waters.

"Now that the sun is gone," Mattan instructed his watchmate, "we can steer by the stars if we lose sight of the coast. We use Rekhubah, the first star of the constellation of the Lesser Wain, to indicate the north, although that is not, strictly speaking, correct. After fixing your course with reference to it, line up the masthead with whatever star or constellation happens to be dead ahead and check your helmsman's course by it. Every half-hour, of course, you must pick another, as the constellations wheel through the sky."

"Everything here is so strange and new to me, it is comforting to guide myself by the old, familiar heavens, and to reflect that they, at least, are the same here as at home in Judea; the same now as last year or in the days of Abraham."

"Ah, but they aren't! Our mariners who have voyaged out through the pillars of Hercules and north in the Ocean to the Cassiterides, the isles of tin, say that as they proceed northward, the southernmost constellations are sunk in the sea; and the old records of the Babylonian observers reveal that Thuban was once the North Star. Even today it is as close to true north as Rekhubah, although some day, centuries hence, Rekhubah will be the true guide."

"So much is unsettling!" sighed Asa. "I am impressed by your knowledge of astronomy."

"I have studied with Berossus, the Babylonian, who set up his school of astronomy at Cos."

Like landsmen generally, Asa had believed professional seamen to be uniformly an ignorant lot; like many another, before and after him, he was astonished to encounter among them a man of wide reading and high intellectual attainment.

He remarked upon this one day, finding himself with Chelbes in the bow while Mattan was busied on the poop.

"Yes, Mattan has had good schooling," the quartermaster agreed. "How, is something of a mystery. I have heard that his mother appeared with him in Tyre when he was still a young child; it is not clear where they came from. She has the manner of a woman of the working classes but has seemed well supplied with money. He does not resemble her, by the way. There is all sorts of speculation about their origin; they claim Cyprus as their old home, and for all I know it may be so.

"He is almost as fine a seaman as the captain and could have had his own command; but he has repeatedly refused it. Abbarus thinks that he is afraid of responsibility, but I doubt it. You will find that he is moody. But always dependable, just the same."

During the ensuing weeks they coasted a hilly desert. When the ships were forced to a distance by outlying dangers, mirages multiplied the scanty shrubbery; but when again they could close with the land, they saw little mitigation of the barrenness of the gigantic furnace. Frequently, at the insistence of their escort, they spent the night ashore, Belnatan and his officers fuming and impatient, but the men glad enough at the relief from the cramping narrowness of the galleys. Sometimes, in waters known to be clear, they sailed through the moon-washed splendor of the inky sea.

On one such night Asa was awakened suddenly by feeling the ship shudder to a violent blow. He went sliding down to port as the deck canted over, in his ears a shrill inhuman scream, to fetch up against the leeward gunwale in a heap with Mattan and Abbarus.

"Start her sheets!" came the shout of Chelbes, who had the watch, then, "Starboard your helms! Brail up, and look alive amidships!"

Asa picked himself up, to find the ship heeled far over to port, the sail straining overhead in a terrific gust of wind, water coming in over the lee gunwale and the surface of the sea a lace of hissing white. Men were in a tangle of bodies, arms and legs. The sheet lines began to crack explosively as the sail flogged them like whips. Lightning flashed continually.

So this was the end of their venture and of his life—here on this maddened midnight sea, far from friends, unseen of any human eye!

But even as the thought came, the lee rail came up as the helmsmen, throwing their weight on the sweeps, swung her head downwind, and the sail spilled its burden of air. The brails began to bunch it up along its spar.

"Bring the yard on deck," came the voice of Belnatan, with astonishing calmness, and Chelbes called out, "Cast off the halyard! Lower away your yard! Abbarus! Set four men to bailing!"

It occured to Asa for the first time that perhaps they were not about to suffer the ultimate disaster. They had shipped very little water, he soon discovered. A large volume of foam had given a false impression. But the continued shrilling of the wind in the rigging, the pressure of it, the whitecaps half-seen overside, and the increasing motion of the boat were very disquieting.

They set a rag of storm-sail; with this, the boat's heading was more readily kept downwind, and she ran to the northward.

"This squall," explained Belnatan, "is frequent hereabout just at this season. It will blow itself out in an hour or so."

And so it proved. Morning revealed the ships of the fleet widely scattered but not completely out of sight. It also revealed the brown mountains of the coast rising in the southeast. The ships regrouped and closed with them.

These Phoenicians, thought Asa, foreigners and idolators though they are, still have something magnificent about them. Officers and men, they are brave and accomplished seamen, as even a tyro could see; all, that is, but the boy Ithobaal and the taciturn Yakinlu, he of the long visage and the burning eyes. But they too were learning.

"Our great danger, Asa," Mattan explained the next day, "is just such a sudden blow as last night's, but with an onshore wind, when we have a rocky coast close under our lee; for then nothing could save us. Usually a storm can be foretold long enough for us to beach the ships on sand, make a harbor or, at worst, work to seaward for a good offing and lie to a drogue. In an offshore squall, however violent, we can anchor in the relatively smooth water under the lee of the shore and ride it out or run off before it. So if you want to see home again, pray your God to avert any unheralded blow that would smash us on a reef. Fortunately that is not too common."

Mattan had been assiduous in the doctor's instruction. But now for several days he withdrew into himself. He continued to discharge his duties efficiently but turned aside any advances of a comradely nature. He did it without giving the impression of a rebuff, which in the crowded conditions of the ship took some doing; he seemed rather to be in a depression, in which friendly intercourse was, for the time being, unwelcome.

The season of the southwest monsoon was drawing to a close, and more and more light and variable the wind became. Especially did it begin to lie in the north. Sometimes, however, they lay up for a day, in harbor or plunging at anchor in a more open roadstead, waiting for an easterly to blow itself out; sometimes in a calm Belnatan drove his thirsty, sweating crews at the oars, *Brant* being assisted by each in turn. Always the heat; always the monotony of the brown, cheerless coast; always the crowding and discomfort; always the tossing of the sea; always the heat, the heat, the heat. Patience wore thin, tempers short.

5

The last day of summer was just behind them when Belnatan pointed to a high, grey, precipitous cliff ending in open sea to the eastward.

"Cape Comorin!"

All gazed with mixed eagerness and foreboding. This was the northeast point of Africa. Once they had rounded it, they would sail right off the charts that showed all that was known of the world. Beyond it was emptiness—darkness—the terror of the unknown, and, if Belnatan was to be believed, the Chaldean fleet.

There was a haven of sorts only a parasang or so this side of the Cape, and into this they put. While the Egyptian galley rested its men, the Phoenicians unloaded their ships and drew them up on the beach.

The hulls were again scraped clean of a month's fouling and carefully inspected for damage. A party walked for some distance along a little-used trail to wells, where the water supply was partly replenished. They located a few date palms; these added their fruit to the ships' larders. All this accomplished, Belnatan assembled his officers again.

"*Morning Star, Seawife,* and *Stag* will be prepared to meet any hostilities that may be offered. We will strip them of all superfluous gear and they will carry eight days' rations each. The material removed will be loaded in *Brant. Brant* and *North Wind* will each retain her captain and four seamen, as well as *North Wind's* boatswain and the supply officer in *Brant.* These will be sufficient to handle them under sail for a day or two. That will release the two mates, the two quartermasters and fifty-five men.

"Captain Ethbaal in *Seawife* and I will each have our crew reinforced to fifty rowers and nine, counting ourselves, as marines and helmsmen. *Seawife* and *Morning Star,* therefore, will be fully complemented as fighting ships with two men at each ten-ell oar, and *Stag* will be able to assist us in case of boarding."

"And suppose there is a calm or an adverse wind?" asked Ieoud.

"In that case, Captain, *North Wind* will be taken in tow by *Seawife,* and *Stag* and *Morning Star* will tow the storeship together."

Ieoud frowned.

"Your three ships, Captain, might, with luck, handle one of the biremes, conceivably two; hardly the whole Chaldean fleet."

"I do not expect to fight their whole fleet at once, Captain Ieoud, and a certain amount of luck is what seamen must count on. In any event, we can do no better."

"For the last time, sir, I formally protest against engaging at such impossible odds."

"Protest noted. We shall sail at dusk and hope to slip past the Chaldeans in the dark. They could ovetake us, but I hardly think they will venture far down the coast. If we are forced to engage, this will be the plan of battle." He prescribed the actions of each ship in detail. "Do you understand your orders, gentlemen?"

Late on the second day thereafter, the ships loaded, the crews rested and embarked, the fleet stood to sea. "Good luck, Captain!" called the Egyptian in farewell. *Brant* and *North Wind* were towed to an offing, and sails were spread to a light breeze from the north. Dark had fallen when they passed the high cape. No enemy was to be seen.

"If they are really here, Captain," said Asa hopefully, "you have given them the slip."

Belnatan smiled grimly and pointed to the Cape. A beacon fire had just blazed forth.

For an hour they stood due east, then east-southeast; at midnight altered course very gradually toward the south, hoping to work up an offing that would put them out of sight of Chaldean lookouts by dawn. The north wind was moderate but steady. On *Morning Star,* Asa was wakeful, as were Chelbes and many of the crew; but Belnatan and Mattan, off watch, slept soundly.

Dawn revealed an empty sea, the mountaintops visible far to the west.

"No sign of them," said Mattan. "Perhaps we've seen the last of them."

"Sail ho!" came from the masthead.

"Where away and how heading?"

"Off the starboard quarter, distant about three parasangs and closing."

A moment later the lookout reported a second sail to port, and from it a signal smoke rose into the air.

"Armorer," ordered Belnatan, "issue weapons and armor."

Grimly Asa accepted helmet, breastplate, shield and sword.

Slowly, inevitably, the gap closed. The Phoenician war-galleys might have made a run for it, but the laboring storeship slowed them hopelessly. The two Chaldeans could have overhauled their quarry in a few hours, but they hung back to be reinforced. Toward the end of the forenoon the other two had joined, and they swept down upon the fleeing Phoenicians.

They made a splendid picture as they drew near in battle array. Their brilliant red and purple upon the azure sea, the lively hues of the rows of shields at the bulwarks, the creaming of their bow-waves and the glitter of helmet and spear were beautiful even to those who beheld doom approaching in this guise. Asa commended his soul to God in the ancient acknowledgment of the Hebrew face to face with death:

"Hear, Oh Israel! The Lord our God, the Lord is One!"

Benanu, the Chaldean admiral, saw his prey within his grasp. His four galleys had assembled in column a thousand feet astern of the fleeing ships. He commanded a force of some two hundred seventy-five men; his opponents, he knew, had only three-fifths as many, and they in ships which individually were smaller and lighter than his own. Of them, the storeship was completely ineffective as a man o' war. A single one of his bigger, faster ships should theoretically be able to wipe out the enemy fleet one by one.

He turned to his flag lieutenant.

"Signal to attack in line astern."

A shield rose to the masthead.

The sails were brailed up. Down came the yards; the masts were unstepped and housed along the deck. The oars, two banks of them on each side, smote the water rhythmically.

"Step up the beat!"

The rowers pulled faster on their oars; the flutist ceased his tune and the time was set by a drum that thudded its death-beats against the eardrums of the foe. The squadron leaped toward the Phoenicians.

Three of the Phoenician ships likewise changed to oars, and, also in column astern, reversed their course and approached him. So they were really going to make a fight of it! They had courage—some of them, at least, because one of the war galleys and, of course, the storeship held their course.

The two fleets approached one another, beautiful in scarlet and purple.

Hello—there seemed to be trouble on the leading Phoenician galley! The Chaldean admiral looked scornfully on as a knot of rowers sprang from their benches and rushed the poop deck. Mutiny! Well, if the cowards thought to earn his mercy in such fashion, they would soon see their error.

The struggle seemed to be over. The Phoenician officers had been overwhelmed. Now the mutineers took over the helms and resumed rowing—but in flight! They passed the other two galleys. Dismayed, these too turned tail. It would do them no good. His faster biremes would soon overtake and crush them.

Meanwhile, the storeship seemed to have lost heart even for flight; she brailed up her sail and, out of command, lay in the trough of the seas to surrender. But he wanted no prisoners whose tale might embroil his king with Egypt.

The three fleeing galleys were now rowing frantically away, still in column astern. The leading one—the ship of the mutineers—headed directly for the storeship, as though to invite Benanu to plunder it and let her go. She swerved, passed under the stern, and momentarily was lost to view behind the larger hull of *Brant*.

He was close, now, to the last of the fugitives, passing under the stern of the storeship in its turn. He was very close—

Around the bow of the storeship swung the prow of a galley, on a collision course for his ship! "Starboard! Hard a-starboard!" he screamed to his helmsmen.

It was too late. With a crash *Morning Star's* beak tore into his galley's side at the waterline, the shock throwing standing men off their feet and tumbling the rowers along their benches. As the Phoenician backed off, Benanu realized with horror that his ship was sinking under him.

The second Chaldean galley drove in for vengeance before the victor could recover her way; but past the first Phoenician sped *Seawife* and met her foe with a shock, bow to bow; grappling lines were thrown; while they hung entangled, *Morning Star* backed off and hurled her fatal beak into this second enemy's side.

Now the third Chaldean and *Stag* came together, each trying to run along the other's side and break her oars, so that, crippled, she would be helpless against the ram. They failed, but the Chaldean grappled her foe and a hand-to-hand struggle began; Ethbaal laid *Seawife* along the other side of the same adversary, while *Morning Star* engaged the fourth enemy in similar fashion. Chaldean boarders poured into her, and iron rang on bronze in a hot melee. Before the issue was decided, the Chaldean captain saw that his only remaining ally was succumbing to the double assault upon her. He called back his boarders, disengaged with some difficulty and fled to the northward. Those of his countrymen still on their feet in the remaining Chaldean ship laid down their arms.

Incredulous at the speed and completeness of their victory, Belnatan's men looked upon one another in amazed relief. Asa disarmed to attend to the wounded; the three Phoenician ships and the captured Chaldean were lashed together while the captains took stock of their casualties and damage.

The first attention was to the hulls; luckily none of them was leaking.

Casualty rates in boarding actions have always been high. *Stag,* who with inferior numbers had borne the first brunt of this phase of the attack, had suffered most severely. In all, thirteen men lay dead in Belnatan's ships, one had been forced overside and drowned, and for another dozen, in the doctor's opinion, death from chest or belly wounds or from massive blood loss was only some days or hours away. In over half that number life clung with desperate but uncertain hold to the lacerated flesh; and there were fifteen with wounds which gave him no cause for serious concern.

The officers had paid, as well as their followers. Ahiram, mate of *Brant,* was dead; Thabion, her boatswain, and Belazar, quartermaster of *Seawife,* were obviously soon to join him. Mattan had received a sword-thrust through his left arm, and Ethbaal lay unconscious with a head wound that proved, in the event, to be of little consequence.

Of the enemy, twenty-eight men, quite or relatively unharmed, had surrendered on the captured galley. Thirteen corpses were pitched into the sea; the Phoenicians drew from the water nineteen men who had been lucky enough to divest themselves of their heavy armor or to find some sufficiently buoyant flotsam. Twenty-three, wounded in various degree, lay under the ministrations of their fellows.

When the patients had been classified according to their status, Abbarus approached the doctor with a few of his men. Indicating eight of the most seriously and painfully wounded, he inquired, "Can anything be done for them?"

The priest shook his head.

Abbarus turned and nodded to his followers. They drew their knives and neatly and efficiently cut their shipmates' throats.

Asa sprang up in horror. "Murderer! What villainy is this?"

The boatswain faced him in indignant surprise. "What is this about villainy? I have done them a favor. They were suffering uselessly—you said so yourself. I did as I would be done by if I were in like case."

The priest had no reply.

A wound that gave him much concern was a scratch on Abu-Tammuz' left eyeball, inflicted by a sword thrust deflected at the last moment. He feared inflammation. He dressed the wound carefully with an ointment of mutton-fat and balm. Some gaping lacerations he drew together with adhesive tape or sutures and bound them with linen. There were some severe but not dangerous hemorrhages which he managed to suppress by compression dressings, and in two cases, by the application of tourniquets. The fourth and fifth fingers of a left hand had been almost completely sliced off and were attached only by some skin; he completed the amputation. He dressed and splinted a bleeding, broken arm.

Meanwhile, Belnatan had been making his appointments. The captains had received his authorization to promote men to the new vacancies of their quarterdecks. Then the commodore turned his attention to the captives, whose loblolly boy had been attending to their wounded.

"How many of you are Phoenicians?"

Two and a half dozen hands were raised.

"Move forward. Chaldeans, aft."

They separated. The captain addressed the group at the bow.

"I can use some volunteers."

As he had expected, all hands were raised. They did not know his intentions—those he could not use would probably be knocked on the head and thrown overboard.

"Who are the artificers?"

"Ship's carpenter, sir." "Sailmaker, sir." "The armorer, sir, is having his head dressed, over there."

"I'll take him, and all the rest of you. Abbarus, have all rations and fuel transferred to our ships. And anything else of use."

"Aye, aye, sir. Shall I have the rest of them killed?"

"We'll see."

By the time the work had been accomplished, Asa was staring curiously at one of the new recruits. The man was scratching continually. Asa walked over to him and made a search for vermin, but found none. On command, the man put out his tongue; Asa pulled down his lower eyelid and stared at it.

"Captain," he said, "I recommend against your taking this man."

"Why?" The seaman was tall, bronzed and of magnificent physique.

"He is a sick man. Despite his fine build, he has a profound anemia. He reminds me of a patient whose blood turned paler and paler, and who finally died within two years. I think that if you set this man to rowing, he would quickly tire."

The other recruits, afraid to lie, confirmed the priest's words. Ever since the start of their voyage, it appeared, the man, despite his seeming robustness, had been failing.

"Well done, doctor!" Belnatan complimented him, and waved the invalid off. The rejected man turned bitterly upon his erstwhile companions. "Betrayers! May the gods curse you, and may your captain drown you as he is going to drown me!"

"I have decided not to drown you," said Belnatan. "You may depart, Captain!"

Incredulously, the remainder of the Chaldean survivors released their craft from the others, picked up their oars and began rowing to the northeast.

"That was a great mercy, captain!" exclaimed Asa.

"I am not so sure. With their losses, they will have difficulty rowing to windward; they are far from home, with little water and no food. They may yet wish that we had sliced their throats.

"On the other hand, they have a chance. They can certainly make shore and perhaps find water, possibly even food—I don't know what lies inland. They will probably head for the rendezvous where they waited for us so as to pick up their shore party.

"If they do manage to return to Chaldea, it will do me no harm to have the Babylonian king learn that I have saved him a ship and crew. I may need a favor from him some day."

"And what of the Pharaoh?"

"Necho hired me to explore, not take up his quarrels. I have no interest in the rivalry between Egypt and Babylonia. Whichever of them comes out the victor will need the services of Phoenician seamen. Our recent enemies tried to stop us, which was their job; now that they have been decisively beaten, they are no longer a threat. It would be pointless to massacre them."

Belnatan disclaimed humanitarianism; nonetheless Asa noted the absence of vengefulness to his credit.

Balsachus approached his commander. "Captain, your tactics were brilliant—brilliant! I have never seen or heard of a victory such as this!"

Mattan turned to Asa. "Now you see why Belnatan was selected to lead this expedition. You are serving, doctor, under one of the great sea captains of all time!"

The immediate need of the fleet was for shelter where the hulls could be surveyed, the wounded nursed and the supplies conveniently redistributed and stowed.

"Slightly south of here," Belnatan told his assembled captains, "there is a long peninsula with harborage to the north from southerly winds, and to the south from northerly ones. We shall proceed to it. There is no shelter for another day's sail down the coast."

The moderate north wind continued to blow, and early moonlight showed them their way under a highland to a bay where they could beach their galleys.

They spent a day inspecting the hulls—which had withstood the shock of battle without apparent damage—and unloading the surplus supplies from *Brant*. But now the dying southwest monsoon revived, and for four days it blew. But none complained. For with it came that tender benediction, longed for, prayed for all over the world, to Jehovah, to Baal, to Zeus—rain!

The silver drops came slanting down from the grey skies. They caressed the leather-dried skins, the sun-reddened eyes, the hot mouths; they washed the brine from the baked decks, the sere and cracking spars; they poured merrily from the catch-cloths into the pottery water-breakers; they made patterns of interlocking circlets in the flattened water, darkened the dust, pattered musically upon the leaves. The rain!

Asa fell upon his knees in thanksgiving. They were far from home, far from the Temple at Jerusalem; but God had not forgotten them!

It almost looked, however, as though He had forgotten Abu-Tammuz, whose eye was fast growing worse. There was no vision in it, even had Asa permitted the red, painful, purulent eyeball to be exposed. He kept it covered with rags steeped in warm oil, but he was growing, like his patient, daily more fearful.

Of the remaining four for whom he had entertained no hope, three were already dead. The fourth, however, transfixed through the chest by a javelin, was not only holding his own but showing miraculous signs of improvement. Two of his borderline cases had gone, one in a rapidly mounting fever, one by a sudden hemorrhage in the night; obviously another pair would soon follow them. A few apparently trivial wounds were beginning to fester, and his hot steeps and poultices were so far not controlling them. The rest were definitely on the mend.

Now the first day of Etanim, the seventh month, was upon him; the day of a holy convocation, when thanksgiving for the autumn harvest was observed in Judea, when man rejoiced in his increase and re-dedicated himself to the Giver of all good. And the tenth hence would be a day of atonement, whereon God searched man's conscience, and sinful man repented and cleansed his soul of evil. As Asa prepared for a day of prayer, of mingled solemnity and joy, he thought of those annual observances in his far-off home and the joyous going up to the Temple in Jerusalem with his fair young wife—that loving and lovely girl whose poor bones were mouldering in the earth of a Judean hillside, far away; and the water came to his eyes.

6

Ever since the rounding of Cape Comorin the heat had seemed less oppressive. On the ensuing day of calm, however, it was again unpleasantly noticeable to all hands.

They got under way nevertheless. Asa, watching the sweating men at the oars, wondered at the wisdom of it.

"True, we don't make much speed," Belnatan explained. "But on ten such days we cover forty or fifty parasangs. It may also mean the difference between making a harbor by dark and having to stand off and on all night. Finally, there's the saving in supplies if we make good a distance in fewer days; although this is not great, for rowers must eat more than idlers."

"It's a pity we can't have full crews, to double our speed."

"We wouldn't double it, doctor. In the first place, water and wind resistance increase too fast; to double a ship's speed would take more than double the effort. What we would do with full crews is what we did during the battle—put two men on an oar. But that doesn't even double the usual effort. One rower sits where, if he moves the oar handle a convenient distance, the blade moves through the pattern of its maximal effect. It follows that a man sitting inboard of him would have the oar loom moving through a larger and more inconvenient arc, and would lose some of his force; for a man sitting outboard, the radius of motion would be smaller, and he would be by that much the less effective. We have determined that two rowers on an oar exert only one and two-thirds times as much useful manpower as one rower; three rowers on an oar exert only two and one-sixth times as much as one. The pente-konters with full crews can do two parasangs per hour in a spurt, one and a third for the long pull."

(Two triple-miles per hour was not bad going, thought Asa.)

"With the half crew that we have, they can make a parasang and a third in a spurt, something better than half of that all day. Assisting the *Brant's* rowers by towing in pairs, as now, we are doing perhaps half a parasang per hour."

"Our mariners have explored some one hundred parasangs south from Cape Comorin. On this much of the coast, few outlying dangers have been reported, and we can carry on night and day, and must, to save time and provisions. Beyond there, all is unexplored. That means that every night must find us in harbor, beached, hove to or anchored on the open coast. So we make all speed while we may—the more, since it is reported that there is an adverse current to be stemmed."

Mattan nodded. "Even if we were willing to pass by parts of the further coast unseen," he explained to Asa, "missing who knows what important observations, we'd come to grief on a rock in the darkness."

Abu-Tammuz's eye was a horrible, shapeless ruin. Worse, the other one had become reddened and painful. To deceive him was both point-less and impossible. He and his physician both feared the worst. The man lay dark and silent, eating little, sleeping little, day after terrible day.

The two worst wounded had died, and so, surprisingly, would a sea-man whose apparently trivial shoulder wound had developed rapidly into a deep abscess, with mounting fever. The withdrawn look and twitching muscles foretold an early end.

The rest were definitely on the mend. Thanks to the new recruits, the expedition was short only two hands as a result of the battle. But four

of the wounded were to have a long convalescence indeed; of them one
with a partially paralyzed arm and one with a recurrently draining
wound in the buttock were to be of limited use in the future.

For weeks the southwest monsoon refused to die, alternating with the
growing power of its foe from the northeast. The winds battled, now the
one, now the other blowing victoriously, with spells of calm in between.
Safe harbors were few on that coast. The ships were driven forward,
then anchored to wait out headwinds, again and again, ever progressing
a little; nights of sickening lurches about the anchors were followed by
spells of back-breaking pulling in the calms. They went ashore but
seldom, and only in the small boats; they grew heartily sick of the tiny,
reeling, overcrowded ships.

Gradually, however, the northeast monsoon became established, and
on one of the last windless days, about a month after their rounding of
Cape Comorin, red sand dunes marked a low point between high land
to north and south. They could see the line of a river. The rowers stood
in slowly toward shore until the masthead lookout sent down the call,
"Shoal water!"

Over went the ships' boats, and Mattan in the longboat, driven by four
oarsmen and with a leadsman in the bow, preceded the galleys. The
leadsman coiled his knotted line; he swung the end of it, weighted with
a stone, and it splashed into the water ahead.

"Five fathoms—five!" he sang out, and "Five!" he repeated again
and again. Then, "Four! And a half three! And a half three! Three!"

"High tide," said Belnatan, with a searching glance at the riffraff
line on the beach. "*Brant*, anchor!" The shallower galleys felt their
way in behind the sounding line and anchored in the smooth water
under the lee of a coral reef.

There were a dozen huts by the drying riverbed, but the inhabitants
had fled. The sailors found scraps of food but none in quantity. The
voyagers would have liked to trade for food; but no native put in an
appearance. Belnatan sat on the beach drawing a chart of the coast on
papyrus. The war galleys were drawn ashore for the monthly cleaning
of their bottoms; in shoal water the emptied storeship was being
careened, and first on one side, then on the other, her bottom would be
methodically scraped.

Asa came to watch Belnatan at work. "Mattan carried off a tricky bit of work, didn't he, sir?"

"Mattan has the makings of a first-rate pilot," the commodore replied. "He is as fine a seaman, for his age, as I have seen, and has an excellent understanding of commerce. He could have gone far."

"Could have?"

"Perhaps he still can. His story is an open secret. He was the by-blow of a princess of Byblos who was, by ill lucks, betrothed to an Aramaean. So Mattan was given to a servant to raise in Cyprus. Plenty of funds went along, and, as you have noted, he has been well schooled. But the anomaly of his rearing by a foster mother never sat well with him. Almost in the flush of success he falls into a mood of doubt and paralysis. Not that he can't be relied on to carry out any assignment! That's why he's here. With this expedition to his credit, all the negative factors should cancel out. At least I hope so!"

At morning muster the blinded seaman was gone. Footsteps in the tide-smoothed sand showed where he had followed the sound of the surf to end his hopeless existence.

Asa, of course, had felt a burden of guilt at his failure, even though reasonably certain that in any other hands the result would have been the same. It was some consolation that Belnatan and the rest seemed to take a similar view.

Naturally, Abu-Tammuz' affliction had pointed up his wistful memories of Tamar. She had, of course, been much in his mind; she had come to represent for him not only woman, but, by association, all the comfort, the softness, the safety which were the antithesis of the rigors of the voyage. Not that he had felt them unduly; luxury, ease and safety were seldom the lot of the Judean hillmen, and seafaring was in many ways analogous to the desert travels of his people.

As they voyaged on, the steady east or east-northeast wind was seldom missing. High and rocky stretches of coast alternated with long, low, sandy shorelines, or much less extensive swamps which the interlaced roots of the mangrove made impassable.

Some seven weeks from the Cape, Belnatan announced that they had sailed off the last of his charts. Islets and reefs of coral and rock thereafter became more numerous. The coastal scene was still for the most part desolate and sere, but brooks and rivers were now more frequent.

There were coconut trees, but landing was for the most part difficult and dangerous.

Belnatan seated himself to write his log. On his lap he placed a piece of board on which was a fresh sheet of papyrus. He sharpened the reed pen, dipped it into the pot of ink—a suspension of charred and fine-rubbed vegetable matter in a watery solution of gum arabic—and wrote as follows.

> *"27th Day Bul*
>
> *Weather clear, moderate east wind freshening in afternoon. High and rocky stretches of coast alternating with low, sandy beaches. Lay to sea anchors during night, rowing twice for offing,* Brant *in tow.*
>
> *"28th Day Bul*
>
> *Weather clear, moderate east-northeast wind. High rocky coast for eleven parasangs, then mangrove swamp. Several inshore reefs and islets. Small rivers. Rain during night.*
>
> *This day we sailed off the last of our charts.*

A complaint new to Asa began to appear among the crews. Men reported with vague feelings of muscular weakness and pain; there was bleeding from the gums; mild bruises were marked by excessively large black and blue areas. Minor cuts were often slow to heal, and in one or two of the worst cases, joints became swollen and painful.

To the Phoenicians, however, especially the more experienced among them, this was nothing new. "This is a disease of sailors," Belnatan told him. "We call it scurvy. It appears only on long voyages when there has been little contact with shore. Some say it is caused by foulness of the drinking water; others, that it is due to the damp or to the ship's continual motion. I do not know how it arises, but it disappears after a stay ashore, particularly in a town. No treatment seems to avail."

"I hope, then, that we can soon get ashore. Most of the men, I think, if not actually sick, are considerably less strong and active than before."

"I know, and I hope that the storms hold off. In a lifetime at sea, I have never known such a prolonged spell of good weather. Thanks be to Baal-Melkarth!"

There had been some hot tempers and quarreling in the intenser heat north of Cape Comorin, and several times Belnatan had had to order the cat. But now the sailors seemed to lack energy to be expended uselessly. The officers were not exempt; Asa himself was aware of weakness and muscular pain, and spat a little blood after a slight bruise to the mouth.

"Captain," said Abbarus one day, "my men need a good long rest."

Belnatan nodded. "I am looking for a more hospitable coast. But within a week, in any case, we will make a halt."

"Now let us pray the gods," said Mattan to Asa, "that we find a good spot for rest and recuperation. But I forgot—you pray only to one God."

"My people acknowledge only one Lord of heaven and earth."

"That reminds me of something I heard from a man of India, whom I knew in one of the ports of Chaldea. The Hindus, you know, worship hundreds of gods. I was some time rebuilding an old ship—ship timbers are not found there, so no salvageable bottom is wasted. He used to read and translate from one of their old writings. There was a story of one of their teachers—Yajnavalkya by name—whom a disciple asked, 'How many gods are there?' He answered with some large number.

" 'Yes,' Vidagda Sakayla went on, 'but how many, really?'

" 'Thirty-three!'

" 'Yes, but how many, really?'

" 'Six!'

" 'Yes, but how many, really?'

" 'Two!'

" 'Yes, but how many, really?'

" 'One!' "

As before on a similar occasion, Asa was troubled. So there was still another people who had discovered the one true God! Was it possible that Israel was only one among many to whom the Lord had vouchsafed His countenance? And if so, how was Israel unique? Were the Hebrews not, after all, a chosen people? The idea was disturbing—humbling.

Disquieting though it be, the chain of thought must be pursued. Well, so the men of India, like the men of Egypt, had known God. Yet they were not monotheists. Like the Egyptians, they had hierarchies of gods, each no doubt with his idols, his priesthood and his form of worship. What, then, had come of their discovery of Him? Nothing.

Israel, however, had not forgotten Him, but had built its entire existence about Him. True, Israel had backslid, Israel had sinned, Israel had broken faith, but had never completely rejected the Covenant. The Israelites had retained the vision of the most High. Amid a hundred vilenesses and a thousand wickednesses, they had kept before their eyes the ideal of the Divine Perfection.

So might Egypt have done—but she did not. So might India have done—but she did not. Instead, they abandoned themselves to the debasement of idolatry, unrelieved.

Israel, then, was indeed the Chosen People—chosen not by God, but by themselves. Perhaps He had revealed Himself to many nations—perhaps even to all—but they had been unable to sustain the concept of utter purity. For Egypt, divinities like Bast the cat and Bes, grotesque in her hippopotamus body; for India, the monkey-god Hanuman and cobra-headed Naga. They had glimpsed the Lord but could not bear His glory. Only Israel had clung to the vision of a Holy Spirit, without shape or form; only Israel had covenanted with Him. Israel had chosen Him among all the gods of the peoples and had chosen herself to serve Him. More truly, then, even than by Divine election, was Asa's a Chosen People! "Blessed art thou, Oh Lord our God, King of the Universe, who hast given us the Law of truth!"

7

A gentle rain was falling as Mattan in the longboat sounded their way into the harbor. About a parasang wide, the mouth was divided by an island. There was much coral about, and the ships crept in slowly behind Mattan. It was not only caution that held down their speed; an outrunning tide opposed them, and all four fifties strained at the storeship's towline. It was all the oarsmen, weary and ill, could do to make slow headway.

"We'll anchor," was Belnatan's decision, "and beach tomorrow, if all is well." Mattan made a survey with the leadline, as a result of which one of the ships shifted her berth to avoid a rock that threatened her after the turn of the tide.

The wind blew at times strongly across the tidal stream; the galleys sailed restlessly about on their cables, now wind-rode, now tide-rode, frequently bringing up with a jerk that threatened to tear an anchor from the ground.

"Keep your helms manned !" ordered Belnatan.

"Why man the helm at anchor ?" wondered Asa.

"The tide is running past us. The ships are moored fast. They are, therefore, in effect, moving through the water, though motionless with respect to the ground. Moving, then, through the water, they can be guided by their helms and kept headed steadily upstream—or at an angle to it, if we wish, even though retaining the same absolute positions. We thus eliminate some of the jerking at the cables."

"Brant seems steady enough."

"Brant is much deeper and heavier than the fifties ; the tide has much more effect on her than the wind. The whole art of piloting, Asa, is the application of the theory of relative motion."

The ships' companies went ashore, leaving only the anchor watch to man the vessels. There were coconut and fruit trees. There was a small village at the other end of the bay ; this time the native men stood their ground as Belnatan and a guard approached with scraps of purple linen and the famous glass beads of Phoenicia as gifts. Ethbaal clutched Belnatan's arm excitedly.

"Gold ! Look at those earrings !"

"Keep cool. You'll alarm them."

The people were of middle height, well formed, with yellowish to coppery skins and short hair growing curiously in distinct little spirals. They had flat faces with broad noses, small ears and daintily formed hands and feet. Some of the women had enormously fat buttocks. Their speech was marked by peculiar clicks. Some of the men bore spears or clubs but no bows and arrows. A few long-horned cattle wandered about.

The natives accepted gifts, but offered no return. Gold was less useful than copper or iron in this remote area; nevertheless, the travelers attempted to trade for such yellow metal as they saw, as evidence for the Pharaoh that it occurred in this part of the world. They were partly successful. More important, the natives reluctantly parted with a few of their cattle. Asa killed them, quickly and painlessly, by slicing their throats with a sharp knife ; he inspected the carcasses and found them healthy. The two conditions of humanity and of sanitation satisfied, a Hebrew might lawfully eat their meat.

They spent a week encamped on the beach. There were no large numbers of natives, and those of the village did not act hostile; so the ships were drawn up for cleaning, and hunting parties went out for game. They brought back the flesh and hides of gazelle-like animals, curious black-and-white striped horses, and a large spotted beast whose long neck brought his head to thrice the height of a man. The meats and fruits alike were welcome; and they gathered a store of green coconuts for use at sea.

The officers fretted at the loss of the good wind but knew there was no help for it. After a week's stay they reëmbarked.

"What are you doing?" asked Asa in alarm as they left port. "You're steering straight for that reef!"

"We are, doctor," Chelbes answered imperturbably. ("Port a bit; now meet her. There is a strong cross tide here," from Mattan. The mate had the con.) "Our real progress," Chelbes continued, "is a resultant of the sidewise motion momentarily imparted by the tidal current and the forward motion imparted by the rowers." And indeed, even as he spoke, the bow was no longer pointing for the reef.

"If you line up that whitish rock on the islet on the port bow with the isolated palm tree beyond ("Steady as she goes!" ordered Mattan), you note that their bearing does not change; as long as they remain lined up, we are progressing in a straight line toward them, regardless of our heading."

Mattan spared them a word and a smile. "Relative motion, Asa! Abbarus, step up the beat!"

The galley leaped ahead in answer to the straining oars. And indeed the men were rowing strongly; the scurvy, as prophesied by Belnatan, had rapidly and mysteriously disappeared.

With the week's rest and change, the better health, the fresh food and the improved condition of the larders, spirits had picked up, and there was a more cheerful air about the ship.

The voyage was four months old.

The pole star had sunk beneath the northern horizon. Ieoud, master of the *North Wind,* approached Belnatan one evening.

"Captain, we no longer have the North Star to guide us. If we should be blown to sea, we will have difficulty in setting a course at night. And our provisions are getting low. The men are growing uneasy."

"Do I have to teach you how to handle your men?"

"No, sir. But to some extent I share their feeling. I believe, sir, that the opinion is growing in the fleet that we should turn back."

"Any more of that, Ieoud, and you will be relieved of your command. By the Queen of Heaven! We are bound for the end of Africa, and to the end of Africa we will go! Even if it means to the end of the world! That will be all!"

Southward they pressed. Now they passed river deltas, where complex channels threaded noisome mangrove swamps; now bold bluffs, or green hills; now low, lush plains. There was no cruising at night; not only was Belnatan unwilling to miss charting the coastal features, but the reefs and islets made it impossibly perilous.

There came a time when all the seamen's skill did not suffice to avert danger. The coast, trending to the southwest, was low and noisome; Belnatan, unwilling to seek its shelter for fear of swamp fever, turned to some off-lying sandy islets. In the failing light, with a shower of rain, visibility through the water was poor; and Mattan's sounding line just missed a pinnacle rock. *Morning Star*, following close on the longboat, passed it safely. But *Stag,* next in line, was not quite on course and drove onto the grating coral. The ship lay half afloat with an unnatural list.

"We're making water, Captain!" reported Balsachus, her commander.

Her crew could not back her off. *North Wind* pressed by the store-ship and passed a line, as did *Seawife*. The three crews, bending hard to the oars, pulled her free.

"Tow her ashore, Ieoud!" called Belnatan, at the same time passing his own towline to the bow of the damaged ship. She lay low in the water, some of her people bailing desperately. She was hurried shoreward and beached in the shallows.

It was three days' work to replace the damaged sections with sound planking and refit for sea.

Mattan undertook quite a different task. He, too, had been worried by the desertion of the north star. With Asa's help he leveled a stretch of sand. At its northern edge he erected a post with a pointed top. When the sun was low above the land to the west, he drove a stake at the point of the shadow. He measured the shadow's length. The following morning, when the post cast a shadow of identical length to the westward, he drove at its point a second stake.

"Connecting these two stakes," he explained to Belnatan and Asa, "I have a line running due east and west. If I bisect it with a perpendicular, I will have true north and south." He did so; and the shortest shadow of the day, at noon, lay along his north-south line in confirmation.

'Tonight," he said, "we shall see what we can discover."

All that night he sighted at intervals along the line, marking star charts on pieces of wood; and the next morning reported to Belnatan.

"We no longer need the North Star," he said. "There is a south star, Achernar in the constellation of the River, that I have diagrammed here. All night it bears due south, with little variation. This star could be seen from Babylon in ancient times."

"Excellent!" exclaimed Belnatan. "This means that here, too, we can steer a true night course on the open sea!"

"It means more than that," said Mattan soberly. "It means that the heavens may be conceived of as a sphere, rotating about a north-south axis; and that, since we raise new constellations as we sail south and leave the northernmost behind us, the earth too is a sphere, with the same axis!"

It was still hot, nor was their discomfort relieved by the frequent rain. Week after week saw them driving south, lying up for the occasional storms, when reef or shore became a thunder of snowy surf. At such latter times they foraged for provision with inconstant success. The produce of the hunt, the trees, and the beach at ebb tide made good the food supplies that Asa from time to time found it necessary to condemn. The increasingly strong coastal current, setting now to the southward, made up for the delays. Even in calms or headwinds it carried them along at a good rate, with only sufficient work at the oars to maintain steerageway.

8

The Babylonian ambassador at the court of Egypt looked up from his third perusal of the letter from the commandant at Perim.

"A visitor, sir," announced the lackey. "Buriash of Babylon requests an audience."

"One of Benanu's captains," Engidu recalled. "Send him in." Then, "Welcome back to Sais, captain! I hope you are here to report that you caught your quarry?"

"We caught him, all right!" said the other grimly.

His manner was disquieting; but Engidu went on.

"Your commander has gone to Babylon and sent you to announce to me that I can forget about Belnatan and his expedition? There were no survivors, I hope?"

"You can forget about Belnatan, all right; he is beyond your reach. Benanu has gone a far longer journey than Babylon; and two ships of ours, with almost a crew and a half, survive." And with mounting amazement and shock Engidu learned the details of the catastrophe.

"But this is incredible!" he exclaimed at last. And then, "And why didn't you go directly to Babylon, to report your failure? Three months have passed, and it will be another three before word reaches the king!"

Buriash laughed his mirthless laugh again. "Do you think I'm crazy? As you said, it is incredible. They would never believe me in Babylon; in fact, I don't believe it myself, though I was there, and saw. But try to convince the court? They'll swear I turned against my commodore for Egyptian gold. I can just see myself being flayed alive at the place of public executions! No, I'll never show my face again in the land of the two rivers."

"And do you think the king's arm will not reach the coast of Phoenicia?"

"I know it will. I'm off to try my luck in the West. If the rest of the crews are wise, they'll do the same. No, don't frown, sir; you don't want this noised about, either. How much the commandant at Perim already suspects, I don't know." He grinned again, this time in real amusement. "I thought of selling the ships at Berenice, to stake myself for new ventures; but I knew my good friend of Perim would inform you of my return, and then you'd have to have my throat cut or never again dare face the king yourself. As it is, you'll just forget you saw me. The project failed, and that's the end of it."

"One question more. If this mad venture of Belnatan's should succeed, when is the earliest that you think he might return?"

"We know he took over a year's provisions, and we know he'll have a hard pull up the west coast toward the Gates of Gades, against wind and current. It will take a year and a half, at least, if it can be done at all. But we're finished with it."

That's where you're wrong, my friend, thought the ambassador. We're not finished with it.

9

Belnatan wrote in his log: "Here are gold, ivory, ebony, slaves, and a great variety of game. Fruits, coconuts, and an abundance of good water are available."

The coast became increasingly foul, with great care in piloting required. Coral reefs, rocks, shoals, and islets grew in numbers; the first became very troublesome, especially when a shower reduced the transparency of the water for the masthead lookout. The rain was still a frequent visitor.

They came to a stretch where the gaps in the shoreline were wide and closely spaced. Belnatan signaled for his captains to join him, Ethbaal guessed the reason for the summons.

"Judging by the discoloration of the water, Captain, we are off the delta of a major river."

"That is my opinion also. We should have a look at this river to appraise its commercial possibilities—and, if they are promising, to consider it for eventual establishment of a trading base. Balsachus, you will be reinforced with a contingent from each of the other ships so as to bring your complement up to a full crew of fifty rowers and ten marines. You will then take *Stag* upriver for four days and return. I shall expect you to report on terrain, ivory or precious metals, useful plants, useful and noxious animals, number and character of inhabitants, and sites suitable for settlement. You will attempt to trade, if you see anything worth trading for, including provisions. You will bear in mind that we are instructed to avoid hostilities with the natives, if possible."

"It is my duty to warn you, Captain," said Asa, "that in my opinion this trip will be accompanied by a considerable health hazard. The land appears to be low and wet. I am afraid that some of the men will come down with swamp fever."

"That is a risk that must be accepted. I do not think that it is too great. Many of my men, in one country or another, have already been exposed to swamp fever, have had it, and can be presumed—or at least hoped—to be relatively resistant. The rest will have to take their chances. But your caution is very proper, and I am glad that you are giving much thought to the health of the expedition."

Shortly after dawn on the following morning. Abd-Melkarth, mate of *Stag,* pushed his longboat into the breakers on the river bar. It was difficult and dangerous work. Only consummate seamanship could make the boat live in that churning sea; the oarsmen pulled for their lives and cursed the ill luck that had made their officers' eyes fall on them. A welter of maddened water seized the stern and raised it till the craft stood almost vertical, as it seemed, on her bow; passing quickly under, the wave let the boat fall with a spine-crushing thud into a trough, when a second snarling, foam-covered mass poured onto the counter. Even as it lapped over the gunwale, it gripped the stern, shook it savagely and flung it aloft at another impossible angle; it sped forward and past, and a green hollow, evilly laced with white, gaped hungrily at the frantic sailors. Hardly could the straining oarsmen and bailers keep their seats; harder yet was it for the leadsman in the bow. Only miracles of equilibration kept the mate, straining at his steering-sweep, erect in the stern-sheets. There was no respite; the longboat leaped and writhed like a crazed horse, and only the superb seamanship of Abd-Melkarth and the superlative oarsmanship of his rowers kept her from swamping and spewing them out to wash ashore, drowned or with broken backs.

But somehow she lived; and a row of buoys now marked a hazardous but possible channel into the rivermouth. *Stag* lowered her mast. Determinedly, albeit with misgivings, Balsachus put *Stag's* prow to the bar. Leaping like her namesake, she negotiated it successfully and brought to in the relatively quiet water beyond to pick up her boat and its crew. With a final wave of her captain's hand, she disappeared among the mangroves.

The fleet anchored in the open roadstead to await her return.

It was again a welcome period of relaxation for the crews. There were rest and storytelling; clothes were washed and mended; in the fortunately rainless evenings, a few harps and pipes appeared, to whose minor-keyed melodies songs of love and war floated down the wind.

"I have been wondering," Asa remarked in the period of pleasant satiety after supper that evening, "what it is that drives men from their homes to this endless, perilous, exhausting struggle with the sea." He lifted up his wine-cup thoughtfully. "The obvious answers I can supply myself. But they are not enough."

"I can tell you very simply," answered Chelbes. "In one word, money. There is more profit in a single successful trading voyage than in ten years—twenty, perhaps—of farming."

"Money, yes," was Belnatan's conrtibution. "But not money alone, or even chiefly. No fortune can repay a man for the years of violent toil and ever-present danger of the sea, especially on a voyage such as this. Most will deny it scornfully, but in the last analysis, we sail for the life and glory—and riches—of our cities, Tyre, Arvad, Sidon and the rest. There is endless war between the powers. Now the star of Egypt, now that of Babylonia, now that of the Hittites prevails, and in the intervals Phoenicia is independent. It makes little difference. They all need ships, and to us they are all one. So long as we Phoenicians control the sea, we will be needed by any who would control the land, and so long will our cities, ourselves and our posterity prosper."

"What you say is true, Captain—" Mattan was speaking—"and yet that is not the last word, either. There are other ways of serving the state than by living in the eternal expectation of drinking salt water and eating sand. And, Chelbes, you know surer ways of wealth than staking your all on the chance of storm or pirates, only to lose everything at the last, as the Cretan sailors did. I think that the Greeks, among whom I lived while studying at Cos, were nearer to the truth. There is in them something forever young, forever joyous. They went down to the sea like a lover to his beloved. To them it was the great game, the high adventure, that beckoned. But that, too, falls short of the ultimate truth. Phoenician, Greek or Cretan, why does a man throw himself into strange seas and strange perils? There must be one universal underlying reason, and I have come to the conclusion that it is this. He wants to see; he wants to learn."

"To see what? To learn what?" Asa asked.

"Himself. And here, I believe, Asa, you have your answer. No man is satisfied until he has tested himself to the ultimate—until he has measured his strength and courage against the Unknown Danger, and he lonely and afar. It is our self-doubt that drives us to the encounter, and it is a doubt that will not down. We test our mettle on the seas.

The Aramaeans do it on their wide-wandering caravans, defying the desert and the marauder. You Hebrews have danger enough at home; so in the name of your Jehovah you dare the gods of all the world—and even Him."

The third evening after her departure, *Stag* was back. Balsachus came abroard the *Star* and saluted.

"Report," ordered Belnatan.

"We proceeded upriver as ordered. The mangroves gave way to jungle. The land was low and wet. We saw numerous crocodiles in the river. Ashore, there was much animal life. There were numerous hoof-prints of various beasts. I saw a gazelle and a pair of small, black and yellow striped horses. I saw also some huge prints that must have been made by an elephant."

"Go on."

"There were many sandbars, and we ran aground continually. Late the first day, while we were shoving off from one of these banks, there came a shower of heavy stones and a few spears from behind the foliage. One man was killed, one knocked unconscious; several were injured, one with a spear through the arm. The attack was repeated on the day following, and two casualties—not too serious—resulted. The enemy evidently traveled overland faster than we could work upstream—the course of the river is tortuous, and there are innumerable sandbars. We loosed a few arrows at random, but could see little."

"And?"

"The mosquitoes were even worse. I have never seen them in such numbers and ferocity. They gave us no sleep. There has been no rain; I worried about the possibility of the river falling and preventing our return, shoal as it is. On account of that and our jungle assailants, I decided by the end of the second day that it would be imprudent to go on. We saw a number of trees with these clusters of long fruit,—some green, some yellow. The yellow ones are tasty and filling. There were no villages. Here is my chart of the river."

"Very well, captain. You may rejoin your ship. Let me have a written description of the river as far as you explored it. Doctor, please see to the wounded."

Belnatan made no reproaches. Stag's captain had had reason enough to turn back; the grand project, the curcumnavigation, was far more important than side explorations, and no ship should be risked in incidental investigations. It was disappointing, all the same.

Later, Mattan spoke to Asa. "That is Balsachus all over. He always turns in a good, in fact a very creditable, performance—but not a winning one."

"Do you mean that he is not competent? Or cowardly?"

"He is very competent, and he is not lacking in courage. No one can criticize him for turning back when he did. But Belnatan would somehow have found the means of carrying out the assignment. I remember hearing, two years ago, of Balsachus convoying a fleet of merchantmen from Sicily. He fell in with a squadron of Corinthian pirates and lost most of his convoy. No blame attached to him—the Greek force was superior, though not overwhelmingly so. But a top-notch commander would have saved the ships. Balsachus has everything but that final spark that makes a champion."

A rope's end, trailing from its pin onto the deck, had turned under the foot of the carpenter's striker; and the man presented himself with a long, profusely bleeding gash where the drawknife had opened his forearm. Asa washed the wound, then drew the edges together with sutures. No fresh meat was available for a dressing; so he packed it with lint saturated with a mixture of grease and honey. He then watched while Benadon applied a neat linen bandage.

"There you are," said the loblolly boy, straightening up, "that'll hold you. It'll heal up nicely until it's laid open again on your next slave raid."

The man grinned his thanks and went forward.

"Have you ever taken part in a slave raid?" Asa asked his subordinate.

"Have I? Many a one, sir, in Africa and in Iberia."

"How do you go about it?"

"Well, sir, that depends. Most of the slaves you get by purchase of war captives. But sometimes you land a large party at night where you've marked a village, surround it in overwhelming force and make your drive. Mostly you get a good yield that way, but sometimes they show fight, and then some of them have to be despatched. Sometimes practically all the young men have to be killed, and you can take only the young women and children. Sometimes, when a shipment of women and girls has been ordered, you make a feast for the natives. Give the men plenty of wine. Then the ones still on their feet can usually be gotten rid of on some pretext or other. Then you grab the girls, hustle them aboard, and it's up and away before any resistance can be organized. I like it better that way, myself—it's more humane, like, and no needless bloodshed. Slaving's a well-paying business, though sometimes risky. There's always a good market."

Asa turned sadly away. The worst of it, perhaps, was the insensitivity of Benadon to the evil. Yet Benadon, essentially, was not—for his environment, certainly—an evil man. He was conscientious in his duty, tender in his care of the sick and injured.

Why did God permit it? Of what atrocious sin would one have to be guilty, to merit the catastrophe of the auction block? Man, he was taught, had free choice of evil or good. If he chose evil, he must be wicked and merit a penalty. But why did he choose it? So far as the priest could see, there were only two possibilities. He was born wicked or he was made wicked by the things that happened to him.

There was, indeed, Divine authority for the former proposition. Had not the Lord Himself said, "The desire of man's heart is evil from his youth?" And if so foredoomed, how was man to choose the good? Or if not evil, but distorted by the lash of circumstance, how again was man answerable for the externality that had made him what he was?

Yet had God said of sin, "Thou mayest rule over it."

Punishment for sin, in any case, could not be the only reason for suffering. The accident of war, the chance of plague, the wholesale clutch of famine fell alike upon saint and sinner as well as upon those still too young to be either.

Of course he had heard other explanations. A life of happiness unalloyed would make a man morally flabby. A good and loving father was never a too indulgent one. He would punish when necessary. More, even in the absence of guilt, a growing lad would be held to the trail of a strayed goat even when fatigued muscles ached their protest and the boy shivered under the searching wind of a winter evening. Only so could his sturdy mountain race maintain itself in the face of hostile man and nature. The restless youngster would be kept at study though his eyelids drooped, or though his cramped limbs longed for the release of field and hill. Only so could they produce a breed of men and women fitted to grapple clear-eyed with problems of right and wrong, wisdom and folly, in a world where other peoples followed the easy path of slavish obedience to hedonistic kings and idolatrous priesthoods—a path that had led nation after nation to oblivion. And was not mankind the creation of their Father, to be led by Him in similar fashion through the toughening regimen of deprivation and pain?

So much had Asa been taught, and so much had he accepted. But he could not stop there; and though his soul shuddered at the awful vistas of agnosticism and doubt that opened to his appalled gaze, he must go on. The Lord had created him with a questioning mind; and to resign his doubts without probing them would, he felt, be the greater sin against the grand Designer.

The earthly father, it is true, tried his beloved children with pain for the greater good of soul and body. But he did so unhappily, with regret, in obedience to the laws of a world which he had not made and could not change. Only God was omnipotent. God could have created a universe in which strength and courage were attained not through pang and heartache but through ineffable joy. Nothing was impossible to Him. He could even have ordained that two and two make five. And that the desire of man's heart be to the good from his birth.

Only with much mental anguish did the priest force his reluctant mind along this line of reasoning. But if he found himself cast in the role of loyal opposition, he could not, upon his soul, resign it. Jonah had tried to turn aside from his appointed road, only to be hurled into a raging sea and the ghastly jaws of the fish. God knew that it was as no supercilious scoffer that Asa grappled with Him, and still less as one taking pride in his puny strength. He labored, as it seemed to him, by Divine command; gladly would he have put off the crushing burden of the train of thought, but he dared not at peril of his soul's peace.

Nor at the peril—of which he was clearly and horribly aware—of wandering as an atheist, forever lost in a darkened universe in which his loving Father was a forgotten myth and his people's noble vision of justice was become a bitter mockery.

10

Day broke over the fleet at anchor in a snug harbor. Rose-hued flamingoes flew off on their foraging; pelicans began to fish. The off-shore wind murmured gently and sent tiny wavelets to caress the line of rock that was their protection. The harbor mouth opened to the north. It was Mattan's and Asa's watch.

"Not much wind," the priest remarked.

"Enough," Belnatan answered. "On the beach, doctor, an onshore-wind always seems stronger than it really is; an offshore wind, on the other hand, has a deceptive seeming of lightness.

"Take her out, doctor!"

Proud but nervous, Asa took the con for his first pilotage. The easier way would be to get under way by oar, then set sail in the clear; but Asa decided to demonstrate his new-learned technique by standing out under sail.

"Tamasus, take your leadline, and keep it going. Stand by sheets and braces! Helmsmen!"

"Ready, sir!" from the two quartermaster's mates of the watch.

"Anchor detail, heave her short!"

"Cable straight up and down, sir!" a few minutes later.

"Cast off your brails! Haul down on your sheets!"

In a moment the sail was set.

"Break out the anchor! Helms hard a-port!"

Partly to the leverage of the steering sweeps, their blades whipping strongly through dead water, but more to the pressure of the beam wind in the sail, slightly forward in the waist, her bow paid off to the northward and she gathered way. A musical gurgle sounded at the forefoot.

"Trim sail! I want that starboard yardarm one ell farther aft!"

Tamasus hove the lead and sang out. "And a half three! . . . . . And a half three! . . . . . Three fathoms!"

"Port a point," Asa ordered the helmsmen.

"Port a point, sir!"

"Meet her!"

"Meet her, sir!"

"Four! . . . . . And a half four! . . . . . And a half four!"

"Half-point to starboard!"

"Half a point to starboard, sir!"

"Five . . . . five . . . . less a quarter six!"

"Steady as she goes!"

"Steady as she goes, sir!"

"Seven . . . . . Less a quarter nine!"

They had cleared the harbor and were standing to the north, the reverse of their desired course.

"No bottom at ten!"

"Secure the lead, Tamasus."

"Stand by to wear ship!" The men at the sheets and braces watched him attentively.

"Hard a-port! Starboard sheet and brace, slack off! Port sheet and brace, haul home, slowly, slowly!"

The ship turned downwind. The sail, originally at an angle of some forty-five degrees to the ship from forward on the port side to the starboard side aft, swung gradually till it arched right across the deck. The wind was now dead astern. The shore was receding. Further the ship turned, through east to southeast. The breeze felt stronger.

"Handsomely, now! Sheet her home to port! Starboard sheet and brace, ease off!"

She began to heel to the wind. The sail now stood again at forty-five degrees to the midline of the hull, but in the opposite direction.

"Belay all lines! Steady as she goes!"

Morning Star, followed by the rest of the fleet, stood into the south.

"Well done, doctor! We'll make a seaman of you yet!" Asa's bosom swelled at the captain's praise, and Mattan and Chelbes grinned approvingly.

It was good, he felt, for a man to win to mastery in a field far removed from his own. (Not, of course, that he could claim to having mastered the seaman's art, as yet. But he was on the way.) It enormously enhanced his prestige in his own eyes that he had two such diverse accomplishments as the arts of healing and of sail. Life was the richer—just as it was the richer for his having gained facility in the Egyptian tongue, even had it had no practical value. Which was not true—he had learned from the physicians of the Nile.

Nevertheless, he reflected ruefully, he had come a cropper on his caution regarding swamp fever. The incubation period of the disease had passed and there was no sign of it in Balsachus' crew. Yet the river banks had been swampy, by their report. Surely the miasm generated by the damp and the rotting vegetation had been there, as well as the warm and humid atmosphere required for its activation. Was there some factor, essential to the generation of the disease, which was lacking in the soil of eastern Africa? Or were the mariners all immune by virtue of early infection or for some other reason? It certainly warranted investigation if white men ever returned to those shores.

The coast continued to trend southwesterly, and hope rose that they were approaching the southern tip of Africa.

At dinner one evening, Belnatan spoke of something that had been remarked before.

"The sun keeps pacing us, or, rather, we the sun. By the calendar, it is the beginning of the winter; yet at noon the sunbeams come from directly overhead."

"Since it must now return to the northward," observed Mattan, "we will be sailing out of its territory. I wonder how far?"

How far indeed? As they set their backs to the receding sun, would they sail out of its living light into those dreadful regions of gloom and darkness that were said to lie at the ends of the earth?

The monsoon was becoming less reliable. Easterlies prevailed. They raised a high surf on this exposed coast; shelter was scarce and landing hazardous. They spent nights drifting on the open sea. To the monotony of the ship's routine and of the diet was added the hardship of continuous close confinement in the crowded ships, and the sea-weary crews yearned for a prolonged spell ashore.

For some time Supply Officer Tabnit had been finding occasional sacks of grain too moldy for use. Such reports were reaching a disturbing number.

To this discouragement, however, the recognition of a southerly current of better than eight parasangs in a day furnished a welcome compensation.

Still Belnatan pressed south.

11

In what back home would be the middle of the first month of winter, they opened a wide, fairly deep bay. At its southern side a promontory offered good shelter. Under its lee, where a rivulet debouched into the salt water, the travel-worn crews moored their galleys.

The countryside was mostly rolling grassland, with occasional trees, single acacias or tiny stands of palm, wild banana and milkwood. The land rose gradually into the northwest, and low wooded hills looked blue in the distance.

In the morning, Belnatan sent exploring parties, well-armed, along the coast and inland. On the following afternoon they returned, one after another, and made their reports. In the evening Belnatan called a council of officers.

"As you are aware, our provisions are one-half consumed. We cannot possibly complete our journey unless we restock. For that matter, we could not even return without restocking—if at all. But we are not going to return. The trend of the coast is more and more westerly, and it may be that we are approaching the southernmost extremity of Africa. Our exploring parties report an abundance of game. The soil looks rich, and the green of the landscape implies plenty of rain. I have provided seed wheat and barley. We are going to break ground, sow a crop, and remain until we have harvested it. Then we push on southwest!"

The fleet supply officer interposed with a question. "What you say, Captain, is of course correct. But with what we have, plus what we can surely obtain from the country, we could push on for another few months before stopping."

"We could, Tabnit. But, in the first place, we do not know what sort of coast lies ahead. It may be desert, or, for some other reason, unsuitable to agriculture. In the second place, the sun has reached its farthest south and has turned northward again. It is winter now at home; but here the rain and the cooling climate suggest autumn. It is late for a sowing of spring wheat and barley but perhaps not too late. Most important of all, we have the rain now. We have no assurance that there may not be a dry season some months hence."

"Winter wheat would give us a larger yield, Captain," Asa put in.

"So it would, doctor, and I should like to have that larger yield. But the points I have made incline me against it. Besides, winter wheat would mean a halt of seven to nine months, instead of five. I am unwilling to lose that much time. And it would mean too long a period of inactivity for the crews. We could not possibly find work enough to keep them busy all winter and spring. A short rest will do them good; but men who are idle too long inevitably get into mischief, and discipline suffers."

"Now I understand," said Mattan, admiringly, to Asa, "why we are carrying ploughs, hoes and mattocks. I thought they were trade goods and thought them poorly chosen. The captain knows what he is doing! But think of conceiving a plan like that for a voyage of exploration! Have you ever heard the like?"

Belnatan's first assignment was to put his little settlement into a posture of defense. Details were set to work constructing a stockade around part of the beach through which ran the little stream.

"We are strictly charged by the Pharaoh," Belnatan told his crews, "to maintain peace with all princes and peoples whom we may meet, in order to lay a firm basis for future relations. In this place of sojourn, our own safety demands that we avoid all hostilities if possible. I shall punish any infraction of this rule promptly and severely. One man's stupidity can put all our lives in jeopardy. You will therefore refrain from any hostile or overbearing act toward the natives. Respect their property; take nothing except what is freely offered or freely sold. Above all, there is to be no woman-stealing. As the older sailors among you know, more blood has flowed over this than through any other single cause. So, unless you make some mutually satisfactory arrangement with husbands or fathers, let the females strictly alone."

Armed parties visited the several villages within the radius of a day's travel to establish friendly relations with the natives. These were short, with olive-colored skins, broad noses and tight spirals of hair. They had cattle and sheep but lived also by the chase and by such fruits as nature offered. Their brush huts were simple, their weapons crude—they too had not the bow and arrow, depending on the spear, the knife and, as would later be learned, the snare.

The reception of the emissaries was cool. One party would encounter indifference and even sullenness. Others found the collections of huts empty, their inhabitants fled.

The stockade and its enclosed cabins completed, the ships were unloaded and dragged ashore within the fort. All hands now turned to clearing ground for planting. Gangs of men were then harnessed to the plows, and the soil of South Africa was furrowed for the first time.

It would have been mid-winter at home in the lands on the Middle Sea; here the climate was somewhat different. The temperature was moderate, warm enough for comfort but not so hot as to make labor a burden; and as at home in this season, the rains spread their benediction upon the sprouting fields. The young green spears of grain appeared—shy, tentative, some hunched cautiously against a strange new world; then, emboldened, they stood erect and began climbing toward the sun.

Belnatan continued his efforts to woo the savages. He was aware of the fact that the numbers of the natives were rapidly and obviously increasing. This was merely the annual rendezvous of the families of the hunters, customary at this time of year; but Belnatan, of course, had no way of knowing this. He had no fear of his fort being overwhelmed by almost any number of the little armorless men with their primitive weapons; but they could certainly harass the workers in the fields, and they could make it impossible to hunt or to forage on the beach. Food was growing short; more spoilage had appeared among their provisions, and a supplemental supply might be needed before the harvest.

Gradually, however, a few of the native men were persuaded to approach the strangers. A couple of them were interested spectators one morning when Asa held sick call. They watched as he dressed a lacerated hand, incised a boil, and administered a purgative of aloes to a man whose facial expression and pointing finger clearly indicated, without need of language, that he was suffering a pain in the abdomen.

Before long an occasional patient from one of the villages wandered in; Asa treated each one as well as he could under the handicap of lack of verbal communication, with Belnatan's enthusiastic approval. Then a few metal knives and pots found their way into receptive brown-skinned hands, and as a result a few fruits and small game were brought to the ships.

The fishermen were taking fewer fish than the cranes that stalked the shallows. Hunting parties went out, with indifferent success. The Phoenicians appreciated the superior abilities of the Africans as woodsmen and trackers; and to the latter, the effectiveness of arrows and iron-tipped spears was a revelation. But no mixed groups took up the hunt.

The accession of distant families, or possibly of some of the voyagers, turned out to be a sadly mixed blessing for the natives. One day, about a month after the ships' arrival, a native beckoned Asa to follow him. Approaching the village, Asa became aware of a sound of wailing and then of a stench. It took him only a minute to recognize that an epidemic had struck.

Sick men, women, and children lay about, in and out of the huts— feverish, hollow-cheeked, their skins dry. The patients moaned as he palpated their bellies. Several, as he watched, rose and walked weakly to the edge of the cluster of huts, where they evacuated their bowels with signs of pain. The stools were loose and watery; there were traces of blood. A cloud of flies was about the area, swarming over the stinking mass, flying back and forth between it and the huts, and settling on the food, the patients, and the babies' faces. Mourners wailed about two or three dead bodies, not yet removed.

This was something he knew how to deal with. As all civilized peoples were aware, a plague was a visitation from on High, a sign that the wrath of Heaven had been incurred on account of the sins of the people. And these benighted heathen, he felt, had plenty to account for.

The obvious thing to do was to lead them into the paths of righteousness as revealed by the law of Moses and of Israel. He could not, now, go into the subtleties of theology, but there were things that he could do, and certain Divine mandates had to be carried out immediately. After much sign-language, he persuaded them to follow his directions.

The people were moved out of the village and the huts were consigned to the fire. The healthy natives established habitations for themselves a good parasang away and built at an equal distance from this spot a quarantine camp for the sick and for all subsequent victims. They dug latrine pits with earth to be deposited, immediately after their use, upon the contents. Asa demonstrated hand washing and indicated that it was routinely to precede eating and to follow defecation.

All of these routine practices of the Hebrew religion, thanks to the sketchy nature of the dwellings, he brought about both more easily and more quickly than might be imagined. Results were better than he had hoped. The new case rate dropped sharply within a week, this drop quickly reflected by a lower morbidity rate. Within a fortnight the backbone of the epidemic was broken.

Treatment of the sick was much less effective, but this failure mattered less than the larger success. Relations between the two groups improved. Tabnit, the supply officer, rubbed his hands in delight as he contemplated the increase in the food supply.

Inevitably, despite Belnatan's warning, brown-skinned girls appeared in the camp, and many a one built a shack for herself and a Phoenician lover. As long as their people showed no resentment, Belnatan did not interfere; indeed, he made his own arrangements. At times Asa was almost alone in the officer's quarters.

This privation, never easy to endure, had been pointed up by the intensely masculine environment and the uncertainty and danger that had made up his life these many months. In the womanless world of the ships, Asa, like many of the rest, had often striven for sleep in vain, under the spur of desires and imaginings that would give him no peace; it was the more agonizing now that he had merely to choose.

So Asa wrestled unceasingly with his flesh. Asceticism was not then, or ever, a Hebrew ideal; man and wife, cleaving together, were pleasing to the most High. He however could not take a woman for a temporary mating and thereafter cast her off.

The fact that the woman might be willing—even eager—was to him irrelevant. He called to mind a famine in Judea, when men and women had been slavishly grateful to a rich landowner who had permitted them to do a long day's work for a handful of flour. The priest had condemned the landowner, and wrathfully, nevertheless.

He could, of course, make one of these savage women wealthy for life with the gift of an iron knife. He could, he reflected, buy off the woman. But he could not buy off his duty.

And, the final consideration, what if the woman conceived and bore him a child? How could he turn his back on his own flesh and blood? And though he were to enrich the abandoned infant with a hundred knives, at what price did one reckon the loss of a father's love?

But all of that did not do away with temptation, and Asa continued to look longingly upon the shapely, almost nude bodies of the graceful girls and their piquant, slanting eyes and laughing lips. For all his driving himself to long walks and exhausting practice with the sling, he tossed upon his bed with aching loins; and a lovely ghost, wearing the shape now of his lost wife, now of Nektanebis, now of a lissome African, now of Tamar, was nightly the ardent sharer of his pillow.

What followed, consequent upon Asa's earlier labors in behalf of his God and of his dark-skinned fellow-men, wrought him as much chagrin as it rejoiced his companions. With spring (by their reckoning) had come the Phoenician festival of Ashtoreth, goddess of love and of fertility, and the natives were the guests of the Phoenicians at a feast in her honor. The sailors set up her idol, and to wild singing and dancing they burned a huge tree, according to custom, to the glory of the Queen of Heaven. The guests followed the example of the seamen in prostrating themselves before her, and as the music and the dancing reached their height they dissolved in an orgy in which couple after couple paid tribute to her power. Disillusioned and sickened at the blasphemous spectacle for which he himself was so largely responsible, Asa reflected upon how easily a missionary may sow the good seed but reap thistles, as many and many a missionary has learned, both before and after him.

12

Nektanebis nodded to the serving-maid, and Muth, high priest of Amun, accepted another glass of Samian wine. Nektanebis was definitely if perhaps unconsciously adopting the manner of a hostess in the house of Engidu, he reflected. There must be something between them. The Babylonian approached.

"The longer I remain in Egypt," he remarked, "the more reasons I find to admire the greatness of His Majesty. Last week, as it happened, I viewed this end of the Nile-Red Sea Canal. The boldness and grandeur of the conception! A lesser king would be staggered by the mounting costs, even if he had the enterprise to undertake such a work in the first place. Over a hundred thousand slaves used up already, and no guarantee that the traffic, when the canal is finished, will be worth it! Most of the coast, after all, is unproductive desert. In my own land, I'm afraid that the king would be unable to resist the demands of the clergy; if he had that much money available, at least half of it would be earmarked for temples and for the support of the priests. But Pharaoh Necho seems to be entirely his own man. Yes, I admire him tremendously!"

The priest frowned. Indeed, he was far from satisfied with Necho's allowances to the church. He was a loyal and patriotic subject of the king, of course, but an Egyptian king's glory was measured by the temples he built, not by such mundane activities as canal digging and seaborne commerce. He would have to do something about that.

13

The extraction of a black, carious snag had not relieved Menachem's tooth-ache. The sailor lay without complaint, but his expression betrayed his agony. The left side of the jaw was badly swollen. His skin was hot and dry, his eyes red with sleeplessness. When Asa reached into the man's mouth and palpated the reddened mucous membrane below the gums, the man gave a long moan of uncontrollable anguish.

Asa spoke to him and to Ieoud, his skipper, facing him over the bed.

"There is an abscess of the jaw bone. It cannot drain, being wholly enclosed by hard tissue. Healing by resolution would be a long, slow process at best. But I do not think that it will heal. Without radical treatment, there will be weeks or months of pain, as severe as now. He will not be able to eat, hardly able to swallow fluids. It is entirely possible—perhaps probable—that he will die."

"Can you do anything?" asked Ieoud.

The priest nodded. "It is a desperate measure, but necessary. I can try to drain it. The operation will be a severe one; it will be hard for him to endure. I can open the bone. But I may break his jaw in the process."

"If that is your advice, doctor, let it be done. What do you say, Menachem?"

"Do something—anything!"

Asa nodded.

He set Benadon, his assistant, to grinding some limestone to a fine powder while he selected, sharpened and washed his instruments. When the grinding was completed, the limestone was put into a deep pottery bowl. Menachen sat with his head over this, and a small tent was improvised about bowl and head.

Reaching under the linen, Asa emptied a flagon of vinegar into the bowl of limestone. As the mixture bubbled, Asa told the patient to breathe deeply. In a few minutes he fell over, unconscious.

Rapidly Asa made his incision. While Benadon held the wound open with hook-shaped retractors, Asa set to with mallet and chisel. Before he was finished, the patient awoke with a moan that became a scream; several men held him while the inhalation process was repeated, and he lapsed again into a coma-like sleep.

There was a spurt of pus into Asa's face, and almost immediately the man awoke once more. His shipmates held him while the wound was dressed, but he did not struggle. In amazement and joy, he announced that the worst of the pain was already gone!

It did not return. Menachem made a rapid recovery. Although he did not know it, Asa's reputation rose mightily with the crews. With the fine illogic of ordinary sailors, they honored him far more for the relief of this single man—which had been as largely a matter of luck as of skill—than for his earlier superb feat. The merit in that had been not so much in knowing how to go about checking an epidemic as in conveying his ideas to a people of unknown tongue, persuading them to accept and act upon them, and then tirelessly and fearlessly supervising and nagging at them to make them see the matter through. He was highly complimented, however, by Belnatan and Ieoud.

Especially by Ieoud. Asa was surprised and touched by the concern that the captain showed for his seaman. Frequently, when Asa visited his patient, he found Ieoud there, deep in some discussion or other which Ieoud broke off to inquire, again and again, about the man's progress.

In fact, every one was feeling more cheerful. The healthy growing fields of wheat, barley, beans and onions gave promise of subsistence for many months ahead. Meanwhile fish, fruit and game offered a richness of repast that they had not known since the start of the voyage. Wine appeared—the materials for a fresh vintage at hand, Belnatan permitted the stores to be broached. The labor of planting was done, that of the harvest not yet upon them; and frequently, of an evening, singing groups gathered about the campfires. Wild grapes grew plentifully among the groves; they were plucked and pressed and the wine-jars replenished.

There was something idyllic about this pleasant pastoral life, away at the end of the earth though it was. The sun and the rain were gracious and the earth bounteous; in this interlude between past and future peril and toil the men took the fullness of the day as it came, and Asa could not find it in his heart to begrudge them their dusky wenches.

The officers, too, relaxed among themselves, sometimes stopping off for a glass and a toast with the men. Ieoud, particularly, was to be found with the crew much of the time. Asa was pleased that Ieoud so retained the common touch; Belnatan was more stand-offish.

In fact, Asa even overheard Belnatan reprove Ieoud, one evening, for his mixing so much with the ratings, and was somewhat annoyed; were the sailors not men like themselves?

Of course all was not well. There was the beginning of a very ugly quarrel between a few overly aggressive sailors of the *North Wind* and the husband and brothers of a broad-hipped slut, but Balsachus happened along in good time and stopped the fight. Belnatan saw to it that a rope's end was put to use on the next day. And there was an occasion when a seaman—again, as it happened, of the *North Wind* —was almost insolent to the commodore. But Ieoud was on the spot, and in a fury that his own man should so shame him, led him off to punishment. And if some of the offender's shipmates were a bit sullen thereafter, who could bother to notice, now that the harvest was upon them?

Equally encouraging was the natives' account of the geography to the southward. Linguistic ability had progressed to the point at which there was little danger of misunderstanding; and according to their informants, the coast beyond extended more and more to the west. Hopes ran high that they had won almost to the southern tip of the African land mass. If so, they might soon round it and head northward for home.

The natives also knew of the river to the north which Balsachus had explored, though none of them had ever seen it. They gave it the name of "Zambezi," which Belnatan duly entered on his chart. There was also, it appeared, another great river, much less far north, the "Limpopo." The fleet had apparently missed it, perhaps in a rain squall.

According to the custom of his people, Asa celebrated the harvest by prayers of Thanksgiving. It was curious, however, as many among them had remarked, that there was no feel of spring in the air. On the contrary, the weather had grown slightly but definitely colder— it felt more like the beginning of winter, home near the Middle Sea. And just as at home in winter, the sun had departed far from the zenith, the difference being that it was to the north rather than to the south.

They worked like slaves to get the precious grain reaped, bound and under cover between rains; and then there were the threshing and the winnowing to be done. While some used flail and fan, others were drying and smoking strips of meat and fish, or collecting fruits and roots for their further voyage.

"When we report back," remarked Belnatan, "that on facing west we had the sun on our right hand, we shall never be believed."

There was a more immediate source of disquiet. The wind was strong but variable in direction, frequently from the south. If this trend should continue, it would cost much time and toil to make their southing.

Ieoud in particular harped upon this theme in his conversations with the other officers. In the presence of Belnatan he held his tongue, but otherwise his reiteration of his worries sharpened the gnawing doubt in the others' minds. Finally, Ethbaal took it upon himself, as the commodore's second in command, to put an end to it.

"You've had your say, Captain Ieoud, upon the state of the winds—not once, but time and time again. You've said enough. If I hear of your opening your mouth upon the subject again, I shall report it to the commodore, with a recommendation for disciplinary action."

So Asa ben Abdiel, the priest, sojourned in the land, with Belnatan, the captain of the ships of Tyre, and all his host; and the Lord blessed them with dew and with rain from heaven, and with the fatness of corn and of wine.

14

The last month of spring (according to the calendar) was upon them when each captain and his ship's carpenter made a final inspection of his hull and pronounced it ready for sea. Some caulking and a few planks had been replaced; *Seawife* had a new mast. The ships were launched and loaded. On a fine, sunny day, with a moderate southeast wind breathing benignly upon them, they set sail and steered into the west.

It was good to be at sea again! Their eyes delighted in the sparkling blue sea, the fleecy clouds, the inexpressibly graceful curve always assumed by every sail, no matter how clumsily cut, how stretched and worn and faded, how unskillfully trimmed. Their nostrils drew deep, deep of the sea-clean air. Even better were the scend and fall of the heaving hulls. But best of all was the promise of the coast, trending more and more to the west, bringing hope that soon they could round Africa's farthest south and steer for the north and home. With favoring wind and current the ships sped swiftly along the rocky shore.

Chelbes and Abbarus took over for the anchor watch that evening. The boatswain posted his lookouts and saw to snugging down for the night. He eyed the sky and nodded in satisfaction. "Now the Kabirim grant us another swift and easy passage!"

Chelbes smiled mockingly. "Let us have a good passage, by all means. But let us not delude ourselves into crediting some silly wooden idols for our good fortune."

Asa pricked up his ears. Had the skeptical quartermaster become a true believer? But Chelbes' next words showed that he had not.

"We are not untaught savages, to believe tales of supposed gods in the empty heaven. In the childhood of mankind such stories had their usefulness, I grant you; and they are probably still of value to keep the more childish among us in line. But the random pattern of human life is enough to convince any thinking man that blind chance rules all things. These are modern times; those old women's tales were good enough for the ancients, but they won't stand in the light of the knowledge of today. Modern man cannot be trammeled by the superstitions of antiquity. He needs a modern set of ideas; and there is no room in it for the theological terrors and abstractions of his grandfather's grandfather. In the world of here and now there is no place for divinity, whether the multiple idols to which you bow, Abbarus, or the imaginary, formless exercise in metaphysics that causes our friend the doctor so much concern."

"And what," asked Asa, "makes you think that atheism is characteristically modern? It has been known since ancient days. In the centuries-old wisdom of my people we find the remark,'The fool sayeth in his heart, there is no God!' "

Mattan laughed. "Put right in your place, Chelbes. And yet there is a certain validity in part of what you say. An ancient theology will not serve for modern man. When your people and mine, Asa, were ignorant barbarians wresting a precarious living from the desert, they had to imagine a superpowerful, personal Helper to defend them against the impossible odds. But we have grown up, and should view the world with the eyes of adults. We cannot today give credence to the idea of a huge Old Man in the sky, as your people once did, or to a whole tribe of such superbeings, as mine did."

"Exactly," said Chelbes.

"But that does not mean that we must conceive of a universe of chance and chaos, as Chelbes would have us do. On the contrary, it is evident, it seems to me, that all creation follows a pattern. The sun invariably rises in the east and sets in the west. From equinox to equinox the count of the days never varies. In big circles or in little ones, the value of pi is always three and a seventh. It is this constancy, this regularity, to which we must be grateful for the fact that human life—or any life at all—is possible. Just imagine, if things should start falling up instead of down! It is this beautiful uniformity, this predictability of known phenomena, that to me is the Divine. When I say God, I mean order. When I say God, I mean law."

"When I say God," said Asa, "I mean God."

For almost a month they coasted along a shore rocky and forbidding but trending ever more to the westward. Progress was unsteady; the winds, colder and sometimes more boisterous, blew more often than not in their teeth. When they had a favorable breeze, therefore, they sometimes ran all night. They spent many days in harbor, adrift, or tossing in an open, uneasy anchorage. Yet when they could sail they made fast speed; and the favoring current was good for some four parasangs, Belnatan reckoned, between dawn and dusk. When they put out one morning from good harborage in a wide but shallow bay, their course along the coast was almost due west.

At sunup the next day, the attention of the officers was at once drawn to Abbarus. He lay struggling where he had slept, a look of alarm upon his face.

"Doctor," he complained huskily, "There's something wrong with my right leg. I can't move it."

"Have you injured it in any way?"

"Not that I know of."

"Has this ever happened to you before?"

"Never."

There was no sign of any contusion or wound upon the limb. It was the same color as its fellow. But it lay inert and flaccid on Abbarus' bed on the deck, and try as he would he could not move even a toe.

"You have suffered a slight stroke," Asa told him.

"Can you cure me?" Hope and fear struggled in his face.

"Frankly, no. But it is not necessary—I am certain that a spontaneous recovery will take place. In the meantime, we must see to it that the limb is moved frequently, by yourself or others; else pressure sores will develop, and they will be hard to heal."

Belnatan, in the bustle of morning duties, managed to draw Asa to the bow.

"Do you really expect Abbarus to recover, doctor? Or were you sparing him the worse truth?"

"I meant it truly enough. But I am not sure that his recovery will be complete. And I am very much afraid that there will be other and worse attacks, from which he will not recover."

Luck, so long their friend and protector, turned from them at last. In the forenoon watch of the following day the southeasterly breeze flagged and died. Briefly they manned their oars, pitching and rolling first in a flat calm, then, under a greying sky, in a headwind from the north-northwest. The breeze grew, and the futile, buffeted oars were shipped and brought inboard. Then for a while they lay to drogues, each ship with a warp stretching ahead to fasten by a bridle to a floating spar. But the murmur of the shrouds, wind-strummed, turned to a whine; more and more viciously the spume struck at their faces; the rising wind snarled in their ears, and the seas mounted and in their growing strength and pride began to climb aboard, in white-streaked, steel-grey masses, over the plunging prows.

No ships were built for such unequal battle. In late afternoon they put about and fled. Watching for a smooth patch of sea, each captain picked his moment. The turning was not without danger; a large wave striking a ship broadside on could swamp her or roll her over. On a signal from the captain, a dozen men pulled the ship smartly forward on her riding cable. Taking advantage of the momentum, the helmsmen flung their weight against the huge steering-sweeps; a dozen oars, put out on the same side, aided as best they could in the broken water. About went the hull. As they brought the wind aft of the beam, a small but stout stormsail rose rapidly and was sheeted home. The drogues came in over the sterns, and the ships ran downwind, help-lessly yielding the precious westing won in the day and night before.

The land disappeared. Except for a giant petrel, or a huge, white bird with a ten-foot wing spread, gliding now and then aloofly through the storm, they saw nothing but the limitless waste of water.

Harder blew the wind and still the sea rose. The shrouded sun for-sook them in the west; they saw a fading seascape wild with riot, and blackness engulfed them in the tumult.

All night they drove downwind in the still increasing gale. The shrouds sang shrilly; the stormwind shouted in their ears. In the bailing-wells men plied the buckets for their lives. Only the strongest could cope with the kicking steering-sweeps; only the most cunning helmsmen could feel on their cheeks the first change of a veering gust, yet not be betrayed into swinging the ships diagonally across the hurtling seas. Had they done so, any wave might have flung itself under the quarter of a reeling ship; might have plunged her bow into some piled water ahead, and about it, fixed as a fulcrum, wrenched the hull aside, till it broached to, broadside to the merciless waves, capsized, filled, and sank.

The dawn, when it came, was almost worse. For now, to the wild pitching and rolling, the shrieking of the rigging, the groaning of the tortured hulls and the ululations of the tempest were added the appalling sight of the monstrous masses of water sweeping endlessly upon them, of stormwrack tearing at their eyes when they looked astern, and of the boundless, daunting horror of an ocean gone utterly wild and agape to swallow. Each ship found herself utterly alone.

Mattan and Asa had the deck when, with a crack heard even above the tumult, *Morning Star's* sail blew out. Its rags almost immediately ripped loose and went kiting to leeward. Almost at once the ship lost so much of her speed that she no longer had steerage-way and began to yaw dangerously, now to starboard, now to port.

"Chelbes, break out another stormsail!" Mattan screamed in desperation, but Belnatan countermanded the order with a shake of his head. "No fabric can stand." He had to shout to be heard, even by those near him, but the captain's manner, Asa noted through his fear, was as calm and unruffled as though he were putting his crew through practice maneuvers. "Trail two hawsers astern!"

It was done, and their drag was just as steadying—or almost—as the sail had been, holding her stern fairly well up to the seas.

Almost all of the crews, Asa included, felt that their end was near. Fear lay cloggingly upon their minds like a blanket upon the limbs of a struggling swimmer; it plunged icicle-like into their spines; it slacked their sinews and kneaded the sickening bowels. Not a man of them but carried on resolutely in its face.

For this was a storm such as few sailors had dared. In the Middle Sea they were used to sailing only in the pleasant summer months; and when a tempest came upon them even then, they knew every cove and headland, every reef and isle that might offer a lee. But on this unknown ocean they were utterly, utterly lost.

The prospect of drowning Asa found unsettling enough; but it was not that that chiefly daunted him and his shipmates. It was the sheer brutal, overpowering wind and waves themselves that through the portals of the senses assaulted the citadel of the soul. Just so might a soldier, quite resigned to the imminence of death, bear up manfully against the idea itself of annihilation, but quail at the glint of his foemen's steel and the thunder of their war cry.

"We'll lighten the ship—overboard with half our food and water!" Belnatan shouted. Then, with a grin, "Doctor, are you ready to meet your end?"

"Ready enough." Asa managed to act outwardly calm. "I suppose it will be soon?"

"I do not think so—not soon, or at all. I checked her fastenings, timber and planking very carefully. I'm confident that she'll hold together."

Except for having to raise his voice over the din of the storm, Belnatan spoke as normally as though he were expounding a point of naval architecture at the dinner table ashore.

Asa gazed at him in admiration. Heathen though he was, this was a hero like unto Joshua! The Pharaoh had chosen well. This was indeed the man to lead them to the uttermost ends of the earth!

All day they drove helplessly into unknown regions, and all of another terrifying night. In the afternoon of the third day the wind began to moderate, and the speed of their flight lessened. But during the night it blew up again. Nevertheless, they slept now in snatches. Sodden, aching, cold, and in terror of death as they were, the exhaustion of three days of unresting battle brought its own mercy, and the watch off was granted a brief oblivion.

Another day and another storm and toil and terror; of belly-wrenching nausea and of cold, raw food; of fatigue, of chill, of wetness, and of eyes smarting from lack of sleep and driving brine. The wind backed slowly into the west. Then suddenly it was southwesterly and dropping. It steadied in this quarter, now moderate. Wearily they hoisted sail and, with the wind on the port beam, headed for land and rest.

It was three days of intermittent showers before they raised the land—a rocky, inaccessible, surfbound coast that they had passed before. Northwest was the best course they could lay, and it would now, if continued, wreck them on the beach. The exhausted crew was in no condition to row, directly or diagonally, against wind and sea; there was nothing for it but to turn back to the eastward under sail until they should find a harbor in which to moor or a sandy shore protected enough for them to beach the ship.

They beached, accordingly, toward evening on a short strip of sand in the scanty lee of a point. The hull had stood the ordeal beautifully, and the gear too needed surprisingly little attention. Belnatan's instructions, in case of separation, had been for *Brant,* the storeship, much the slowest of the fleet, to continue at her best speed; the others were to wait for four days, lest she be somewhere astern, and then set about overtaking her. They settled down accordingly to wait.

As Asa composed himself to peaceful sleep at last, he murmured,

He spoke, and He raised the stormy wind, which lifted up its waves.

They mounted up to heaven, they went down again to the depths; their soul was melted because of trouble.

They reeled to and fro, and staggered like one drunken; all their wisdom was vanished.

Then they cried unto the Lord in their trouble, and He brought them out of their distress.

He calmed the storm into a whisper, and stilled were the waves of the sea.

And they rejoiced because they were silent. So He guided them into their longed-for haven.

15

During the days of storm and terror Asa had made his devotions reg-
ularly, after the custom of his people. But he had not cried unto the
Lord for rescue. In the fact of his doubts, it seemed to him that he had
not the right to do so. With a deep inherent piety, he refused to offend
God and himself by calling for succor when he could not do so out of a
full heart and an untroubled faith. So he had called upon his puny
human courage and denied himself the release of a plea for deliverance
from on High.

He did not feel called upon to explain all this to Mattan when the
latter asked him how often he had prayed for aid, but put the mate off
with a half-truth.

"He who decreed the flowering and the death alike of Jonah's gourd
and of the thousands and thousands of people of Nineveh, that great
city, knows whom He wishes to preserve, and whom to cast down. He
has not forgotten me, His servant. If it be good in His eyes that I live,
then live I shall, through what dangers soever; and if He had decreed
my death, then nothing can save me. He knows my merit and will save
or destroy according to my deserving. 'The judgments of the Lord are
true and righteous altogether.' "

"Granting that," asked Mattan, "can you not pray for mercy?"

"Is it needful? His mercy endureth forever. If it be well that I be
shown mercy, He knows it, and will be merciful."

"You might have asked mercy for the rest of us."

"The same thing applies. Shall I teach God mercy? How should I
dare? 'Should mortal man be more just than God? or a man more
righteous than his Maker?' I wonder whether one should ever pray
for the favor of Heaven. I am beginning to believe that prayer should
consist only in the glorification of God and resignation to His will.
Shall we instruct Him in what is to be done? There is a time for living
and a time for dying. Do we know our seasons? It almost seems to me
that in prayer we should approach the Lord as a hurt child comes to his
parent, not expecting the parent to do away with the hurt, but seeking
solace in the parent's love and concern and in the knowledge that there
is One to whom we belong and who shares our griefs and our joys."

So the priest spoke; but his heart was troubled. Was there indeed

One who listened? From the atheism of Chelbes he recoiled aghast. He would not, could not, believe that there was no Power in heaven who had wrought the grandeur of creation, but that all things had spawned themselves in the lifeless womb of time; that men fall uselessly in their uncounted millions, with none to mark the righteous or the doer of evil; and that the great thirst for justice and mercy was doomed never to be slaked—the vision of the kingdom of Heaven was only a lying dream in the night.

Even less could he embrace the abstract divinity of Mattan's ideas. Was man to give over the ideal of Holiness for the cycle of a self-regulating sun? Instead of trusting to his warm and loving Father, should he sing hosannas to the abstract value of pi? This was even worse than the other.

Asa ben Abdiel had wandered a far trail from the Temple at Jerusalem; and its chanting rang but faintly in his ears.

Nevertheless, it was the hour for evening prayer, and Asa ben Abdiel was a Hebrew of the Hebrews. He bent his head and began to pray with the psalmist's words.

He sent from on high, He took me;
He drew me out from many waters.

The doctor's prognosis or forecast regarding the boatswain had been proved correct. Abbarus was up and about again, only a dragging limp remaining of his disability. With a rested and restored crew they waited impatiently for the other ships to join.

On the next day *Seawife* and *Stag* came in together.

They were, by Belnatan's reckoning, but little past the bay which marked the beginning of the westward trend of the coast; and on the second day thereafter, the ships and gear being fairly well dried and an east wind springing up, the commodore's impatience set them in motion. Westward, then, they cruised, peering hopefully to seaward and ahead for the sails of the two absent vessels, anxiously scanning the rocky beaches for signs of wreck. "Although," said Belnatan, "it is hardly possible that we will see anything on the rocks. If a ship has been overwhelmed at sea, its wreckage would never have drifted onto this shore; and if any ship has regained the coast, as we did, there has

been nothing in the weather since to make her a casualty of the sea."
At night they anchored, tossing off the unprotected coast, lest they run
by their companions in the dark.

On the second morning they opened a narrow cove, and there was
Brant, riding easily to anchor. *Morning Star* tied up alongside, and
Stag and *Seawife* moored together; the cove was much too small to
offer scope for four riding cables. *Brant,* deeper in the water, had not
been driven as far to leeward as the war galleys, and her deck had made
her less susceptible to swamping; nevertheless, Abdemonos had judged
it necessary to jettison stores enough to bring up her freeboard by an
additional foot. The loss was unfortunate, but the safety of the bulk
of the provisions—to say nothing of her crew—was the greater consideration.

Of *North Wind* there was as yet no sign.

That same day at noon they put to sea again and stood to the west.
But with the promontories of the cove still in sight, the easterly failed.
And it blew again from the west, and strongly; and, cursing, they put
their helms over and stood back to the cove. And there came *North
Wind,* fighting her way under oars from the east; they entered together,
moored as before, but with *North Wind* on the other side of *Brant.*
They snugged down for the night.

It was late in the first watch—toward midnight, in a rising wind—
that the men standing anchor watch became aware of strife on *North
Wind.* Two men and then a third tore free and flung themselves yelling
onto the adjacent ship. Belnatan, awakened, heard their tale grimly.
Ieoud and his crew, so it ran, had their bellies full of the voyage. They
had plotted to cut loose the other craft from the storeship, to overpower
and kill its sleeping crew, and to seize it and make their way back up
the coast toward home, there to offer their services to the Chaldeans
or to turn pirate, as might seem best. And even as they spoke, *North
Wind* under oars dashed for the harbor mouth, hoisted sail and was
gone.

Belnatan's first impulse was to pursue, but even as the orders leaped
to his lips he repressed them. "Let them go," he said instead. "I had
my suspicions and tripled the watch on *Brant.* I had not really looked
for such a brazen attempt, but let them go! Catching them will be a
doubtful business, and I'm not going to risk another ship. They have

failed to capture extra supplies. With them, they might have stood far out to sea, eluded us, and conceivably made their way back. Without them, there is small chance that they will ever see home again. Even so, that's safer for them than to stay here and hang as mutineers. We can wring one bit of consolation from the business—our supplies will last the longer for it !"

For a week the westerly held them harbor-bound while they fretted and consumed their provisions. Then a southeaster arose, and for two days they cruised along the coast. Then the wind veered into the northeast for another day of progress. But again a howling westerly gale was upon them, and they fled downwind for their lives with their goal receding further and further behind them. When after days and days the wind stood again in the southeast, it was cold—piercingly cold to these men garbed for the lands of sun—and the rains beat down upon them. The favoring wind came often in terrific gusts, so that they were forced to shorten sail before it and lose some of the benefit of the progress it might have brought them.

Weeks went by, endless weeks, while they struggled along that iron coast and battled that lawless sea. No other seamen in the world could have kept those tiny craft afloat ; indeed, no others would have had the daring to try. The hands were in a state of dull misery and despair. There was, most of that wretched time, no resting ; no peace or warmth for sound, unbroken sleep while high winds deprived them of the shelter of deck tents ; and of course no fire for cooking. The officers were no better off. Even Belnatan was gaunt and grim but never wavered in his fight to win every possible tiny bit of westing.

Fear, fatigue, cold and hunger were exhausting them. The helmsmen could no longer stand to the tillers for their full trick ; they had to be relieved four times in a watch. The men moved more slowly, and more of them were needed to haul at sheets and braces. What with the violence of the motion and the increasing clumsiness of the tired crews, injuries became more frequent. A stumble resulted in a broken arm. A rope of palm fibre snaked around an ankle and jerked ; the man went overboard, and in that sea no maneuvers for rescue were possible. A swinging spar fractured a thigh. A fall brought a man's belly violently down upon the top of a samson post ; he lay moaning with internal injuries. To the difficulties of diagnosing and splinting in the hellish up-roar were added the more nauseous details of nursing attendance upon prostrate, helpless men. An older crew member died quietly during the night.

It was during this time that they completed the first year of the voyage.

Why, Asa wondered dully, for the fiftieth time, was he such a fool as to be here? He could be sleeping, warm and full and comfortable, in his house in pleasant Judea, far from any peril of storm, with a woman by his side, pliant and soft and loving; yes, and with the likelihood of growing old and being buried, full of years and honor, by his children and his children's children. Instead, he was off here on this fool's errand in the midst of primeval chaos, in misery of mind and body; and he was soon to sink down in the suffocating brine, down, down into its icy depths, forever, with none to mark his passing; and his very name would be forgotten.

Every other man aboard was having the same gloomy reflections—including Belnatan.

But still they battled toward the west.

16

Far south of the southernmost tip of the continent, *Stag* tossed alone upon an empty sea. Where he was, and how far away and in what direction rode the rest of the fleet, Balsachus had no idea. For an eternity of days he had been running before this unending northwester. His crew—and he himself—had reached the limit of endurance.

But now at last the violence of the gale—praise be to Atergatis!—was moderating. And the wind seemed to be shifting—yes, it was defi-nitely moving into the west. Rapidly, with the broadening day, it contin-ued to veer, and by afternoon a strong southerly was blowing. Balsachus raised a tiny trysail, and slowly the ship began moving toward the north.

It was high time. Dry rot had gotten into her timbers and her fasten-ings were beginning to pull out of the softened wood. The working of the hull under incalculable stresses had opened her seams, and the bailing was desperate and continuous. He was not sure that she would live to reach the coast. He was not sure that he cared. Through his rain-soaked garments the wind blew cold.

In late afternoon the rain-clouds parted, and the horizon was clear in every direction. Suddenly a cry rang out—"Land, ho!"

Balsachus looked up in astonishment. It was not possible—they were far from the coast! But the men were peering astern. Far to the south snow-covered mountains rose from the sea! Land was near!

What the captain did not know was that the cold south wind had forced its way under the mass of relatively warm air from the north. The layered atmosphere, with different refractive indices at different levels, had acted as a huge lens, curving the rays of light and lifting into view immense masses of ice from far, far to the south.

During the night the wind hauled further around, into the east. Balsachus considered carefully. It was doubtful whether he could make the African coast, and in any event his recent experience had led him to believe that the wind was likely to be northerly again within a short time. It would be better to head for the nearer shore for rest and repairs. He ordered the quartermaster to keep her south.

So south she drove again, the strained hull opening wider under the stresses of a beam wind. They passed an old sail under her hull, pulled it tight, and partly checked the rising water. The easterly held, and all day they drove on.

The wind backed into the southwest; but Balsachus, sure that he was close to land, lay to a drogue and made as little northing as possible. It was incredibly cold.

For a whole week the winds toyed with him, then, tiring of the sport, rose toward an evening to make an end. The wracked hull, tortured beyond endurance, gave up. The crew could do no more.

As the water rose toward the coaming, they got the boats overside. Some of the weakened crew were unable to transfer to them. Some didn't try. A wave washed into the sluggish bow. The hull foundered; suddenly, in a moment, it was gone. They were horribly alone on the endless, angry sea.

Balsachus and two of his men were in the gig. In the deepening twilight they saw the overloaded longboat suddenly disappear. There was nothing they could do.

It started to snow. The freezing wind blew fiercely through their soaked clothes. The captain, weak and shivering, doubted that his boat would live till morning.

He was wrong. The boat was still floating staunchly four days later. But to the three ice-stiff corpses aboard, it made not the slightest difference.

For the last time Balsachus had turned in a good but not a superb performance.

17

Morning Star, Seawife, and *Brant* crawled painfully along the coast on a west-southwesterly course. The wind was on the starboard bow; they could not lay a course to clear the point ahead under sail without standing far out to sea. By hugging the lee of the shore, they found water smooth enough to use the oars; all three crews were rowing, the two pentekonters with towlines to the storeship.

Ahead, what looked like a promontory stretched for half a parasang, as they judged, into the sea. It bore two rocky hills; the higher reared some five hundred feet in the thin sunshine.

Only with every bit of manpower could the exhausted crews make headway against the pressure of the wind and the drag of the deep hull of the storeship. On each galley, the captain and the mate manned the steering-sweeps, and the rest of the officers toiled unbidden with the men.

Asa pulled wearily at the six-ell oar. He depressed the loom, lifting the dripping blade clear of the water; he brought the blade forward; he dipped it; then gave a long, hard pull through the viscous brine, and repeat. He was bone-tired, sleepy; his muscles pained him. But others had been pulling longer than he, and he would not give up.

A man toppled off his bench. The doctor did not even break rhythm. What the man needed was the medicinal force of nature—rest, sleep, warmth, good meals, rest. A physician could not supply them.

Pull...pull...pull...pull, and drive the punished body beyond what it believed it could endure. Pull, and rub the blistering skin over the brutal wood of the oar. Pull with the aching back; pull with the heaving chest, with the hammering pulse.

He did not know how properly to cushion the hard bench; his

buttocks ached atrociously. No matter. Pull. Pull. If Phoenicians could endure the grueling labor, so could a Judean.

It was, he realized, a foolish pride. He should not measure himself against them in their own fashion. On a mountain trail he could easily give them a third the distance, he knew, and win; but they had been bred since boyhood to the toil of the oar. And even they were suffering. No matter. Pull...pull.

Slowly the long morning wore by. The oarsmen did not turn from their tasks, but Belnatan reported to them how the promontory grew near. Now he could see detail in the rocky masses. Now individual shrubs stood out upon the bleak hillside. Now he saw the riff-raff line of flotsam and jetsam, snaking its way along the sandy stretches above high tide level. Pull.

Then—oh, hope and relief that burgeoned at the words!—the captain called, "Abbarus, stand by to moor!" And then the joyous, the sweet, the blissful words, "Way enough!" followed by, "Let her go!" and the anchor splashed, and the toil was done.

They lay in the angle of the promontory and the shore. As long as the wind held in its present quarter, they could rest secure. But let it shift and blow anywhere from south to northeast, then their anchorage was exposed, and they would have to get underway and along the coast lest a sudden gale crush them on the rocks.

"Mattan," ordered the captain, "I want a dozen men, armed and armored, for the longboat. Would you like to go with me, doctor? I'm going to climb the hill and take a look at the offing."

Exhausted as he was, Asa accepted the opportunity to leave the confines of the ship and get earth under his sea-weary legs, if only for an hour.

It was a hard climb for the tired men up the rough, steep hillside, under the weight of their metal. As their heads cleared the hilltop, they saw the coast, on the other side of the promontory, trending as far as the eye could reach in the clear air—some eight triple miles—to the west— northwest. But due west was neither coast nor cape nor island— only the openness of the sea.

Belnatan seemed to grow taller as he stood there. Into his eyes came the light of triumph. "The South Cape!" he cried. "The furthest end of Africa! Beyond," he waved to the south, "is only the endless ocean, that rolls around the world!"

"How do you know," Asa asked, "that this isn't a large bay, with a further southern extension of the coast beyond the horizon?"

"By the waves. It takes a long, long fetch to work up a sea like that. I have seen it only here and off the western coast of Europe—in the open ocean!"

His men in a moment were frantic with joy and pride. They cheered— they leaped—they clashed their weapons—they stripped off garments and waved them on high; until in the ships far below men noted them, and guessed at the joyful event; and they too laughed and yelled, and set up an exultant clamor; and for the first time the clash of iron and bronze affrighted the gulls of those far-off waters, so that they flew up and about and added their cries to those of the joy-crazed mariners.

Then sang Asa, son of Abdiel, priest of Israel,

If I ascend up into heaven, Thou art there:

If I make my bed in the netherworld, Thou art there.

If I take the wings of the morning, and dwell in the uttermost parts of the sea,

Even there shall Thy hand lead me, and Thy right hand shall hold me.

If I say, "Surely the darkness shall cover me, and the light about me shall be night,"

Even the darkness is not too dark for Thee;

But the night shineth as the day; the darkness is even as the light.

That night Belnatan's name rang again and again over that uneasy sea, as his adoring crews drank and feasted and pledged their commander. No more wandering off into the dark and the nothingness afar. The mythical terrors of the ends of the earth were laid forever. From now on every parasang further on their journey was a parasang nearer home!

18

"I found out what you wanted to know, darling," said Nektanebis, as Engidu embraced her in greeting. "The stoppage of work on the Nile-Red Sea Canal will be permanent. The priests of Amun warned the Pharaoh that the gods would not smile upon his project and that, in any case, he was only building for the barbarian."

"Now I wonder what put that into their heads? Although, on second thought, the unprecedented expense may have had much to do with the decision." He kissed her. "And now, my dear, we'll hold a feast. Somehow, I find myself in the mood for revelry. And we'll have the jeweler in and buy you the finest necklace in his wares."

The next day he summoned a courier. "You are going back to Babylon," he announced. "Here is a letter which will be the official reason for your journey; and if it is intercepted or read by the Egyptians, no harm will be done. But the real purpose of your trip is this.

"Say to the king that his servant's efforts have been successful. The king of Egypt has abandoned the canal. The waters of the Southern Sea will be for all time a Babylonian lake! And get word to Epikrates the Phocian that I want to see him."

It was on the second day thereafter that Nektanebis, on this occasion unexpected, turned in at the gate of Engidu's mansion. She instructed the footman who accompanied her to wait outside, entered, and ordered Engidu's steward to fetch a stoup of wine for her suddenly sick servant. He left the hall on his errand, and Nektanebis, neither knowing nor caring whether he was deceived, took the familiar route to Engidu's bedroom.

So it came about that, as Engidu and the Phocian strolled into the former's antechamber, she overheard a surprising conversation.

"I am about to leave Egypt," the ambassador began. "This is still secret, but my royal master is honoring me with the hand of one of his sisters. I tell you this that you may repose the greater confidence in my authority for what I have next to say. You will shortly learn, if you haven't already, that the Pharaoh has lost interest in the Southern Sea. This being the case, he has, by the same token, lost interest in Belnatan of Tyre and his fleet. So it is now safe to carry out the project we spoke of. When you reach the West, pass the word that the pentekonters *Seawife, Morning Star, North Wind* and *Stag* and the storeship *Brant,* or what is left of them, all under the command of Belnatan of Tyre, may be entering the Middle Sea through the Gates of Gades. They will make a rich prize for the brethren of the coast, but only if every one of them is sunk and all their crews accounted for. Two or three of the more articulate among them are to be spared and delivered, properly secured, to Lycaon, tavern-keeper, in Ephesus. Even if, as is probable, the ships are empty, Lycaon will pay an enormous reward. It may be very profitable indeed to hug the straits and snap up what you can out of Tarshish and Gades."

The Greek dismissed, Nektanebis hurriedly put herself to rights and skipped out of the house. It was only a short time later that Engidu, informed of her visit, made a search for her through the house. The search was not wholly in vain. Part of a familiar glass bangle lay on the floor of his bedchamber.

Nektanebis was no longer in love with Asa ben Abdiel, even if she had ever been. But she had once been fond of him and some of that quiet affection persisted. True, it had been disconcerting to have her proffered favors turned down. But in no sense had she been made to feel scorned, and in priest-ridden Egypt it was easy to understand a motivation of divine, or presumably divine, origin. Whether in love or war, an unconquered antagonist arouses a certain respect.

And now she was, if not—as she honestly admitted—heartbroken at her lover's impending desertion, more than a little irritated at his duplicity.

But Engidu was nobody's fool. Thus it came about that when Nektanebis, after sundry soul-searchings and a rather rueful laugh at her own sentimentality, put a hired assassin on the trail of the Phocian, he found the latter always under the shield of a four-man bodyguard. When Epikrates sailed a week later, the agent quietly moved upcountry without reporting his failure to the Egyptian.

19

Northwest they stood along the rocky coast. All were in high spirits —almost all, that is. There is a discontented soul in every ship's company, and here it was Yakinlu, always somewhat apart, who several times complained about the distribution of food and twice made the patently ridiculous charge that someone had stolen his knife. But the water sparkled cheerfully in the clear cold sunshine and white clouds paced them overhead. A reach with wind abeam, at that temperature, would have been a miserable business; but the favoring wind, coming over the sterns, seemed scarcely swifter than the galleys themselves and did not search their garments for the precious body heat. The hulls soared rhythmically over the regular seas, rolling at their crests as though yawing; but the sea-wise helmsmen spared the steering-sweeps, and the fleet made good way. Heaven itself seemed reaching to draw them on; with every week the southward-marching sun had been rising to a higher zenith.

The commodore looked thoughtfully ahead at the flaming sky of sunset. There was no shelter in sight. To lie to all night was certainly the course of prudence, and there might be a useful harbor just ahead which should be investigated and charted. But they had wasted precious weeks in rounding the South Cape, with great consumption of supplies without advance. While the easterly wind blew, infrequent in this clime and season, he should take every advantage of it. And all signs betokened the continuance of good weather.

He made his decision. They would continue to run.

So run they did through a fine moonless night. The seas soughed under each stern and gurgled out from under the forefoot; the sail arched dimly over the deck, on which the sleeping figures were shrouded under their sailcloth tent. The peacefulness, after weeks of storm and striving, was heavenly.

They kept a good offing, lest some cape or outlying reef should reach with rocky fingers for their destruction; or, more subtly, an inshore set of current drag them unaware into the surf. But moonrise and then dawn found them safely offshore. In the fine weather they kindled cooking fires and breakfasted on grains hot-roasted and greens.

So on they drove until in the second day, with the wind hauling into the northeast, they opened a wide bay, where they unloaded and beached on the western shore to scrub hulls. This bay had the three sides of a square, seven parasangs to each, open at the south, and was well sheltered from all but southerly winds.

A half gale arose from the northwest. In this region northeasterly winds seemed to forerun such gales, which hauled to the southward to blow themselves out. They scrubbed bottoms, found them not very foul, and dug various shellfish.

A hunting party encountered some natives with peculiar bulging brows, speaking a language vaguely similar to that further east.

On the fifth night the wind hauled to southward, diminishing. The day dawned clear with moderate southerly winds. They stood to sea, doubled the cape, and stood northwest along it. There was no land to the west. A high sea was running.

In the afternoon watch they put into a large bay opening to the southeastward. At its head was a remarkably flat-topped mountain, like a table, between three and four thousand feet high, as well as a mountain to the northeast and a sharp peak to the southwest. This bay offered shelter from easterly and southerly winds, though exposed to north and northwest.

Midway in their charting someone called their attention to the boatswain. Abbarus lay on his back, breathing stertorously, his eyes half shut. He could not be roused. A prick, or a blow over a sensitive area provoked an automatic withdrawal of the left arm or leg; but on the right the limbs lay flaccid, immovable, like lumps of dead flesh.

The doctor rose from his examination. "This time, captain, I do not think he will recover."

"Is he dying?"

"It might be better if he were. With good nursing care he could live for months—years, perhaps, though I doubt it. But a complete or even a fair measure of recovery is extremely unlikely. And when and if he recovers consciousness, it would not surprise me if he was unable to speak."

"He has lost his mind, then, as well?"

"Not necessarily. He may retain a measure of understanding and be able to communicate by signs. But for our purposes, and indeed for his own, he is as good as dead. And, in fact, he may actually die within a day or two, though I think not."

Belnatan sighed. "He was a fine seaman. If there were anything at all to be done for him, I would not count the cost, but if, as you say, it is hopeless, I am not going to keep him on board here, where he will be very much in the way and where he cannot easily be cared for. *Brant* has much more room, and we'll transfer him. Bodo!"

"Sir?"

"You are promoted to acting boatswain."

"Thank you, sir! I'll do my best."

Asa admitted the wisdom of the transfer. To *Brant's* loblolly boy he gave full instructions for feeding and cleaning the helpless patient. He particularly warned about the avoidance of bedsores and emphasized the necessity of massage to preserve as much as possible the vitality of the affected tissues.

Despite his reluctance to waste the still southerly wind, Belnatan decided to spend a few hours investigating the bay. The lumbering *Brant* he sent ahead under escort of *Seawife*. And indeed the exploration was worthwhile; for the mouth of the bay opened into a northerly and southerly arm, the safest and most commodious anchorage he had as yet charted in that whole region.

On his return to the anchorage, there was Ethbaal in *Seawife* with bad news.

"Just as we had cleared the harbor, Captain, I noticed that the top of the sternpost was forward of where it should be by half the thickness of a finger. On investigating, I found that the apron from the foot of the starboard kingpost to the sternpost had split along its fastenings to the keel and ribs; and the sternpost, therefore, has been receiving the full power of its thrust."

This was serious. The tremendous, continuous pull of the brace, which transmitted fully a quarter of the drive of the sail to the king-post, had been passed to the sternpost; and the fastenings of the *scarph* joint between it and the keel had pulled. Without repairs, the ship might founder in the next blow.

"It will take you four days to unload and beach your ship, make repairs, launch, and reload," said Belnatan. "*Morning Star* will join *Brant*. You will soon overtake us."

It was nevertheless with considerable though concealed perturbation that the two crews parted. Still, the harbor was a snug one, the natives few and unwarlike; and after their experiences of the past few weeks, the fleet should certainly use the sternwind while it lasted. *Seawife* would as certainly soon overtake *Morning Star* and the slower storeship.

Onward, therefore, they pressed, along shores where a high surf pounded low rocks or sand dunes fronting barren hills quite different from the broken shoreline they had so recently left. The sea water was cold, very cold, but abounded in fish; and whales frequently rose from the depths about them. The climate was changing; the rain became less frequent, and the land assumed again the dreaded appearance of a desert. Rivers there were, now and again, but usually guarded by bars or reefs that the ships could not attempt.

From what distant rains, for how many weary weeks had those lonely rivers flowed to Ocean? And for that matter, thought Asa, why were the dwellers in one land blessed with rains and dew, while those in another, no less deserving, struggled endlessly with starvation?

Again the soul-wearying round. But no—not again. He was finished, he decided suddenly, with the ceaseless speculation. Let others fatuously deem themselves to have mastered the Great Mystery. He could not know the unknowable, and he was through trying. He dismissed the whole field of metaphysics as unprofitable. A Hebrew he was and a Hebrew he would remain; and he would continue to acknowledge and pay his devotions to the God of Israel. Whether or not his prayers were heard, and indeed whether or not there was One to hear them, let others debate.

So he reflected in the late afternoon; and as he gazed shoreward toward a distant hill, the reflected light of the sun glared angrily upon him as from a mountain of burning gold.

Days passed. The seas were large, but without cresting they presented no perils. Still the wind blew fair. Southerly or southeasterly it blew, less often from the southwest; on one day a hard westerly held them in the uneasy lee of a rocky, guano-covered islet. Harbors were few and mostly afforded but imperfect shelter; but with this fine homeward breeze, who would want to linger in a thirsty wasteland like this?

Fog, however, was a frequent visitor. Day would break over them, moored in some cove under shelter of a point; but closed in by an impenetrable wall of grey, they could see even less than at night. On the first couple of days on which this occurred, Belnatan waited impatiently until, late in the morning, the fog would lift. Thereafter, however, he put to sea despite it. They felt their way out with the questing lead, blindly following the unseen contours of the bottom as with an elongated, probing finger, ears alert for the snarl of surf or for the whisper of the tide-run past a rock. Once they had worked up an offing, they found themselves in the clear light of the sun.

Thrice the fog came up around them while they were at sea. They continued on their course, taking their direction from the sun, dimly perceived, or from the wind. Once they almost came to grief when, after running for hours at half speed through a grey obscurity, white water appeared suddenly close on the starboard bow. *Morning Star's* helmsmen threw their weight desperately to starboard upon the look-out's frantic cry; there was a sickening bump as the trough of a wave dropped the keel momentarily upon a rock, and then they were free and standing out for sea-room. *Brant,* forewarned, turned in time and followed them to deep water.

They lost a day and a half in a tiny, poorly protected bay, rolling uncomfortably to seas reflected from a low cliff, while they waited out a northwester.

In *Brant,* Abbarus, a pitiful wreck of a man, lay like a vegetable, his dead right side confining him to his narrow strip of the afterdeck. From his mouth came unintelligible sounds; his eyes looked about in torment or poured forth helpless tears.

It was just over two weeks after they had parted company with *Seawife* that her sail rose over the horizon astern. The three ships were reunited in the safe and commodious shelter of a long, low, sandy spit that made into the sea to the northward for almost two parasangs.

This time it was to the fleet surgeon that Ethbaal took his tidings of trouble.

"Five days ago," so Esmunazar, *Seawife's* loblolly boy, began his history, "the yard fell and struck the mate on the head. He was knocked unconscious and has been in that condition since. He had blood on his head and cuts in his scalp. There was a dent in the top of his head. I could feel many pieces of bone. I could feel his soft brain underneath and its pulsation."

A compound comminuted fracture of the cranium was serious indeed, and Chrysor was in desperate plight. Asa made his examination. The mate was in poor contact with his surroundings. He responded neither to questions nor to orders. He was not paralyzed; occasional voluntary movements of arms and legs occurred. His skin was dry and warm, his expression vacant. On exposing the bandaged skull, Asa saw a bulge as large as the palm of his hand. It was soft but resilient under his fingers, like a water-filled bladder.

It was doubly unfortunate that the accident had happened in the physician's absence and on the ship with the least competent of the loblolly boys. It was possible, for instance, that Esmunazar had felt, as he reported, the pulsation of the brain; more likely he had imagined it or felt the pulsation of his own fingers. There might have been many bone fragments, but there had probably been few or one. And a better attempt might have succeeded in inducing the patient to take fluid during the first days; his skin was dry, his lips cracked and scaly. He had not vomited, and that was a good sign.

It was, of course, the soft swelling of the cranium that most worried the priest. The differential diagnosis lay between herniation of the brain under its membranes and mortification of the deeper tissues of the scalp with suppuration.

The differentiation was of the highest importance. If this were a mortification, it was poisoning Chrysor's whole system, and incision and drainage of the pus, without delay, might be a life-saving procedure. There was a rapid pulse, as might be expected with much pus retention. But the scalp is a tissue highly resistant to purulent affection. Still, this could and did occur.

But if this were a herniation of the brain, operative intervention would probably be swiftly fatal. The surgeon's fingers could detect no pulsation. That might be due to the presence of increased cerebral fluid. There was certainly every sign of brain damage.

The physician weighed the evidence in deep perturbation of soul. Chrysor would probably die, he realized, in any case. But that made no difference. If the surgeon did his competent best and lost his patient, his hands would be clean. But if the patient died of some error of omission or commission that should not have occurred, the Lord would surely require that blood of his hands. Despite his new doubts, the priests's mind followed its accustomed paths.

It was now dark and he would observe his patient in the morning. But there was no sleep for Asa that night. He lay staring into the sky, debating the case with himself again and again. He felt terribly alone.

Mattan and Chelbes had spoken to him about the loneliness of command; about the authority and responsibility that cast an aura of remoteness about the most easy-going of sea captains. But this, Asa reflected, was as nothing compared to the loneliness of the ship's surgeon in a detached command. The captain could, and on occasion should, ask the advice of his officers; he could consult with them and in the exposition of the problem perhaps find its solution. At worst he could find strength in the understanding and support of his fellow-professionals, subordinate though they were.

But the surgeon at sea was utterly isolated. There was no one to aid him. His responsibility admitted of not the slightest sharing. And life or death hung on his judgment.

In the morning Asa made up his mind. With a bronze scalpel he made a deep incision into the swollen scalp. With inexpressible joy and relief he saw a great spurt of pus and blood. His diagnosis was confirmed. He washed the wound in decoction of willow and bound it up.

Two days later, with the glory of the noonday sun directly over his unseeing countenance, Chrysor died.

20

Far to the eastward, off the other side of Africa, *North Wind* struggled up the coast. Ieoud, after his desertion, had run easily eastward. At the end of their provisions, they had arrived at the haven where they had spent four months. It had not been difficult, at the proper moment, to fall upon the natives after their welcome and seize what scanty stores of food were to be found in the huts. Discipline had gone with the resentment of the men at his misleading (naturally, they never thought of blaming themselves). In the ensuing night of riot and debauchery, the brown men, reinforced, had attacked; and a Phoenician or two fell while the rest fought clear.

But now, though the winds were, in the main, favorable, the east African current that had served them so well in their southing was adverse; and they made slow progress indeed. Recriminations were bitter. In the course of a disagreement, a sailor slipped a knife neatly between the captain's ribs, and when he went overside, three of his supporters would have been sent for company but that the mutineers realized they needed rowers.

Hunting, fishing, and foraging, they could supply themselves with food; voyaging, they could not. On desperately short rations, therefore, they sailed slowly north along the coast, with frequent stops for food.

When they reached the mangrove swamps and the jungle, provisions were much harder to come by. They could get fish and shore food but not in adequate quantity. Fruits and game were scarcer.

There were fights over food. A couple of killings occurred.

A hunting party failed to return.

Weakened by hunger, a boat's crew capsized in the surf of a difficult landing. Some drowned. The others swam ashore but could not rejoin the ship. The ship could not pick them up.

With half her crew, *North Wind* finally succeeded in entering the river that Balsachus had tried to explore. They anchored in the estuary. There was plenty of game, but hunters were picked off, by ones and twos, by the inhabitants of the land.

The rest stayed aboard and starved to death.

21

Belnatan and his fleet stood north along a generally desert coast. Sandy beaches were backed by low or, infrequently, higher hills. Tiny sand-choked rivers and poorly protected bays (a few, however, were snug enough) broke the shoreline. The temperature had risen but little, but on the ships, running with the steady southerly breeze, it seemed much warmer since they had rounded the last of the southern capes.

Gradually, too, the wind had fallen lighter; in fact, Mattan and Chelbes speculated anxiously about the possibility of the existence ahead of a belt of calms. Nevertheless they still made fair progress, and Belnatan established that here too a favoring ocean current helped to bear them along. The wind, generally southerly in the morning, gradually shifted westward in the course of the day; they made good use of it.

On a rare windless day they lay at anchor in a wide-mouthed, poorly protected bight. One of *Brant's* hands, overhauling the masthead gear, suddenly sang out, "There's a dark line to seaward, Captain! It's coming this way!"

Was a squall upon them? No sign of it. In a moment they descried a gigantic wave rolling shoreward with incredible speed.

Men sprang to the oars and to the mooring cables in a desperate effort to get deeper water under them. There was no time. The incredible comber struck up their bows with a terrific heave. It tore loose the tiny moorings; it swept the helpless fleet shoreward. Another surge followed and another. *Brant,* anchored well out in deeper water, was not carried quite to the shallows; had she been, her heavy hull and load would have crushed the timbers beyond repair. *Seawife* grounded, but gently, and escaped damage; but *Morning Star,* moored off a projecting spit, was flung ashore, high and dry, with a crash that stove her quarter and three of her frames.

This time it was Ethbaal who, in *Seawife,* shepherded the storeship on her way; while Belnatan, his crew reinforced by the ship's carpenters and carpenter's apprentices of the other two, remained behind to rebuild his shattered stern. It took nine days of fast, hard work before he pronounced her again ready for sea.

Twice more on that coast they were to encounter this mysterious phenomenon of the giant rollers; but on the one occasion they were under way well off shore and the rollers passed harmlessly under them, and on the other they lay safely behind a long sandbar, on which the waves broke.

Another difficulty that they had been finding on this coast was a confusion of distant visual perception, due to some trick of light and atmosphere. At a parasang's distance from the land they were generally safe from reefs and shoals. But what with the refraction and mirages, an estimation of their offing was difficult and uncertain.

The coast trended due north, then gradually fell away to the northeast in a great, shallow bight. As the two galleys made good the parasangs, the sun was moving rapidly southward. Gone were the short days of southern storm—the hours during which the sun looked down upon them were now as long as those during which it was hidden beneath the sea. It was becoming appreciably warmer. Rain began to fall—seldom at first, more frequently and in greater quantity as the weeks passed. The shore, too, was changing in character. It became bolder. Twice more they saw mountains gleaming brightly in the westering sun. Was it granite? mica? or gold, perhaps? They could not explore ashore, but Belnatan duly noted them in his log. White cliffs, too, began to appear; but of greater interest was the reappearance of forest verdure in increasing quantity. They were leaving the desert behind.

Scurvy became manifest again, and the two captains were eager to recruit the health of the crews by a brief stay ashore. But Belnatan's orders were to press on.

Issuing from a deep bay one bright dawn, Ethbaal's little squadron saw *Morning Star* on the southern horizon. She had spent the night hove to off an inhospitable stretch of coast and was coming up rapidly with a fresh dawnwind over her quarter. It was two weeks and a half since she had been left behind.

They ran in company along a coast of moderate elevation, now wooded, now more or less bare. Again the trend was to the north-northeast. The shore was steep-to, with depths too great for anchoring; except for the few nights when they were lucky enough to find harborage, they were compelled to heave to during the hours of darkness. Each dawn, it seemed, revealed a denser, more continuous forest.

While they had been cruising off the desert there had been no sign of human inhabitants. But with the beginning of vegetation they saw an occasional smoke. Now they began to encounter men. At first they saw a single boat fishing in the tideway at the mouth of a bay. As *Morning Star,* leading the fleet, opened the waterway and the Phoenicians and Africans became visible to one another, the natives immediately took fright, paddled shoreward and disappeared. But the sailors encountered more and more of them.

22

They came to a broad, fair estuary some eight or nine parasangs across. This must be the mouth of a mighty river, indeed—as far as the masthead lookouts could discern, the sea was discolored by a turbid outflow. There was a fishing fleet of considerable size. The canoes drew together for protection; then one of them boldly stood out to intercept the Phoenicians, who altered course for the encounter.

The native craft was a dugout, some twenty feet in length. The three men of her crew were, in contrast to the dwellers in the south, tall, very dark-skinned, with abundant woolly black hair. Their language was quite unlike any that the travelers had heard. The climate was now warm, and they wore scanty loin-cloths and ornaments at wrist, neck and ear; the explorers' interest quickened at the sight of ivory pieces and a trinket of gold among the shell and bone. The bearing of the natives was dignified but friendly. Belnatan pointed inland with an expression of inquiry; one native uttered what sounded like "Zaire."

"Probably the name of the river," guessed Mattan. After distributing a few trinkets, the Phoenicians sailed shoreward.

Three parasangs in, the inlet narrowed rapidly to two, then to one parasang across. They had crossed a bank of heavy swells and had stemmed the outward current with increasing difficulty; beyond this point the southerly breeze could not drive the deep, beamy storeship against the rising current. The shores were flat, with mingled palm and mangrove trees; beyond them rose low, grassy hills. They anchored, and Belnatan summoned his captains for a conference.

"This is obviously the largest stream we have encountered since leaving the Nile," he began. "It should be investigated. Reduced, as we are, to only two war-galleys, I hesitate to risk one. We have seen gold and ivory, however, and the Pharaoh will want a report on the harbor and the country; especially since this is the first river we have seen without a bar and deep enough for a trading ship to enter."

"Do you think, Captain, that a trading voyage will ever be profitable at such a distance?" Abdemonos queried.

"Not by the way we have come, certainly; but we do not yet know what lies between here and the Gates of Gades. If the route is fairly direct and if the winds have the same seasonal variation that they have in the ocean to the east, and above all, if the gold here is plentiful, it might be worth while. At any rate the Pharaoh will want full information. If the natives ashore seem friendly, Mattan will take the longboat with a full crew, completely armed and provisioned for four days. He will start upriver on a flood tide. We will beach for scraping while he's gone."

"Captain," put in Asa, "we have a few men ill of scurvy, as you know, as well as the fracture case and Abbarus. As we stood in, I noticed that the point to the south is high and would catch the sea breezes. It is as far as one could get from the swamp airs that breed fever. I think a week ashore might do my patients good. May I land them?"

"It looks like an isolated spot. Permission granted."

"Thank you, sir. After my fiasco on the eastern coast, I hesitate to warn you again of fever; but I am still afraid of it."

"Perhaps you may yet be proved right, doctor. A word of warning is always in order. In fact, I take your caution seriously enough that we'll lie out in the open part of the river, especially at night, and go upstream only as necessary to seek supplies."

On the following day Belnatan took a boatload of well-armed men ashore. There was a sizable village of brush huts, whose occupants were neither friendly nor hostile. A few iron knives were exchanged for fruit and game, but the abundance of ivory was the most welcome discovery. There was gold but in no great quantity. Most important, there was no evident disposition to resist the landing. At the village across the river Abdemonos had a similar experience.

At dawn thereafter, accordingly, Mattan set out upriver, his men rowing on the feeble flood. The vegetation closed about him.

These Negroes were of a very different type from those in the southeast. The men were tall and strong and bore themselves proudly; though not quarrelsome, they had obviously no fear. When one of the sailors, out of his officer's eye, chucked a wench under the chin and proffered a propitiatory axe-head to the nearby male, the African's eyes blazed, he struck the axe-head to the ground and made an unmistakable gesture with his spear.

Asa and his patients, with the two loblolly boys, were landed on the south point, and camp was set up at the head of a low cliff. Belnatan established active communication with the beach, and the monotonous fare was varied with its produce; the parties afloat turned to fishing with considerable success. On the third day Ethbaal bore triumphantly aboard two gold bracelets for which he had bartered an axe. Their intercourse with the indigenes was going well.

On the morning of the fourth day a longboat from *Seawife* made a last visit to the shore for fresh supplies.

While the boat's commander dickered, without benefit of common speech, for what commodities he wanted, two of his oarsmen slipped unnoticed up a jungle trail. As they hoped, they encountered a young woman.

Before they were missed they were again at the boat.

Scarcely had it returned an hour and a half later when a high-pitched keening rang out. Another voice joined in, and another. A few minutes later canoes put out, two headed upriver, one across. Belnatan sent Chelbes with a crew to investigate.

Chelbes' boat was soon returning. The foam flew at her bows, and the stout oars were bending under the urging of her rowers. Something must be very wrong.

Ethbaal, in answer to a summons, joined Belnatan just before the mate climbed aboard to report. "As soon as we got ashore, Captain, I noticed everybody looked sullen. They kept away from us. I followed the sound of the crying and saw a knot of women lamenting over a dead girl. Her throat, even through the dark skin, was blackish—it looked as though she'd been strangled. Fortunately there were few men around. We got back here as fast as we could."

Belnatan's face darkened. "I want the names of the boat's crew that was ashore there. If I find out who was responsible, he dies—for disobeying orders and for jeopardizing the safety of the fleet! The officer will be punished in any case." He paused and thought for a moment. "Ethbaal, I am taking five of your men, and I'll pick up five more from *Seawife*. You will send a longboat immediately, with a dozen armed men, to pick up the doctor's party. You and Chelbes will row your ships downriver and wait where you can make sail for sea and safety if you are menaced. You'll be short of rowers, but the tide is beginning to ebb. I'm staying here aboard *Brant* to try to save Mattan and his boat's crew—if he comes. *Brant's* high sides make her better for defense than the fifties. If I don't join you by"—he hesitated—"by sunset, you will put to sea and resume the voyage. Under no circumstances are you to return here to attempt a rescue. Understand?"

"Aye, aye, sir!" from Ethbaal and Chelbes together. "Good luck!"

Within minutes *Brant* lay alone.

Then the drums began. Out from the inscrutable green forest thudded their beat. The deep tones rolled over the waters, and the day became chill. They beat at the eardrums—they reverberated within the skull—they assaulted the heart in its constricting bosom. The seamen glanced at one another nervously. From near at hand came the rhythmic beat, from afar the throbbing answer, and further yet, unseen hands took up the motif; then close aboard the rumble resumed once more.

On their point, far away, Asa and his men looked up in disquiet.

"Them drums don't mean nothing good, sir," Benadon remarked. "They sound like war drums to me."

It was about an hour later that Ben-Hodesh landed with *Seawife's* heavily armed boat's crew. He informed Asa of what had happened.

"*Seawife* and *Morning Star* are coming downstream, doctor. You are to be evacuated immediately. We haven't room for your whole party in the boat, and Ethbaal didn't dare to weaken himself by sending off two boat's crews, so we'll have to make two trips."

"Can you take all the sick and injured and the guards?"

"Well—I guess so."

"Take them, then, while the two loblolly boys and I break camp and pack the gear. Come back for us as quickly as you can."

"I certainly will, doctor."

The longboat soon disappeared around a point, and the three fell to their work.

It was a half-hour later that Benadon pointed to the south, away from the river side of the headland.

"Look yonder, sir. That don't look like no fishing party to me."

The doctor's glance followed the pointing arm of the loblolly boy. A long canoe with some two dozen paddlers was heading toward the point.

"That's what the drums mean—war," Asa murmured. "They have summoned reinforcements from the coast and from the jungle."

Benadon threw down his hands in despair. "Then we are dead men. We are only three."

There was a sickness in Asa's stomach. So he was to die here, on this remote rock far from the dear hills of Judea, in consequence of the crime of some brutal, self-indulgent seaman! Well, he must say the prayer of the dying. He closed his eyes and his lips moved.

"Here's your armor and weapons, sir," came Esmunazar's voice.

The priest looked around. The loblolly boys had armed themselves and were grimly awaiting the attack.

"I don't want them. We can't win."

"No, sir. But we can kill a few of them before we go down—maybe half a dozen, even."

"I don't want them, I say."

Asa saw Esmunazar gaze at him with a mixture of amazement and contempt. Well, let him. There was not much point in trying to explain. Life was sweet, and if there had been any prospect of success, the priest would not have hesitated to shed blood in self-defense. Or if this were an unprovoked, murderous assault, his anger might well have driven him to such fierce, last-ditch defense as he could make, and woe to the victims! But these wretched heathen were reacting to intolerable outrage, and he could not find it in his heart to vent his bitterness in pointless killing.

At a hail from down on the beach on the river side, all three rushed across in joyful relief—only to have their despair return. For there, to their consternation, were the returned sick! And the boat had again disappeared!

On their way, a patient explained, they had seen fishing canoes clustered about the approaching ships, although at a distance. Fearing lest he might have to fight his way through, overloaded and encumbered with non-combatants, Ben-Hodesh had decided to land the patients once more. Then, seeing nothing of their new peril (for none of them had anticipated attack from the seaward side), he had set out to reinforce his captain.

"In the name of God, no!" the priest exclaimed. "My patients are not going to die! Benadon, Esmunazar, Abdelim"—the last was the least disabled of the sick—"I want a heap of fist-sized stones, as smooth and round as can be, at the head of the path leading up from the beach. On the double! If we can hold them off for a while, Ethbaal will come to our rescue!"

As they ran to do his bidding, Asa cut a length of wide bandage some three feet long. He picked up a stone, fitted it into the bight of the cloth, whirled and let fly at a mark on the beach.

By the time a little pile of ammunition was ready, the canoeists, brandishing spears and yelling, were splashing through the shallows. There was a steep climb from the beach. Asa shouted in warning, waving them back. As they pressed forward, he let drive. It was a lucky shot. The foremost checked, and his left hand flew to his right arm, which dangled uselessly.

Ithobaal cried, "The ships! The ships!"

Asa spared a glance upriver. *Seawife* and *Morning Star* were coming to the rescue! He might delay their assailants long enough to win safety.

His next two shots were clean misses. But then a savage went down, killed outright by a stone to the head.

He had the range now, and his sling was causing casualties among the climbing warriors. They drew back and held a brief conference; they reembarked and paddled to the nearest thicket. Here they cut withes and bound them together to form shields. This done, they attacked again.

But now Phoenicians were landing from the ships; and suddenly the African warriors saw the bluff crowded with enemies. They fled.

"Kill! Kill!" cried Abdelim fiercely, but Asa shook his head.

"I have done too much killing today. The danger is gone, and our patients and ourselves are safe. Let them take their dead and their wounded and depart. I, a priest of Israel, have shed human blood. It is well that I am not of those who serve the Altar at Jerusalem; for if I were, I could never approach it to make sacrifice for my people again."

About noon, the watchers on *Brant* saw Mattan's boat, the rowers pulling hard, appear around a bend in the river. They counted heads— all were present, though a couple of men were obviously wounded. Behind the boat trailed a canoe; then another and another, paddling fast, hove into sight. As the desperate boat's crew neared *Brant,* a crowd of canoes came in view.

The fugitives pulled for their lives and got aboard with scant minutes to spare.

"Ready to get under way, sir!" said Abdemonos.

"Too late," Belnatan answered dryly. "There's no wind in here, and your men cannot fight and row at the same time."

"Do we fight it out at anchor, then?"

"Hopeless. Within an hour the river will be swarming with savages. We have not men enough to hold them off indefinitely. But we can defend the deck for a time. There is a strong ebb running—we'll simply drop down on the current to sea and safety."

"But the ship will be out of command—we'll drift ashore and be helpless!"

Belnatan grinned at him. "You fight your ship, Captain—I'll take her to sea. Give me two men at the anchor cable and one to help me at the steering sweeps, and see that we are defended."

Abdemonos set about disposing his crew for defense. He knew his job.

There was just time before the assault was launched. Like a swarm of bees the warriors attacked. High decks, metal weapons, and armor gave the Phoenicians, man for man, a tremendous superiority; they too knew their jobs. Still, it would only have been a question of time before they were overwhelmed.

Belnatan paid no attention to the tumult. At a wave of his hands, the pair at the bow hauled in on the anchor cable, shortening it until it entered the water at so steep an angle that the fluke could no longer grip the bottom effectively, and the ship began to glide downstream. She approached a sandbar, and Belnatan ordered the helms to port. Hampered by the dragging hook, the ship moved less rapidly than the current. Although drifting backward, therefore, she was, relatively to the water in which she floated, moving forward in it. A ship floating freely could not be controlled by her helmsmen; but the water, running by her steering-sweeps, gave them purchase, so that Belnatan had a considerable degree of control. In a more sluggish current the maneuver would have been impossible.

But here the river was shallower, and the line of the cable was nearer to the horizontal; the anchor gripped the bottom once more at the more favorable angle, and the ship lost way. Again Belnatan signaled, and the sweating pair at the bow hauled in; and progress was resumed. Past the shoal, however, the hook hung almost straight up and down in a deep spot. No longer under control, the drifting ship began to spin. Belnatan signaled again, and the anchor detail let out cable till the hook caught and kept her head upriver once more.

It was hot work at the bulwarks. Each man had some six or seven feet to defend, and where there were no warriors thrusting at their throats, the assailants in the further canoes kept up a rain of stones and darts, not all of which missed their marks. Men began to fall, and red pools marred the decks. Ever more canoes were arriving to press home the attack. It was a nightmare of thrusting, hacking, and screaming. Spears were wrenched from the defenders' hands, and they fought with swords, axes, knives, and even fists.

Hard pressed as he was, Abdemonos detailed two men to climb the mast and lie out on the yard, one to either side. Two more he sent below to fetch ballast rocks. These were then hoisted one by one and dropped overside. They plunged through the fragile canoe bottoms. The small craft were suddenly swamped, and their fighters found themselves struggling in the water. The yard was braced round, and the areas further forward and aft were brought within range. The wreckage prevented other canoes from closing, till the current swept it away, and fresh canoes came to be sunk in turn. Thereafter the canoes kept clear of the waist of the ship, and the fighting became relatively limited to stem and stern. The defenders were enabled to close ranks and concentrate there. It was high time; the Phoenicians at the bow of the ship, first target of the missles from the native reinforcements, were giving way, the Africans had gained the deck and Belnatan and his three men had had to snatch up their weapons and thrust for their lives; but now, reinforced, they drove the dark-skinned assailants over the side.

Now the banks of the river were drawing more widely apart as they debouched into the estuary. The men on the yardarms felt the breath of the southerly air on their cheeks and hailed the deck with the welcome tidings. In a moment the bowmen, working desperately, had hauled the anchor clear of the bottom, then collapsed in exhaustion; the topmen came sliding down the mast and unbrailed; the sail was set and sheeted home, and *Brant,* leaving the war-parties astern, issued triumphantly from the forest-girt river. There were *Morning Star* and *Seawife*!

Abdemonos and his crew gazed at Belnatan in admiration and relief. He had achieved the impossible for them once more.

23

The fleet stood up the coast. With the tremendous volume of the river added to the ocean current, they were making great time past the low shore. On *Brant,* Asa and the three loblolly boys were attending the wounded. There were six corpses in the bow, and two men were breathing their last. Tennes, the mate, lay with a fractured skull; Asa hoped to bring him round. The sailmaker and one other had lost so much blood that recovery seemed doubtful. A barbed spearhead had entered a man's back at an angle and was embedded under the shoulder-blade. Because of its position, it could not be pushed through. While four men held the victim down, Asa made his incision and, working rapidly but blindly in a field of welling blood, cut the bone loose along its inner and lower sides, folded it out toward the shoulder, and dissected free the weapon of staghorn. He replaced the shoulder blade, put in some sutures and applied a pressure dressing.

"You'll do," he told the sailor with a grin. "A civilized man would bleed to death or die of mortification of the wound. But you salts of Gebal are indestructible."

The rest of the miscellaneous stabs, slashes, and contusions gave no great concern.

Morning Star led *Brant* and *Seawife* into a bay. Like most of those they had found on this coast, it opened to the northwest, with a long spit offering shelter from southerly and westerly seas. When the hooks were down, Belnatan boarded *Brant* to hold commodore's mast on her roomier deck. He was joined by the officers of *Morning Star* and *Seawife.*

Mattan had already made his report. He had told of battling upriver against strong currents and baffling eddies; of a confusing maze of channels through swampy lowlands, then hills, some grassy and some granite; of mosquitoes in almost unbearable numbers in the damp, rainy air; of crocodiles, elephants and birds of all kinds; of wretched hovels in riverbank villages; but never a town, never a sign of civilized man. A gorge impassable with whirlpools and eddies had finally blocked their further progress.

"Doctor," Belnatan began, "it is my pleasant duty to commend you, and most highly, for your defense of the wounded. In fact, I cannot speak to well of your prowess and courage. You have saved the lives of several men and increased the confidence of all three crews in yourself and, incidentally, in all their officers. Rest assured that I shall make report of it to His Majesty."

Asa was at once embarrassed and deeply pleased. "Thank you, sir. But your good opinion, is worth more to me than His Majesty's. I am through with Egypt. But there was really nothing else, under the circumstances, that I could do!"

"True. But it was well done, nevertheless."

"Thank you, sir, again. But I think more credit should go to the men with me—Benadon and Esmunazar. They just stood by and took my skill with a sling on faith. To say nothing of yourself and the crew of *Brant*. And Mattan."

"I am not forgetting any of them, doctor!"

There was a press of smiling faces and outstretched hands toward Asa. It was a heart-warming experience, and again, as often before, he felt a burst of affection for these tough, idolatrous, sin-ridden mariners.

"Now, Captain," said Belnatan, "I'll hold commodore's mast."

He questioned Yahu-melek, who had become boatswain of *Seawife* on the death of Chrysor.

"When you took the longboat ashore this morning, what control did you maintain over its crew?"

"I ordered them not to stray off individually, Captain, while I bargained for provisions and the natives collected them."

"But you did not keep them all under your eye?"

"No, sir."

"Did you keep any of them under your eye?"

Hesitation, then, "Yes, sir—Melchi-Osiris."

"No one else?"

"Not all the time."

"Did you know where the others were? Or what they were doing?"

"I told them to stick around the village."

"But you don't know, for certain, what they did or where?"

"No, sir."

"If it weren't bad for discipline, I'd have you flogged. Take your gear to the waist. You are relieved of your boatswain's duties as of now."

A cross-examination of the boat's crew, together and separately, was not fruitful.

Yakinlu was the next to be summoned.

"Your quarreling has become a nuisance," Belnatan told him. "This morning, in the midst of our troubles, you picked a fight. Have you anything to say for yourself?"

"They're all against me, Captain! They call me an eater of camels. I never did like Sidon anyway. Why should I serve Sidonians?"

Belnatan frowned in perplexity; then, "Twenty-five lashes. And I want no more trouble out of you!"

When the doctor made his rounds on the next morning, he was more than gratified by the condition of his patients. They were doing well; even Tennes was holding his own, despite the skull fracture of which Asa was quite certain. All were doing well, that is, but Abbarus; the tormented spirit gazed out of a gaunt, wrecked visage and strove in vain to reassert its old domination of the flesh that closed it in.

There was also a minor annoyance; Tubal, in *Morning Star*, who had been out of sorts for a day or two, had shown up at sick call with an almost unendurable headache and backache as well. He was pale and without appetite. Wine and cold compresses did not seem to help.

That evening two more of Mattan's exploring crew appeared with similar complaints, one of them suffering a severe chill.

"Are you sure you are feeling quite well?" Asa asked the mate, anxiously.

"So far, quite well. Do you think it's swamp fever, after all?"

"It does not look like the swamp fevers I have known from the Jordan valley. The incubation period has been much too short, for one thing—swamp fever takes three times as long to develop. Besides, there has been no fever—though Tamasus is beginning to develop one—and the chill was not nearly as intense as you would expect. It is of course possible, however, that a different type of swamp fever prevails in these parts."

By the second day thereafter all of the men who had gone upriver save Mattan himself were obviously sick. Tubal had developed a moderately high fever; his face had become red and swollen, his eyes watery and irritated, with swollen lids. Pulse was moderately rapid; there was severe pain in back and limbs. The others were obviously taking the same course. Appetites were gone and so was sleep. They complained of a high bellyache, and several were vomiting colorless or slightly greenish fluid.

"This is definitely not swamp fever," Asa reported to Belnatan. "I don't know what it is. If we were ashore, I should isolate them for fear of its spreading; here, isolation is impossible. We can only hope that it is not contagious."

Belnatan nodded worriedly. "Let us hope not. The crew is becoming alarmed. We are lucky, at least, that we don't need the sick men at the oars."

There was indeed no need for rowers. The wind, mostly on the beam, was driving them northwestward along the coast at a good fourteen or fifteen parasangs a day. The weather was fine, somewhat overcast in the mornings but clearing at noon. Occasional showers freshened the hot atmosphere.

The coast was variable, now flat, now marked by low hills, some wooded, some bare. Harbors there were, but often difficult to distinguish against the unbroken green of the beach. The river-mouths were often closed by bars on which the surf broke in fury; nor did they care to risk their health by venturing again into this inhospitable forest. Only the tropic birds, with their incredibly long, incredibly beautiful white tails, cruised at will between sea and shore.

On the fourth day of the epidemic, whether through Asa's ministrations (which he doubted) or otherwise, Tamasus was feeling and looking better; and, to the doctor's inexpressible delight, the other sufferers enjoyed a like remission soon thereafter.

Tamasus continued to improve; not so the rest. Their fevers returned and so did the vomiting. But this time it was not of the same character. The vomitus became a thick, blackish fluid. The whites of their eyes, then their skins, turned yellow. Purple spots appeared; there was slight bleeding from the mouth.

"Make up five ro of powdered dates, five of dart, and fifty of water," Asa ordered Benadon. "Boil down to three-fifths of the volume. We will administer it warm, a mouthful at a time."

It did no good. Indeed, most of the patients could not even keep it down. In vain Asa tried every febrifuge he knew; the fevers became more marked and so did the yellowing of the skin.

"I have never seen anything like this yellow fever before, either in Judea or in Egypt," the doctor confessed to Belnatan. "Nor do I remember anything like it in the medical literature of Sais. I am helpless. These men are going to die and I am of no use to them."

"Don't feel so guilty, doctor," Belnatan comforted him. "I have known many sicknesses and many physicians; I am satisfied that no one could do any better. In other hands, more of the wounded would have perished as well."

The first death occurred on the fifth day, in a coma which passed almost imperceptibly to its terminus. The second man died in convulsions, and a third; the fourth succumbed after a severe diarrhea.

By the tenth day, of the nine who had comprised the exploring party, only Mattan and Tamasus were left alive.

"I am completely at a loss," Asa said miserably, for the fifth time, to Mattan, "even for a diagnosis, let alone a cure. And I have no idea why you alone escaped the contagion, whatever it was."

"I have an idea on the last point, Asa. The mosquitos were ferocious, I had an Egyptian mosquito net that I bought in Sais. With it, I managed to get more sleep than the men. It may be that fatigue wore them down to a point at which they could not resist the miasm or whatever it was that attacked them; being better rested, I escaped."

"It may have been that," admitted Asa.

The Congo was to claim two more victims.

While Asa picked unhappily at his evening meal, a request came that he visit *Seawife* to see a patient. As soon, accordingly, as he had finished eating, he was rowed over to Ethbaal's ship.

"Show him your hand," the captain ordered Sanduarri.

The seaman was reluctant. "It is nothing."

"Show him! He should have complained before but was foolish, and only by chance Ben-Hodesh noticed something amiss."

"How did you injure it?" the doctor asked.

"A spear thrust in the fight," the seaman mumbled.

Asa inspected the curved row of lacerations in the swollen, greenish, putrefying flesh. "That doesn't look like a spear thrust," he remarked. Thinking aloud, he went on, "It looks more like a bite. In fact, only a human bite is likely to mortify in just this fashion."

Ethbaal started. "I want the boat's crew that went ashore on our last morning in the river mustered at once!"

Elimination quickly identified the seaman who had been Sanduarri's companion of the other day.

"Row us to *Morning Star!*" Ethbaal ordered sternly.

Further denial was useless, and under Belnatan's grim eyes the two men confessed.

"Bcause you two had to have a woman," said the commodore, "almost a dozen of your comrades are dead, *Brant* narrowly escaped, the sick would have been massacred but for the doctor, and the whole expedition might have been lost. Three hundred lashes."

Asa burst forth, "But that is death!"

"And they deserve it!"

"True. But not such an agonizing death! Let them be killed quickly!"

"I am going to make an example of them. Every man in the fleet might well have perished through their fault. Discipline and punishment are my province, doctor, not yours."

"I am not questioning your justice, Captain. I'm imploring for mercy. Give them a quick death! As a personal favor to me!"

Belnatan frowned; then his brow cleared. "You have earned a favor, doctor. Very well. Let them be bound back to back and thrown overboard to drown."

"No one," the priest remarked later to Chelbes, ruefully," has said a single word in condemnation of the real crime—the rape and murder of an inoffensive woman. And no one has expressed any sympathy for the many natives whom we killed or wounded only for trying to obtain justice."

The quartermaster shrugged. "What's one barbarian wench more or less, doctor? And for the rest of them, set your conscience at ease. That was only a spark that touched off a ready-laid fire; they were less interested in justice for their dead girl, I dare say, than in the plunder in our ships."

But the priest was no less troubled. "Either way, there were suffering and death, and all for naught! It is a hard thing to try to understand the Divine justice; and to see the Divine mercy, harder still."

Chelbes laughed. "You seek what does not exist, doctor—a divine plan. There is none, because there is no divinity. Life struggles blindly on earth, but there is not even a blindness in heaven. You tell yourself fairy tales because you are afraid of the dark."

"I am afraid of the dark—yes. But it is neither the same fear nor the same darkness that you speak of. Man that is born of woman is full of trouble as surely as the sparks fly upward. His trouble he can bear. But if he bear it in vain, and if there is no scheme and no fulfillment in the universe but only this incessant, hideous struggle of life against life, what does the struggle, or even the victory, avail? Far better that man, and beast, too, had never been created!

"They weren't created. They arose of themselves."

"A fish—a worm—a fly—and a man suddenly arose of themselves! And how does your philosophy explain that?"

The quartermaster shrugged and was silent. But the mate took up the discussion.

"When I was studying with Berossus at Cos, he was visited by Thales, a philosopher born at Miletus (of a Phoenician mother, by the way). He was still a young man, but I remember well the brilliance of their discussion—like sparks flying in the night! Thales believed that life infused all things and that life forms as we know them originated in the sea; and that all living creatures developed, in stages, therefrom."

"By themselves?"

"By themselves."

"I cannot believe it. But let us grant, for the sake of argument, that it could be so. Let us further grant, which I find still harder to believe, that the power of thought and imagination could be self-acquired by mankind, at need. But how—" he flung out an arm—"do you explain that?"

"The sunset?"

"Not the sunset itself, but the joy we take in it. The aesthetic perceptions—our delight in the glory and the colors of the sky and of the flowers—in poetry—in music. There is nothing purposive in it. No materialistic cosmogony will account for it. But there it is, and who would want to exist, on however refined or brutish a level, without it?"

"Ask that of the shades of the men who died of fever, and of those who went before them."

Asa shook his head. This was no answer. And yet, there he was again brought back to the evil and pain that hung like a sombre cloud between man and his quest for God.

He had told himself that he was done with such fruitless theological speculation. But he could not leave it. To penetrate into the essence and purpose of the universe—that was to say, of the Godhead—was the Great Quest, and no other of the goals of man even approached it in urgency. Without it, he was adrift in a malignant darkness, being driven helplessly and hopelessly through pointless suffering to oblivion.

No, he could not leave it. He who wrestles with an angel must endure even until the dawn.

The crews had supped while a beautiful sunset flamed and died and the last light was fading from the seascape. There was no sign of a harbor; they had put a fair bit of water between themselves and the vanishing strand, and Belnatan had decided to spend the night lying to. The current had slackened to a degree that promised little drift during the hours of darkness. The sail was brailed up along the yard; Chelbes set his watchkeepers, and the rest composed themselves for slumber. A cry rang suddenly out:

"Captain! The North Star!"

Morning Star's crew was up and agape in an instant, following the lookout's pointing finger. Sure enough! A lone star glowed faintly just above the horizon. The rest of the constellation, like the Great Wain with its pointers, was below the rim of the earth at this hour, but there above were Cepheus and Cassiopeia. A cheer ran through the ship; *Seawife* was hailed to share in the good news. They had sighted a well-loved beacon, an old and true friend to light their long way home!

For his own professional reasons, as well as those common to all of them, the doctor rejoiced in the prospect of their return to northern waters. It was hard enough to deal with those diseases with which he was familiar; the exotic ills of the south were utterly beyond him.

And even some of the familiar complaints seemed more frequent in these strange seas. Rodent ulcer of the skin, for instance, with whose occasional appearance on nose or brow among the farmers and herdsmen of Judea Asa was familiar, was common, he had learned, among seamen, but commoner yet on this voyage through the torrid seas. He treated it successfully with an arsenical ointment that ate away ulcer and surrounding skin together; the treatment was painful, however, and he would be glad to see the incidence drop to a normal level.

24

The crews gazed about them in delight. They were standing up a magnificent sound. On the mainland a glorious mountain range stretched to where, northwest of them some twenty parasangs, an immense peak towered into the heavens. To the east, a like distance over the blue water, a great island raised its green masses almost as high. In the fine visibility that had followed days of rain they could clearly make out every detail of the landscape for an incredible distance.

For the first time on this voyage the men of Phoenicia looked upon a terrain like to that of their homeland, and something of the joy of homecoming filled their hearts. Despite the heat of the sun, the very sight of those verdant, wind-swept hillsides was unutterably refreshing.

"If this is a bay, Captain," Mattan speculated, "we may have some trouble getting out again against the wind. And it would not surprise me if it were. For some days I have thought that the northerly set of the current was diminishing."

"My observations have been the same. But I don't think it's a bay. And if it is, we'll get out. The sound narrows up ahead—keep her further out toward the island. I would rather moor where there are fewer natives and under a good lee from this southwest wind."

By afternoon it began to appear that the land to the west, now quite close, was indeed an island—the sound apparently opened to the northwest. But Belnatan's gratification was subdued as he studied a bank of dark clouds that had appeared. It grew as its center lightened.

The tornado struck in a white fury. One minute all was calm and quiet after the dying of the breeze; the next, the ships shuddered to a violent blow from starboard. Over heeled *Morning Star* and *Seawife,* their racked shrouds shrieking, over—over—till the sea lapped over the lee gunwales and capsize seemed imminent. *Seawife's* sail split down the middle with a loud report and was reduced to rags in a twinkling. Relieved of the pressure in the sail, the hull righted. Her crew worked frantically to bend a trysail before the wind and rising seas should smash her on the rock-bound island shore.

On *Morning Star,* Chelbes and Tamasus had managed to cast off sheets and braces; she, too, regained an even keel. Her helmsmen were heaving desperately at the steering-sweeps to bring her around and put the wind on her quarter. Belnatan was about to order a storm sail broken out, when he saw the storeship.

Brant was in desperate case. Far heavier, deeper, beamier and there-fore more stable than the others, she had heeled relatively little to the onslaught of the wind. Her spars and rigging had had to absorb the shock alone. It was too much. A jagged stump of mainmast projected some eight feet above the deck; the rest of her tophamper dragged in a sickening tangle over the side. Abdemonos, axe in hand, was already starting to cut it loose, while he bawled to his boatswain to heave both anchors in the futile hope of holding his ship off the hungry rocks.

Belnatan issued his orders calmly and rapidly. "Bodo! I want a heaving line bent to a hawser, and the hawser to our bitts. Mattan! Belay sheets and braces again. Helmsmen! We'll pass close aboard *Brant* on her lee side. The weather side would be better, but we can't make it," the latter aside to Chelbes, who stood next to him on the poop.

"She'll never carry that sail, sir, in this wind!"

"Then she'll carry it away. We can't hope to tow *Brant* under re-duced rig. Bodo, stand by to heave!"

Heeled far over to starboard under the pressure of her sail, *Morning Star* leaped toward the stricken storeship. Her poop deck even with *Brant's* beam, ten feet away, Bodo swung the weighted monkey's fist and gave a terrific heave. Had the distance been greater, he could never have made it against the wind; as it was, the line just reached the other deck. It was snatched up, and *Brant's* men tailed successively on the heaving line, then on the hawser, running with it and returning, one by one, to snatch hold and run again. The bight of the towing hawser was slipped over the samson post; Abdemonos himself ran forward with his axe and parted the anchor cables. There was a frightening wrench; *Brant* spun slowly around and followed *Morning Star* at the end of her line. The two ships, with the gale howling on the port side, stood southwest along the isle. They were quickly passed by *Seawife* under her storm sail.

A ship towing another of her own size or greater is not under the command of her helm. The towed ship does the steering.

So *Brant* strove to keep *Morning Star* and herself from closing with the beach. But she was heavy—far too heavy for *Morning Star* to drag rapidly or efficiently through the water. A vicious sea arose with incredible rapidity. Every wave pushed the two ships a little closer to destruction. Lashed and stung by the driving spume, the helmsmen used all their cunning to hold every bit of their offing. Hard by to leeward, reef, point and islet roared in the surf, reaching hungrily to crunch the frail timbers and planks. About the hulls was a snarling welter of white.

They were just able to hold a course parallel with the beach, neither gaining nor losing distance from it. Ahead lay open sea and safety. Over their weather quarters was the howling enemy. On the lee was death.

Proudly, tenderly, Belnatan caressed the gunwales of his ship. She was making a magnificent fight, and he murmured to her love words that he had never used to a woman. Shackled by that enormous dragging weight at her stern, far greater than her own, she could not rise in time to the mounting seas, and men labored in the bailing well to throw overside the brine that flooded in over the gunwale.

A ship running downwind relieves, by her speed to leeward, the pressure of the wind in her canvas. It often happens that only when she alters course to a reach do her crew realize the weight of the wind. Slowed by her tow, *Morning Star* had little speed with which to diminish the labor of her sail, too large in the first place for a tornado. The rigging was being subjected to stresses which her designer had never envisaged. It could not endure.

But it was not the linen fabric that gave. The yard, arcing forward under the strain, had pulled and chafed the lines that held it to the mast, until they parted. There was a daunting crack in the ears of the crew; as they looked up in horror they saw the yard angling with a break almost through its middle. To carry on so meant the complete loss of yard and sail and destruction in the surf; to haul down the yard for repairs meant to be driven even more immediately onto the beach.

Mattan snatched a line, bent it about his middle, and went up a shroud hand over hand. On the line an oar with which to fish the broken spar was sent aloft to him, and he proceeded to lash it along the yard as a reinforcement. It was dangerous work; if the yard went while he was at its middle, he would drop into the rolling ship and suffer serious injury perhaps, perhaps death; if it went as he worked his way outboard, he would be flung into the sea, and it would be utterly beyond their power to pick him up. There was no time for him to lash himself to the masthead.

But the yard held while he lashed the ten-ell oar along it, and then another, and another. Then he laid below to the deck.

"Mattan," his captain shouted in his ear, "that was one of the finest feats of seamanship I have ever seen. If the wind doesn't get any worse, we'll make it."

The wind did not get any worse. But it shifted. Against them. Only a point—the thirty-second part of a circle—but that was enough. The captains of both ships, looking ahead, knew that they would just fail to clear the next promontory.

Abdemonos went forward in *Brant*. He knew his business. He lifted his axe and brought it down upon the towline. He turned toward *Morning Star* and raised his arm in a last salute. Granite-faced, Belnatan saluted him back.

Freed of her burden, *Morning Star* shot forward toward the sea and safety like a bird released. She quickly lost sight of the storeship in a torrential rain.

Brant turned and started bow first for the beach. Abdemonos conscientiously went through the motions of breaking out and heaving another anchor, and another. They didn't hold her. He hadn't expected them to. With a mind-shattering crash, the ship struck on an outlying reef. In a moment, her deck was being swept by the large seas that had been raised with astonishing rapidity.

There is a strange madness of compulsion that seizes upon the people of a stranded ship. The history of the sea is full of accounts of wrecked ships whose crews would have survived if they had stayed with the wrecks until the storm had blown itself out. They have seldom done so. By boat, raft, wreckage, or swimming they set out frantically for shore—a shore that would be friendly were it not for the raging surf whipped up by a violent wind. And they drown. By whole ships' companies they drown.

So it was with *Brant*. Once she was hard on the reef, her people made frantically for the beach. She was a strongly built ship and still held together when, an hour later, the tornado had subsided. One man fell and broke his arm when she struck. He lashed himself to the wreck and was rescued next day. One man, swimming strongly, gained a quiet cove down along the cliffs and was rescued with the other. The rest drowned or were battered to death by the surf against the iron shore.

Abdemonos perished while trying to rescue one of his men.

So Abdemonos slept with his fathers; and the days of his years were two score and eight; and he was a valiant captain before the Lord.

25

Deep gloom pervaded the two ships. One-third of their number had just perished—three crews out of the original five would never see home again. More selfishly considered, there remained fewer than five dozen men to assist one another in emergencies or to fight off an attack. Worse, their storeship was gone; they were far from their destination, in a land of pestilence and death, with but a month's supply of food between them and starvation, and no possibility of rescue. The officers kept up a show of confidence, with determinedly cheerful words on their lips, but the tight, grim lines of their countenances betrayed the truth that they too knew themselves in desperate straits.

Only Belnatan, that man of tempered bronze, looked, as he was, undaunted. His fleet was reduced by three-fifths? The remnant would suffice him. Their supplies were gone? He would provide a replenishment. He would complete his voyage as he had set out to do—in the teeth of death, disease, hunger, storm, enemies, and untold distances between him and his goal. The sea was his element, and he was its master.

His first necessity was to put the crews to work, not merely for the sake of the tasks that were so urgent, but to give them no opportunity to brood over their losses and the desperate hazards still facing them, and to sink, idle, into a morass of self-pity and despair.

Almost immediately after the rescue of the two survivors, and while a temporary base was being fitted ashore, the wreck had slipped off the reef into deeper water, to lie some six or seven fathoms under the surface. Belnatan set them about salvage operations nevertheless. The galleys could not be risked so close to the rocks, so divers prepared to work from *Seawife's* longboat and from a hastily constructed raft. (*Morning Star's* longboat had been a casualty of the storm; threatening to batter herself to pieces against the slowly moving stern, or to foul the steering sweeps, she had been cut adrift, to be seen no more.)

The proximity of the reef caused the small craft to toss dangerously, and the longboat was with difficulty prevented from shipping water. They sacrificed almost the last of the oil, carefully hoarded for medicinal purposes, and each diver pulled himself down along a weighted line with his mouth full of the fluid. This, released in the depths, floated upward to diffuse itself upon the surface and flatten the breaking waves.

It would have been not too hard to cut away the numerous hatch covers and expose the interior of the hull. The difficulty and danger of the work, however, were enormously complicated by the broken and splintered wood which presented tangled chevaux-de-frise against the divers' assault. Also, the violence that had been inflicted upon the hull had smashed jars and ripped open many of the sealed leather bags, already deteriorated from the effects of the prolonged wetness. The amount of food that could be recovered, therefore, was disappointing. They did succeed in salvaging a quantity of iron, bronze, and copper hardware, weapons and domestic utensils, almost the whole of a knocked-down longboat, and various planks and timbers from *Brant's* sea stores; well weathered wood, in that perpetually humid climate, was a prize. And *Morning Star* and *Seawife* both had need of it; they had been leaking considerably of late, and repairs were in order.

While *Seawife* stood by the diving operations for assistance and defense, Belnatan took *Morning Star* on a survey trip around the island. It was, he found, roughly quadrilateral, some twelve parasangs by six, extending from northeast to southwest; everywhere well wooded and with numerous coves and brooks of good water.

It took only a few days for the divers to retrieve all that, under the circumstances, they found practicable. At the end of that time, the squadron had at its disposal an amount of provision only slightly in excess of their full load.

Belnatan called a council of his officers.

"How far we have still to go," he began, "I have, no more than you, the least idea. By my reckoning we are still at least five hundred parasangs south of the Gates of Gades, and almost as far, perhaps, to the east. How much to the west of Gades Africa extends, I do not know." He deliberately refrained from voicing the possibility that the coastline might force them once more to the south, as well.

"We are by no means in such bad case as one might think. When we started out, each galley carried six weeks' food for her thirty-three man complement. Our numbers have been reduced by battle and sickness, so that the two ships' crews now total only fifty-four men. That means that the same amount of food will now last us for fifty days. With what we have salvaged from *Brant,* we have almost two month's provisions.

"We can sail day and night, from now on—our explorations will be less thorough, but by that means we can make two-thirds to three-quarters additional distance on the same rations. And by cutting rations by a third, we can go still further. By the time our provisions are gone, we may have arrived at Gades and safety. I say, we may—but I doubt it. We have had a favorable slant of wind for a long time. It cannot last. It may already be at an end; the wind has been, for the most part, southwesterly, and we have a lot of westing to make. In fact, the coast just ahead seems to trend toward the west. We also have to work a good deal further north; the wind at the Gates of Gades is prevailingly northerly at all seasons. We don't know how far down the coast it blows. And, as I said before, we haven't the vaguest idea of the length of the journey still remaining; the coast may run directly from here to the Gates of Gades, or there may be an enormous bulge to the westward."

"Then what do we do?"

"We must, as I see it, count on having to get more food. There is still enough seed grain. Against this very contingency we divided it between all the ships. The point at issue is whether to proceed until our provisions are gone, or almost gone, and then hope to live off the country while we grow a crop, or to plant it here and now. In favor of continuing is the faint possibility that we may finish the journey without having to plant, and, more important, that if we should have to plant later, then when we start again with the limited cargo-carrying capacity of the pentekonters, we'll be that much nearer Gades.

"And home, too," said someone.

"On the other hand, we have reasons for breaking the journey at this point. There are the same ones as last year. We have here land that is obviously fertile and well-watered, and at this time we have rain. Ahead lies the desert. How far ahead, we don't know; but we do know much of north Africa to be rainless. Then, too, this is an island, which means we will find only a limited number of potential enemies in it. Since our numbers are so reduced, and since we no longer have a reserve supply of provisions in the storeship, I invite your opinions."

"Captain, we want no more of that yellow fever," said Mattan.

"We certainly don't. But we don't know that the yellow fever prevails here as well as on the mainland. And we don't know that we won't find it further along."

"The yellow fever may be a good reason for stopping here, Captain," Asa suggested. "We found it in the river. There are no rivers here. Yellow fever, like swamp fever, may be a disease of the lowlands. Here for the first time, the mountains come down to the sea. We could establish an upland plantation and hope to avoid an epidemic—hill country is generally healthier than the lowlands."

"A very good point, doctor. And judging by the forest, there is as much rain higher up as at sea level—likely more."

"But as you have said, sir, our cargo capacity is limited." *Morning Star's* quartermaster was speaking. "If we stop off here and raise a crop, we'll be able to carry little more than we have now; and we'll have only our labor for our pains."

"Not correct, Chelbes. As I pointed out before, our original provisioning will suffice our present crews for 50 days. That is on the basis of one and a half sep of food, one sep of firewood and five and a half sep of water (including the weight of the jars) per man per day. If we cut only half of the fuel, that gives us two sep for food, with a hot meal every second day, while the wood lasts. As long as we are sailing a well watered coast, we can cut our water supply by more than half. We can water (and refuel) at least every three weeks. That gives us, say, four and a half sep of food—enough for 150 days. If, further, we add 3000 sep to replace the weight of worn-out ship's and personal gear, and to load the ships a little deeper than before, that's another 70 days' rations—a total of provisions for 220 days. We can always jettison some of it if we run into dirty weather. By the time we come to the edge of the desert, we'll have used up enough provisions, most likely, to be able to carry more water again. If not, we'll just have to abandon some. We can, if necessary, throw overboard armor, most of our arms, and boatswain's stores. Have you anything further to say, gentlemen?"

Silence.

"Then I have decided. We do our planting here. We will put the ships ashore in a bay in the island."

26

Belnatan wrote in his log,

12th day

... *Selected for our base a bay on the north coast, about two-fifths of the length of the coast eastward from the northwest corner of the island. Its mouth is a quarter parasang across, its length somewhat greater. This bay open to the northwest. It is well protected from northeast winds by a long, rocky point that makes out to the north, then to the northwest, on the eastern side. The lee of this point is shoal in its outer, but steep-to in its inner portion. The west shore of the bay is formed by a shorter, wider point and a cluster of rocky islets, some forty feet high. The entrance is clear of dangers. To the east of the bay is a stream of good water. To the west is a smaller bay, also fairly well sheltered, except from the northwest. To gain it from the former, proceed due west, favoring the north side of the channel to avoid a reef making out from the point, along a line from the point on the east side of the great bay to that on the west side of the lesser; when the easternmost of the islets bears due north, turn sharply to port and enter. To the west again is another watering place.*

13th day

Anchored for the night in two fathoms.

Light rain during the morning watch. This day dawned with light overcast, moderate southwesterly wind. Sent Ethbaal with twenty-five men, fully armed and provided with three days' rations, to explore the hills. Foraging parties sent along the beach. Some fish taken, and shellfish. Observed kingfishers, pelicans, and falcons. Light drizzle in the afternoon. Red sunset.

14th day

"This day dawned clear. Scouting parties proceeded a short distance inland. Few natives—one small village."

At midmorning on the fourth day the exploring party returned. Following game trails, Ethbaal had climbed through the verdant forest. He reported an amazing profusion of flowers. The upper third of the mountain bore no trees but was covered with shrubs and grass. He had passed through a tiny village which had been deserted at his approach. At an altitude between 1200 and 1500 ells, he had found some land suitable for their purpose—a natural level clearing in the forest with shrubbery and ground cover but no trees. It was less than half large enough, but it would not be too difficult to clear some of the adjacent soil, and another similarly open field was nearby. The area was well watered and well drained.

They set to work immediately to unload and beach the ships. Despite the health hazards of the lowland and the greater vulnerability of a small party to attack, it was easy to get volunteers eager to serve as shipkeepers rather than undergo the grueling labor of packing supplies and equipment up the hills and clearing the land. These immediately began the construction of a blockhouse.

The rest took the path to the heights.

The island was not thickly inhabited. Its dwellers were of the type they had met on the forested Zaire. The Phoenicians could afford to be generous with the pots, knives, and other gear salvaged from *Brant*. They could not take it away with them, in any case. Good—at least, satisfactory—relations were established. With the Congo misadventure fresh in their minds, the crew did not need Belnatan's fierce promises of dire punishment to make them circumspect in their dealings.

The possibility—though it did not seem great—of pursuit and vengeance could not be overlooked. So Belnatan kept the waters to south and east under continual surveillance from the heights. Paradoxically, the same danger led him actually to encourage, this time, liaisons between the mariners and native women—always, of course, by purchase from or permission of the men. It had happened more than once, as he knew, that some isolated garrison had been saved from massacre by a timely word of warning from an indigenous concubine. Or the girls might have some value, in the event of trouble, as hostages ; while, should they suddenly disappear, that would be enough to put the voyagers on their guard.

Even more disquieting in the ensuing month was the weather. From the first, the abundant rains began to diminish. By the winter solstice, some five weeks after their landing, they estimated that the number of days of rainfall and its amount had dropped to only half of their previous level. If this trend continued, their crop would fail.

It did not continue. The grain, onions and legumes could indeed have done with more moisture ; as it was, however, there was no serious lack, the humid atmosphere prevented undue drying of the leaves, and the great heat fostered almost a forced growth.

Olives were their great lack. Oil for cooking had long since been exhausted. It was to all the dwellers about the Middle Sea a staple which, when absent, was sorely missed. It was, however, replaced in this wise.

Abdelim, one of the shipkeepers, had made arrangements for the services of a tall, well-built wench at his bed and board. So far as his shipmates were concerned, at least, she was even more valuable in the latter function than in the former. For when, one day, oil appeared in his repast, he inquired in pantomime as to its source.

The islanders, he found out (by her demonstration) were wont to gather the clustered fruits of a species of palm tree. These were pulled apart and boiled ; light reddish oil separated and rose to the surface, to be removed by skimming.

Once this had been ascertained and communicated to Belnatan, he detailed men to the preparation of a supply of oil for their voyage ;

there was no difficulty about its procurement. It was of good quality and was welcomed equally by the crew for the larder and by Asa for his drug chest.

One of their wants was met by another of this astonishing group of trees. Their wine had been exhausted, but the sap of the unripe flowers of a certain type of palm, they learned, fermented readily and produced an acceptable if inferior substitute.

Besides these, valuable timber trees—ebony and lignum vitae, as well as the ubiquitous acacia—abounded.

Game was fairly plentiful. There were many types of monkeys; a large scale-covered mammal that apparently ate only ants; an enormous rat, of whose flesh, to the officers' disgust, the natives were very fond. Of animals permitted by the law of his people to Asa there were a species of deer, smaller than a goat, and a gazelle no larger than a medium-sized dog. Their arrows and snares took the dove, the pheasant, and another ground bird hitherto unknown to them. The air was in fact alive with birds—among them parrots and parrokeets, humming-birds more colorful than those at home, the rosy flamingo, and a bird whose call was strangely like the cry of a child.

The priest drew down upon himself some feelings of irritation, especially among the lazier and greedier of the men, in his uncompromising condemnation of all meat that was more than twenty-four hours old. There were some who, gourmet-like, preferred their game rather high. But in all matters of hygiene he insisted upon observing the ritual of his people; and indeed they had to admit that the incidence of gastric and intestinal disorders had been lower than on any other expedition within their experience. Yet, here, as will be noted, the laws of Kashruth—fitness—served them less well than hitherto.

A cat, attaining in some cases the size of a leopard, frequented the mountains; fortunately it was less aggressive than that animal. The asps and vipers were more dangerous, but fortunately no one was bitten.

So in this interlude ashore the voyagers attacked the strange, savage, flamboyant jungle, to wrest their subsistence from its dank soil.

But the jungle defended itself.

It fought back with the steamy heat of the sun. High in the southern heavens at their arrival, the sun advanced day by day until directly overhead it sent its oppressive rays upon the naked, sweating backs of the seamen.

The jungle fought back with vermin—crawling, biting, loathsome creatures that invaded their food—gnawed all clothing and accoutrements of leather or wool—attacked their very bodies by day and by night.

It fought back with itchings and burnings. Half the crew reported at sick call with raw, red, weeping areas of skin that drove them wild with the constant irritation. There was no beer left to be compounded with onion crushed in honey, the favorite prescription of Irj for dermatitis; and the doctor rejected in disgust the revolting smears of human and animal excrement which were so highly esteemed in Egypt. Although skeptical, he procured, with much diplomacy, the milk of a woman who had borne a male child, and boiled cedar shoots in it; but even this favored treatment of the Saite physicians was ineffective. So he fell back on his dessicating powders and fatty applications, which afforded a measure of relief.

The jungle fought with its inexhaustible fertility. It seeded the bare earth between stalks of the growing crop, and backs ached and arms wearied with swinging the hoes, lest noxious weeds compete for the sun and the water needed by the grain and beans.

It fought them with its damp. Rheumatic pains attacked the limbs and stiffness and soreness impaired their agility and made them walk and move like aged men. In vain the surgeon applied his poultice of black knife-stone, fat, honey, and saltpetre, or of locusts ground up in a mortar with honey and spices.

It fought them with diarrheas, severe though brief and non-febrile. At Asa's orders the loblolly boys compounded mixtures of one-eighth onion, one-eighth fresh gruel, one-eighth oil, one-eighth honey, one-sixth wax and one-third water, boiled and administered thrice daily for four days; by which time there would be a remission of symptoms.

And it fought with fever. Asa's advice that they establish their plantation in the hills had been wise, for down at the beach men began to fall more seriously ill. First one, then another, came down with fever after a brief period of lassitude, lack of appetite or headaches. Chills then made their appearance. In some, they developed a forty-eight hour periodicity, the victims blue and shivering violently with an intense sensation of cold, belied by the heat of their bodies under the examiner's hand. They piled on garments but could not become warm. There followed in a hour or so a high fever with thirst, severe headache and sometimes vomiting. A few hours later came a sweat, whose profusion soaked the clothes of the sufferer and the bedding on which he lay, but brought relief. Then ensued a moderation of symptoms, a profound sleep, and a feeling of well-being until the second day thereafter.

"This is the authentic swamp fever," the doctor reported to Belnatan. "I shall try a Babylonian remedy for fever and chills that is highly regarded." He made a decoction of tamarisk wood, mashtakal plant, shalalu reed, alkali, cummin and date wine, all boiled in water with an amethyst ring lent by Chelbes. This was poured over the bodies of the sufferers, which were then rubbed seven times with a mixture of ground makhanu root, sale, ukhkhulu plant and sweet oil.

The results, if any, were not dramatic; and with considerable chagrin Asa so reported to Belnatan. The commodore, however, was less disturbed.

"You have accomplished much, doctor, by your advice that we plant in the highlands; as it is, the disease is confined to a few."

"We are probably fortunate, also," said Asa, "that the rains have diminished; in a wetter season, the morbidity rate would have been considerably higher. The relative drought is a blessing after all."

Two of the patients, a fortnight or so after onset of their illness, lapsed into a coma, one after a spell of delirium, the other after bloody vomiting and diarrhea, and died.

There were of course the usual injuries and illnesses such as had always appeared at daily sick call. Cow's milk and butter, the basis of so many remedies in the pharmacology of Egypt, were of course unavailable.

As heretofore, Asa's abstention from the delights of wenching was the subject of discussion among some of the men.

"Funny that the doctor don't grab himself off a cute little piece. Must be something wrong with 'im."

"Naw, there ain't nothing wrong with 'em. I seen 'im looking at the girls, hungry-like. Mebbe he's scared of females."

"Yer both wrong. It's something about his religion—his god laid a ban on sex, or something. Them Hebrews is queer—they're plumb god-crazy."

"What d'yer mean, god-crazy? If you ask me, they don't care nothing about gods. They just pretend. Ever hear of one of 'em burn his son alive to the glory of his god, like we do?"

"Yeh, I heard of it—that is, to the glory of Moloch, not of his own god. But you're right—it ain't like they do it generally. It's against their law or sumpin'. But the doc's all right, just the same. I'm for 'im."

"Oh, sure—we're all for 'im. He's a first-rate sawbones and a damned fine officer. But like you said, them Hebrews is queer people."

Asa tossed yearningly on his couch and conjured up visions of lost Michal, and lost Tamar, and nameless seductresses fair-skinned and dark. And his manhood and his strength were an agony to him in the scented velvet of the night.

The good grain grew. They had harvested the onions and the beans. Now the barley and the wheat were topping out. Once the labor of clearing the land was behind them, the shipwrights had been set to work on the beach paying a seam here and there with the last of the pitch, replacing an odd timber of plank which was found soft with dry rot or cracked by contact with some coral head or rock. Standing and running gear were overhauled, oars were scrutinized for checks. The shipwrights slept at the tip of a rocky point to windward in the hope that the swamp fever miasm might not reach them. This proved, in large part, successful.

Others were set, with the assistance of the women (whose practiced hands, indeed, did almost all of it) to plait palm-fronds into sails, to spare the last of their fabric. Belnatan set up a rope-walk, and a crew spun new line out of palm fiber. The rest of the men who were not needed in the field were kept foraging—hunting, fishing, digging shellfish, and searching through the forest for its edible fruits.

Seawife was the first to be readied; Ethbaal was to take a look at the mainland shore to the northeast, in the angle of a huge coastal bight, so that Belnatan might chart its main features.

"Do you notice anything strange about *Seawife's* mast, sir?" Ethbaal asked his superior.

"Yes, I do. It has developed the slight twist that they all do, as they dry—but in the opposite direction."

"Could that be, Captain, because it was set up and dried so far to the south?"

"Perhaps. The turn is with the sun, both here and in the north." Belnatan chuckled. "This, too, will not be believed."

But there was even stranger to believe when, a few days later, Ethbaal was back from his survey.

"Here is my chart, Captain. There is an estuary, with a rather narrow mouth, as you see; it is fed by several small rivers. There are shoals upon the coast." He paused, with the expression of a man who has something sensational to announce.

"Well?"

"There was a fight, Captain. We lost a man and killed one. Oh, no—you need not fear attack, sir—they're very different from the people of this island—from all other people, in fact. It was unavoidable—we accidentally cut this man off, and he attacked. Six of my men tried to subdue him without bloodshed—we didn't forget your orders—but he was far stronger than all of them, and mauled and bit them badly, killing one. Really, sir—I saw it, and finally speared him. There was nothing else for it. It took three of us to lift his body. I brought it for you to see."

Belnatan looked into the beached ship, and his eyes widened in amazement. Never had he seen a man who looked remotely like this one. He was huge—moderately tall, but immensely broad and heavily muscled, with stumpy legs but long, terrible arms. The entire naked body was thickly covered with short, blackish hair, except for the scalp, where the hair was reddish. The face was flat and bestial, the nose had no bridge, the forehead low—almost absent—over great brows, and the teeth! The huge, frightful teeth in the powerful jaws!

"I believe you, Captain. It could not be avoided. For once, when we return, our story of a strange race of man will be the truth—but it will be branded a lie!"

27

Far to the north winter was upon the Middle Sea. The halcyon days were gone. No longer did warm blue waters sparkle under the Zephyr's kiss; cold spume blew off the grey wave-tops to the whine of a rising gale. Ships were laying up ashore for the season, and in Sybaris, in

Crotona, in Syracuse, and in Massalia ran the rumor: there will be a massing toward the straits, just inside the Gates of Gades, in the spring. There will be prizes—rich prizes—ships of Tyre with an Empire's ransom riding on their thwarts!

28

The men of Phoenicia, like the Hebrews, had been born in a land of hills; unlike the latter, they spent their lives in coastal towns or on ships (except when in caravan), and took no joy in the rigors of a mountain trail. Among the crews, therefore, only Asa had looked upon the heights of the island in eager anticipation of stretching his sea-cramped legs among them.

It was disconcerting, therefore, when he discovered what inroads the many months of shipboard confinement had made into his pedestrian prowess. He tired, not as quickly as his companions, but much too quickly by his own standards. Frequent trips between farm and shore toughened his calves and thighs. Often from the shipwrights' camp on the promontory he had looked yearningly to the heights.

It was not alone the measure of his strength against their massiveness that he desired. From time immemorial among his people, men had retreated into the hills and the deserts to seek spiritual sustenance where there was little for the body. Although the priest had adjusted well to the crowded conditions of shipboard, he was aware of a growing yearning for a brief spell of solitude, that he might look uninterrupted into his own soul and commune with the Illimitable.

There had been no hostilities with the natives; so Belnatan granted the doctor a few days' leave. Taking some food, a light axe, a woolen cloak, a bit of sailcloth and a fire smouldering in a cow's-horn container, the priest set forth. This was quite different from striding the open hillsides of Judea. Brook beds and game trails gave passage, but in places he had to force a path through the thicket. Drenched in a sweat despite the continuous shade, bitten and stung by insect pests, he climbed steadily.

High noon came and went while he worked a slow upward way. Birds and butterflies of gorgeous colors illuminated the endless green; now and then he glimpsed a monkey peering curiously from a high branch; lizards and rodents scurried across his trail; he passed lumbering tortoises and once shrank back in alarm as a venomous serpent, half a foot long, fell from a tree beside him.

In the waning afternoon he made camp. He spread the sailcloth over a bit of well drained ground, found a little firewood, ate his meal and, somewhat to his own surprise, fell promptly asleep.

It was considerably cooler by morning. He noticed presently that the trees were smaller; then they began to thin. Quite suddenly he came out of the forest.

He emerged onto a hillside of scrub trees, shrubs and grass. A cold wind was blowing. A thousand feet up, the mountain disappeared into a grey mass of cloud, which grew as he watched. He knew from his youth how easily one loses his bearings on unfamiliar terrain in the clouds, so he settled himself to wait out the expected rain.

Hillmen and seamen, who live close to nature, develop great resources of patience; and Asa prepared to wait out the downpour without fretting. He first retired to the forest; sheltered there from the searching wind of the heights, he made his camp.

Toward evening it cleared, and after his supper he strolled again into the open. The well-remembered constellations shone in the alien sky, and he gazed long despite the deepening cold.

Incredibly bright and close at hand they seemed. How far were they in reality? His imagination soared through the realms of space to where creation had set the sun to rule by day, the moon and stars by night.

And beyond the stars? Space, infinite space. But Asa, finite man that he was, could not conceive of infinity, though he strove to do so. Send his imagination soaring ever so high, somewhere it halted, at the surface of an invisible sphere; to dart forward, obediently, again and again, but in a succession of definite, limited bounds. It could not rise in sustained flight. Man can not endure or understand infinity.

No more could he conceive of a finite universe. Beyond the furthest reaches of his imaginings, space must go on. And on. Even though it be empty—void and desolate as at the Beginning—wherever his mind took its stand, it gazed out into further and further oceans of the empyrean. Man cannot conceive of a finite universe.

His brain reeled dizzily from its exploration of the firmament. What could an earthling understand of the skies? "The heavens are the heavens of the Lord, but the earth He hath given to the children of men."

If here were a logical paradox—for surely the universe must be either finite or infinite—it represented, obviously a failure of his human intellect. If the intellect failed at this, why might not the logic which made the evil of the world incompatible with the concept of an omnipotent and benevolent Deity, also represent merely his human inadequacy? In the beginning God had created the heaven and the earth. If man could not imagine the creation, how could he hope to understand the Creator? The priest knelt in prayer with an overflowing heart. "The Lord is gracious to all, and His tender mercies are over all His works."

And yet . . . and yet . . .

The morning dawned clear. Some three thousand feet above him, sharp against the sky, towered the peak. Without breakfasting, the priest set himself to the ascent. He climbed strongly, reveling in the play of his leg-muscles as in his Judean homeland. Stride after effortless stride took him up the steep slope. Behind him lay the jungle, and utterly far beyond and below it the flawless blue of the sea. The brilliant sunlight and his own efforts warmed him in the cool breeze. Oh, it was good to be alive! Alone on the height he strode strongly toward his goal. Eyes, skin, and limbs shared in his delight.

As he climbed, he thought of other mountains he had known—the grey-brown hills of home, the Mount of Olives by Jerusalem, the incredibly jumbled, incredibly waste mountains of Moab across the Dead Sea, and Mount Hermon, high, white, and pure in the north. How remote they seemed! How remote his life among them! How remote the people he had known in the past—Shmuel, the headman of his village, Azariah his teacher, ben Ittai, the ambassador, Tamar his ward—Tamar? No, curiously, Tamar alone did not seem remote. She stood out in his mind's eye like a living being amid a cloud of ghosts.

An hour passed. His climbing was no longer a conscious pleasure. It had become mechanical. He noticed a soaring eagle and wondered at the perfection of the plan which allotted to each creature its appointed path. And he thought, as he had often thought before, of the saying of Solomon, wisest of kings, "Three things I do not understand —the way of the eagle, the way of a snake upon a rock, and the way of a ship at sea." He smiled humorously at the great king's afterthought —"and the way of a man with a maid."

Up, up, up. His climb had become a toil. He was panting in the cold, thin air and every step was an effort. He could feel the labored throbbing of his heart. Well, not much farther to go. The scrub trees were long since gone—the shrubs were disappearing, and only scanty tufts of grass sprouted between the blackish masses of rock. Once he found himself standing stock still, without any recollection of having willed himself to do so; with an effort he addressed himself again to the ascent. A protecting shoulder of rock fell away, and a strong blast of cold wind leaped at him. He snatched the cloak from his shoulder, wrapped it about him and pressed on.

Up, up, up. All greenery was gone from the naked rock. The massive cone lay contemptuous and bare beneath his intruding steps. He forced his left foot forward, his right, his left . . .

If he should fall, now, and break his leg or his ankle, he would die of exposure on this windswept upland. Well, he must not fall.

Up, up, up.

He forgot his fatigue as his head, then his body rose above the summit. In his eyes were the grandeur, the chaos and the terror of Creation. At his feet the summit was hollowed into a huge, bowl-shaped depression, hundreds of feet across. Twisted rock forms lay all about. Beyond, the mountain fell away into a jumble of ridges and chasms, out of which, far to the south, rose a second peak, not quite as great as this. All about the green of the island lay the sea—as placid-seeming, at this distance, as a sheet of polished lapis lazuli. To the east, across the channel, rose the massif of the mainland in a wild mass, culminating in the north in a monstrous heap that towered even higher than the one on which he stood.

Here in these dizzying heights was the raw material of which the world had been fashioned—chaotic and formless, as when it was evening and it was morning on the First Day. And of this stuff, void and desolate, was he to believe that impersonal Nature had wrought the gentle slopes of pasturage and tillage for beast and man? Could this rock, unaided by any transcendent Will, have transmuted itself into the exquisite hue and texture of blossom and butterfly wing? Was he to assume that wood was fuel for fire and that water could quench the flame at man's need without reference to any Divine Plan? If so, he must make a thousand assumptions more, unsupported by any demonstrable fact. But as a believer, he need make only one: after that pristine thunder of "Let there be light!" all things that followed became reasonable, credible and logical.

Almost all things.

The priest began to gather stones. Only in the Temple at Jerusalem was it lawful to make sacrifice, but a prayer one might offer anywhere. He built a rude altar on the mountain peak, and standing before it he began,

Hear, O Israel, the Lord our God, the Lord is One.

It was past noon and time to begin the descent. Asa doubted that he could find his way through the jungle back to the plantation, but the outline of the shores was visible and, tiny in the distance, the curving finger of rock that was the eastern side of their harbor. He would strike downhill, to reach the north coast somewhere to the east of the bay, then make his way as best he could westward along the shore (fortunately it was not a mangrove swamp) to the base. If he erred and came out too far to the west in the first place, the northwest corner of the rectangular island would soon apprise him of his error.

Lest, in consequence of such error, he might be benighted in the fever-breeding lowland jungle, he camped that evening at about the same altitude as the plantation. He reached the bay on the following forenoon without incident.

Now that the harvest was at hand, the rains were returning. There had been just enough sunshine to ripen the ears, and it was with great anxiety that they looked for dry weather enough to let them get in the crop without its being spoiled by mildew.

An interlude of sunshine came along before the critical time was past. Some of the crop was lost; but enough was harvested, dried, and gotten under cover, so that they had a good ten months' supply of provisions.

So Asa ben Abdiel the priest sojourned in the island of the sea with the Sidonians, even with the men of Tyre; and the Lord showed kindness unto them, and made fruitful for them the land; and He blessed them with fullness of grain, of wine, and of oil.

PART iv

THE WESTERN OCEAN

As a bird that wandereth from her nest, so is a man that wandereth from his place. His soul longeth for his habitation; his bowels yearn toward the wife of his bosom and the secure walls of his kindred. But the waters rage between, and the seas roll endlessly to his shore. He hath voyaged and sought, but in vain; he lieth empty and forlorn among the empty isles.

Canst thou by searching find out God? Canst thou learn the completeness of the Almighty? It is as high as Heaven; what canst thou do? It is deeper than the Pit; what canst thou know? Larger than the earth is its measure, and broader than the sea.

1

WITH THE SUN almost directly overhead and the vernal equinox upon them, they took departure from the high northwesterly promontory of the island. The wind had lain in the northeasterly sector of late, but now it returned to its old quarter, and as they stood to the northwest to close with the mainland, it blew on their port beam and drove them at a good parasang an hour. They looked with delight over the illimitable undulating blue to seaward and past the voluptuous bellying of the sails to a magnificent peak that thrust upward far to starboard; they reveled in the kiss of the breeze on their sun-soaked bodies and joyed in the rhythmic scend of the long, lean hulls. It was good, good to be at sea once more!

"Of all the creations of man," Mattan rhapsodized to Asa, "there is none so utterly beautiful as a ship! No wonder that we lovers of woman see a ship in her image. For a ship is female; lovely and as feminine as any devotee of Ashtoreth. But it is not only on account of her grace and her curves of hip and bosom. In her behavior as well, a ship is completely woman. Bedeck her with color and with well-cut new fabric and she moves lightly, joyously as a daughter of the wave. But if she is dirty and foul, she shambles disspiritedly on her shameful way; she shrinks visibly under the glance of men. Tend her devotedly, and she will love you to the end; through all hardships and all perils she will bear you in safety and ask only your love in return. Neglect her, and she will avenge herself; she will turn on you and whelm you and herself in a moment of despair. The caprice of woman is hers; one day you will put hand to helm to guide her through an accustomed measure of the dance, but she will not. A thousand times she has followed your lead, but today she will not and cannot be persuaded. You will wheedle, beg, cajole; threaten, storm, and curse the day that laid her keel; but there is no help for it, she cannot be persuaded; until you are fain to believe, against testimony of your own memory and intelligence, that the evolution is beyond her powers. Yet on another day, under identical conditions of wind and sea, she will perform it as prettily as you please; and with her air of seeming innocence have you half convinced that her former fault was your imagining. When you are with her, you may tire of her exactions and her service; but when you are from her, you are impelled to fly to her arms and lose yourself in the delights of her bosom."

"Very beautifully said," Asa applauded with a smile, "and I can more than half believe it. Can you?"

"Why, no," laughed the mate, "but what of that? Do you believe only the credible?"

"Well and trenchantly put. Obviously the ideal ship lures many a man from the embraces of her fleshly counterpart."

"The ideal ship is like the ideal woman—she lives only in the dreams of men."

"Meanwhile man must be content with what he has."

"Man may well be content with what he has."

"True—true—indeed, true," murmured the priest, his memory flashing back for an instant of anguished sweetness to the wife of his youth. "But while we are waxing philosophical, what of your mariner? Does he deem himself worthy (lubberly seaman, dullard, craven, perhaps, though he may be) of this living, exquisite, idealized creation that floats amid the foam?" And immediately answering his own question, "Even as every youth expects a bride with the beauty of Sarai, the tenderness of Ruth? And, in a sense, he gets one."

"We must all cherish some illusions about ourselves, Asa, or we could not endure our imperfections. Yes, every man in his secret dreams sees himself as the matchless lover, the incomparable hero who flashes upon the favored maid like Gilgamesh in the Babylonian tale, at sight of whom even the goddess Ishtar was seized with a hopeless love. So every sailor plays in his mind's eye, and sometimes, even more or less consciously, in the eye of the world, the master mariner, seawise and dauntless, who struts among the landlings like a stag among cattle. There was something of that in Abdemonos," he added reflectively, "though in truth he made a noble end."

"I suggest," interrupted Chelbes, who, like the rest of them, had been up most of the night making all ready for sea, "that you irresistible lovers and incomparable captains take the con a while and shut up, so that Bodo and I can snatch a little sleep."

The western wind that blows around the world harries the waters of ocean with ceaseless compulsion. It raises the white-capped rollers and sends them charging out of the west. Through wastes of open sea they sweep, to batter in frustration the coast of Gaul and the misty isles of Britain. With them, under the same resistless urging, flows a mighty river in the ocean. Off the coasts of Europe it turns, seeking an outlet to the south; and the wind turns with it. Faster and faster drives the mighty stream; past Iberia, past Mauritania, past the mighty westward bulge of Africa; then eastward again, into the very heart of the great Gulf of Guinea; where it turns back at last and seeks the sunset shores from which it came.

Off the low, wooded coast with its distant surf the discolored sea again betrayed the presence of a great river. The northeast wind had blown for twenty-four hours, and they still made their parasang an hour, as they judged, through the flotsam-strewn water; but their progress westward along the shore was disappointing. It was, of course, hard to judge off this featureless coast; but breakers upon occasional outlying shoals gave them, now and then, a point of reference.

By morning they found themselves off the numerous creek-mouths of a mighty delta. But by morning they also found themselves in a flat calm.

Belnatan wrote in his log:

1st Abib

Faint northeasterly during night. Weather clear this day, flat calm. Still off river delta. Sighting on shallows gives an easterly drift of a good third of a parasang. Very hot. In forenoon, at oars; made good about one-third parasang over bottom.

2nd Abib

Night clear, calm; at anchor. Land wind at dawn good for almost a parasang under sail. Coast still low, wooded, featureless beyond river-mouths. Calm; under oars in forenoon, to keep crews in good trim. Anchored in afternoon, but made about a parasang with sea breeze at sunset.

3rd Abib

Night clear, calm. Moderate southeasterly this day; made good approximately ten parasangs westing.

4th Abib

Southeast wind continued through night, dying at dawn. This forenoon at the oars.

So the flutist piped his tunes, to which the slender oar-blades kept time, and the galleys crept painfully on. The reduced crews were just too few to man all of the oars, even with officers at the helms. It was back-breaking work, pulling the deeply laden vessels in that windless heat; and heartbreaking as well to mark the snail's pace of their progress by the beach. Against the current, a ship running under sail before a fresh breeze makes good, over the bottom, all but a small fraction of her progress through the water; but at the lower speed of oarsmen, in the same time, half of their toil and sweat is expended for naught.

Weeks went by—weeks of slow, slow westing against currents of wind and water. What they gained by painful labor at the oars, they largely lost to the remorseless current; so for the most part, Belnatan forbore to hold them to the rowing, more than to keep their muscles and the skin of their hands toughened to its requirements. Occasionally, when they could almost but not quite lay a course on a south-south-westerly slant of wind, he had them pull a short leg straight out to sea; and then, setting sail, close gradually with the land again, making a bit of westing in the process. It was discouraging work, past low beaches whose sameness made it hard to mark any progress. There seemed to be the same mud, then sand, the same low, green front of the illimitable jungle; and to the south, of course, the same empty ocean, its cobalt blue stretching to meet the hardly more delicate cerulean at the horizon.

They got an infrequent air out of the southeast, or, even less often, the northeast, with the rank, fetid smell of Africa lying heavy upon it; and they made good headway briefly along the coast till it died.

Still the continent stretched endlessly to the west.

2

In the court at Sais the vizier made but slow progress in the complexities of diplomacy. He could, not too frequently, manufacture an atmosphere in which his opponents were slightly more pliable. This was such an occasion.

Ranofer's reception was the big social event of the season—big in size as well as in display. The entire diplomatic corps of the brilliant capital, ranking officers of the army, the elder members of the priest-hood, the aristocracy of Sais—all these and a host of others attended.

It should therefore arouse no astonishment that Tamar found her-self strolling arm in arm with Nektanebis; nor that at this moment the steward announced Epikrates, owner and commander of a squadron of galleys of Phocis. The two ladies were still together when a knot of bystanders asked his news.

"I'm but lately come from Massalia," he answered. "We are doing a good business there in furs and amber from the northern regions. When we can, we get a shipment of British tin or Iberian silver from the galleys of Tyre and Carthage. Gallic slaves are always available. There is a strong demand for Egyptian metalware, cosmetics, and toilet articles."

"Is there any word," Tamar broke in, "of Belnatan the Tyrian and his fleet?"

The Greek flashed a keen look in her direction. "None, my lady, nor do I look for any."

It was shortly thereafter that Nektanebis challenged her companion with a query: "I thought I detected a more than casual concern in your inquiry regarding Belnatan. I suspect that your interest is less in the success of that doughty seaman than in some more personal matter—shall we say, the welfare of a certain physician of your nation?"

"I'll answer that if you'll tell me why you stiffened so suddenly when Epikrates the Phocian was announced."

"Yes, I'll tell you," after a long pause. "Because it means that even if they have succeeded in their project, Belnatan and his crews will never see their homes again." And the Egyptian told Tamar as much as was needful of Engidu's intrigue and her own unsuccessful attempt to thwart it.

3

Not in years had the fleets from Lusitania, Tarshish, and Cornwall suffered so from the onslaughts of pirates. The overworked war-galleys of Gades and Olisipo had to keep the sea almost continuously; and there was hard fighting in the homing convoys. Pirate after pirate was sent to the bottom of the sea or perished in lingering pain in the stocks; but more than a few stout Phoenician mariners were sent to join their foes. On the exchanges of Tyre and Byblus, Sidon, Arvad, and Gebal, fortunes were lost and proud families gave place to upstarts whose shoestring ventures had met with better fortune.

4

Seaworn, ill fed and weakened, Belnatan's fleet was no longer the matchless fighting force that had wrecked Benanu's power. Nothing could have saved it from the Greeks at this time but the hated head-winds that kept it far from home.

They made better progress, of course, in the absence of slow, heavy *Brant*. And there was one other slight gain. In the warm waters in which they were now voyaging, the weed grew rapidly on the sub-merged surfaces of the ships. The labor of the monthly beachings to scrape bottoms was tremendously lightened by *Brant's* absence. The fifties were quickly unloaded at high tide and dragged, if necessary, far enough up the beach for the hulls to be exposed at low water, then refloated on the subsequent high. The emptying of the huge hull of *Brant* had been a far longer and harder job, and even so it had been necessary to careen her to get at all the points of her bottom.

Yakinlu had always been an ineffectual sort of person. Without close family ties in youth, without the facility of making friends in manhood, he had gone his solitary way. People, he believed, did not like him, and the discipline which had been meted out to him on the voyage had done nothing to change his opinion. More and more, he felt, he had become an object of dislike and suspicion to the crew. He saw them gathering in whispering knots to ridicule and revile him. When an officer ordered the rowers to quit soldiering and put their backs into it, he knew that it was for him alone that the admonition was meant. More and more often his ration, he could see, was slightly but definitely smaller than those of his fellows.

When, in outbursts of righteous indignation, he refused to tolerate the injustices which were inflicted upon him, the officers always took a stand on the side of his oppressors. Belnatan himself regarded the seaman with a dour eye; and when, one evening, the officers held a low-voiced conference, it was perfectly apparent to Yakinlu that they were plotting his death. As the conference broke up, the man next to him laughed. No man of spirit could be expected to tolerate the deliberate taunt, and Yakinlu broke a billet of firewood across the fellow's head. At the immediate mast, the captain, as he had expected, revealed his enmity.

"Your offenses have been repeated and aggravated," Belnatan said to him. "One hundred lashes."

The doctor interposed. "Captain, I don't think Yakinlu is responsible for his actions. An evil spirit from God has entered into him, and overthrown his reason. He is a sick man."

Belnatan looked at Asa in irritation. "And how do you propose to deal with a chronic trouble-maker? Coddle him?"

"Yes, sir—he needs coddling. I can assure you that a flogging will do no good."

"In that, at least, you're probably right. Very well—sentence suspended. He is in your hands, doctor—but Melgarth help him if he comes to my notice again!"

Organically, Asa could find nothing wrong with his patient. Neither history nor physical examination suggested any bodily defect, but the man was sick in his soul—of that the priest was certain. Asa could think of only one therapeutic medium that might be useful—musicotherapy. Accordingly, the flutist spent an hour morning and evening, at the doctor's request, playing to the unfortunate the songs and dance tunes of his native Byblos. Whether it was the influence of the music or the evidence that some one took a friendly interest in him, Yakinlu became, for a time, more amenable and behaved himself in better fashion. Although officially on the sick list, he did his share of the ship's work, if not well, at least well enough; and Belnatan had no cause for complaint.

Merbal, a spare man of some fifty years, was another source of worry to the doctor. He had long complained of severe and more and more continuous pain in his stomach region. He had begun to vomit bloody fluid, and his feces had the appearance and the consistency of tar. He was pale, with yellowing of the whites of the eyes, weak, and losing weight. The doctor found marked tenderness to pressure between ribs and navel. There were large hemorrhoids. Signs and symptoms suggested inflammation of the abdomen; the suppression of the flow of yellow bile by the hemorrhoids, Asa reasoned, had caused the disorder. A poultice of flax stems and milk was indicated, but neither of these materials was available.

The weather, aside from the frequent rains, remained fine.

Every evening that it was practicable, Belnatan and Ethbaal worked out of the sea breeze every bit of progress that their craft of years made possible. The land breeze they could use less often; given any wind that could possibly serve, they ran well out to sea at night to avoid any outlying dangers, while lookouts kept anxious watch for the flash of surf on reef or shoal, or the loom of an island bulk, blacker against the blackness of the night. And sometimes, now, the breaking day revealed a smoke-like haze that hid the shore from view, and only warily would they close with it, ears strained for the sullen roar of breakers on the beach.

Somewhere, sometime, that endless coast must turn to the north. With all their hearts they longed for that point; with all their eyes they searched ahead, each dawn, to see it appear. How would they then fly homeward on the wings of this southerly wind! So they toiled and sweltered, smiting the viscous brine under that cooking sun, or running hopefully in spells of favoring breeze, making their slow westing against the stubborn flow; but the wished-for cape was long in coming. The current had quickened, too; sometimes as they strove to pull round a promontory, they were actually set astern.

They began to lose heart.

5

Tamar obeyed the summons to her guardian's bedside. She observed with anxiety the feebleness of his voice and the tremor in his wasted hands.

"I am a very sick man, Tamar," he told her, "and must reckon with the possibility that I am about to die. No, don't interrupt—I have no strength to waste. I did not say that I thought it probable, but possible it certainly is. That being the case, I think I must pass on to you now your marriage gift from your father. I have told Asa ben Abdiel and others that there was none; and indeed it is not a princely sum, but neither is it negligible; and here is the deed that conveys the property. Guard it well."

Malachi did not die, but word of his serious indisposition reached his capital and he was ordered home. Ranofer arranged for his passage by sea to Jaffa, that the strain of a trip by caravan might be spared him. The vizier stressed the reliability of the captain he had chosen. Tamar was emboldened to open the following conversation.

"Do you plan to visit the west again, captain?"

"Yes, my lady; as soon as I have dropped your party off at Jaffa I shall return to Crete for a cargo of bronze and wine." The Lydian looked at her searchingly. "Surely you do not have business in those parts?"

"I have a commission for you, captain. I should not dare to entrust it to you if Ranofer had not praised your honesty so highly. Do you read Hebrew?"

"I can make my way through a Phoenician bill of lading, but no more than that."

"This is a deed to a house in Jericho. You can verify its value and authenticity at Jaffa. I will sign it over to you. In return, as soon as you reach the west. I want you to spread the word among shipmasters far and wide that Lycaon of Ephesus has withdrawn his offer of a reward for the destruction of the ships of Belnatan of Tyre and that he has no further interest in them and their crews. As to why I am doing this, that is my affair."

6

The jungle had a long arm. Its dangers and discomforts were far astern, and the sick were well at last—or reasonably so; but still its vengeance followed. The precious cereals wrung from its reluctant soil at such cost of labor, illness and even lives began to spoil. In pottery jars, in sacks, in woven baskets they deteriorated. The least objectionable was alive with bugs and maggots, crawling and nesting and breeding among the golden grains. Some was slimy with mildew or mold. Some simply fermented where it stood, giving forth a sour, offensive gas that hung like the invisible atmosphere which it was about the ships, except when a beam or quartering wind carried it away. Their incompletely dried or smoked meats slowly putrefied.

They ate the nauseous messes. Bad, spoiled food these tough, enduring men had always accepted as the natural lot of the mariner; what made this harder to endure was the certain prospect of months of it, growing steadily worse and without the possibility of relief.

The water, too, turned rapidly foul and stinking. The ships would anchor and the boats row in to the dangerous surf-swept bar of a river mouth, towing the empty jars astern; and like as not, after negotiating the entrance, they would find themselves in a wide, long lagoon, between jungle shore and an off-lying bank of sand, where the water was brackish and unpotable.

Even worse was the prolonged confinement in the tiny ships, almost a score and a half of men in a space thirty ells, six ells at its widest point, the footing too uneven for walking.

The crews were sullen. Tempers flared. Off the angry southern Cape of Storms the men, worn down by the incessant toil of keeping their ships afloat and fighting toward the west, had been too weary to quarrel. Here, however, the long hours at anchor or under sail when the wind served, allowed them enough rest so that they could vent their anxiety and resentment upon one another. These were the most trying days for discipline, and the skippers had to follow the fine line between indulgence and strictness that would keep the men the cooperating, cohesive force that they had been.

Physically, however, they stood it very well. Not quite all of them, of course. On *Seawife,* Melchi Osiris was causing Asa some worry. The man was obviously failing in weight and strength. His appetite seemed insatiable—he was forever complaining of the ration that sufficed even men considerably heavier than he. The doctor persuaded Ethbaal to allow the seaman an extra half-ration. He seemed always to be thirsty too—he drank as much water as any three of his fellows and urinated accordingly.

"He'd better get over that before we reach the desert," said his captain. "No one gets extra water then."

Tapeworm was a possible diagnosis, and the doctor prepared herbs-of-the-field and natron, baked into a cake with cow's bile. The tapeworm, if present, was not expelled. Nor was pomegranate root any more effective.

Merbal, the patient with the pain in the abdomen, was no better. Asa palpated a firm mass in the belly. He diagnosed a malignant growth. There was little to be done.

The coast had definitely changed character. There were still sandy beaches, but they were broken by numerous rocks, cliffs, and promontories. Some of the coves, Belnatan guessed, with the construction of a jetty could be made into practicable harbors, but he could not see that their development would be worthwhile. But he did catch the gleam of gold in a rare one of the few canoes encountered that did not flee at his approach.

"Captain," Ethbaal said one day, "fever or no fever, I'll have to give my men a period ashore before very long. They can't take much more of this without a chance for rest and recuperation. They are getting stiff and crippled from the long confinement. They're covered with bruises from knocking about in close quarters, and the caked brine on everything makes their cuts and scrapes smart and burn without let-up."

It was almost three months since they had left the isle when with a good beam wind they approached a rocky peninsula. The land about and behind it was low. Rapidly they approached and rounded it—at a good distance to avoid the reefs on which the sea broke heavily and perhaps others which they could not see. Beyond it, the coast fell away at long last toward the northwest!

Exhilaration spread through the ships at the double omen. The favorable signs might be reversed on the day following, but Belnatan ordered an extra wine ration for both crews. There were laughter and singing in the galleys. They had turned the corner! They had beaten Africa! They had won past the Cape of Heat as they had won past the Cape of Cold—in spite of wind, water, bad food, and disease. With started sheets they were running for home!

Chelbes, winecup in hand, pounded Asa's shoulder. "In two weeks— a month at most—we'll be in Gades! You'll see wineshops and wenches such as we haven't had since leaving Tyre! I'll educate you, doctor! I'll break you down, and for once in your life you'll cut loose! Ho, for home!" and he launched into a rollicking and bawdy ballad of the waterfront.

Asa turned incredulously to Belnatan. "Are we really so near the end of the voyage, Captain?"

The captain smiled grimly. "Yes—very near, I think, in distance. But ask Mattan to tell you the Greek story of the short homeward voyage of Odysseus. He was closer to home than we are—but it took him twenty years to get there. However," and his voice lightened, "let them have their moment of illusion; they need it, and they have earned it. If it turns out that I am unduly pessimistic, so much the better."

7

It seemed, indeed, that Belnatan had been unduly pessimistic. Day after glorious day they ran swiftly northwestward along the coast, a fine quartering breeze coming in from seaward. If the brief favoring current no longer aided them, neither was there one in opposition.

The torrential daily rains that soaked their clothes and their equipment could not dampen their joy. On they sped, past beaches becoming gradually more rugged, with frequent rocky promontories and low headlands, occasional rising hills behind, breaking the monotony that had dulled their faces. Coves and streams offered the promise of shelter; but, sea-weary though they were, what enticement had this alien strand for a homeward-bounder? Twice a squall struck viciously offshore, but they lowered sail, rode it out, and resumed course even before it had subsided.

So for almost a week they drove—till it fell calm one evening, and all night they tossed uncomfortably, and all the next day, till Belnatan's impatience led him to risk working close inshore with the oars, that they might be ready to make the most of the expected sea breeze of evening.

And then it struck—their greatest danger, that they had watched for unremittingly for so long. They saw again a lowering bank of dark cloud build up offshore, saw it lighten swiftly in the center, and with a howl of hate the tornado pounced upon them.

There was scant sea-room. Working with incredible speed they got in their sails of woven palm, not without damage to them, and set the linen trysails. To heave to would be to crash in wreckage in surf gone suddenly mad. So northward along the shore they drove in furious career, heeled far over to starboard, bailing frantically as hissing combers climbed aboard and blown spume stung their faces; northward, till the terrifying cry of, "White water! Dead ahead!" was torn from a dozen screaming throats at once, and a reef rose hungrily to bar their passage.

"Wear ship!" called both captains; and wear ship they did, by prodigies of seamanship; turning shoreward and then south again, at the cost of a few hundred feet of precious offing.

Now southward flew the struggling ships, leaping and bounding like panic-stricken horses fleeing over uneven ground; southward through the shouting seas, and the shrieking tempest, and the tortured screaming of the bow-taut rigging.

Along that murderous shore they sped till again through the murk the lookouts spied the flash of white ahead, where rocks smashed the charging seas into fountains of foam and barred their further way.

There was only one thing to do. They wore again, and, closer to the beach, retraced their way until the former peril snarled again before their bows; and they wore ship and reached back southward, and wore, and wore again, until the waves became high and steep beneath them in readiness to break, and that thundering strand prepared to crunch the gallant ships and crews together.

And then, when the surf reached in evil triumph for the keels, salvation came. With a suddenness almost equal to that of its rise, the high wind fell. The rain poured down, the waves subsided quickly, and they seized the oars and pulled to sea and safety.

The coast was becoming increasingly broken. While this meant numerous offshore hazards to navigation, it also meant harborage, to which, on sign of the approach of dirty weather, they might repair. Inland hills between two and three thousand feet high stood out against the rain-washed skies.

A westerly wind on the port bow began to appear—not oftener than one day in three or four, but enough not merely to keep them at anchor for that much lost time, but to cause them to wonder, uneasily, whether more headwinds were in store. Also disquieting was the persistence of the adverse current. No longer did it have the same force as further down the coast, but it was there and might gain strength again.

Worse, the shoaling of the sea now forced them far offshore.

The continental shelf off this section of coast, as the mariners were discovering, has the most gradual slope of all of Africa. To cruise within sight of land, therefore, would have necessitated a course through waters so shoal as to be everywhere dangerous and in places impassable. The commodore therefore directed the helmsmen to steer through what was much of the time open sea with a completely landless horizon circle. They were guided only by the sun and the stars, frequent casts of the sounding line and the wearying chant of the leadsman.

In five fathoms, therefore—a purely arbitrary depth upon which Belnatan decided—they groped their way blindly along that hidden coast. And it was an eerie sensation to lie at anchor in open sea far from any sight of land, while the night-wrapped ships tossed and jerked at their uneasy and unaccustomed anchorage.

Again luck was turning against them. The wind lay increasingly in the west and north, and very soon they were spending three or four days fretting at anchor to one of progress. And still the set of the current—sluggish, more of a menace than a hindrance—was in their teeth.

Belnatan awoke in the dark with a feeling of disquiet. While part of his mind automatically checked the course by the constellations spread overhead in brilliant array, another part explored his sensations to discover the source of his uneasiness. It required less than half a minute for him to be consciously aware of the jerky motion of his ship in steepening seas. He leapt erect.

"We are standing into shoal water, Chelbes!"

A word from the officer of the deck sent the sounding line plunging overside. "Three fathoms—three!" the leadsman reported.

"Put about," Belnatan ordered, and "Hard aport!" shouted Chelbes.

With that most terrible, most sickening of all sensations to the seaman, the ship struck. The captain looked about him by the light of the moon, now in its last quarter. The shoreline could not be seen. She swung around on the unseen barrier, her stern carried down upon it by wind and sea, bumping in the troughs of the waves, till she lay fast upon it with a list to port. Her sail was rapidly brailed up to the yard, the steering sweeps raised out of harm's way. Some of the crew were set to bailing out the water that was coming in through her bottom.

A blast on a ram's horn, meanwhile, had signaled *Seawife* to anchor, barely in time for her to escape the like disaster. A boat carried *Morning Star's* anchor out to the windward, and they tried to assess the damage in the darkness. An inadequate palm-oil light flared in the wind. Seas hissed dauntingly by. Water sloshed thigh-deep in the bottom of the ship, the floatable items of her equipment washing to and fro about the legs of her people. With great toil they shifted cargo aft until Bodo was able to work his way under the bow deck to feel her forward bottom. It was dangerous; if she should roll off the reef, her metal—ballast, anchors, arms and other items—would sink her, and he might well be trapped in the hull and lose what chance of safety *Seawife* could offer.

Presently he reported the portside garboard plank (next to the keel) and the one outboard of it stove in and water rushing in through a jagged hole. Mattan and he went again with armfuls of clothes to wedge into the opening. The flow lessened.

There was nothing more to do but wait for daylight.

That was the danger of running coastwise at night in unfamiliar waters. But it could not be helped. Since the loss of the storeship, it had become necessary to accept this additional hazard in order to stretch their meager cargo capacity to its limit of distance, if not of time.

Dawn broke to reveal a line of treetops barely raised above the landward horizon. Ahead was a cluster of islands large and small. As far as the eye could reach they stretched across the course; and even back along the way they had come, but to seaward of their route there were a couple of islets.

They had struck at half-tide, fortunately during the ebb. They lay along a hog-back reef, high and dry for the time being. About them, as far as they could see, was a maze of reefs and shoals, some exposed, some betrayed by the breaking of the seas above them. They had blundered into a perfect mare's nest in the darkness.

Obviously, the thing to do was to make temporary repairs at once, then beach the ship on one of the islands for a more permanent job. Battens were nailed across the hole, and outside of this framework a double thickness of oil-soaked sailcloth was tacked tightly in place. Over it they nailed boards as protection against any further contacts.

Ethbaal meanwhile was not idle. While Belnatan supervised the repair, *Morning Star's* stores were transshipped to *Seawife*. The latter was dangerously overloaded. A squall now would mean destruction for both.

Seawife's longboat was scouting ahead, buoying the channels toward the nearest islands.

The rising tide floated *Morning Star* a few hours after dawn. She weighed anchor and pulled for the land, her sister ship close in her wake. Belnatan would not willingly subject his ship to the stresses of sail-carrying until he had thoroughly surveyed the damaged hull. She leaked, but not too much for the bailers to control.

Ben-hodesh, mate of *Seawife*, was having no easy time of it in the longboat. Until now it had been a simple matter to pick their way; any waterway that would float the longboat at low water would do for the ships when the tide was in. But at the present high tide he had to proceed blindly, guided only by the questing lead; again and again he blundered from side to side of a channel, was forced into sharp turns, and twice groped his way along a submerged ridge till its ending cleared a way toward his objective. Twice, too, he had to reverse course when he found himself in a cul-de-sac.

Darkness fell with a third of the distance uncovered. They moored for the night, and Ethbaal hoisted a recall signal for his boat.

For *Morning Star's* people it was a miserable night. Besides the watches they had stood during the night previous, all hands had worked frantically for its last few hours. They had toiled all day at the rowing and the bailing; and now, in a bare hull with bottom awash, clothes soaked, cold food and little of it in their bellies, imminent disaster in their minds, sleep was far from them. They took turns at the incessant bailing and watched for morning.

Dawn broke on that confusion of rock, sand and water. Weary as *Morning Star* was, the men pulled oars with desperate energy to reach safety before any coming storm. By the middle of the forenoon watch the wind showed signs of rising. The tide was rising, too—and the higher the water rose, the less effective was the protection of the shoals. Huge seas could not exist there, but even a chop was hazardous in their crippled condition, and breaking waves were all about them. While these helped to point out to Ben-Hodesh many a lurking reef, they were a constant menace to the longboat as well as to the crippled ship. Only these superb seamen could have threaded the maze of those murderous shoals and lived.

In the early afternoon, with a rising wind, they reached a fine, hard, sandy beach on the lee side of an island. Trees had to be felled and trimmed to serve as rollers; the island had to be scouted; *Seawife* had to be unloaded. They missed the tide, of course, but roaring fires and hot food put strength into their bodies again.

It was well past midnight when, the ships beached above high water mark, *Morning Star's* crew turned in. They slept the rest of the night and most of the next day, while *Seawife's* crew took the watch. Then they ate, congratulated themselves on being alive, and slept again.

The only seasoned lumber available was that of the oars. Several of these, therefore, were split to furnish new planking. Green wood was good enough for replacements and was there for the cutting. Their supply of most items of hardware was long since exhausted. The smith had to burn charcoal, set up a portable forge and make new fastenings. Linen strips were dried at the fires (everything was soaked with the heavy rains), twisted into wicking and soaked in coconut fat to serve as caulking material.

And all the while they worked with the sickening knowledge that there were more of the shoals among the islands ahead; whether they stretched for five parasangs or for fifty or more, Belnatan had no way of knowing.

There was also the fear of fever.

They were five days on the island. At the end of that time, Belnatan pronounced his ship seaworthy.

It took three more days of careful piloting, with the lead going constantly, before they were clear of the islands and their shoals. Then followed a week of alternately favorable and adverse breezes, with the trend of the coast turning more to northward. Low red cliffs began to appear and vegetation was definitely less abundant. Again and again they found themselves passing through shoal water, occasionally while out of sight of land. It was an anxious time. Once they waited out a northerly in the protection of a deep river-mouth, once in a tiny cove that made into the southern side of an islet.

The dreaded fever did not appear.

On a day when they were pulling against a light northeasterly air, they raised two islets close together and far ahead. As the hours wore on, these resolved themselves into two hills at the tip of a westward jut, some seven parasangs long, from the coastline. On closer approach, this was seen to form a long, half-moon shaped bay with a sandy beach. Its recurving tip rose in a dark-faced rocky cliff.

From the outer part of the concave curve of the bay, a small point made out to the northeast and offered shelter from all directions. They sounded their way in.

Belnatan, with Ethbaal, Asa and a guard went to one of the two hills, some three hundred feet or more high. It was a two hour walk through the sparse shrubbery and thinly scattered baobab trees. From the hill-top, they saw in the sunset that they stood on a promontory reaching out into the ocean. To the north curved a more barren stretch of almost unbroken beach backed by sandy hills. But it trended also toward the east. This trend might be deceptive—it might reverse itself further on. But Belnatan knew, with the intuition of greatness, that this was the westernmost reach of Africa!

8

In ten days they had made good only some sixty parasangs of north-ing. There was no longer any doubt about it. The southerly wind, that had carried them all the way from the Cape of Storms far to the south, was failing them. They were running into a belt of northerlies and would have to fight the rest of their way along the coast. An occasional wind still came from the southwest to their aid, but more and more it blew against them. The current, feeble though it was, still set to the south.

And the scurvy was back. Their fortnight's stay ashore, for whatever reason, had not arrested it. Men were bruising easily and bleeding from the gums; a few of them had lost a tooth each. Joints were becom-ing stiff and painful.

Belnatan held council again.

"We are making little headway. If we are caught in a storm on this coast, the men are no longer physically able to fight their way through. Our provisions are low. Even if the weather remains good, it is doubtful, at our rate of progress, whether they will stretch till Gades. We passed a fairly large river five days ago, only one day's sail to the south. I propose to turn back and enter, if the bar is practicable. We will wait for a change of wind; if it comes, we will have lost little time, since most days we have to wait out adverse winds at anchor. Meanwhile, we can, perhaps, live off the country, at least in part, and spare our supplies. And the men, I hope, will be restored to health."

Perhaps the bar of the rain-swollen river would not have been negotiable in any case. Perhaps Mattan made an error of judgment. Perhaps the six oarsmen, weakened by months of poor food and fatigue and by incipient scurvy, were unable to keep her head to the seas in a moment of crisis. However it was, the eyes watching from the ships saw, horror-stricken, the longboat turn end over end in the surf and disappear. In that broken sea it was too far to perceive the heads of the swimmers, if indeed any lived in that evil water.

Ben-Hodesh pulled over in *Seawife's* longboat for permission to go in to rescue any possible survivors.

"No," said Belnatan, deliberately turning away from the priest's anguished eyes, pleading for Mattan, "I am not going to risk another boat's crew. They are all probably dead. I will float in a week's supplies, marked by a flag, on the flood tide. Then we will turn south for the harbor under the West Cape without them."

It was a run made in deepest gloom. The deaths of the boat's crew preceded only by a little, perhaps, the end of all of them. They were exhausted and sick, on a harsh coast, with failing food supply, and even the very heaven had turned its winds against them.

Once at their former anchorage, Belnatan set the men to foraging. The fishing was not too good, the game not very plentiful; still, results were far from negligible.

It was almost a week later that, as Asa sat brooding by a fire, he felt a hand on his shoulder, and a familiar voice pronounced his name. He leapt to his feet in sudden joy and embraced Mattan—Mattan, weary, dirty, but alive!

Mattan and Tamasus had been two survivors of the longboat's capsize. They had recovered the supplies sent drifting in, and, guessing the commodore's plans, had started the long trek down the coast on the following day.

It had been slow going, trudging through the sand with the heavy load, but the trip had otherwise been without obstacle. There had been a few crocodile-infested creeks to be forded. Twice they had passed through tiny villages whose few occupants had seemed unfriendly but, eyeing the excellent weapons, had refrained from hostilities. They were bone-weary, not alone from the march, but from the strain of sharing a nightly vigil. But they were safe, and a measure of cheer returned to the encampment.

A month went by. The sun approached from the northward to shine directly overhead once more, but the heavy rains continued. The scurvy disappeared, as usual on a stay ashore. But the wind blew even more steadily from their destination.

Yakinlu had had enough of the blundering and stupidity that marred the conduct of the expedition. More specifically, he resented being sent in search of clams, which he disliked. He was in no hurry, therefore, to obey the order; and when Ben-hodesh gave him an impatient push, his fury plucked out his knife and thrust it straight for the officer's heart.

The blade, fortunately, was vertical and dulled with long neglect. It engaged in the ribs, and a minor cut resulted from what had been intended for a fatal stab.

His trial for mutiny and attempted murder was immediate. Belnatan sentenced him to hang.

Asa pled for him. "Captain, the man is not responsible. It was the evil spirit of his sickness, not his own will, that struck the blow. In the name of justice, I beg you to lessen the sentence and spare his life."

"Request denied. No, not another word, doctor—that's an order." Then, "I wish I could do as you ask."

Mattan was not sympathetic to the priest's outraged expostulations. "Look here, Asa. The captain is deeply concerned with problems of navigation. He is concerned with the condition of the ships. He is concerned with the health of the crew. He is concerned, and very deeply, with the problem of supply. He simply cannot afford to be concerned with problems of disaffection. We are in bad case, and it may become desperate case. If he condones, or appears to condone, a murderous assault upon an officer, there will be no more discipline. And if discipline goes, there will be speedy and complete disaster. Now let me tell you something else. I know, as well as you, that Yakinlu was the helpless victim of something he could not control. The captain knows it. Furthermore, all the men know it. But the captain, in the grip of necessity, was no less helpless. Everyone knew that the safety of all depended on prompt and merciless punishment."

"But he was my patient."

"Wrong. He had been your patient. In any case, Asa, consider this. To all practical intents and purposes, the man died a year ago. And one final point, Asa. Are you quite sure that in your bitterness at Belnatan, you are not transferring your own feelings of guilt at having failed to cure your patient? For which nobody blames you—I have never known a physician to succeed with a patient who had lost his reason."

Bodo baited his hook, cast in the line, and settled himself as comfortably as might be on his rocky perch. Asa did the same.

"As soon as you feel a nibble, doctor, give a yank to set the hook. Then haul in."

"Right."

"Now if only I was doing this back home in Sidon, with a flagon of good wine at my side, life would be perfect."

"I don't suppose you'll be shipping right out again, when we get back?"

"Not for a while. When we're paid off at Sais, I'll have enough to keep me for quite a while—especially if the Pharaoh adds a good big bonus, as certainly he should. I'm hoping that I can keep my boatswain's rank. O' course, that depends on the captain. There are ships enough."

"I'm sure he'll do what's right, and I'm sure you deserve to keep your promotion."

"One thing I'm sure—I ain't going to blow all my money like some of them dumb ratings—and officers, too. Oh, I'll go on a good drunk, all right, for a week or two—I sure as hell need it! And go down the line with the girls. You know, I think I'll get married. On an officer's pay, I'll be able to keep a wife."

What was Tamar doing? Married, no doubt, long since, and likely a mother. For the thousandth time he brought her to his mind's eye—the graceful figure, the pleasant if not beautiful face, the gentle voice . . .

"One thing more," resumed his companion. "If I'm given a choice of signing on for here or Hades, I'll take Hades. But I sure doubt whether there'll be many voyages to this—pull 'im in, doctor! Pull 'im in! Steady—steady—ah, too bad! Like I was sayin', there ain't nothin' here worth goin' so far for. Although we seen gold, further back. And people. But you couldn't hardly go slaving so far away, and make it pay. Although at the rate the Pharaoh was using up slaves on that Nile-Red Sea canal of his, he might have to."

"What do you mean—using them up?"

"Like I said. He was digging that canal, you know. Well, I guess he figgers it's cheaper to replace 'em frequent than to take care of 'em. Anyway, what with the labor in that heat, an' shortage of water—it costs a lot o' money to carry water in the desert—an' little food—he worked over a hundred thousand slaves to death on it. An' it not done."

Asa turned horror-stricken eyes. "Worked over a hundred thousand people to death?"

"Oh, don't look so shocked, doctor—it don't cost much to get more slaves. Africa's full of 'em, an' Asia, too, an' Europe. We can supply 'em at such a low cost per head that it don't hardly pay to feed an' rest 'em proper."

The priest felt sick. He remembered the pity with which he had looked at the wretched slave gangs toiling in the burning sun, the brutal-faced overseers, each with his lash, the aloof and indifferent engineers; but little had he realized the hellish doom that had been unfolding before his eyes. Over a hundred thousand! Dying in the desert of overwork, of thirst, of hunger, of the lash! For this their mothers had born them in travail, their fathers had toiled; lovers had kissed that aching flesh; and now their places knew them no more, and those who had loved them were left in unassuageable grief.

Was the Pharaoh's heart of stone? How could men who in infancy had sucked the sweet breasts of women endure to inflict such wholesale agony on their fellow-beings?

And what of Him above? He heard this swelling chorus of intolerable woe; nay more, from all quarters of the world rang the cry of man's agony, beating in futile despair against the throne of his Creator. There was the crushing, the irrefutable fact; what cleverly analytical dialectic would explain it away?

As to sin, what of the sinless? What of the children, barely coming into knowledge of good and evil, whose lives were hopelessly broken in their morning?

And if this were not so—even if all mankind dwelt as brethren in amity, and even if the beasts of prey turned to the insentient grass for their food; but somewhere a single fledgling uttered a despairing squeak as the hail battered out its little life—would not that one cry be sufficient to darken the radiance of the Lord of the Universe and to rend the very heavens, the guilty judgment-seat of the Eternal? There could be no Righteous One who in his omnipotence permitted the anguish of His creatures. It was a delusion, and a lie.

And yet—and yet . . .

In a towering rage, the captain sent for Chelbes.

"You were in charge of the wine! How do you account for Melchi-Osiris getting at it?"

The quartermaster looked at him stupidly. "Nobody got at the wine, sir—it's been under constant guard!"

"Go and take a look at him!"

Asa went with Chelbes. At the edge of the camp Melchi-Osiris was being questioned by Bodo. The seaman held himself erect by a tree. His speech was thick, his mind clouded; he understood with difficulty and his answers were vague. Bodo turned to them.

"Smell his breath!"

There was the fruity odor of wine.

Something about the drunken man bothered Asa. The seaman had been going downhill for months. He was thin and pale. If, in despair of living to see Tyre again, he had snatched at an opportunity to forget his wretchedness in a last carouse, who could blame him?

But it was not that that made the doctor thoughtful. Certainly the man looked and acted drunk. But that slurring speech reminded him vaguely of something. The odor, too, was somehow different from that of the usual vinous breath—suddenly Asa snapped his fingers. He went and fetched a pot.

By dint of much patient repetition of the order, he induced Melchi-Osiris to urinate in it.

The doctor regarded the pungent-smelling yellow fluid with distaste, while he battled to overcome his reluctance. Some nasty duties fell to the lot of the medical man! Well, it had to be done, and there was no one to whom he had the right to delegate the unpleasant task. So, after a grimace, he raised the pot to his lips and took a sip.

He moved his tongue through the nauseous mouthful, considering. Yes! The seaman's weakness, the loss of flesh, the inordinate hunger and thirst, the present symptoms—they all fitted in! He spat out the disgusting fluid and rinsed his mouth with water, again and again. Then he went to Belnatan.

"Captain, I have just examined Melchi-Osiris. He is not guilty of stealing wine. He—"

"Are you telling me that I don't know a drunk when I see one?"

"Yes, sir. Melchi-Osiris is not drunk. He has—"

"Doctor, I'm getting tired of your interference with my disciplining of the men. I'm telling you for the last time; keep your hands off what does not concern you!"

"I'm sorry, sir, but this does concern me. The man is not drunk. He has the honey-flowing sickness—his urine is sweet, and he is going into coma. You cannot punish him."

"When he has sobered up tomorrow he will be flogged within an inch of his life! In the meantime, doctor, you will confine yourself to your quarters."

"Yes, sir. But he will never sober up. By tomorrow Melchi-Osiris will be dead!"

He was.

9

There was no longer any doubt about it. The southerly wind, that had carried them all the way from the Cape of Storms far to the south, had failed. The autumnal equinox had come and gone, and a fortnight thereafter the wind was still blowing almost uninterruptedly from the north. Day after day, on arising, the men looked eagerly at the weather and cursed vociferously at the adverse breeze. Day after day they scanned the heavens before their night's slumber, seeking some promise of change, and dropped, weary and disconsolate, onto their earthy beds.

Until the day when Belnatan called a council again—not, this time, of the officers alone, but of the entire ships' companies.

"Men of Phoenicia!" he began. "For two months we have been waiting here for the change of season. The rains have practically ceased. Another autumn has begun. But the wind still blows from the north. It may be that the wind will yet change. But I do not think so. I think that we have arrived at the belt of eternal northerlies which blow from the Gates of Gades down the coast of Mauretania. We have been able, in large part, to live off the country. There has been a continuous drain on our supplies nevertheless. We still have about two months' provision remaining. Three possibilities exist. First, we can get under way and proceed, as best we can, to the north. On the exceptional slants from the south that blow once in a while, we can sail, and in the infrequent calms or light northerly airs we can row. Frankly, I do not think that we can get very far. We are too few to man all the oars. And ahead of us lies the desert. We do not know the location of oases or water holes, and I think that we would die of hunger or thirst."

Ethbaal gave a nod.

"In the second place, we can remain here, with abundant water and a certain amount of fruit, fish and game, and hope that the wind will yet haul to the south. Our supplies will last longer. Even if I am wrong, and the southerlies do come to our rescue, they may be too late. If I am right, and they don't come, the best we can hope for here is to drag out a miserable existence; or we might starve if the game disappears, though it will take longer. We have no more seed grain. There is a better choice. Not all of the air in the world can blow forever to the south. Somewhere, it must turn to the north again. Somewhere, there is a favorable wind. We are going to find it. With the skill and courage of Phoenician mariners, it can be done. It will be done."

He paused for effect.

"You are the finest body of seamen alive. With you I can take these ships through any waters in the world. With your skill and your courage we will find our wind. We are going to do what man has never done before. Today we load our ships. Tomorrow we sail—west! We are going to sail straight out into the Western Ocean and keep going until we find our wind! Many of us have sailed blue water before. Ethbaal and I have taken ships right across the Bay of Biscay to northern Gaul, and from there to the Cassiterides in the tin trade. I have crossed the Arabian Gulf many times, and so has Mattan, in the whaling industry. I have sailed from Chaldean ports straight across the Bay of Bengal to India. Some of you have made such voyages, and all of you have crossed and recrossed the Middle Sea. The Western Ocean is simply more of the same. We who have weathered the Cape of Storms can face anything that the Ocean may have to offer. But we must start now—before our food supply is exhausted and before we run into the continual gales of winter. We are doing this because we must. But I would not have it otherwise. Our names will go down in story as the first men who sailed into the sunset reaches of the Western Ocean, to the glory of ourselves and of the navigation of the cities of Phoenicia! I bid you, therefore, be of good cheer and good courage. We have idled windbound long enough. Tomorrow we start for home!"

The two ships had dropped the shore of Africa below the horizon. Heeling well over under a brisk beam wind, they stood into the west. There had been doubting and fear in the darkness of the night; but now, in the brilliant sunshine, a feeling of boundless confidence and pride possessed the crews. The wavetops wore ruffs of the most exquisite of white laces, shading off into the incomparably deep blue that characterizes the brilliant sunlit waters of the southern seas; but in the shadows of the ships this was enriched to an incredible purple. With the steadying effect of well-filled sails there was little roll, and the beam seas raised bow and stern in the same moment, so that there was no pitching; the ships rose evenly to each crest before sliding with steady decks into the trough. Fleecy clouds chased across the sky, and an infrequent flying fish rose under a prow, glided for a few hundred feet through the air and dropped into a wavetop.

The more articulate among seafarers had tried in the languages of many lands—Crete, Egypt, Phoenicia, Assyria—to express the dichotomy presented by what was at once the sameness and the infinite variability of the waves of ocean. One was, barring unimportant variations in size, much like another, under any given conditions; they behaved alike, a ship felt them as like, and they offered the like study in harmonics of shape and motion and in color change from ultramarine to milky white. And yet, when gazing upon the wind-stirred seascape, the eye perceived no two of them the same in any instant of time, nor any one of them from one second to another. They advanced, growing constantly or shrinking, yet never changing markedly in size; they extended to the sides, divided, approached one another at the most obtuse angles and fused in little evanescent pyramids of water; and upon each, smaller wavelets appeared and disappeared, played round each other, climbed on one another's shoulders to collapse in a churning of cream. White, too, boiled the wakes, stretching far astern, and white the bow waves; but above the latter arched the fairy hues of perfect little rainbows, waxing, waning, disappearing, and suddenly once more present to delight the gaze as much with their vividness as with their transparency.

Afternoon wore on and fire was lighted on the sand pans; they supped frugally on gruel, a morsel of dried meat or fish and a cupful of palm wine.

Later, much later, when the last lingering glow had faded from the evening sky, the shrouded sea wore a different beauty. Black now were its waters, and hidden, save for three things: the vague lightening of the tumbling wave-crests close aboard; the sheen and sparkle of phosphorescence in the disturbed water of bow-wave and wake; and the brilliant glitter of the moon-path, longer and brighter as the moon lay lower toward the dim horizon. Above was the aching loveliness of the low constellations, wheeling slowly round the pole-star, faithful in the north. And gently through the planks came the gurgle of the water until slumber stopped the ears.

By day the helmsmen steered by the visible signs of wind direction—

the waves, or the flutter of a tell-tale in the rigging, keeping the square sails full, angled at forty-five degrees across the deck. By night it was simpler, having put the wind on their beam, to sight along stay or masthead to some friendly star, and steer for it as their goal till the revolution of the heavens in a half-hour or an hour brought that star too far to the north, when they would ask of the breeze for another bright point in the firmament. But in the eyes of the ships the anxious lookouts peered incessantly for the darker dark of a land mass or the flash of white water upon a reef.

Morning brought the rising and the bailing out of what sea water had leaked through the hull or come aboard as dollops of spray over the sides; and the setting up of standing and running rigging; and the cold breakfast of parched grain and tepid water; and then the turning to for the cleaning, and the carpentry, and the sail mending, and the many little tasks of the day.

So westward and to the north they reached, day after brassy day and through the arching splendor of the night. Sometimes they could lay a course to west northwest, or even due northwest; but ever further they sailed into the vast reaches of the empty ocean, where never men had been before, seeking their homing wind. And with them fared those far-wanderers, the porpoises, pacing the prows with ineffable grace, the sea-dwelling friends of man; and they saw the great whales. In their dreams the black-tressed women of Phoenicia stretched out their arms and urged them to haste; and the men of Arvad and of Tyre prayed to the dread Kabirim, and to Egyptian Osiris, and to fish-tailed Dagon of the Philistines; for favoring winds and peaceful waters they prayed. The gods seemed to answer their prayers, for the weather was fair and the wind blew no longer from the north; gradually it hauled into the east, and after ten days they had made good, Belnatan estimated, some three hundred parasangs to the northwest. It rained hard most of a day, but the sun shone for the rest of the time. Once they tossed futilely through half a day of calm, and once they hove to for a day's recurrence of northerly wind.

For now the wind began to blow from every point of the compass in turn; and they used it as they could to sail, as nearly as might be, to the north.

As day followed day, however, and the ocean unfolded ring after ring of its emptiness, a certain disquiet arose. True, they had expected nothing else; but the enormousness of the waste of ocean had a daunting impact. The cheery exchanges, the banter, the songs gradually disappeared. While not frightened, or even quite depressed, the men were appreciably subdued. They gazed longingly for the land which they half feared they would not see.

The grain was, even to their unselective palates, almost inedible. Its rate of deterioration had speeded up. Some, in fact, had to be discarded despite their need. When they were two weeks out, Belnatan put the men on half rations.

The nineteenth day was drawing toward its close when the cry of "Land, ho!" sent a wave of eagerness through the ships. Sure enough, there on the northern horizon, almost dead ahead, was an unmistakable speck of something more solid than sea and sky. All night they ran toward it, visible as a point of ruddy light. Daylight revealed what seemed a cluster of islands thrusting their several peaks above the horizon. From one of them a tower of volcanic smoke and flame proclaimed afar the presence of the intruding land within this giant circle of empty sea.

The highest of the peaks, the one with the active volcano, proved to be near the western end of an island which extended to the east as far as the eye could see. A short distance to the west rose a lower, smaller isle. On the southeasterly wind they approached.

From the lofty, smoking peak a red and glowing river of fire led down the side of the cone, gradually cooling and losing its glow among the dark grey ashes which covered miles of hillside. But further east, above the rock-bound shores, the hills were green; and the westerly isle was green likewise.

"This is incredible," Asa exclaimed, "these mountains rising out of the empty sea! Fire springing out of a world of water, and solid rock from among the unsubstantial waves! I almost expect them to dissolve before my vision!"

Mattan nodded.

"There is that about an island that has always invested it with an aura of fascination. Man gazes across water and sees a bit of earth unconnected with the mainland. Small, perhaps, but self-sufficient, it pursues its independent existence, indifferent to the massive continent, the devouring waters, the conquering tread of man himself. Therein, perhaps, lies the nature of its magic. For every man dreams of himself as a lone champion, fearing naught. dependent upon none. Yet no man, in sober fact, is isolated like unto an island; for he is bound to his fellows by a silken skein, and the weal or bane of any is transmitted through the web to each and every of its tenants. Yes, Asa, even I realize that well. The isle, therefore, is the embodiment of a dream which man can never realize in his proper person."

"True," said the doctor.

"When, therefore, you fling a bridge across the strait so that the island is isolated no longer, it loses at once its unique charm. Lovely, pleasant, desirable it yet may be; but its pristine fascination is gone. If this be true of those isles which nestle close under the shore of a continent, as a sort of extension or afterthought to it, how infinitely greater is the aura of mystique about the isles of the sea! Remote and lonely, in mid-ocean they rise. From the time of creation they remained untrodden by man, until the last days; in splendid majesty they rise almost unbelievably from the abyss. They are fortresses, beleaguered by a thousand thousand years of storm yet enduring on their unassailable bulk all the accumulated hate that the frenzied elements can offer."

Asa fell in with the mate's musing. "There they stand, since first the Creator set mete and bound between the waters and the land. Hail, thou Rock, that proclaimest amid the surges the power of the Lord!"

10

Belnatan wrote in his log:

27 Bul

"The volcanic peak is somewhere between three and four thousand ells in height. The coast is rocky and inhospitable. The wind being easterly, we ran westward along the shore for some two parasangs to the extremity of the island; then across a channel, a parasang in width, to the smaller isle, some two or three parasangs, as it seemed, across. This too is mountainous, although not over two thousand ells in height. In its southeastern side is a commodious bay, offering good protection from all sides. The entrance is wide and free of dangers. Here is good water. We landed at this

place at the end of the afternoon watch. Great numbers of hawks
noted. To the northeast, some three or four parasangs, another
isle extends toward the east. This isle is as pleasant a place as
ever I have beheld. The soil seems fertile. Beech trees are abun-
dant. Heavy shower in the afternoon.

28 Bul

Showers during the night. Continued moderate southeast wind.
These isles would make an excellent base for exploration to the
westward; ships could water here and, after the establishment of
plantations, revictual. There is a lake of fresh water in the middle
of the isle. All shores except the one by which we landed are pre-
cipitous.

The two days' interlude ashore was most welcome. A longer time, because of the failure of their food supply and the elemental threat of the advanced season, Belnatan would not allow. In his judgment, they had made northing enough to be able to sail due east and fetch the Gates of Gades, perhaps even the Lusitanian coast above them. He resolved, however, not so much because he doubted his reckoning as to hedge against the possibility of their being carried southward on their way to the Middle Sea, to stand to the northward for two days more when and if an easterly wind should prevent his homeward progress.

It so befell that on the morning when he again put to sea the wind was from the northeast. The ships stood accordingly northwestward. Hill after hill, mountain after mountain they dropped below the horizon, yet at nightfall that sentinel peak still flamed astern. By the following dawn, however, the seascape was once more unrelieved. The wind blew steady, and they held their course through another night.

The following day broke with an angry red sky. The mariners set up their shrouds apprehensively and looked to their lashings. By mid-morning the sky was overcast. The breeze hauled southerly, then circled rapidly into the northwest. It settled there and began to blow.

The sea, leadenly reflecting the sullen grey of the heavens, became restive under the lash of the quickening air. It began to snarl, whitened fangs snapping for prey. Still the wind rose. The sea flexed its muscles in anger; its surface rolled and heaved in great, grey, roaring windrows of water. Rain fell.

The two ships drove before the rising storm. Downwind they rushed, the great square pinions carrying them southeastward in headlong flight; until the strain and the motion became too violent, and the captains, eyeing bending spars, took the sails in and hoisted storm canvas in the evening twilight. The light went out over the expanse of ravenous water under a starless sky, and darkness was upon the face of the deep.

Before midnight they were running under bare poles. Despite the crashing of the storm, they could hear the fearful wailing of the rigging, the groaning of the timbers, the rattle of the flung rain and spume. The helmsmen were assisted by warps towing astern, as off the dread Cape of Storms; but even so, they steered for their lives to keep the ships from broaching to. In the bailing wells the toil never slackened.

Dawn disclosed a maddened welter of surging, white-topped water. The ships had lost one another. Each was flung wildly hither and yon; at times their people had to hold on desperately lest they be hurled overside to perish. With difficulty, a small, soggy ration of island-baked bread and some wine were served round; drenched and shivering, they forced it down.

These were the ships and these the men who had fought a similar gale off the Cape of Storms and won. But the ships were older now, sea-wracked and weary; the men were tired with an eternity of voyaging, they were ill-fed, they were discouraged. And they were fewer. But they battled for their lives as before.

Cold, very cold they were, though this was not the bitter cold off the Cape of Storms. But, then they had been buoyed up by the knowledge that land and shelter were not too far away; whereas now they were in the midst of the emptiness of ocean whose very vastness was a frightful maw for their swallowing.

The great grey immensity of the seas, their endless procession, the sheer unbounded power of them as they shouldered at the slender hulls, filled the heart with helpless terror. Surely these waves were irresistible, and surely they would follow one another to the end of time! The intellect's feeble attempt at rally was overborne, beaten down by the terrific ululation of the storm, the all but overwhelming pressure of the wind, so that each man moved in dumb but anguished despair. But they fought nevertheless.

All day they bailed desperately in a grim fight to stay afloat. *Morning Star* managed to keep ahead of the inpouring brine, but in *Seawife* the level of the bilgewater began to rise. They jettisoned arms, armor, ship's gear, even food, to lighten the ship.

By evening the storm began to moderate. But by then Ethbaal knew that his ship was breaking up.

"We'll have to frap her!" he shouted into the ear of his mate.

Ben-hodesh nodded and dived into the chaotic mass of gear sloshing back and forth in the half-foundered hull. Somehow he came up with some fathoms of stout line. Somehow they got a bight of it, and another, and another, about the bow of the galley (it called for miracles of equilibrium while holding on by the toenails) and passed them aft. The two ends of each piece, coming up from under her bottom at intervals on either side, were tied together. A stick was then passed through a bight in each line and twisted, tightening the line about the hull with terrific force. The planking was thus pressed in upon the frames, the gaping edges of the seams brought together again.

It worked. The weary men kept the upper hand of the leaks. It made little difference, Ethbaal reflected. They had lost *Morning Star,* and his ship, he knew, would never live to see Europe or Africa again. He could not sail her, held together only by pieces of line, for days and weeks across the ocean, with the waves working her every loosened joint and prying relentlessly at every seam. Even if they had food enough—and they didn't.

A pity to perish when they were so near the end of the voyage.

With a brisk wind on her starboard quarter, *Morning Star* stood to the eastward. Except for the watch-standers, her people were asleep, and Chelbes, both yawning and shivering, wished he could do likewise. Well, they'd all be awake soon. The eastern sky had begun to pale a little bit, and the stars were less bright than before. The pallor spread westward through the sky and then downward, and suddenly the ocean, grey and restless, was revealed to his sight. He roused out the cook, then extinguished the light which had been set in the hope that *Seawife* might be somewhere near in the darkness.

The daylight brightened and the sleepers were called. Now the sky was blue again. To west and north the ocean was empty, but southeastward two island peaks rose from a bank of haze.

Suddenly, dramatically, a sliver of gold appeared on the eastern horizon. It widened, rounded above, was the edge of a circle, then a halfcircle; then the full orb of the sun rose from the rim of the world in token of a new day.

Belnatan looked at the two peaks, the glitter of their eastern sides just visible. His food was dangerously low—there had been more spoilage (from salt water), as well as loss, during the gale. To investigate those mountainous shores would cost him a day—which, if another gale caught him, might mean a week's or a month's delay, which might well mean forever. But it was, he supposed—he knew—his duty. The captain suppressed a sigh.

"Helms down and set course for the nearer of the islands. You can just lay it on a reach."

He chewed his half handful of grain. By the time he had set the morning's tasks for the crew, the sun had burned away the mist so that a single long island, with several peaks, lay under his gaze.

By afternoon he was coasting along a forbidding shore. From the beach or from the tops of basalt cliffs green slopes rose to central heights. A shallow bay offered a stony landing place; with the wind in its present quarter, it was a weather shore, and calm. He gave order to land.

Asa stepped ashore and bowed his head.

The waters saw Thee, O God!
The waters saw Thee, they were troubled;
The depths also trembled.
The clouds flooded forth waters;
The skies sent out a sound;
Thine arrows also went abroad.
The voice of Thy thunder was in the whirlwind;
The lightnings lighted up the world;
The earth trembled and shook.

Thy way was in the sea,
And Thy path in the great waters,
And Thy footsteps were not known.

With the dwindling food supply, the captain dared not delay long. On the afternoon following they re-embarked and stood down the coast to the eastward. It was almost dusk when the hand at the masthead sang out for a fire on the beach. Sure enough, there was *Seawife*! The search had paid off. They stood in to the cove and moored.

"We came in at noon," Ethbaal explained. "Our timbers, as you will see, are completely riddled by shipworm, and all the fastenings have pulled in consequence. The wood was in worse shape than our survey had indicated. Being blown back toward the islands was a great stroke of luck. I had given us up for lost when we sighted this bit of land. It was my hope to find forage enough to keep us alive over the winter; meanwhile, we would burn *Seawife* for her hardware and use it to build a new ship, if we could find suitable timber."

"We will have to forage anyway," Belnatan replied. "It was doubtful whether *Morning Star* had enough food to make the coast and keep us strong enough to work the ship when we got there; with your crew, as well, it is impossible. Tomorrow we send out hunting, fishing and food-gathering details."

The island, they soon discovered, was beautiful, with gently rolling hills, lakes, hot springs and flowers even this late in the season. The soil, too, was obviously fertile and could be made to yield richly. At present, however, it offered but little in the way of sustenance. There were no beasts to hunt. Some birds were taken of types known in Europe and Africa, whose scanty, rank and stringy flesh and tiny eggs were of some little use. There was a species new to them, a little grey-green bird with a very melodious voice, too small to be worth taking. There were eels in the short, rapid rivers. Plant food was almost entirely wanting; they did, however, find a sort of plum tree similar to those of the Iberian peninsula, and abundant whortleberries.

The sea was more generous. They took bonito and mackerel and once a tuna. It looked as though they might maintain themselves from this source, but, without more boats, they could not hope to catch and preserve a surplus.

"Never fear," Belnatan encouraged them. "I'll get us our supplies," and he made his preparations.

They had been on this island for a week when their big chance came.

It was mid-morning. The fowling, fishing and fruit-gathering parties had dispersed for their labors. At the camp were a few men, including Asa, variously occupied, when Belnatan, with Mattan at his side, came rushing at top speed downhill toward the beach.

"All hands aboard the longboat! On the double!" the Captain shouted. "Sperm whales offshore!" Mattan tossed some equipment from the beached *Morning Star* into her longboat. A sick but ambulant seaman was sent to assemble a crew to follow in *Morning Star.*

Altogether, they were seven men.

The Phoenicians seldom hunted sperm whales; usually their whale-men sought less dangerous prey. But in their present necessity they could not choose.

Afterwards, the priest's recollections of the chase were confused; and of all his experiences up to date, this was the most incredible. There was the long, tiring pull to approach the prey; then the low-voiced demand from Belnatan, at the steering sweep, to step up the beat; the mustering of reserve strength that he did not know he possessed; the sudden, terrifying glimpse of the huge sea-beast, half as large as *Morning Star,* arcing through the water; the lurch, as Mattan, in the bow, hurled his harpoon; the wild, perilous, exhilarating dash through the waves as the maddened giant took them in tow; the second approach, and Mattan thrusting with his lance for the very life of the monster; the huge impending flukes, Belnatan's cry, "Jump," and, even as he was still in the air, the crash as their cockleshell was demolished; the flurry of the great fish dying in blood and foam; and then *Morning Star's* approach and rescue of (miraculously!) all of them from their wreckage.

There was feasting that evening and for two days thereafter, while Mattan told yarns of the whale fishery, and they smoked and dried meat over the fire and pried out the huge teeth (sperm whale teeth, it seemed, fetched a high price in the markets of the Phoenician cities).

"The merciful Lord has been mindful of us," reflected Asa, gorged and comfortable for the first time in weeks.

Chelbes turned a skeptical eye. "Has he? What, then, of Balsachus' crew, and that of Abdemonus? Were they less righteous than we, less deserving? Unlikely. Was it not chance, then, that blindly cast the dice of life or death?"

"As to the relative piety and righteousness of the four crews, I cannot speak. But certainly little can be said for the high moral principles of Ieoud and his men—who are almost certainly dead by now."

"That only supports my contention that righteousness and wickedness both cut across religious lines and are to be found among believers and non-believers alike. Will you maintain that your own people, despite their vaunted religiosity, live lives of honesty and selflessness?"

It was on the tip of Asa's tongue to answer, "Yes." In general, that was. But in particular—and he remained silent as he reviewed the conduct of one unscrupulous, acquisitive Judean farmer or stockman after another.

Chelbes pressed his advantage. "For that matter, your pious folk are the greatest hypocrites alives. How often have I heard them try to justify, in terms of divine command or sanction, one piece of knavery after another! And so have you."

The priest nodded sadly. "And so have I. But—" and he raised his head—"may not that very unwholesome circumstance serve to support my position? I have never seen a villain conscious of and rejoicing in his villainy. Always there is some attempt at justification—some invocation of a moral law, however perverted, to bolster the rightness of his action. Why should he bother, unless he thereby acknowledges, however reluctantly, a Divine code and a moral order in the universe?"

Now Chelbes could think up no reply.

"For that matter, let us accept, tentatively, your original proposition, that one falls or prospers by blind chance, regardless of one's good works or their lack. Are there not, nevertheless, in your country as in mine, countless people who follow the right as they see it, whether it make for their weal or their woe? Look at Abdemonus—he threw away his chance for life rather than endanger us further. Were he an Egyptian, you might argue that he did it in expectation of a joyous hereafter. But he was no Egyptian.

"No, it seems to me that the whole fabric of ethics rests upon a certain stubborn integrity of the individual, without fear of punishment, without hope of reward. Every shepherd who freezes with his flock through the winters, rather than take his comfort with the plunder of his spear—every pretty woman who sweats in the vineyards rather than take the easier path of the streets—is a living rebuke to the concept that mankind, and indeed all creation, is naught but a whirling of motes of dust swept up by the winds of chance."

To himself, he added, "I hope."

11

The flood of merchant shipping inbound through the straits had thinned to a trickle. More and more of the Grecian seawolves were turning toward home—those of them that were left. Winter was coming. And Callicrates the Lydian was spreading the report from ship to ship that the golden prize for which they waited was no longer theirs for the taking—Lycaon of Ephesus, ostensible tavern-keeper but actual Babylonian secret agent, had withdrawn his offer for Belnatan's fleet.

But there is an old saying that has been current in all of the navies of the world since seafaring began.

"There's always some poor son-of-a-bitch that doesn't get the word."

12

The eastward passage was a boisterous one. The winds had waxed with the advance of the autumnal season, and the ship danced in lively fashion over the sea. For a day and a half it blew hard from the southwest; *Morning Star* was obviously on the outskirts of a full gale, and she had to run with just a scrap of steadying sailcloth.

As heretofore, the wind came at different times from all quarters. With any air on or abaft the beam, they laid a due easterly course. With northeast or southeast breezes, they could obliquely approach the continent. But for two days, while the wind shifted between east and east-northeast, they lay to a sea anchor, hove to, in order to lose as little easting as might be.

More and more, however, the wind was in the northern sectors— which indeed they expected to be so from their knowledge of the prevailing weather off the Gates of Gades. Rain was frequent and the sky more or less cloudy more often than not; but they did not mind such inconveniences, close as they felt themselves to civilization, while the brave ship rushed onward like a weary horse that scents his stable.

And if the imperfectly smoked and dried whale meat grew steadily higher and the remnants of the grain were almost inedible with mold and acid, these too, to these men who had endured so much, were annoyances as trivial as they were temporary.

It was slightly harder to put up with the unaccustomed crowding. There were over forty men aboard, rather less than the normal complement of such a galley; but even at the start of the voyage, the ships had carried a total of only thirty-three officers and men each and had long been reduced, by violence, accident and disease, below that number.

At dawn of the twelfth day, when a man of the morning watch laid up to the masthead to take a look about, he hailed the deck with the cry of, "Land, ho! To the north'ard! A red, rocky bluff, it looks like!"

Was it Africa? Europe? Another island?

Belnatan laid aloft to look for himself. The headland fell off toward the east; ahead he could see nothing.

"Lusitania!" exclaimed Belnatan. "I know this cape! Men, we're in Europe! We have returned to our own world at last! Five parasangs north of here is the port of Olisipo, on the Tagus river! Sixty parasangs south and east is the port of Tarshish! And a day's sail beyond— Gades!"

"We have beaten Africa. We have beaten the boundless Ocean itself!"

13

Usous, factor of the Tyrian trading post at Olisipo, gazed disconsolately at the lean, sickly hogs in his pen. A wretched lot his confrere in Sardinia had foisted on him! He could not feed his staff on them this winter without supplemental purchases; and yet the home office expected him to show a profit! The worst of it was that every possible buyer in the settlement knew about it, so that it would be difficult for him to dispose of them except at a severe loss.

A slave hurried to him. "Master, a vessel is standing into the harbor!"

Usous hurried around to the front of the establishment. Sure enough, there was a ship—Phoenician, of course, by her lines—but what a ship! There was not a spot of paint upon her topsides or spars—or, as she came nearer, upon her decks. Her faded sail was incredibly patched and mended. Now she brailed it up, and out went her oars—oars devoid of any trace of color. He went down to the wharf as she was laid alongside. The seamen who were belaying her mooring lines were almost naked in their rags; they were gaunt and hairy.

"I am Usous, factor, representative of the King and of the Worshipful Company of Iberian Merchants of Tyre. I bid you welcome to Olisipo."

The man who stepped ashore to answer was as ill attired as his crew, and as wild-looking, but he moved and spoke with dignity and assurance.

"Thank you, factor. This is the ship *Doe of the Dawn,* Belnatan of Tyre captain, in the service of His Majesty Necho, Pharaoh of Egypt."

"Whence come you, Captain, and whither bound?"

"Baal-Zephon to Sais. This is a survey expedition around Africa."

"I see, Captain. We shall be pleased to put at your disposal—*where* did you say you'd come from?"

"Baal-Zephon."

"But that's on the Red Sea."

"Correct. I shall want food for my crew—we have none—and clothing. Here is my authorization to draw on the credit of His Majesty." The outlandish-appearing captain relaxed in a smile. "It is long indeed since we have had civilized fare at table."

"I can well believe it, Captain." But not, the factor reflected, this fable for ignorant yokels about having sailed here from the Red Sea. However, the seal on the letter of credit looked genuine enough, and that was all he cared about. "The seamen's barracks are the stone building yonder, and that pretty little frame house is the bachelor officers' quarters. I shall have the cooks turn to at once." Inspiration came upon him—why, this ship was heaven-sent! By the looks of them, and according to what her captain had said, they would not be too discriminating!" I'll venture to say, sir, it's a long time since your men have tasted pork! We have a fine lot of fat hogs—I'll have two killed, dressed and roasted whole, at once, and as many as you like salted down for your voyage to Sais. The shipyard will be available for any work you care to have done."

"Thank you."

"It will be my special assignment to see to it that all your wants are met as completely and expeditiously as possible. Nothing is too good for a captain sailing under the orders of His Majesty of Egypt!"

The fall was near its close and the season of gales was upon them. During that time the prudent mariner left off his voyaging; only the most urgent of errands could induce him to slide his keel into the waves of winter. But Belnatan's impatience to complete his mission as well as the confidence borne of his unparalleled voyage were enough to determine him to hasten on to Egypt before the weather had quite reached its worst.

Had he attempted, however to proceed without allowing his crew time for a good debauch, he would have been faced with mutiny. Nor, indeed, could he find it in his heart to do so. He yielded gracefully to necessity, therefore, and enjoyed, along with his crew, a week of the first complete relaxation he had permitted himself for almost two and a half years. Only the dying Merbal ate and drank little.

They began, of course, with a feast of heroic length and volume. Usous' two hogs and a third were consumed on the first evening, with the kindly aid of sundry ladies of the port who were persuaded to join in the revelry—with the pork eaten in a very under-done state by reason of the eagerness of the famished crew. They enjoyed the good wheaten bread almost as much. And jar after jar of the sweet, dark wine of Lusitania and Spain was brought and emptied. Far into the night ran their carouse. They slept, woke to gorge, drink, and make love some more, and slept again. And again.

Small wonder that after a day or two, more than half of them were nauseated and vomiting, with cramps and with running off at the bowels. But, as every drunkard knows, the ills of drink can be drowned in more drink, and the colossal binge went on.

Olisipo was taken apart and put together again, the wrong way, several times.

To Asa, of course, the flesh of swine was forbidden. In fact, he was not even too familiar with the appearance of pork. He had not scrupled to eat the equally unfit meat of the whale, but that was under circumstances of necessity. Now he had a choice, and he purchased in succession a kid, some lamb, and a brace of squabs on which he dined quite well. Nor did he refrain from looking long upon the wine when it was red, but he did not drink himself into sottish oblivion.

Nor did Mattan. The mate was no abstainer, but most of his exuberance was not of the grape.

"I'm a new man, Asa!" he confided to the doctor. "When we return, our reputations will be made. I think you know that I've never felt free to take the place I can earn. Well, that's ended. From now on, I feel that there's nothing that's beyond my reach!"

If the temptation to drunkenness and to indulgence in swine's flesh had little effect upon the priest, it was a different matter when it came to girls. Chelbes had kept his word and thrust more than one willing and well-favored lass across Asa's path. It was almost more than flesh and blood could bear. But Asa did not deceive himself. Even in the heat of the struggle, he knew that its outcome had been predetermined by his personality and his training.

So the priest went grimly off by himself. He conjured up heated imaginings of Tamar. And a golden girl from the north of Lusitania. And an African. And Tamar. And Michal. And Tamar.

"I don't laugh at your convictions, Asa, as Chelbes does," Mattan said earnestly one day. "You may even be right in your philosophy of sex. But what of it? Relax, man, relax!"

"I cannot relax and enjoy myself at some other human being's expense."

"And we who can, therefore, are wicked men?"

"I would say, rather, that some of your deeds are evil. One of the most perplexing facts in human life is that so many of the good deeds are done by the wicked, and vice versa. How many a time have I seen a judge make a decision which I considered subversive of right and justice; yet I knew him well for an honest and well-meaning man but myopic and of little understanding. And if Abdemonus and his crew were sinners all, it is no less true that we owe them our lives! Life would be far simpler if we could categorize evil men and good, and if we knew that from the former, we could expect evil, and from the latter, good. But it is not so."

"How, then, do you say, is man to attain the good, and to happiness?"

"Happiness can never be approached directly. Happiness is always a by-product—the result of righteous living."

14

It was a sorry-looking crew that set sail for Gades. All through the week the doctor had been dressing broken heads, broken ribs, slashes, loosened teeth, and broken noses. In addition to these and other injuries, he had to deal with the aftermath of the week of intoxication.

The symptoms, as might be expected, were more severe than usual. Well, as Belnatan assured him, and as he knew, they would quickly disappear.

But they didn't. The weakness, the lassitude, the lack of appetite persisted in many of them. Within the next day or two a few complained of chills and fever. The doctor looked anxiously toward their arrival in Tarshish.

But headwinds delayed them on the way and stormy weather held them harbor-bound for days. The symptoms became bizarre. A couple of the sufferers, including Belnatan himself, began to cough painfully, bringing up bloody sputum. A number complained of sore throat, with great pain on chewing or swallowing, and even, in two cases, difficult and painful respiration. But by far the commonest complaint, by the end of a week, was severe muscle pain and tenderness, increasing to the point where the men were practically helpless. Their faces swelled, especially the eyelids. Some had pain in the eyes themselves.

Ashore, Asa would have prescribed hot packs and hot baths; but here he could do nothing for the soreness. The pains in the eyes called for a preparation of xet-tree sap, a farmer's urine, and elderberry, all mixed with honey for a poultice. The priest gladly omitted the second item; the rest, along with other replenishments for his medicine chest, he had procured from the factor.

Only Asa was unaffected. It seemed clear to him, since the only ones spared were the two who had eaten no pork, that the meat was incriminated, especially in view of the gorging that had taken place. He condemned the remaining supply and prevailed upon the captain to have it thrown overboard. For the time being they would eat no more swine's flesh.

Only a quarter of the crew were fit for duty when they met with a pair of Phoenician biremes proceeding up the coast, their two banks of oars on a side flashing in the sun.

"Captain, have you seen a Greek bireme?" one of them asked as the three ships stopped for a parley.

Belnatan, sick and pain-wracked, rallied to answer. "No—what would a Greek be doing here?"

"He was blown westward, we believe from Massalia, toward the straits. He plundered a village and the alarm was raised. We thought we had him, but under cover of a rain squall he eluded us and slipped through the Gates. We're hunting him down. He can't get back past the guard at the Gates; we're afraid he'll land in some little cove with a village, kill the people, seize the supplies, hold up and poke his nose too far into our business next summer. He must have passed you during the night. We'll catch him. Good luck, Captain!"

"We must make all speed for Tarshish," Belnatan said to Asa. "The Greek may be up the coast, as they think; or he may be just over the horizon at sea. We are in no condition to fight."

But neither were they in condition to row, and a calm held them motionless for a day. When on the morrow they got a favorable slant, Belnatan collapsed in helpless agony.

"I can do no more,' he said. "Doctor, you are the only officer still able to carry on. Here is your chart. Try for Gades if you can—or anchor, till the rest of us recover or die."

Ethbaal and Chelbes were moaning and helpless; Mattan was in a coma. Not a man was fit for duty.

Asa went to the mast, weighing the almost superhuman effort of sailing single-handed against the certainty of disaster should a freshening of the light air drag her from her mooring and smash her, helpless, on the beach hard by. Halyard in hand, he scanned the horizon mechanically, and stiffened.

A ship under sail was standing in from seaward on his starboard quarter.

Could it be a friendly merchantman? But no, the season was too advanced for such traffic. One of the pair of Phoenicians of the day before? But they would not have separated; unless, indeed, the Greek had already been caught and crushed; but he knew in his heart that it was not so.

In confirmation of his intuition, the stranger struck her canvas, then her mast; he saw the oars go out, and she surged forward to the attack.

The priest dropped his hands in despair. This was final, irretrievable disaster! Nothing could save his patients from massacre. The Greek could not fail to overtake *Morning Star* on this forsaken coast. And, when he found them, he would—he must—kill. Harried and hounded by Phoenician men-of-war, he dared not leave any witnesses of his passing or he was lost. *Morning Star's* crew, prostrated, could neither fight nor fly. And here came the enemy, as resistless and inevitable as wind and tide, to—.

"The tide!" he exclaimed aloud. That was his hope and his chance! The Greeks came from the tideless Middle Sea—perhaps they had not yet learned the ways of the rhythmic rise and fall of the ocean! He studied his chart. There was another harbor entrance a little way down the coast. An area of about half a parasang square, to be filled to a depth of eight feet by an incoming tide, almost in mid-flood, through a narrow opening—let's see, the current should work out, roughly, at a parasang and a third! And the line of rocks extending out to sea— yes, there was a chance. It would require nice timing. But it was possible that he might be able to decoy the Greek ashore. The Middle Sea sailors knew how to allow for a river current; but it might not occur to them, until too late, that there was often a strong set upstream with the rising tide.

Asa gave one longing glance toward the shore—he could reach it and probably make his way overland to Gades and safety. But that would mean the abandonment of his helpless shipmates, and he put the thought aside.

He rushed aft and seized a steering sweep, and with the gentle westerly filling her sail, *Morning Star* stood along the shore.

The Greek was ready to fight. The Phoenician was a smaller, lighter vessel, and had, as it seemed, a very small crew. There would be no serious resistance. He wanted no survivors to betray his passing.

Morning Star stood along the coast, the Greek oarsmen gaining on her rapidly.

Asa headed his ship for the rocks. Right here his chart indicated a gap with deep water through which he could pass. He flung his weight desperately against the heavy sweep, trying to compensate by a sculling stroke for the lack of a second helmsman. The tide was running strongly inshore; he headed out at an angle against it. Relatively to the inrushing water, he was moving diagonally out to sea, but relatively to the bottom, he was making good a crabwise passage through the gap in the rocks.

The Greek captain pursued at twice *Morning Star's* speed. The Phoenician thought that he would not dare follow her among the reefs, eh? Well, he was no tyro when it came to piloting. He could go anywhere the other could go—given, of course, an ell or so more for his greater draft. Leadsmen singing, he drove into the passage.

"Port! Hard a-port!" he cried in panic. The tidal current was sweeping him inshore, and the landward reef was suddenly, unaccountably under his gunwale. His helmsmen obeyed, but it was too late. With a shock, his ship struck—and water poured into a hole in her side.

Whether or not he managed to beach his ship would make no difference. He would, he knew, be given no chance to repair her. His men could swim ashore. But they would never see the green hills and sparkling waters of Greece again.

Morning Star swept on, passing in a huge arc along the south Iberian coast. The doctor was utterly weary but dared not rest—he must get to harborage and help. Day waned and the darkness was upon him. Through the night he steered that ship of the sick and the dying over that weird ocean.

The first man died at dawn.

Through the interminable day Asa stood to the helm, supporting as he might his wearied legs against the bulwark. Noon came and went; he snatched a drink and a bite as he could, but dared not leave the ship to herself long enough to tend the sick.

Toward evening they arrived off Gades. Asa, drunk with fatigue, opened the scroll of the "Periplus" and read:

"When entering Gades Harbor from the northwest, keep one half parasang off the western point. Enter fairly close to the western side of the two-parasangs-wide harbor mouth; then pass inshore of the line of reefs and shoals, keeping a cluster of trees on an islet in line with a rounded hill to the north, till a long, north-south sandbar begins to bear due east. Then steer southeast to the town."

The wind shifted northwest, and it breezed up as he approached the harbor mouth. He could not point high enough to make the entrance with the east-running tide.

"I must have help," he called, "to make harbor! Who can pull on a line? Sheets and braces! Trim sail!"

There was weight in the wind, and it was touch and go whether she could be handled, well as the square sail balanced.

It was Merbal who raised himself with difficulty. He threw his weight upon the port brace and the yard swung round. They belayed the lines again and stood into harbor. Merbal vomited blood and died.

With the last of the daylight, *Morning Star* reached Gades and help. Asa, worn out with an unintermitted three-day vigil, turned over the care of his ship to the port captain and of his sick to the resident physician.

But Mattan, Asa found, was in coma no longer. Despite the interdiction against priestly contact with a corpse, Asa clasped his dead friend's head to his bosom and sobbed aloud.

15

It was the first day of spring. Deceptively bright sunshine flooded the south Iberian coast. From the harbor of Gades, *Morning Star* stood east for the entrance to the Middle Sea. Belnatan would not wait for the protection of the slower convoy that was ready to leave, but made for Egypt, seven hundred parasangs away, with all speed.

To his shipmates, the conclusion of the voyage would mean, presumably, reward, and then a series of new voyages—shorter, easier, and less perilous, to be sure, but essentially without a break in their way of life. But to Asa it was to be the end of an interlude utterly removed from the normal course of his days. He tried to formulate plans, but the future, even in his musings, remained in shadow.

Only one image stood sharp and clear-cut in his mind's eye. Tamar. He would see her—he found his heart beating a little faster at the prospect—to wish her happiness with the husband and child or two that by now, almost certainly, she had. Or so he told himself.

These were familiar waters with known and reliable ports of refuge and supply. The season was not yet settled, and twice they waited weatherbound in harbor, and once ran before a blow in open sea. But the voyage was relatively uneventful.

West of Egypt, the north African coast was almost wholly Phoenician. They made many halts for water and supplies. They rested for two days at Carthage while a Levanter blew itself out; shortly thereafter, pulling their hearts out in a calm, they made harbor at Melita, between Sicily and the African coast, a few lengths ahead of a piratical squadron of Syracusans.

They made good time and entered the mouth of the Nile some six weeks out of Gades.

16

As the ship lay moored to the bank that evening, Asa stepped ashore to stretch his legs. Belnatan joined him.

"How soon do you start for Judea, doctor?"

"As soon after our arrival at Sais as I can secure transportation, Captain."

"You might think about coming with me to Tyre. A great career awaits you there, Asa." The captain did not often, the doctor reflected, address him in this intimate fashion. "In Judea you will be only one more physician—perhaps, even, by virtue of your study in Sais, a prominent one. Judea, though, is a poor country."

"It is," Asa admitted.

"But in Tyre you can rise to the top of your profession. We have brought back about a quarter of the men who sailed with us from Baal-Zephon. There is no doubt in my mind that, if it had not been for your sanitary discipline, our numbers would have been weakened to a point at which we should have been too few for any to survive. For that alone I could recommend you highly—and my word has weight in Tyre. But in addition you have achieved as much understanding of seamanship in these two and a half years as many men do in a lifetime. As I have said before, your escape from the Greek galley was masterful. You can sail with me as a master's mate for a year or two, spend a like time in a shipyard, and then qualify for an independent command. Or you can hope to become Chief Surgeon of all the fleets of Tyre, and stand at the left hand of the king himself! Both fame and wealth are waiting for you. And if you are inclined toward domesticity, there is hardly a family in Tyre that will not give you a daughter. Settle among us and get your sons!"

"I am honored—very, very deeply honored, Captain—and I should be telling less than the truth if I said I was not pleased that you think so well of me." The words, Asa felt, were stilted; but it is always difficult to reply gracefully to direct praise.

"But I have been away from my own land for almost four years. I have a great longing for the hills of Judea. I do not think that I could settle happily in a foreign land."

"You may have no choice, doctor. What I am about to say may sound unpleasant, but consider the facts of international life rationally. Judea is a tiny country. It has been shrinking steadily since the days of Solomon. The break-up of the earlier Egyptian Empire, the better part of a thousand years ago, enabled your people to set up as an independent nation, but times have changed.

"We are in an age of imperialism, and the new Egypt is not the only expansionist power to be reckoned with. If Egypt totters, there is Babylonia; to her north and east, the Medes and the Persians are restive; the Greeks are pressing into Asia from across the Aegean Sea. Small nations will no longer be able to survive. They will be ground to dust in the clashings of the Great Powers. Face it, doctor—Judea is doomed. Only the cities of Phoenicia will survive forever. Our maritime prowess will be needed by any power that seeks to control the sea, whether for commerce or for war. Either independent, or serving foreign kings, the sea-captains will ride their wooden horses as masters of the deep. As long as mankind has need for ships and shipmen, there will be fame and riches for the men of Tyre and Byblos, Arvad and Sidon and Gebal. But within a generation—I would not be offensive, doctor, but anyone with an eye to international affairs can see it coming—Judea will be no more. You are a tiny nation and, as I said, a poor one. Your people have no architecture, no sculpture, no history of far-flung conquest, such as Egypt and Babylon have achieved, to preserve your national consciousness; within a century the very name of Hebrew will be forgotten. For the sake of your children, and of your children's children, Asa, come with me to Tyre."

"You may be right, Captain, about the evil that is to come upon my people. I am not sure. But I am sure of this. If I live in a foreign land, far from the temple of my God and with none of my people about me, then my children or my grandchildren will inevitably fall away from the faith of their fathers. I too would not willingly give offense, Captain. But rather would I die without seed and without remembrance than have my daughters act the harlot in honor of Ashtoreth; rather see my sons lying dead at my feet than have them burn their babes alive to the glory of Moloch."

Belnatan shrugged. "In an intelligent and educated man like yourself, doctor, I find these lapses into fanaticism hard to understand. I do not decry religion. But, bred though I was to the beliefs of my own people, I can respect those of others no less. Good and evil, Asa, are relative, depending on time and place. What shocks you may be right and proper in another milieu."

"I think otherwise. I believe that there are eternal verities. Oh, I admit, of course, that details of morality and of philosophy may legitimately vary. But in its broad outlines the path of man from barbarism to blessedness stands clearly revealed. There can be, as I see it, no debate on the propositions that love is better than hate; that mercy is better than cruelty; that right is better than injustice."

"And yet, if I remember my history, your people have slaughtered their enemies without scruple, even as the rest of us."

"They did so, Captain, before our prophets had taught us that all men are brothers. 'Have we not one father? Did not one God create us? Why, then, do we deal treacherously, one with another?' And even in modern times, I am afraid that the hands of our warriors have been red. But we do not kill for love of killing. Sometimes, even in ancient days, my people spared their enemies—who subsequently gave them cause to regret it. I do not know—perhaps the massacres of olden time were inevitable. I hope that they will not continue. In any case, the most terrible thing in the world, I think, is the wanton infliction of suffering upon a fellow creature. And there, I maintain—forgive me if I take a superior attitude—our God has most clearly demonstrated the holiness of His law. We do not rejoice in pain. We do not celebrate our triumphs by the torture-death of the populations of whole cities as our neighbors do. (It has happened, I admit it with shame, but very rarely.) We have never blinded children before the eyes of their parents. Even our criminals are not subjected to prolonged agony before we grant them the boon of death. When we kill, we kill quickly. Our women are not the helpless instruments of our pleasure—they have rights, and they are honored. The happiness and welfare even of a slave are precious in the sight of our lawgiver Moses. We are commanded to use the very beasts with humanity and mercy, and there is a code of laws to that effect."

"You will be telling me next that you are commanded to love even your enemies."

"We are not commanded to love our enemies, and we do not love them. But we are commanded to do good unto them. 'If thine enemy thirsteth, give him to drink—if he hungereth, give him to eat.' "

"And do you?"

"Sometimes. We are imperfect in the observance of our laws, as you are in yours. But the ideal is there, and perhaps we may some day approach it more closely. Wherever men live together, there must be some concept of right and justice. But only we—" and the priest drew proudly erect—"have learned that mercy is more precious. Only our God has taught that man must be holy, for the sole and sufficient reason that He is Holy. I think that mercy, which is loved and practiced by the crude tribesmen of the Judean hills to an extent not even imagined by the urbane, cultured city dwellers of Egypt and Chaldea, is the clearest proof that God alone is God, and all other faiths—your pardon again, Captain, but I speak what I believe—are a delusion in the darkness. And I believe that it is not an impossible ideal, but that only so can man live in happiness and peace, and study war no more."

He paused for a moment, then added, "And I believe that it would be an impossible coincidence that only that people which apprehended the Deity would be, purely by chance, the only people to set its face firmly against the deliberate infliction of misery and pain. I believe that that association is the strongest evidence of the existence and the holiness of God."

17

Two years and eleven months after he had quitted it, Asa stood in the Judean embassy at Sais.

"Sholom aleikhem, Kohane!" the ambassador, Menachem ben Shimon, greeted him.

"And unto you too be peace!" was the priest's reply. "I had looked to find Malachi ben Ittai here."

"My friend ben Ittai was recalled last year by reason of ill health, and I was his replacement. You are most welcome, ben Abdiel—the more so, because you were long since given up for dead. But we will talk later. You have just time to bathe before joining us to ask the Lord's blessing upon our sabbath meal. Eliezer! See to the comfort of our guest!"

The exchange of news came later.

"Ben Ittai has made a good recovery from his attack of kidney stone," said the ambassador, "and is in attendance at the court in Jerusalem. His wife too is well, he writes. His daughter Zeruiah married Joel ben Eliphas and is the mother of a fine young daughter."

"That is good news," said the priest. His throat was suddenly tight. "And Tamar, his ward—whom did she marry?"

Menachem shook his head. "A very headstrong girl. Malachi had a good marriage arranged for her, but she would have none of it. A shameful thing in Israel, that a maid should live unwed and without hope of issue! She is the only one, by the way, who has steadfastly refused to believe that you were lost. In every letter there is an inquiry from her for news of you." If Menachem guessed more than he said, he gave no sign.

A delicious feeling of warmth flooded the priest's bosom. His imagination leaped over the space and time that separated him from Jerusalem; his mind's eye pictured the dark-haired girl waiting in Malachi's house, and he was filled with a deep, quiet happiness.

"Your voyage, I'm afraid," the ambassador went on, "was all for naught. The Pharaoh seems to have lost interest in the undertaking. He had been, as you know, building a canal from the Nile to the Red Sea. Well, one of his heathenish soothsayers told him that he was building only for the barbarian. These Egyptians, you know, for all their resplendent culture, are a superstitious lot. At once, despite all the gold and all the lives that had been spent in the undertaking, he abandoned it. All this you know. Apparently his interest in maritime development has since gone the same way. Oh, you people will get your wages, I doubt not, and perhaps a little over, but there will be none of the glory that you had a right to expect."

Asa thought of the prodigies of skill and toil with which Belnatan had brought them through. He thought of Ieoud's poor, wicked, deluded, lost crew; of Balsachus' ship's company, swallowed up, no doubt, in the stormy seas so far away; of brave Abdemonus and his men, sacrificed to save the rest; he thought, with a pang, of Mattan.

Menachem continued. "I know, of course, of the circumstances under which you left Sais. I can understand why you so impulsively shipped with the Phoenicians. Well, you're older and wiser, now; but those years are gone from your life, and the memory of I can't guess what sufferings and terrors remain. Believe me, ben Abdiel, you have my deepest sympathy. I can't tell you how sorry we are for you."

The priest looked up, surprised; and the glint of sunlight on far-off seas gathered in his eyes.

"Sorry for me? Sorry? I have been where never man has been before. I have thirsted on burning seas, and I have seen the treasury of the snows sailing as huge ice-mountains in the great waters. I have stood on a reeling deck in storm and have toiled to bring a sinking ship into strange harbor. I have learned the ways of sail and wave. I have fought mighty foes on the breast of the hungry Ocean and have matched wit and prowess with strange dark men of farthest Cush, and with the men of Javan in their pride. I have seen the blood of Leviathan spurt red to the lance! I have heard the voice of the Lord in the whirlwind on the waters, and I have seen His fury lashing the great deep. Five beautiful ships and over eight score men there were that set forth in their strength, and we only, eight and thirty of us in one galley, are returned alive to tell thee. I have sailed with the Sidonians and have physicked the wild brown men of the uttermost ends of Africa. I remember the menace of surf on forlorn beaches, and storm on wintry seas far, far away."

A conscious bit of language-play, he realized with some embarrassment, and yet the sentiment was sincere enough!

He strode to the window, and looked out upon the gaudy city of Sais.

"And you are sorry for me?"

When Asa bade farewell to his shipmates, he was unable to speak. His throat was full and his eyes wet. He loved them. How could man look upon the foreigner as a foe? They were one flesh, and all the flesh was dear. To *Morning Star's* crew the parting was almost as painful; not quite, for they remained together. But they blessed one another, and went their ways.

And as to Belnatan the captain of the Sidonians, and all the rest of the things that he did, are they not written in the book of the chronicles of the kings of Tyre?

18

Now it was the end of the spring harvest, and the Feast of Weeks was at hand. So all the people went up to Jerusalem, to the temple, to sacrifice unto the Lord. And Asa ben Abdiel, the priest, went with them, to make atonement unto the Lord for all the trespasses which he had done. He walked again among his people, and he looked with love and happiness toward the white-domed roofs of the city. "How goodly are thy tents, O Jacob! Thy dwelling places, O Israel!"

First he would purify himself at the Temple, and then he would be free to go about upon the business of men. And as he drew nigh to the sanctuary on Mt. Zion, he heard the chanting of the Levites, faint but clear.

The earth is the Lord's, and its fullness; the world, and they that dwell therein. For He hath founded it upon the seas, and established it upon the floods. Who shall ascend the mountain of the Lord? Who shall stand in His holy place? He that hath clean hands and a pure heart.

The well-remembered melodies made his bosom melt as wax, and the happy tears came to his eyes.

That evening Asa knocked again at Malachi ben Ittai's door. The strange maidservant who admitted him had just told him that the master was not at home when Tamar came out into the courtyard and asked her who had come. He silenced the woman with a quick gesture and sang from the lovesong of Solomon:

If thou know not, Oh fairest of women,
Go thy way forth by the footsteps of the flock
And feed thy kids beside the shepherds' tents!

"Asa!" and then unnecessarily, for her cry had told him all that he needed to know, "My beloved is mine and I am his," and never had he known that the words of the song could ring so sweetly and so true.

Later that night, alone again after Malachi and his wife had discussed the wedding which was to follow the festival, Asa gave thought to the future. It was given to the priest, in that moment, to look deeply into his own heart. He saw himself through the years as a steadfast son of his people and an unswerving servant of his God, but the old, unquestioning, wholly satisfying faith was gone past recovery. He knew that he would never learn the Answer. He knew that he would never quite find his way back to the close-by, loving, all-powerful Father that had been his.

But he knew that he would never give up the search.

AUThOR'S NOTE

The historicity of this episode rests upon the quotation from Herodotus given at the beginning of the work. In the fifth century before the Common Era, Herodotus had traveled the world known to the Greeks of that time, but he knew nothing of the southern hemisphere. The point on which he bases his skepticism—the sun's being in the north, on the right hand of the voyagers, at their southernmost point—is strong evidence for the authenticity of the account. Miracle-mongers would have invented more striking wonders—such as giants, pigmies, and monsters.

To reconstruct the voyage, the writer has called upon oceanography, meteorology, history, the science of shipbuilding, geography, as well as other disciplines. If the voyage south from the Red Sea had been started at any other time of the year (give or take two weeks) the mariners would have had to row their ships hundreds of miles against strong winds along barren, poorly watered shores in the hottest seas of the world. Such an undertaking makes no sense.

The association of a Hebrew with Phoenicians in a maritime venture need occasion no surprise. These three Biblical references are well known:

> *And king Solomon made a navy of ships in Ezion-geber, which is beside Eloth, on the shore of the Red sea, in the land of Edom. And Hiram sent in the navy his servants, shipmen that had knowledge of the sea, with the servants of Solomon. And they came to Ophir, and fetched from thence gold, four hundred and twenty talents, and brought it to king Solomon.* (I KINGS :9 :26-28)

Jehoshaphat made ships of Tharshish to go to Ophir for gold:
but they went not; for the ships were broken at Ezion-geber. Then
said Ahaziah the son of Ahab unto Jehoshaphat, Let my servants
go with thy servants in the ships. But Jehoshaphat would not.
(KINGS I: 22:48-49)

For the king's ships went to Tarshish with the servants of Huram:
every three years once came the ships of Tarshish bringing gold,
and silver, ivory, and apes, and peacocks. (II CHRONICLES: 9:21)

There is much internal evidence in the Bible of an intense preoccupation with the sea. The most detailed listing of the materials in a Phoenician ship is supplied us by one of Ezekiel's sermons (27:5-9). Recent archeologocial evidence has been added to all this. Aymar's *Marine Museums** illustrates a model of a Judean merchant ship.

The exact year of the expedition cannot be established.

There are several possible details for those who wish to carp. It has been widely stated, for instance (by the *Jewish Encyclopedia* among other sources), that the physicians of Judea were not priests; but very little evidence is adduced. There is a reference to a king who perished because he trusted in the physicians rather than in God; but even the most conceited priest would hardly have identified himself with the Deity. Yet it was almost a universal custom among primitive peoples for the priesthood to be the repository of medical knowledge; and indeed, the one very definite medical diagnostic procedure mentioned in the Bible (for leprosy) is very specifically assigned to the priests. For medical details the author has drawn chiefly on the Bible, the Ebers and Edwin Smith papyri, the writings of Hippocrates, and occasional Babylonian notations. It is not generally realized that the modern medical specialty of Public Health has introduced only one principle not treated in the Bible—vaccination. Otherwise, meat inspection, food preservation, pure water, disposal of human wastes, isolation, sex hygiene—they are all there.

Naval architects are generally agreed that such a voyage as described in this book was not beyond the capability of the ships of that day. In

---

* B. Aymar, *A Pictorial Treasury of the Marine Museums of the World.* New York: Crown Publishers, Inc., 1967.

science we are prone to require a positive and a negative control. Both are available. On the negative side we have a tale told by Herodotus of a fourth-century Persian noble who ravished a lady of the court and was sentenced by the king to death by impalement. The noble's mother persuaded the king to commute the sentence to a circumnavigation of Africa from west to east. The offending prince started down the west coast but found it impossible successfully to oppose the northerly current off southwest Africa (Vasco da Gama 2000 years later with infinitely better ships accomplished a passage in this direction only by standing across the Atlantic to South America and thereby evading it). The ill-advised princeling returned to his royal master with the news of his failure, and was impaled.

On the positive side, we have an account of a voyage soon after da Gama's day of a Portuguese sailor in a small boat making a successful journey from the Indies around the Cape of Good Hope and north to Portugal.

The author has credited the Phoenicians with slightly more extensive geographical knowledge than they were known to possess. This is defensible. The Phoenicians were notoriously closemouthed, like the Iberian kingdoms in the Age of Discovery.

The writer has taken only one liberty with the facts. He has disregarded the changes due to erosion and siltage and used the topography of the present day African coast. In justification he pleads that the changes are likely to have canceled each other out in different areas.

Only the reigning monarchs are factual persons.